JUST A DREAM

Cheated out of her inheritance by a willful stepmother, Lady Elizabeth Stanton follows Nathaniel O'Connor to America—eager to accept the dashing shipbuilder's proposal of marriage. But it is a stranger who greets the penniless miss at her intended's door—the *true* owner of the grand Boston mansion, Nathaniel's handsome, secretive and insufferable older brother, Morgan.

JUST ONE KISS

The cruel treachery of a disloyal sibling left Morgan angry and bitter—but he takes in the cad's forsaken fiancée nonetheless. And when one stolen kiss threatens scandal, he offers to wed the proud, golden-haired beauty himself. But Elizabeth is devoted to a rogue. And Morgan must first conquer his own pain and suspicion to know a passion that can thaw a frozen heart . . . and a love that can heal all wounds.

SAMANTHA JAMES

JUST ONE KISS

An Avon Romantic Treasure

AVON BOOKS ◆ NEW YORK

JUST ONE KISS is an original publication of Avon Books. This work
has never before appeared in book form. This work is a novel. Any sim-
ilarity to actual persons or events is purely coincidental.

AVON BOOKS
A division of
The Hearst Corporation
1350 Avenue of the Americas
New York, New York 10019

Copyright © 1996 by Sandra Kleinschmit
Inside cover author photo by Almquist Studios
Published by arrangement with the author
Library of Congress Catalog Card Number: 95-94929
ISBN: 0-380-77549-2

First Avon Books Printing: March 1996

AVON TRADEMARK REG. U.S. PAT. OFF. AND IN OTHER COUNTRIES, MARCA
REGISTRADA, HECHO EN U.S.A.

Printed in the U.S.A.

RA   10   9   8   7   6   5   4   3   2   1

Prologue

~~∽◯◯∽~~

Boston, 1830

The smell of brine lay heavy in the air, as heavy as her heart. For the time had come when she could deceive herself no more . . .

She was dying.

Within the room were two young boys, the sons she held so near and dear to her heart. A spasm of pain tore through her, yet it was as nothing compared to the ache in her heart. And deep in her chest swirled an agony of dread, for how was she to tell these two sweet lads she would soon be lost to them . . . and they to her, for it mattered little to their father that his sons were dirty of hand and ragged of clothing.

Silently she mourned. Alone, the three of them were, for Patrick O'Connor spared neither a care nor a penny when it came to his family. More often than not, he was in the barroom below, as drunk as his patrons. Loretta's soul cried out at such injustice. What would happen to her sons when she was gone? Their father scarcely acknowledged their existence.

1

A shudder passed through her body. Lord, but the world was so unfair! She would be robbed of life . . . and her sons of her. As the thought passed through her mind, a cry of both torment and rage welled in her throat.

Yet no more than a wheezing breath escaped. At the sound, small, thin fingers stole into hers. A frail smile crossed lips that were pale as a winter moon; Loretta O'Connor squeezed as best she could. She held on, for she could not yet bear to leave . . .

Her husband shouldered his way through the door. He came to stand above her, no hint of warmth in his eyes. Instead, he snorted, his lips curled in disgust, then spun away to snatch a shirt from a peg on the wall. He spared her no further word or glance, nor the boys who lingered near. Always it was so, Loretta thought with heartbreaking candor. Always it would be . . .

Her heart wept. As her husband left, the sounds of rough male voices and grating laughter filtered up the narrow stairway to the rooms above, but the trio paid no heed.

Loretta's gaze dwelled longingly on her sons, Morgan and Nathaniel. For a heartbeat, the faintest of smiles graced her lips. One would never have known the pair were brothers. Yet brothers they were . . .

One was fair as a golden field of wheat, the other as dark as the blackest moon. The younger was Nathaniel, born to the world but four years past. At ten, Morgan was the elder. He was somber and thoughtful, ever observant and knowing. She had always marveled that the two were so very different . . .

A stark pain twisted within her. *Dear God*, she cried out in silent agony, *who would guide them when their path should stray?* She gave thanks that the babe born between the two brothers had died, for she dreaded what their lives might become when she was gone. Praise the saints above that her Morgan possessed a quick mind and strong constitution! Yet Loretta could not help but fear for Nathaniel; lively and sweet natured, he certainly was, but at times he displayed a reckless, stubborn spirit—his father's, blast the wretch!—that well might land him in trouble throughout the coming years.

There was a faint rustling near the end of the bed. Clutching a handkerchief to her breast, Loretta glimpsed Nathaniel peering across at her, his eyes huge and uncertain. He had grown quiet— ah, but it was so very unlike him!—a quiet that seemed to reach into the heavens and beyond. Young as he was, he sensed that all was not well. She tried to smile, yet she could not.

The end approached.

Loretta's breath grew papery thin. All at once there was so much she longed to say . . . so little time to say it.

Her gaze shifted to Morgan. Were she able, she would have screamed aloud at the pain that wrenched her heart. Above the hollows of his cheeks, Morgan's beautiful gray eyes were damp and red rimmed, yet he did not cry. No, for it had never been his way to cry, no matter how badly he'd been hurt.

Trembling, for the effort nearly sapped the last remaining strength in her body, Loretta squeezed his fingers. Her lips parted. With her eyes she silently beseeched him.

The boy leaned close.

Lovingly her gaze roved over his thin, pale features. "Morgan," she said faintly. "Oh, Morgan, my brave young lad . . . how I will miss you. How I wish I could be with you. How I wish I might stay . . ."

The boy's eyes filled up with tears, yet still he did not cry.

"Morgan, it is up to you now, to watch over your brother. Oh, I know I ask much of you . . . but I know you can do this—"

Frantically the boy shook his head. "No, Mother, I—"

"You can," Loretta cried weakly. "You are the elder, Morgan. Nathaniel is so young. He is not so strong or brave as you—"

Again the lad shook his head.

"No, you are! You are and I am so very proud of you!" Seeking to reassure him, Loretta clasped his hand to her breast. "Morgan, please! You must do . . . what I cannot . . . what your father *will* not . . . Your brother is so young. What if he should become one such as your father? Oh, he will need someone, Morgan, someone like you . . . Guide him. Protect him." Her breath wheezed in and out of her lungs. Her expression was tormented as she clutched her son's hands. "I beg you, Morgan, please do not fail me! Promise me you will do this or I will never find peace!"

The boy swallowed, seeking to keep the tremor from his voice. "I-I promise. I will do this. For you, Moth—"

"No, my son. Not for me. For Nathaniel." Her voice grew weaker. "That's a good lad. Oh, Morgan, be brave. Be strong and courageous, for yourself and for Nathaniel. Have faith in yourself, and in God Almighty. And may He bless you, my dearest sons . . ."

At this last, all strength was bled from her. Her eyes fluttered closed, even as her grip on the boy's fingers grew slack and limp. Morgan held tight to her hands, as if to hold on forever to the life that had already departed. His throat burned and ached like fire as he fought back tears, even as anger welled and threatened to explode within the hollow of his chest. He wanted to shout, to scream and vent his fury and grief . . . most of all, his fear. Instead he remained there, his shoulders stiff, his form as rigid as a soldier's.

Nathaniel crept close to his brother. His expression forlorn, he peered at his mother. "Morgan," he whispered in a small voice. "Is Mama asleep?"

Morgan did not speak. He could not, for he was hurting as never before . . . hurting as he somehow knew he would never hurt again.

His mother's voice echoed in his brain. *Be brave. Be strong and courageous.*

He swallowed. *How?* he wondered. *How?* "No," he answered hoarsely. "She's dead, Nathaniel. *Dead.*" There was a terrible pause. "Like the kittens that Papa drowned."

The younger boy began to weep. "What shall we do?" he whimpered. "Now we have no one to love us. No one to take care of us. Papa—"

Hesitantly—awkwardly—the lad called Morgan patted his brother's shoulder. "Don't worry," he said. "You'll have me, Nat. You'll always have me."

So the lad said ... and so it was.

Months passed. At such a tender age, Nathaniel's grief and his memory of his mother soon faded.

But Morgan didn't forget so easily.

Nor did he forsake his promise.

He'd sworn to their mother on her deathbed that he would protect Nathaniel ...

And so he did.

Their father remained as before, petty and mean, his moods ever vile, his liking for drink as lusty as ever. By his twelfth year, his father saw to it that Morgan had little time of his own—he spent most of it in the barroom and kitchen. Nathaniel was often left to himself ... Little wonder that he was a daring little rogue who often strayed into mischief.

Midnight was but a fallen stroke of the hour when Patrick O'Connor burst through the door on this particular night. He staggered across the room like the drunken sot he was, a stubble of candle clutched in one beefy hand. In the lumpy pallets that bumped the far wall, the two young boys stirred, then went utterly still. They both held their breath and their silence, for they knew better than to alert him to their wakened state.

It mattered little. Patrick O'Connor swayed and stepped before the bureau. His bloodshot gaze swept idly across the surface, then narrowed abruptly. A roar of rage ruptured the silence. In but an instant, both his sons had been rudely wrenched from their pallets.

He stalked back to the bureau. "There were six

gold coins here this morning. Now there be but five!"

Nathaniel stared at his father with huge blue eyes. His tongue came out to moisten his lips. Timidly he spoke. "Could it have fallen on the floor?"

Patrick O'Connor bent his considerable form low to the ground. His gaze scoured the chipped wood floor. He straightened. "I think not!" he growled.

"Then, Papa, perhaps you are mistaken—"

"I am not!" the man shouted. Rage contorted his features. "This is hardly the first time I've noticed a coin or two missing. But I warn you, lads, I swear it will be the last! So tell me and tell me now! Which of you took it?"

No answer was forthcoming. Morgan did not back down from his father's boiling anger. Instead he tipped his chin and regarded his father with an evenness that far belied his tender years.

"Answer me, brats!" O'Connor's voice vibrated from the very ceiling. "Which of you took my coin?"

The floor creaked. Patrick O'Connor took but a single step forward. Sheer temper flamed in his eyes. Next to Morgan, Nathaniel inhaled sharply. A vision flashed through Morgan's mind—Nathaniel's grubby palm closed around a handful of sweets only this afternoon. At the same instant, fear leaped high and bright in Nathaniel's eyes. Cowering, he shrank to his knees.

Morgan stepped forward. Bravely he raised his chin, praying his father would not see that his knees were shaking. "I took it, Papa."

"Blast you, boy!" he cursed. "How dare you!"

Morgan's shoulders tightened. "I fetch and toil

just as your barmaids do, yet I earn no—"

"I put bread in your belly and clothes on your back, you ungrateful little wretch!" A vile oath scorched the air. "God knows I get little enough in return, and yet you dare to steal from me! Well, no one steals from me, boy ... no one! Now, come here!"

But Morgan did not move quickly enough to please his father. A rough hand clamped his narrow shoulder and yanked him forward; his shirt was ripped from his back like the frailest of cloth. A brutal snarl twisting his lips, O'Connor jerked the tattered remnants around the boy's wrists, binding them behind his back.

Thrust to the floor upon his knees, the boy stiffened at the sound of a cane being snatched from a hook on the wall.

It was a sound he knew well.

The first blow blazed through him like fire up the chimney. The lad called Morgan closed his eyes. He was the elder, he told himself, as his mother once had. He must be strong. He must be brave.

He must protect Nathaniel.

He braced himself for the next blow.

The whistle of the cane tore through the silence again and again, but the boy made not a sound, not a whimper or a cry. He could bear it, for this was for Nat, he reminded himself.

Always for Nat ...

Chapter 1

Beacon Hill, 1854

It was too late to turn back.

Odd, that the thought should chain itself in her mind now, when she had come so very far. Indeed, across the vastness of an ocean...

Lady Elizabeth Stanton cast one last, almost pleading glance at the carriage from which she'd just alighted. As she watched the vehicle totter around the corner, a flurry of dust and fallen leaves rose in its wake.

Clutching her reticule, grasping her courage, she turned.

In one sweep, her anxious glance took in the sight before her. Elizabeth couldn't help it. There had been such pride in Nathaniel's voice as he'd described his home to her—and no wonder. She caught her breath, for the house that loomed before her was as grand as Nathaniel had promised. Indeed, she marveled, it was surely the height of Victorian grandeur, as stately as an English country mansion, as elegant as the finest London town house.

An ornate iron fence enclosed the whole of the property, yet despite the stark outline of tree branches and frozen lawn, it was not so very forbidding. Elizabeth could well imagine what it would be like with the bloom and brightness of spring upon its face: buds of flowers and trees stretching toward the sky.

The house itself was gabled and huge. She caught a glimpse of wispy white lace framing wide, stained-glass windows and resisted the urge to curl her white-gloved fingers around the iron and stare in sheer delight. She gave a tiny little laugh. Of course, she was being silly. Nathaniel was a highly successful American shipbuilder. Of course, his home would be beautiful.

As she stood there, a sight to brighten the late winter twilight, little did she realize the picture she presented. Her traveling dress was of dark gray silk, a trifle wrinkled perhaps, but the height of London fashion. Yet it was scarcely her clothing that made her stand out like a jewel among coal . . .

No, for her coloring was far too striking. Hair as shiny and brightly gold as a newly minted coin lay coiled beneath her hat. Her eyes were the vivid green of an English meadow in spring. No pale, fragile flower was Elizabeth Stanton. Sweet natured though she was, her carriage was one of pride and hinted at hidden strength. Yet all at once, Elizabeth did indeed feel small and insignificant . . . and very, very lost.

No, she thought again, grasping for the spirit that had sustained her these many weeks. It was too late to turn back. And she had yearned to see Nathaniel for so long now.

Memories sifted into her mind, one by one. So much had happened, she reflected with a faintly wistful sigh. So very much . . .

He'd taken London by storm, this brash young American named Nathaniel O'Connor. Handsome as sin, as charming as the Pied Piper of Hamelin, blond and bold and dashing, he was all the rage in London: No fewer than a score of women proclaimed themselves instantly in love with him. But of all the beauties in London, she was the one he pursued.

The one he'd wanted.

He'd been an outrageous flirt, of course. At first Elizabeth had thought his attention to her a grand joke. She was hardly irresistible and most certainly not the type to swoon over a man! Yet secretly she'd been flattered, for indeed, she considered herself no beauty at all! And so she'd teased him as unmercifully as he'd teased her, certain his interest would surely wane.

But over the next few weeks, his interest did not wane. And though she'd always considered herself possessed of a steady, level head, Nathaniel O'Connor proved a temptation she could not resist.

It made her tingle inside to think of him. She remembered the first time he'd kissed her. They'd been dancing at Lord Nelson's birthday celebration, a lively, vivacious waltz that left her breathless and laughing. He whisked her out onto the terrace and onto a small stone bench near the garden. Slowly the laughter left his face. With his fingers he cupped her nape, tilting her face upward. There, with the sweet scent of roses swirling all around, with her heart leaping wildly and her pulse pounding madly in her ears, he'd kissed her—a kiss that was something she'd never expected, yet all she wanted.

It wasn't so very long after . . .

They were sitting in the parlor of her father's London town house. Nathaniel took both her hands in his. "Elizabeth . . . something's come up, love. I'm afraid I must leave for Boston sooner than I expected."

The day had wrought such awful news already—little wonder that Elizabeth gazed at him, stricken. "Oh, Nathaniel, no! When? When must you leave?"

"Tomorrow, love. I sail with the morning tide." His hands gripped hers more tightly. "Elizabeth, please. Come away with me . . . marry me. Be my wife. I'll make you the happiest woman on this earth, if only you'll consent to be my bride."

Even as Elizabeth's heart soared as high as the stars above, it was burdened by a heaviness she could scarcely put aside.

"Nathaniel. Oh, Nathaniel, I want to . . . you don't know how much! But this day has brought us nothing but heartache! You know that terrible cough that has so troubled Papa these many weeks? Nathaniel, he is gravely ill . . ."

She was caught squarely between heaven and hell. As the only daughter of the Earl of Chester, how could she leave? Never had she seen Papa so sick—so weak! It frightened her. True, he was not alone. He had Clarissa, his wife of the past two years. But she, Elizabeth, was his only child, and she could not desert her father! At such a time, her place was at his side.

"When Papa is well, I will come to you in Boston. I promise, Nathaniel, as soon as I am able."

"I'll be waiting, Elizabeth. That, I promise."

When Papa is well . . . Faith, but she had come to regret those words!

For Papa had remained ill for nearly a month. But his health was even more delicate than she had feared.

They'd buried him nearly six weeks ago.

The soft line of Elizabeth's lips tightened. Yet another memory returned unbidden, but this one was like a burr beneath her skin.

Elizabeth's mother had died of a lung infection when Elizabeth was a very young girl. For many years it was just the two of them, Elizabeth and her father. But as she grew to womanhood, she began to understand all of which her father never spoke. His loneliness. His yearning for a woman's companionship. For those reasons, she hadn't been surprised when the earl eventually married Clarissa Kenton, a widowed baroness from the neighboring shire.

Unfortunately, she and Clarissa had never come to be close, though the Earl of Chester was not aware of it. Though it was not in Elizabeth's nature to be mean-spirited, she found the new countess rather dour, ever practical, and occasionally condescending.

And never more so than on the day the earl's will was read.

Elizabeth was still half-numb with grief. Although it had pained her to say farewell to Nathaniel—indeed she had clung to him almost shamelessly—'twas with the certainty that they would soon be united. But she would never again see Papa, feel the comfort of his nearness, the warmth of his voice and laughter . . .'Twas that very thought that refused to be extinguished as she watched his coffin sink beneath the earth.

So it was that her mood was somber and she remained quiet as she and Clarissa sat in Papa's study, listening to the droning voice of Papa's solicitor, James Rowland. Her thoughts were vague and dull.

"Elizabeth!" Clarissa's voice rang out sharply. "Are you listening? I believe this next pertains to you."

Behind his spectacles, Mr. Rowland glanced between the two women. Had Elizabeth been more herself, she might have caught his unease. "Shall I continue?" he queried.

"Please do," Clarissa snapped.

Mr. Rowland cleared his throat and began to read. "Some of my most precious memories of my life are of my daughter, Elizabeth, and the time we spent together at Hayden Park, my country estate in Kent. For this reason I wish Hayden Park to pass to Elizabeth on the joyous occasion of her marriage, in the hopes that she and her new husband will continue to keep residence there."

Elizabeth was not surprised. She had expected that Papa would leave the bulk of his holdings to Clarissa, and so he had. But Hayden Park had always been special to her. She smiled in wistful remembrance, for she, too, carried many fond memories of happy days there.

Rowland continued. "In these, my last days, I have but one regret—that I will never see Elizabeth wed, for indeed, seeing her wed and provided for are my last remaining concerns. For this reason, I have charged the task of finding a husband for Elizabeth to my dear wife, Clarissa, for I know that she will see my wishes carried out."

Her slender hands folded neatly in her lap, Elizabeth had gone very still. When she spoke, her tone was very quiet. "Please explain, if you will, Mr. Rowland. Precisely what does this mean?"

Rowland's ruddy cheeks grew redder still. "Legally it means that possession of Hayden Park will not pass to you until you marry—"

Elizabeth's voice cut across his. "Does this also mean the choice of husband lies in my stepmother's hands?"

He had no time to answer. "Indeed it does, Elizabeth." Triumph abounded in both Clarissa's tone and her bearing as she turned toward her stepdaughter. She smiled, a smile that sent needles winging down Elizabeth's spine.

"But you need not worry, dear." Clarissa wasted no time in making known her intentions. "I have taken care of everything. Lord Harry Carlton is quite agreeable to marrying you. Indeed, I daresay he was quite happy when I approached him."

Elizabeth was stunned. At the age of twenty and one, she'd had several offers for her hand. Although Papa had at times been frustrated, he had not pressed the issue.

She knew Lord Harry, of course. He was the youngest son of the Marquis of Salisbury. His weight no doubt exceeded his girth; but it was not his appearance that had always disturbed her. No, the man was a lecher. It was there in every look, in the greedy way he eyed whatever woman might pass his way.

She felt sick—sick at heart. There was an awful tightness in her chest, a fear she could not give voice to, for then it would surely be real.

She prayed unknowingly. *Merciful Father, this cannot be. Let it not be true.*

The hands that had been folded so primly tightened in her lap. "I would understand you, Clarissa. You would have me marry Lord Harry?"

"Of course!" Clarissa smiled sublimely, yet her eyes were hard. " 'Tis an exceedingly good match, don't you think?"

Elizabeth filled her lungs with air. The fires of anger sizzled in her veins. By God, she'd not give herself over to a stranger—a man she did not love—a man chosen by her stepmother!

But she did not show even a hint of her fury. Instead she chose her words carefully. "You would make me do this, Clarissa? You would have me wed a man I have no desire to wed?"

Clarissa's smile withered. " 'Tis long past time you married, Elizabeth. And you'll do no better than Lord Harry." She folded her arms across her ample bosom and glared at her stepdaughter.

It was then Elizabeth saw in her stepmother's eyes the naked truth, the venom she had always sensed . . . the dislike Clarissa no longer masked. Clarissa hated her. Her concern was a travesty. Now that the earl was gone, she wanted nothing more than to be rid of her stepdaughter.

Elizabeth squared her shoulders. She angled her delicate chin high. If that was what Clarissa wanted—to be rid of her—she would most certainly see the deed done.

She allowed a faint smile to grace the fullness of her lips. "You are right, Clarissa," she stated coolly. "I will marry, but it will be to a man of my own choosing—and it will *not* be Lord Harry."

Clarissa snorted, a distinctly unladylike sound. "Who then? If you wait any longer, you may as well resign yourself to spinsterhood!"

"Nathaniel O'Connor asked me to marry him before he left for Boston," Elizabeth stated very quietly, "and I have already accepted."

"Nathaniel O'Connor? That bold, young American who lacked all semblance of grace and manners?"

The elder woman's disdain was more than evident. Though a burning retort simmered on her tongue, Elizabeth thought it best kept to herself.

"We disagree as to his character, Clarissa, but yes, he is the one."

"If he intended to marry you, then why did he return to Boston?" Clarissa's tone was one of sheer triumph. "And why did your father and I not hear of this?"

"Nathaniel has a business to which he must attend." Elizabeth faltered slightly, praying her stepmother wouldn't notice and wishing Nathaniel had given her a more detailed explanation. "I did not go with him because Papa was sick. And I didn't tell him for the very same reason."

"Ha! It was because you knew he would disapprove!"

Elizabeth battled an inkling of guilt. Somehow

she managed to continue to hold her stepmother's accusing gaze. So what if Clarissa was right? She'd not let the old witch know it, not now, not ever!

"Papa was ill," she repeated. "I merely wanted him to concentrate on getting well that he might *see* my wedding to Nathaniel."

"Your father would never have permitted you to marry a—a Yankee nobody—and one of Irish descent yet! Such a marriage is hardly suitable!"

Elizabeth shook her head. *A suitable marriage.* She cared little about that. But she was well aware that Clarissa didn't understand the fires of youth, the fires that burned in her breast whenever she was with Nathaniel.

No, she thought. *No.* She would not marry Lord Harry—not to please Clarissa, nor to please anyone. For if she did, she would lead a stifling existence, a life she could not bear.

Nor did she delude herself. If she remained, Clarissa would do all she could to force her to her will. Indeed, she sensed in Clarissa an unyielding purpose that was almost frightening.

Slowly she rose to her feet. "I regret that it must be like this," she said calmly. "But I think you will agree that perhaps it is best I leave for Boston—and Nathaniel—as soon as possible."

Clarissa leaped to her feet as well. Her cheeks turned a mottled shade of red. "By God, girl, you always were a willful, spoiled child, but your father would never believe me! I told him you'd lost your senses to this Yankee! I told him you needed a strong hand to guide you, but he would not concede until he lay dying. And now

I thank God that he is dead, for he would be scandalized by your behavior!"

Elizabeth ignored her, extending a hand toward James Rowland. "Thank you for your help, Mr. Rowland. I trust you'll understand if I remain no longer. I've passage to book, you see."

Rowland was on his feet as well. "Lady Elizabeth," he pleaded. "Lady Elizabeth, please! I beg you to reconsider. Surely the two of you can work something out. Indeed, you stand to gain much. Your father made provisions for an extremely generous allowance—"

"An allowance to be determined by me, Mr. Rowland. And by God, she'll get not a farthing. Not a farthing, do you hear?" Clarissa's voice vibrated with her fury. "Without me, you are as poor as a church mouse!"

Rowland fell silent. Elizabeth knew then it was true. Papa, she thought sadly. Oh, Papa, why did you do this? He had taught her to think for herself. She needed no one to guide her, to control her, as Clarissa seemed determined to do.

After a moment, she tipped her head, the merest wisp of a smile on her lips as she spoke softly. "You don't understand, do you, Clarissa? Papa's money does not matter to me. True, I love Hayden Park, but my life is my own—and means far more to me. And I would rather be poor than wed to a man I do not love."

That was the last she'd seen of Clarissa.

And so she had said farewell to her father, farewell to England . . . to her life as she had known it.

For a time there was no help for it—she'd been secretly crushed. She couldn't help but feel that by placing her future in Clarissa's hands, Papa had betrayed her. But during the long voyage across the sea, she'd come to realize Papa's only fault was in trusting so easily; trusting Clarissa to look out for his daughter's best interests.

Yes, she thought once more. *Yes.* She'd made the right choice. The *only* choice.

For to marry as Clarissa commanded would have been unbearable.

Slowly Elizabeth released a long pent-up breath. Her mind returned to the present . . .

And Nathaniel.

She coughed, aware of an unfamiliar tightness in her breast. Her chest had begun to ache again, as it had the past few days. She brushed it aside distractedly. It was nothing but the memories, she told herself.

Grasping the strings of her reticule, she glanced once more toward the house. A twinge of uncertainty marred the smoothness of her brow. Nearly three months had passed since she'd last laid eyes on Nathaniel. Would he be pleased to see her?

She gave a little laugh. Of course he would. He loved her. Her fears were silly. Besides, it wasn't him she was afraid of, simply the future. And little wonder, for her life had certainly been unsettled of late.

Still, a nagging thought persisted. Had she been unwise to come here first? The driver had known where the O'Connor residence was located. But she must still find lodgings, and she'd thought it best to seek a recommendation from Nathaniel. Her funds were scarcely limitless— she'd sold off several pieces of jewelry to pay for her passage. But if all went right, she needed only find a room for a week or two at most. It was indeed her most fervent wish to be married as soon as possible—she prayed Nathaniel felt the same!

Her mind thus engaged, Elizabeth patted her bonnet and straightened her spencer. She felt decidedly dusty and disheveled after a month at sea. A half smile curved her lips. Indeed, she felt a bit of a waif as she glanced down at the small portmanteau at her side. She'd left her trunks at the ship's docks, in the hope that Nathaniel would send someone after them, perhaps tomorrow.

Bolstering her courage, she started down the brick walkway. Her booted heels clicked as she mounted the stairs. There, before two wide double doors, she reached out with one slender, white-gloved hand and curled her fingers around the ornately carved brass knocker. Outwardly calm, inwardly shaking, she tapped smartly upon the paneled wood.

Footsteps immediately echoed from within. The door swept wide. A stoop-shouldered, gray-whiskered man appeared—the butler, from the look of him.

Elizabeth summoned a smile. "Good day," she said pleasantly. "Is this the O'Connor residence?"

Shaggy brows rose. "Indeed it is, madam."

Her smile relaxed. "Good. Then I'd like to see Mr. O'Connor, if he's in, please."

His gaze encompassed the length of her, and apparently found favor. "Who shall I say is calling, madam?"

"Lady Elizabeth Stanton." Her laugh was rather breathless. "Please forgive me for arriving unannounced, but my ship docked only this afternoon, you see." Elizabeth felt compelled to explain. "Circumstances were a bit muddled when I left London. I was in such a frenzy, I'm afraid I had little time to write and inform Mr. O'Connor of my arrival. And . . . oh, perhaps I should have waited, but I'm so very anxious to see him again!"

There was the slightest pause. "Mr. O'Connor has not yet returned from the shipyard, though I expect him within the next quarter hour. Would you care to wait?"

Her anxiety fled. "Oh, yes! Please."

The butler stepped back. "Please come in, then."

Elizabeth followed him to the drawing room, just off the massive entrance hall. As she stepped inside, her gaze silently approved the large, comfortably inviting furnishings.

"My name is Simmons, madam. If you'd like, I could bring you some tea."

Though his manner was faultlessly polite, and rather formal, his eyes were kind. "Thank you, Simmons," she said with a smile. "I'd like that very much indeed."

He gave a slight bow and retreated.

As the door closed, Elizabeth seated herself on a large, overstuffed wing chair across from the fireplace. A young girl soon returned with a silver tray, introducing herself as Millie. Elizabeth poured herself a cup of tea, thinking it would refresh her, but after several sips she felt as if she were hot as the fire that burned in the hearth.

She rose, restlessly pacing the length of the room and back. Now that the time was nigh upon her, both excitement and fear warred within her breast. She caught sight of herself in a small, rectangular mirror decorated with small rosettes at each corner. Two spots of rose stood out on her cheeks. Her eyes shone brightly, vivid and green. She frowned, thinking they seemed almost overbright . . .

Her reflection seemed to waver, then abruptly righted itself. She frowned. In the last hour, her breath had grown rather short, but surely it was just a case of nerves.

The rattle of a carriage sounded just outside.

Elizabeth flew to the window. Through the filmy lace, she glimpsed a tall, spare figure striding up the walkway.

Her heart began to sing. *It's him . . . it's Nathaniel!*

Voices echoed in the entrance hall. She linked her gloved fingers together before her to steady her hands. She had to stop herself from whirling around in joy.

Footsteps approached. Simmons knocked, then opened the door just a crack. "Madam, the master will be in shortly."

Elizabeth nodded. Her mind sped onward. Would Nathaniel be surprised to see her? No doubt. Would he be pleased? Oh, surely he would! After all, he'd asked her to be his wife! Bliss descended in full bloom. She sighed, picturing what would happen when Nathaniel strode through the door.

He would gaze at her with that ever-present smile of his, laughter shining in his eyes; her lips curved in sweet remembrance. And then . . . then he would take her in his arms, and kiss her as he once had.

The door opened with a creak. The outline of a man flashed before her eyes—elegantly attired, taller than most, powerfully wide shoulders, incredibly narrow hips . . . and hair as dark as night.

Poised to fly across the room, Elizabeth halted with a gasp.

Her smile froze. Her heart seemed to stop. Her mind blurred. Suddenly she felt so weak, she could barely stand. She blinked, certain that her eyes had surely deceived her. Surely this could not be . . .

For the man before her was not Nathaniel.

Chapter 2

His business concluded, Morgan O'Connor strode out the entrance of the Commonwealth Bank. An extremely well-dressed middle-aged lady was just preparing to enter. Morgan graciously swept the door wide. Stepping back in silent invitation, he tipped his hat in greeting.

"Good afternoon, Mrs. Winston."

The woman spoke not a word. She marched by in a swirl of frills and lace. The plume in her hat dipped and turned. An icy glare was the only acknowledgment of his gesture. Morgan cocked a brow and lifted one broad shoulder in a shrug. Thank heaven, he decided with acrid humor, his bankers were not so fastidious as Mrs. Winston. They were, in fact, only too eager for each and every transaction.

It hadn't always been so, Morgan reflected, climbing into his carriage. When he'd been clawing his way up from his days as a seaman, financial supporters had been few. But the day had come when all had changed. And while he'd not been openly embraced by the city's upper crust, for many a year he'd at least been admitted into Boston's wealthiest drawing rooms—and given the pretense of welcome.

He'd thought the days had passed when Boston's crème de la crème considered him a nobody—merely the son of a drunken tavern owner. Riffraff. *Shanty* Irish. But in essence, little had changed. For within the stroke of an hour, he'd been once again branded the outsider. The unworthy.

No longer was he so foolish. So blind.

And although Morgan was loath to admit it, even to himself, deep inside the knowledge grated. He'd struggled year after year, long and hard, to better himself and his circumstances. He had earned what so many of Boston's so-called elite had been born to—or had handed down from father to son. But in all honesty, the city's blue bloods were no better than he.

They merely thought they were.

With a flick of a finger, Morgan motioned his driver forward. And though his lips still carried the trace of a smile, his silvery eyes were hard as stone.

As the carriage rounded the corner, the choppy waters of the Bay came into view. Curiously his gaze lingered.

God, but he'd grown to hate that tiny little tavern by the sea where he'd spent his youth. But the sea had been his salvation. And it was there he'd finally found sanctuary. *And* his fortune.

His only regret was that he'd been unable to share it with his mother.

A mocking smile touched his lips. His father had been gone nearly ten years now. It was no accident that he'd chosen to demolish that wretched tavern scarcely a week after his father's funeral. And it was there he'd founded the offices of O'Connor Shipbuilding.

Shrill laughter outside the carriage snared his attention. A group of children playing along the street called out and waved at his driver. He smiled faintly, wondering idly if they knew how lucky they were. His own childhood had hardly been rife with such lightheartedness. No, he'd left the carefree laughter to his brother, as he always had.

Nathaniel . . . It was inevitable that his mind should turn to him. The train of thought caused Morgan to steel himself subconsciously as if for battle.

Nathaniel . . . the brother he'd so loved. The blackguard he'd trusted with his life . . . with his *wife*.

Nathaniel's charm had carried him far, Morgan reflected cynically. Indeed, so much so that many were wont to forgive him his transgressions.

Not everyone.

Morgan's lips grew thin. A dark hole seemed to burn in his chest. He'd had precious little contact with Nathaniel the past five years; that was the way he preferred it, and little wonder. He could scarcely excuse his brother for all that had passed between them. Never had he dreamed his brother would betray him so . . . Never had he dreamed his brother would *hurt* him so.

So much had happened. Too much to forget. Too much to *forgive*.

But never again would Nathaniel hurt him so.

Nor would any woman, even one as lovely as his wife, Amelia, had been . . .

Another vow he would not forsake.

Twisting restlessly against the rich cushions of the carriage, Morgan admonished himself fiercely. *Enough of Nathaniel,* he told himself. Because to think of his brother . . . was to think of *her.*

And he would indisputably rather think of neither.

Yet oddly enough, both still lingered in his mind when he arrived home a short time later—his dead, faithless wife, and his wretchedly tormenting brother. One of the downstairs maids admitted him; he gave her a nod and proceeded straight to his study, where he poured a liberal amount of brandy into a crystal glass. He swirled the liquid in the glass and stared at it intently, his mood as darkly morose as his thoughts. But even as he contemplated it, he knew he wouldn't drink it . . .

A knock sounded on the door.

Morgan was sorely tempted to ignore it—but such was impossible, as he soon discovered.

The door opened a crack. "Sir?" It was Simmons.

Morgan paused, long fingers curled around the rim of the glass. "What is it?" He didn't bother to disguise his irritation.

The door opened wide. Simmons stepped inside. "Sir, there is a lady in the drawing room who wishes to see you."

"Oh?" There was the faintest sarcasm to his tone. Most of his female callers bypassed the drawing room completely and simply proceeded to the bedroom.

Simmons nodded. "Sir, she's from London." There was the faintest pause. "I gather from what she says that you are expecting her."

"A woman from London?" Morgan's tone was curt. "Hardly. She's come to the wrong house, Simmons. Please show her out."

"Forgive me for saying so, sir, but I do believe you should see her. She seems most anxious. She said there wasn't time to write to inform you of her arrival."

Morgan's gaze narrowed.

Simmons hastened to add, "Her name is Elizabeth Stanton, sir. *Lady* Elizabeth Stanton."

Morgan's reply was both blunt and brief. "The name means nothing to me, Simmons. I tell you, she's come to the wrong house."

Simmons neither moved nor spoke. He merely cleared his throat and rocked back on his heels.

Morgan grimaced. Lord, but Simmons could be incredibly stubborn at times. But far more annoying was the woman waiting in the drawing room, *Lady* Elizabeth Stanton. He pictured a plump, dowdy matron with hips nearly as wide as she was tall. With a name like that, how could she be anything else? God in heaven, he thought. What now? What in hell could a woman like that possibly want with him? Normally he wasn't a man to invite trouble, but Simmons seemed unusually persistent.

He set his glass down on the table with a *thunk*. "Fine," he muttered, already striding through the wide double doors. "I'll see her." Ten paces took him to the drawing room, where he was afforded the first glimpse of his caller.

He'd been dead wrong. It flashed through his brain that here was no dowdy matron. Instead she stood near the mirror, a slender, smartly dressed figure in dove gray. She half turned, at last facing him fully. No, Morgan thought vaguely, she was not at all what he'd expected . . .

Clearly she felt the same.

He was, in fact, totally unprepared for his effect on her. Huge green eyes grew wider still. Her expression was a strange mixture of confusion and unquestionable disappointment. Vexed though he was, he was also unwittingly amused. Her eyes locked on his.

"Dear God," she gasped. "Who the devil are you?"

One winged brow quirked upward. "Simmons informed me you wished to see me."

"You? Why, I don't even know you!"

"I might say the same of you," came his dry response. "But it was you who came to my home. Therefore I trust you have business with me. I confess, however, I am most curious as to the nature of that business."

Her eyes had yet to waver from his. Morgan had the oddest sensation that she thought him the devil himself.

"There must be some mistake," she said faintly. "I was told this was the O'Connor residence."

"And so it is."

She stared at him as if he were half-mad. "No, you don't understand. I'm trying to find the man who owns O'Connor Shipbuilding."

Morgan linked his hands behind his back. The merest smile lurked about his lips. "The very same, madam."

"No. No, that cannot be." She looked as if she might burst into tears at any moment. "I-I've come all the way from London! I-I can't go back, I just can't! I have to find Nathaniel O'Connor."

Morgan's smile vanished. In the instant between one breath and the next, everything changed. He spoke gruffly. "Well, you won't find him here. It's my understanding he's not in Boston."

Her fingers clutched at the strings of her reticule. "You know him then? You know Nathaniel?"

Morgan's laugh was gritty. "Oh, yes, I know him well. I am his brother."

She paled visibly. Her lips parted, yet no sound escaped. Then to his utter shock, before he could say more, she pitched forward into a dead faint.

It was lucky for her Morgan's reflexes were so quick. He caught her mere inches before her head struck the floor. Twisting her around, he slipped an arm beneath her knees and lifted her to the nearest settee.

"Good Christ!" he muttered. "What next?"

Morgan's first thought was that the girl's collapse was nothing but a ruse—a display of feminine wiles—whatever the reason might be. Curbing his impatience, he sat beside her and gently slapped first one cheek and then the other, fully expecting her to vent her anger with an outraged shriek.

She moved not a muscle.

Morgan frowned. Had the girl simply laced her stays too tight? Why women wore such contraptions, he didn't know. To men who wanted to dispense with a woman's clothing as quickly as possible, they were nothing but a nuisance. Easing her to her side, he nimbly unfastened the myriad hooks on the back of her dress until he was able to reach inside and loosen her laces . . .

Again, to no avail.

It was then he noticed for the first time the warmth emanating from her body, even through the silk of her dress. What the devil was wrong with her? He pressed the back of his knuckles to her cheeks once more. He swore suddenly. Christ, what an idiot he was! The girl was burning up with fever!

She moaned then. Morgan gripped her shoulders and gave her a little shake, fumbling a little as he sought to recall her name. "Elizabeth! Elizabeth, wake up! Are you ill, girl?"

Her eyes opened slowly, dazed and glazed with pain.

"Elizabeth, tell me," he demanded. "Where do you hurt?"

Her fingertips came slowly to her brow. "Here," she said faintly.

"Anywhere else?"

Her hand fell to her breast. "Here, too." Her whisper was feeble, as if the effort cost her every bit of strength. "It hurts to"—she swallowed—"to breathe." As she turned her head aside, her lashes fluttered closed. She coughed, the sound dry and hacking. Morgan knew she'd slipped into unconsciousness once more.

This time he was almost glad, for he suspected she would have been appalled at what he was about to do. Tugging the bodice of her gown down over smooth, creamy shoulders, he bent low, putting his ear to her chest. Her breath seemed to rattle; air made a whistling sound in and out of her lungs.

Morgan swore. He was on his feet in an instant. "Simmons!" he shouted. "Send a man for Stephen! This woman is ill!"

An hour later, his friend Dr. Stephen Marks stood beside the bed where his patient had been taken. He was short but broad of shoulder, his easygoing nature reflected in the readiness of his smile and the warmth of his eyes.

He stepped back from the bedside, glancing back over his shoulder where Morgan watched him quietly, strong arms folded across his chest.

"She came from London, you say?"

Morgan nodded. "So she told Simmons," he said briefly.

"There's no question it's a lung infection," Stephen said. "Probably from the damp sea air. But she's young and appears healthy, so that's in her favor. Right now the best thing we can do for her is to try to bring her fever down and keep her dry." He replaced his instruments in his bag, then cast his friend a teasing glance. "I must say, Morgan, she's a bit of a change from your usual."

Morgan's mouth turned down at the corners. "Don't bother speculating," he said dryly. "It wasn't me she came here to see at all."

"Who, then?"

There was a moment's silence. "Nathaniel."

The twinkle slowly faded from Stephen's eyes. "What on earth would a woman from England want with Nathaniel?"

"That," Morgan stated grimly, "is what I'd like to know. And there's more, Stephen. Simmons said she introduced herself as *Lady* Elizabeth Stanton."

Chestnut brows shot upward. "Britain's upper crust?"

"So it would seem." Morgan's gaze rested on the figure in the bed. "When the lady wakes up, we'll just have to ask her, won't we?"

Stephen said nothing, merely watched his friend closely. "Where *is* Nathaniel?" he asked finally.

The lines of Morgan's features had gone hard. His reply was blunt and instantaneous. "We both know I'm rarely privy to his whereabouts. I haven't seen him in months—which is just the way I prefer." He nodded toward the girl. "Will she be all right?"

"I suspect so," Stephen said thoughtfully. "But it will likely be some weeks before she's back on her feet again." He chuckled as he watched a thundercloud darken his friend's face. Reaching for his jacket, he shrugged into it. "You may as well become accustomed to the idea, Morgan— you'll be having a houseguest for a while."

That, Morgan thought blackly, was not what he wished to hear.

Stephen strode toward the door, then stopped suddenly. "I have a suggestion, though. What if

I sent over my housekeeper, Margaret, for a time? She's not only an excellent nurse, but she'll keep tongues from wagging should it come out you've a young female residing under your roof. The last thing you need is another scandal.''

A cynical half smile curled Morgan's lips. He shook his head. ''It's not necessary. Heaven knows my reputation is the last thing that concerns me. Besides, God knows it could hardly be sullied any more than it already is.''

Stephen reached for the door's ornately carved brass handle. Seeing the gesture, Morgan turned toward him, but Stephen waved him away. ''No need, old man. I'll see myself out.''

With that, he was left alone—alone with his uninvited houseguest. Moving back to the bedside, he glanced down at the girl. Her profile might have been etched in marble, she was so still and white. Her closed eyelids were the palest pink, almost translucent. Lashes like Indian ink curved across her cheeks. Her brows were slender and arched with a distinctly piquant slant.

But it was her skin that captured his attention the longest. It was unbelievably smooth and unblemished. He had the strangest urge to reach out and stroke the girl's cheek, to see if it was as soft and creamy as it looked . . .

He'd done it again, he realized. Why did he persist in thinking of her as a girl, when she was hardly that? Perhaps it had been something in her wide-eyed, almost pleading expression when she'd discovered he wasn't Nathaniel, for indeed, she was hardly so very young—he guessed in her early twenties.

His gaze wandered further, lingering on the thrusting roundness of her breasts beneath the satin coverlet. He'd stripped her of her petticoats and stays before Stephen arrived. She was clad only in her chemise. Though she was tall and slender, her body was full and ripe and womanly. Impersonal as he'd been, it was impossible not to be aware of her warm sensuality.

Ah, yes, she was a lovely one—if one cared for blondes, which he definitely did not. He'd found most were generally too insipid for his tastes, often with personalities to match.

She stirred then, a fitful toss of her head upon the pillow. Morgan bent low, for a breath of sound escaped her lips ... a word ... ?

A name.

Nathaniel.

Morgan straightened. His thoughts were firmly unrelenting as he spun away. Whoever this woman was, he didn't appreciate her presence here in his household. Yet here she was, a reminder he could hardly ignore—a reminder of all that was best left alone.

But he would do all he could to ensure that she was given the best of care. With luck, she would soon be well on her way to recovery, for he was determined to send her packing as soon as she was able.

She moaned, drawing his gaze back to her despite his best intentions. As her fingers curled around the edge of the counterpane, he caught the glint of gold. His eyes fastened on the source.

A gold band circling the third finger of her left hand.

A vile curse erupted. Christ! What the hell had

Nat done now? Morgan balked at the obvious. Nat could barely keep himself out of trouble. God forbid he'd taken a *wife!*

Damn! he thought, striding from the room, furious all over again. *Damn!* Why was Elizabeth Stanton here? And what was her connection with Nathaniel?

He had the feeling he wouldn't like the answer.

Chapter 3

⟡

For Elizabeth, the next few days passed in a haze of pain and the strangest sense of unreality. Yet deep in the foggy recesses of her mind, she knew she was wretchedly ill. A smothering heat enshrouded the whole of her body. Her head throbbed and every breath seemed to drag at her insides. She was hazily aware of tossing and crying out, of being urged by an unfamiliar voice to sip and drink. Often there was a hand at her brow; a damp, blessedly cool cloth ran over her neck and shoulders. Voices swirled all around her.

Then one day, she became aware of bright sunlight trickling directly through the window before her. Wakefulness returned in slow degrees. She tried to turn her head against the brightness, but there was no escaping it. She knew from the murmur of voices that she was not alone. She wanted to protest that something was wrong— in both the London town house and her room at Hayden Park, the window was angled behind the head of her bed.

She let her hand fall against her eyelids. "The light hurts," she muttered.

Full, throaty laughter sounded above her. "Well, now, I'm glad to see you're back with us again."

The voice was a stranger's. Bewildered, Elizabeth opened her eyes to find herself being scrutinized by a man with thick, chestnut hair and twinkling, golden eyes almost the same color as his hair. A part of her recoiled in horror—she was hardly accustomed to men in her bedchamber! To make matters worse, he sat in a chair scant inches from the bed in which she was lying.

"Wh—who are you?" The voice that emerged was nothing like her own. It came out a dry, rasping croak.

The man chuckled. "I'm Dr. Stephen Marks. I've been taking care of you the past few days." He tipped his head to the side. "I confess, being an American, I'm not quite sure how to address you. Should I call you *Lady* Elizabeth?"

As hazy as she was, Elizabeth had already decided she liked Dr. Stephen Marks. There was a warmth and friendliness to his manner that made her trust him immediately.

Ignoring her parched throat and cracked lips, she smiled. "Elizabeth is fine."

"Good. And you may call me Stephen." There was a pitcher of water on a table near the head of the bed. He must have known of her thirst, for he poured a glass of water and offered it to her. "Here, allow me," he murmured, helping her to sit and adjusting pillows behind her. He handed her her white silk wrapper, then discreetly turned his back while she slipped it over her shoulders. Elizabeth smiled gratefully when he returned to tip the glass to her lips. She was embarrassed at how weak she was, yet her muscles seemed to have turned to gruel.

When she'd finished, he said briskly, "Do you know where you are, Elizabeth?"

Memory rushed in at her from all sides—she recalled waiting for Nathaniel in the drawing room. Only it hadn't been Nathaniel who had come—it was that tall, fiercely elegant stranger . . . Turning her mind to the question at hand, she bit her lip, her gaze touching on the richness of the room's furnishings.

"From the look of it," she murmured, "not in a hospital. Therefore I assume I'm still at the home of Nathaniel O'Connor."

He hesitated, a faint frown lining his brow, then nodded. "So tell me, Elizabeth. How are you feeling?"

In her entire life, she didn't know when she'd felt so awful; as if she'd been battered and bruised from the inside out, and so she said. After a moment, she asked, "What day is this?"

"Sunday morning."

Her eyes widened. Her ship had docked Wednesday afternoon. "Oh, my," she murmured, precipitating another kindly laugh from Stephen. She bit her lip and glanced at him hopefully. "Do you think I might get up for a bit?"

He started to shake his head, then glimpsed her crestfallen expression. "I suppose we could see if you're up to it—certainly a few steps would do no harm. Here, let me help you." He swept back the counterpane, taking care to avert his eyes from the sight of her bare limbs.

Elizabeth eased her legs to the floor, secretly surprised by how wooden they felt. Nonetheless, she was determined. Stephen slipped an arm around her waist. She smiled up at him gratefully and sought to rise to her feet. Her expression quickly turned to one of startled bemusement when she discovered her legs refused to hold her.

She sank back down. "Oh, dear," she said with a laugh as shaky as her legs. "I'm afraid I'm not up to this after all."

Stephen merely shook his head, his lips curved upward as he swung her bare feet back to the mattress. She leaned back against the pillows, all at once feeling absurdly tired and weak for having slept nearly three days, and disliking it heartily. "What's wrong with me anyway?"

"Pneumonia, I suspect. And though it appears the crisis has passed, you're still very ill, Elizabeth." He rose from the chair. "Which is why I'll leave you to rest. I'll have the cook send up some broth, and we'll see how you do with that. Some nourishment should begin to make you stronger. In the meantime, if you need anything, don't hesitate to ask."

Even as the doctor exited, another figure entered . . .

It was *him*.

The door clicked shut.

They were left alone.

A fleeting panic assailed her. Odd, for Elizabeth would never have considered herself a coward, but the prospect of facing this man was almost frightening.

There was scant resemblance to Nathaniel, she noted distantly. This man was taller. Leaner. The elder, by the look of him. He was not smiling, as Nathaniel surely would have been. And there was no laughter in his eyes . . .

Instead they were fixed on her, coolly remote. His clothing was severe yet elegant—dark trousers, a plain black satin vest and jacket. He wore no jewelry but a watch and chain. For an instant, all she could think was that he was austere and forbidding in manner—and in looks! Long of nose and keen of eye, his hair as dark as ink. But those eyes . . . They held her as if pinned. She saw in them a haughty condemnation, a cool, dismissive appraisal . . . and then she saw nothing, no hint of anything at all.

More memories brushed at her. Of falling into darkness. Darkness and warmth. Of being held in a man's arms . . . *this* man's arms. She recalled the smell of bay rum, of being carried up a flight of steps, the touch of warm fingers brushing at the neckline of her bodice. On the warm skin of her breast . . .

Her hand flew to her throat. "You touched me." The accusation came out in a breathless whisper. This man—this *stranger*—had undressed her. Touched her as no man had ever done, as no man had a right to, not even Nathaniel.

Nathaniel. Dear God, this was his brother. His *brother*, a man she had never dreamed existed— a man she hadn't *known* existed.

"Unavoidable, under the circumstances, I'm afraid." He sounded not the least apologetic, she noted indignantly. Her chin came up as he approached the bedside. Then, to her utter shock, he gave as courtly a bow as one would find in London.

"I do believe we should reintroduce ourselves," he said smoothly. She found her fingers encased strongly within his grip—oh, if only she were wearing gloves! The feel of warm, faintly callused skin against hers disturbed her immensely. "Morgan O'Connor at your service."

His brows slanted devilishly, he awaited her response. "Lady Elizabeth Stanton," she stated breathlessly. Even as she spoke, she sought gently to tug her hand free. But to her discomfiture, he refused to release her. Years of breeding took their toll; she was too much of a lady to make a scene.

Thank heaven there was no need to persist. He released her fingers abruptly and stepped back.

"I hope you don't mind, but I took the liberty of having your trunks delivered here from the docks."

Elizabeth raised her gaze. "My thanks," she murmured. Despite the obvious richness of his clothing, there was something distinctly predatory about him that put her on guard. Warily she watched as he proceeded to pull up a chair to the bedside.

He gave a half smile, a smile that did not reach his eyes. "You must forgive my colonial ignorance, but I find myself intensely curious as to why you are called *Lady* Elizabeth Stanton."

Did he mock her? She couldn't be sure. Nervously she wet her lips with the tip of her tongue, unmindful of the dark gray gaze that tracked its movement. "I am the daughter of the Earl of Chester. As such, I am known as 'lady.'"

"I see," he murmured. "I confess, Elizabeth, that merely makes me all the more curious as to what a woman of the aristocracy should want with my brother."

As he spoke, he crossed stylishly shod feet at the ankle. Though the movement was offhand, the omission of *lady* was blatant. Elizabeth had the strangest sensation there was nothing unstudied about the man.

Her delicate chin angled high. She would be no one's patsy, and it was time he knew it. "The reason is simple, really." She folded her hands in her lap and smiled directly into cold gray eyes. "I came to be his bride."

"Indeed. And what does your husband think of this?"

Elizabeth was caught wholly off guard. "My husband," she echoed. Her tone turned indignant. "Why would I wish to marry Nathaniel if I were already married? Why, the question is preposterous, sir! Of course I have no husband!"

"No?" His hand shot out, encircling her wrist like a shackle of iron. Though his hold was not hurtful, his movement was so sudden and unexpected that she nearly cried out. "Then why do you wear a ring," he demanded, "if you are not wed? Indeed, I wonder if you are truly who you say you are. Perhaps Lady Elizabeth Stanton is just a guise—a means to an end. Well, I warn you now, whoever you are, you'll gain little from my brother."

Elizabeth gasped and wrenched her wrist free. The gall of the man was unmitigated; she was not used to being the object of such suspicion. "I am who I say I am. And since I traveled unescorted," she informed him haughtily, "I had no wish to fend off unwanted advances from the ship's male passengers. I thought the easiest way to avoid such unpleasantness was to pretend I was already wed—thus the wedding band."

His eyes narrowed. "Why would a lady of your station travel unescorted?"

"I'm not certain it's any of your business," Elizabeth snapped.

"You are in my home," he pointed out curtly. "That makes it my business."

"*Your* business . . . *your* home." Elizabeth sputtered with ire. "You ungrateful wretch! I am no fool! You may live here, but this is Nathaniel's home!"

A smile that could only be called cutting spread across his hard lips. A single word was all he spoke. "No."

Elizabeth glared at him. "No? What, pray tell, do you mean, sir? I know full well this house is Nathaniel's—I knew as soon as I arrived! He described it to me quite well, and it was exactly as I expected!"

"Indeed." Morgan's tone was light, but his features were hard. "I suppose he regaled you with stories of O'Connor Shipbuilding, too, along with tales of the thriving business he has built over the years."

"And what if he did? I daresay he has every right to be proud of his accomplishments!" Faith, but Morgan O'Connor was far and away the most arrogant man she'd ever met.

A dark brow cocked high. "My dear lady," he

drawled, "my brother has scarcely done a day's work in his entire life, most certainly neither *at* nor *for* O'Connor Shipbuilding. Perhaps you already know, but there are some who would say Nathaniel is a liar. A cheat."

"I know nothing of the sort! And I am given to wonder what kind of man would so malign his own brother!"

"You have only to ask the servants to know that I do not lie. You're under a grave misconception if you believe otherwise. For I assure you, this house is solely mine. O'Connor Shipbuilding, too, is solely mine."

He spoke with quiet brevity. All trace of arrogance vanished from his manner. Elizabeth stared at him. Her brain scrambled for clarity. Her head had begun to ache abominably. As the seconds marched slowly by, a sick feeling began to gather in the pit of her stomach. All at once, she was no longer so sure of herself—or Nathaniel.

But by God, she'd not let Morgan O'Connor leave this room feeling he'd bested her.

She watched as he moved to stand before the fireplace hearth. Casually he turned to face her, resting an elbow on the mantel. "So," he said. "You are truly who you say you are? Lady Elizabeth Stanton?"

Her gaze was silently detesting, her tone filled with icy disdain. "Come now, sir. First you refuse to believe I am who I say I am. Now it seems that you do. So which is it to be, I ask?"

His answer came, but not in so many words. "And you wish to wed Nathaniel?"

"He asked for my hand in marriage. I accepted. Unfortunately, my father was ill and I was unable to accompany him when he returned here from London." As she spoke, Elizabeth calmly folded her hands upon her knees, drawn up beneath the coverlet—it was hard to feel dignified when she was dressed only in night rail and wrapper.

"To my knowledge, Nathaniel has never before proposed to marry." He appeared to consider the possibility. "The daughter of an earl no less, eh? Yes, Nathaniel would like that. It becomes quite clear now. No doubt you possess a fortune."

Elizabeth reeled. His insult appeared directed more at Nathaniel than at her, yet she felt it just as keenly.

But he was not yet finished, the brute! He continued, his tone smooth as oil. "A lady of breeding," he mused almost thoughtfully. "A lady of quality. A lady of the English aristocracy . . . Why, Nat's outdone himself this time."

Storm-gray eyes wandered over her, lingering with blatant approval on the roundness of her breasts, making her feel as if he stripped her naked. Deep inside, she was horrified at his effrontery, for never before had a man made her feel so—so common and cheap.

His eyes locked with hers. "Yes," he said softly. "I do commend my brother's taste. But of course, he would want to assure himself that he would not lose such a prize as you." He paused, a cynical half smile flirting on his lips. "Tell me, Elizabeth. When is the child due?"

At first Elizabeth didn't comprehend. But when his gaze dropped to her belly, she felt her face flame hot as fire, first with embarrassment, then with anger.

She trembled with outrage, small fists clenching upon the counterpane. "By God, were I able, I would slap your face."

He laughed, the scoundrel, he laughed! "When you are able, Elizabeth, then you may."

Rebellion blazed within her. "It's Lady Elizabeth to you!" she cried.

He made no sign that he heard as he sauntered away. In her heart Elizabeth was appalled at her unladylike behavior. Never in her life had she shouted at anyone, not even her stepmother, though many was the time she longed to do so.

But that didn't stop her from glaring at the door he'd just passed through. No wonder Nathaniel had never spoken of his brother. He was surely the most hateful man ever to have been born.

It was only later that she realized . . . She still had no idea where Nathaniel was.

Chapter 4

When Morgan emerged, Stephen awaited him in the corridor outside. Arms crossed over his waistcoat, his mouth tight with disapproval, he wasted no time venting his displeasure.

"I couldn't help but overhear." Both Stephen's tone and manner were stiff. "Elizabeth is scarcely up to doing battle with the likes of you, Morgan."

Battle? Morgan was unwillingly amused. Even as he spoke, deep in the recesses of his mind, he envisioned her fiery glare. It struck him that Stephen was wrong—he suspected Elizabeth Stanton would stand up to Queen Victoria herself if she so chose—and without batting an eye.

No, he thought again. No spineless weakling was the lady.

Morgan deliberately kept his response light. "What! Surely you jest, Stephen. I was hardly 'doing battle' with the chit, as you choose to put it."

Stephen remained vexed. "Nonetheless, I would remind you, she is my patient."

51

"And I would remind you, she is in my house." Though his smile remained fixed in place, there was no mistaking the steel in his voice.

Stephen grimaced. "Oh, come now, Morgan. You know I'm not one to interfere, but it will be some time before she's fully recovered. It's my duty as a physician to make that happen as quickly as possible. She needs to concentrate on getting well—no worries, no strain."

A dark brow rose. "Well, then, Stephen, perhaps we should continue this discussion in my study, lest the lady hear us and become upset."

"Yes . . . yes, of course, you're right." Stephen fell into step beside his friend.

Morgan's study occupied a goodly portion of the east wing of the house. Wide windows looked out upon the garden, which in spring and summer bloomed in riotous color. Though he'd commended Amelia's tasteful decoration of the remainder of the house, this was the one room that bore none of her touches and all of his own. The furnishings were of mahogany and dark, rich leather, totally masculine and wholly unpretentious, designed for a man's comfort.

Striding to the side table, Morgan poured brandy from a crystal decanter into a glass and handed it to Stephen. Watching as Stephen raised the brew to his lips, he said casually, "Correct me if I'm wrong, Stephen, but it would appear you're quite smitten with the lady."

Stephen chuckled, his good humor restored. "Oh, come now. Appealing as the prospect may be, I think it's a bit premature on that score."

"Good," Morgan remarked. "Because I'm afraid she's already spoken for."

Stephen sighed and made a face. "Ah, well. I should have known." He sprawled into the nearest chair but suddenly sat upright. "Good God! I was going to ask who the lucky fellow was, but . . . she came to see Nathaniel—don't tell me it's him!"

His gaze sought Morgan's. Morgan gave a wordless nod.

Stephen blinked. "He certainly has an eye for a pretty face, doesn't he?" He frowned suddenly. "Do you think she really expects him to marry her?"

Morgan gave a short, harsh laugh. "Obviously she is hardly acquainted with my brother's changeable sense of purpose. Do you know she came here believing this house was Nat's? And the business, too, God rot his soul—he told her it was his!"

"Looks like he's up to his old tricks again." Stephen studied him. "You still haven't forgiven him, have you?"

Morgan's shoulders stiffened. Though he spoke not a word, his silence was all-encompassing . . . and all-telling.

Stephen shook his head. "Sometimes, Morgan," he said softly, "I wonder what's happened to you."

Morgan was hardly disposed to wonder. His thoughts were as dark as his mood. Time had aged him, he thought. Life had hardened him.

One side of his mouth curled upward in a sardonic half smile. "And I wonder that you've chosen to remain my friend, Stephen."

"Why?" Stephen said bluntly. "Because I'm one of those Boston blue bloods you hate?" His family lines went back over two hundred years. His good name was among the oldest and wealthiest in the city.

But Morgan hadn't always hated the "blue bloods" of whom Stephen spoke. Even while he considered the city's elite pompous and stuffy, a secret part of him had envied them. Many was the time he'd wished he were one of them, especially as a boy.

Once, while his mother was still alive, she'd taken him and Nathaniel to see the "grand houses on the Hill," as she'd called them. There had been one immense home under construction, nearly finished but not quite. When the workmen had gone, the three of them had strolled through the empty rooms, imagining that they lived in this magnificent house. From that day on, he'd gone to sleep dreaming that someday he, too, would live in a house that was just as grand.

And now he did.

But he could never escape his roots. It was a lesson in truth that had proved painful to learn.

His mouth still carried a trace of a smile. "In all honesty, Stephen, your loyalty astounds me, but I value it, just as I value your friendship. And of course, you are right. Elizabeth Stanton's recovery should be the foremost concern. Her care is in your hands, my friend. You have my word that I will distress the lady no more."

The next week passed quickly. Elizabeth was still weak and largely confined to bed, though

she grew stronger with every hour. The majority
of her time was spent sleeping or resting—the
best medicine, according to Stephen, who continued to check her progress daily. He was, as she
discovered, a most engaging, witty man, very
easygoing and friendly. She came to like him immensely.

And it was from Stephen that she learned Morgan spoke the truth—this lovely house was un-
disputably his. O'Connor Shipbuilding also
belonged solely to him.

For Elizabeth there was little peace of mind.
The seed of doubt had been planted and refused
to be banished. Nathaniel—her gallant, chival-
rous charmer—had lied. Yet another disturbing
thought reared high in her mind. *I love you*, he'd
proclaimed. So sweetly. So sincerely.

Was that a lie as well?

She took a deep, fortifying breath. No, she told
herself forcefully. She would have known. Surely
she would have known.

Or would she?

Now, as Stephen escorted her to the parlor to
sit for a while, a dozen questions flooded
through her.

"I-I don't understand it," she said, settling herself on the seat he offered. "I don't understand
why he should do such a thing! Do you think
perhaps he thought I might think less of him
were he to tell me the truth? And he said Boston
was his home."

Stephen hesitated. "And so it is," he said
slowly.

"Then where is he, I ask . . . where?" Elizabeth's troubled gaze sought Stephen's. Dis-

traught as she was, she had yet to glean his reluctance.

"Elizabeth, I must confess, I'm uncomfortable talking to you about Nathaniel. Somehow I feel as if—as if I'm a naughty schoolboy telling tales."

"Nonsense," Elizabeth said firmly. Her tone turned pleading when he remained silent. "Tell me, Stephen. Please tell me. You are the only friend I have here."

Stephen sighed. "Elizabeth, you place me in an awkward position. Please, go to Morgan with your questions."

Morgan's image flashed behind her eyelids. Elizabeth couldn't help it; just thinking of that piercing gray stare made her shiver.

She bit her lip. "Oh, Stephen, I-I would, but I cannot help but feel Morgan has no liking at all for his brother! And though I was not blessed with brothers or sisters myself, I find that very strange."

"That's true," Stephen admitted. "They are no longer close. But it wasn't always so." On seeing Elizabeth's eyes widen, he shook his head, anticipating her query. "I'm sorry, Elizabeth. I can say no more, except that the answers to your questions should come from one of them." He hesitated, then laid his hand atop hers where it rested in her lap. "It may not be wise to expect too much of Nathaniel."

Such a cryptic warning. In the end, she had no choice but to do as he suggested—go to Morgan.

She'd seen little of him, which suited her quite well indeed, since she found Nathaniel's brother a most odious man! He left early in the morning, and often was gone well into the evening. He'd made no effort to see her, other than to inquire as to her health when she'd chanced to see him one afternoon as he emerged from the library. Oh, he was polite enough, but beneath the smooth exterior he presented her was a faint mockery that riled her usually placid temper.

Later that afternoon, she learned from Simmons that he was in his study. As she stopped before the set of massive oak-paneled doors, she couldn't help but feel as if she were about to enter the lion's den. Why she should react so strangely, she didn't know. She knew only that with but a single encounter he had unnerved her as no one had before.

But that was nonsense. He was just a man—a most disagreeable one, at that!—but he was still Nathaniel's brother. Chiding herself for such foolishness, she squared her shoulders and knocked firmly on the door.

"Come in," called his deep male voice.

With a courage that was pure bravado, she opened the door and walked forward.

He was seated behind a huge desk that was strategically placed near the windows. He was once again garbed in black. An unguarded surprise flickered in those startlingly light gray eyes as he acknowledged her.

With one lithe movement he was on his feet, and then it was her turn to be surprised when he rounded the corner and approached her. "Why, Elizabeth, this is quite unexpected," he said, reaching for her hand.

For the space of a heartbeat Elizabeth could neither speak nor move. She caught the scent of bay rum—odd, but it seemed almost familiar! But his very closeness was overpowering; despite the stylish elegance of his clothing, there was an unmistakable aura of primitive male vitality that was somehow almost frightening. And her skin seemed to burn where his hand locked firmly around hers.

Something faintly akin to panic raced along her spine. She tugged almost frantically, vastly relieved when he released her hand. Unable to think of an appropriate reply, she said nervously, "I do hope I'm not intruding."

His gaze, coolly assessing, swept the length of her. The merest of smiles curved the harshness of his mouth. "Not at all. I'm glad to see you looking so well."

Elizabeth drew herself up sharply. Did he mock her? Drat the man, she couldn't be sure!

"Would you care to sit, Elizabeth?" He indicated a nearby chair. Elizabeth nodded, and allowed him to assist her. Smoothing her skirts, she watched as he strode toward the window. He stood for a moment, hands linked behind his back, then turned to face her. It appeared the beast had been caged, Elizabeth decided cautiously, at least for the moment.

Clearing her throat, she folded her hands in her lap. "I fear I owe you an apology, Mr. O'Connor. It was quite rude of me to shout at you the way I did at our last meeting."

One broad shoulder lifted. "My dear girl, I'm hardly offended. To be honest, I'd not given it another thought. And I certainly gave you cause to react that way."

His reminder made her grow hot all over

again. What was it he'd asked? *When is the child due?* Lord, that he could even think she would do such a thing! She could count on the fingers of one hand the few times Nathaniel had kissed her. Besides, such frankness between man and woman was unheard of. She was shocked that he could speak of it so casually.

It also seemed she judged too soon.

His eyes had lowered to her lap. "Ah," he murmured. "I see you've removed your wedding ring."

Elizabeth flushed. She didn't appreciate his reminder of her dishonesty. Her chin rose a notch and her eyes flashed mutinously.

"I came here to thank you for your hospitality, sir, but you make it exceedingly difficult."

He inclined his head. "I accept your gratitude, Elizabeth. But I have the feeling there's more."

Elizabeth sat very still. Lord, was there nothing this man did not overlook? It was as if he could see right through to the marrow of her bones.

And it was a feeling she heartily disliked . . . as indeed, she heartily disliked *him*.

Her tone was clipped. "I shall come directly to the point then, sir. My illness was most unfortunate, for it waylaid my purpose in coming here." She paused. "You said the day I arrived that Nathaniel was not here. But you are his brother, and the only one to whom I might turn. And so I would ask you again . . . where can I find him?"

"And I shall come directly to the point. I do not know, for I am hardly his keeper."

Elizabeth was undaunted. "But surely you

must know something . . . You must have some idea when he will return."

His expression had turned as hard as stone. She held her breath, for she feared he would refuse to answer. But then he spoke.

"No, I do not."

"But this is his home—"

"Yes, Boston is his home. And I suppose you are right. No doubt he will return. He always does, sooner or later."

"And will he return here? To this house?"

Again that damnable silence. "No," he said at last.

Still she persisted. "The two of you don't share this house?"

"I thought I made that quite clear."

"You are both unmarried. Why not?"

"That is none of your business."

Elizabeth caught her breath. His tone was quite rude. By some miracle she maintained a pleasant countenance. "I beg to differ, sir, for I believe it is my business. Nathaniel will be my husband. You will be my brother-in-law. And if you are privy to his whereabouts, so should I be."

"My dear Elizabeth," he drawled. "My attorneys see to it that my brother receives a more than generous allowance, yet for Nathaniel it is not always enough—I see him only when he is in need of excess funds. He lives for the moment, through the generosity of others. Or did he neglect to tell you this too?" A jet brow rose high. "Why, should the two of you actually marry, I wouldn't be surprised if you found it necessary to pawn the very ring you wore on your journey here. So tell me, Elizabeth. Does that change your perception of my dear brother?"

His manner was sheer arrogance. Elizabeth's temper began to simmer. "It changes nothing," she retorted. "And you, sir, are unforgivably rude."

His lips twisted. "No, lady. I am unfailingly honest, unlike my brother." Their eyes tangled fiercely. To her dismay, Elizabeth was the first to look away.

He said nothing for a moment, merely stood with his arms braced across his chest. "What do you intend to do?"

She squared her shoulders. "Wait."

"For Nathaniel?" The sound he made was one of sheer disgust. "Good God! You're determined to see this through, aren't you?"

"He asked me to marry him," she said levelly. "He may not be here, but that doesn't change the fact that he proposed to me."

"And what if he is not the man you thought?"

"Ah, yes—the rogue again." They were on dangerous ground, she reflected. She hated the doubt that pricked like a thorn beneath her skin, and willfully brushed it aside. "Whatever Nathaniel may have been in the past," she said with soft deliberation, "he has changed."

To her surprise, the look he gave her was long and searching. "A word of advice, Elizabeth. Leave here and never look back. Forget you ever met my brother. Believe me, if you don't, he'll make you regret it." He paused. "If you like, I can arrange passage—"

"No. No, I say." There was no question he was vastly perturbed by her vehemence. Lest he grow angry, she took a deep breath and sought to explain. "You once asked if I possessed a fortune. Well, sir, I tell you I do not. I've been disowned, and I would rather not discuss the circumstances right now, if you please. But the fact of the matter is, I cannot return to England."

He didn't bother to hide his skepticism. "Come now. You truly expect me to believe you are destitute?" Four steps brought him within reach. His disdainful gaze swept the length of her, taking in the watered silk day gown she wore. "Yours, my pampered young miss, are hardly the clothes of a pauper."

His mockery cut deep. Perhaps he didn't lie. Perhaps Nathaniel had once been a scoundrel. But surely she was right. Surely it was just as she'd said. He had changed . . .

To her utter shame, her certainty began to slip away like sand beneath the sea. For just an instant, resentment blazed within her. How she wished she'd never set eyes on Morgan O'Connor!

But the anger she would have welcomed simply would not remain. She began to tremble. Her head began to pound. She raised ice-cold fingertips to her forehead and bowed her head low, feeling perilously near tears.

"Elizabeth? Are you ill?"

His voice prodded her. She didn't see the lean hand that hovered just above the shining coronet atop her head.

Her composure badly shaken, she fought the hot ache that threatened to close her throat. "No," she whispered faintly, hating the betraying wobble in her voice. " 'Tis just that . . . I came here expecting to find Nathaniel. I never dreamed he wouldn't be here." She shook her head. "You must have some idea where I can find him."

His hand dropped to his side. "None," he stated flatly.

"I—I cannot believe that." Slowly she raised her head, blinking back tears. "There must be something you can do."

The silence dragged on. His thoughts were a mystery to her. He appeared frozen as he stared down at her, his expression as rigid as stone.

She gestured vaguely. "Please," she said, very low. "I am alone here. I have no one else—I can turn to no one else. But . . . there must be a way to find him." Her gaze locked with his, full of the plea she could no longer hold inside. "Can you help me? *Will* you help me?"

Time spun out endlessly. Her fingers strained against each other. This time Elizabeth didn't look away. But her heart plummeted as she watched his lips thin further, as his features grew ever more dark and forbidding.

His words were not what she expected.

"I know a man . . ." he began slowly, then stopped. "I will make no promises," he went on. "But I will try."

Elizabeth's lips parted. Dear God, it was all she could ask for! "Thank you," she murmured, and then again, "I—I thank you." She shook her head as if to clear it. "In the meantime, I'll not trespass on your generosity any longer. I shall find lodgings elsewhere until Nathaniel returns."

"There's no need," he said curtly. "Particularly if you are in the financial straits you claim to be."

She felt a warm flush creep into her cheeks. She almost wondered if it was his deliberate aim to embarrass her. She summoned her dignity, for indeed, at the moment it was her most treasured possession.

"I have some money," she told him quietly. "Not a great deal, but enough to—"

"Nonsense. Nathaniel's bride-to-be in a hotel? No. You may stay as long as you like. Indeed, I insist."

He was once again cool and detached. Elizabeth studied him as he rounded his desk and resumed his place behind it. Certainly she had no wish to remain beholden to him, yet if the truth be told, her money would scarcely buy lodgings for more than several nights.

"I truly appreciate your offer," she said slowly. "But I am well now and it isn't proper for you and I"—she faltered—"that is to say, for the two of us to . . ." She stopped, unable to continue.

To her surprise, he gave a harsh laugh. "And what if I were to tell you the good people of Boston expect no less from me? Propriety be damned! The matter is settled and I'll hear no further argument."

Elizabeth hesitated. Oddly, that was not what bothered her the most. "I do not mean to argue, sir. But I am already in your debt and have no wish to—"

"For pity's sake," he growled, "you are hardly beholden to me. But if you wish, I will make you a bargain."

Elizabeth blinked. This was the last thing she expected. Still, she couldn't entirely erase the assumption that leaped to the fore. Morgan O'Connor was young, handsome, and unmarried. But he was still a man, no doubt a man with an appetite for the opposite sex . . .

"Wh-what sort of bargain?"

Little did she realize she might well have shouted the thought from the rooftop. "God in heaven," he said impatiently. "You are hardly to my taste, so you needn't look at me as if I expect you to exchange your body for the bed you sleep in! This, my dear girl, is the bargain I propose. Simmons grows old and is unable to do as much as he once did, though he would never admit it. I merely ask that you assist in matters of the household—planning meals, overseeing the maids' work. Now, do we understand each other?"

By now Elizabeth's face was flame-red. Yet curiously, she felt wounded without knowing quite why. "Yes," she managed.

"Then do we have a bargain?"

Her nod was jerky. It was all she could do.

"Good."

He swiveled his chair. Reaching into a drawer, he dropped a sheaf of papers on the desktop. She'd been forgotten, she realized.

Rising, she gathered her skirts in one hand and fled the study. Outside in the hallway, she stopped and leaned back against the wall. A nervous laugh escaped. How silly she was to think Morgan O'Connor might find her attractive and take advantage of her situation.

But he would send someone to try to find Nathaniel—that alone was worth having faced the dragon in his lair. Why it was so, Elizabeth had no idea, for he was a complete enigma. Indeed, she would swear he was less than pleased at the prospect. But even as she wondered what had happened that he disliked his own brother, relief flooded her veins. He had relented, and she would ask no more of him.

All that was left to do was to wait and hope . . .
And pray that Nathaniel was found soon.

Chapter 5

Hours later, Morgan still sat in his study, a black cloak of darkness surrounding him.

Lord, but he was a fool.

Damn . . . *damn!* He cursed himself vilely, even as he cursed her. He'd felt himself weakening, feeling sorry for her. Yet he almost hated her for it, for bringing up the past, reminding him of all he longed to forget.

Christ, he thought blackly. If she only knew . . . How could she be so blind? Nathaniel was anything but noble. But he *was* a charmer, Morgan reflected bitterly, particularly with the ladies.

A twinge of guilt bit at him. It wasn't in his nature to lie. And he *hadn't* lied, he told himself . . .

Yet he hadn't been entirely truthful either. True, he didn't know *where* Nathaniel was. But Morgan had no doubt he'd find him in the arms of his latest whore, and what would the elegant Lady Elizabeth Stanton think of that?

A vision of her flitted through his mind's eye, as she'd appeared only hours before. Vulnerable and pleading. Tears standing high and bright, turning her eyes to shimmering emerald. Tears he had sensed cost her no little amount of pride . . .

He shouldn't have cared. By God, he *didn't* care. But the damage was done. He'd made a promise, and he wouldn't go back on his word.

Early the next morning, he hired a detective named Evans; Evans left that very morning to attempt to track down Nathaniel.

God, but he hoped Evans wouldn't find him.

As for Elizabeth, he would put her from his mind . . . an impossible task, he soon discovered.

The days turned. A week passed, then another, and soon a month had gone by.

Her presence in his home—in his life!—was a distraction he hadn't counted on. His awareness of her was tremendously vexing, so much so that he stayed in his offices longer and longer every evening; their paths crossed but seldom. Yet the more he resolved to ignore her, the more her image lingered in his mind—an unfamiliar rustle, a soft sigh, a swirl of scent the moment he walked through the door was all it took. And then there were those eyes, wide, deep pools of vivid green that grew dark with wariness whenever they chanced to meet—that, too, he found vexing. Yet when they spoke, they were both politely formal. Still, Morgan couldn't deny the air of quiet dignity that always surrounded her— and even that both disturbed and impressed him.

Christ, where had Nat ever found her?

He suspected she made every effort to avoid him, dining alone in her room, often retiring before he arrived home. But already he could see the difference her presence had wrought upon the household. Meals were hot and well prepared, and offered far more variety. Where there had sometimes been a veil of dust coating furniture and furnishings, there was none. Thank heaven Simmons didn't mind her assistance. Indeed, the old man appeared almost fond of her.

And it was from Simmons that Morgan learned Stephen was a frequent early evening visitor. It seemed the pair spent a good deal of time together, a situation he found highly annoying—yet for the life of him, he couldn't precisely say why it was so.

But all the while he hoped Evans would not find Nathaniel.

Unfortunately, his hopes were in vain.

Evans appeared at the shipyard one bright spring day, just when he'd begun to think the detective was well and truly stumped in his search for Nathaniel.

A burly, heavyset man who looked more like a salty old seaman than a detective, Evans swept his hat from his head as Morgan's assistant escorted him into his office.

"Sorry to come unannounced, Mr. O'Connor, but I thought you'd want to hear what I found right away."

"That I do." Morgan waved him to the chair opposite him and resumed his place behind the desk. He waited until the other man was seated before he spoke. "So tell me, Mr. Evans. Were you able to find my brother?"

Evans's head bobbed up and down. "I did indeed, sir. Yes, I did indeed. He spent the first of the year in Pittsburgh, then moved on to Philadelphia." His grin was rather tentative. "Seems he met a real fancy widow from New York while he was there."

Morgan arched a brow. "I see. And where is he now, Mr. Evans? New York?"

Evans's grin faded. He looked startled. "You mean you knew all along?"

Morgan's smile was tight. "No. But I do know what my brother would do in such a situation. Tell me, is the widow rich?"

Evans rolled his eyes. "Lord, yes."

"And no doubt my brother has relieved her of a goodly portion of her riches."

Evans's grin reappeared slowly. "From the looks of him, he keeps the tailors busy. And just last week he bought himself a fancy pair of Thoroughbreds. Paid more for those horses than most people make in a lifetime."

Of course, Morgan agreed with derisive scorn. As long as he was spending someone else's money, it was nothing but the best for Nathaniel.

A glint had appeared in Evans's eye. "I got pretty friendly with one of the house maids. She had some wild tales of how your brother keeps the widow too busy to miss her late husband, if you know what I mean."

That he did, Morgan thought silently. He had not a single doubt that Nathaniel and the widow were lovers. But he conceded the fact that most women who fell in with Nat were no more ill used than he.

His mind strayed to Elizabeth. An odd feeling tightened his gut. He couldn't help but wonder how many a sensuous escapade she and Nat had shared. Forcing himself to relax, he reminded himself he shouldn't judge her for falling in with the likes of his brother. Outrageous as he still found it, her only fault lay in the fact that she truly seemed to believe Nathaniel intended to marry her.

Once again he leveled his gaze on the burly man. "I trust you didn't make yourself known to my brother, Mr. Evans. *Or* your purpose there."

"Not at all," Evans said quickly. "I didn't say a word. I came back to Boston to report to you, just like you said."

"Good." Morgan briefly tapped the tips of his fingers together. Rising to his feet, he extended his hand across the desktop. "I thank you for your assistance, Mr. Evans. I'll instruct my bank to have your draft ready at your convenience."

Evans reached for his hat. "You don't want me to return to New York and bring him back?"

A split second's hesitation . . . "No, Mr. Evans. That won't be necessary."

He saw Evans to the door, then slowly closed it. For the space of a heartbeat, he wondered if he'd been wrong . . . Perhaps he should have instructed Evans to return with Nathaniel. After all, he owed Elizabeth Stanton nothing. Why should it matter if Nathaniel leapt fresh from the arms of his latest whore into hers?

But he couldn't do this to her, or anyone. She was better off not knowing where Nathaniel was—worse yet, *what* he was doing.

Yes, he thought. This was the best way, the *only* way. The sooner she was gone, the better for all of them. All that remained was to convince her to board a ship back to England.

That particular subject was still very much on

his mind when he arrived home a short time later. As Simmons took his coat and hat, the sound of mingled laughter, feminine and masculine, reached his ears.

"Stephen?" he queried.

Simmons nodded. "Yes, sir. He and the lady are in the drawing room."

And it was there Morgan directed his steps. The pair sat on the sofa, near each other but not touching. Their heads were bent together as Stephen pointed out something on a small map stretched between them. Morgan paused in the doorway, feeling very much the intruder, and disliking it intensely. Neither was aware of his scrutiny.

"Excuse me," he said.

Both looked up at the same time. He could have sworn a flare of something akin to panic lit Elizabeth's eyes, yet it was gone in an instant.

Stephen was clearly nonplussed. "Morgan!" he greeted heartily. "A tad early for you, isn't it?"

Morgan's response was decidedly cool. "Not all of us are born to a life of leisure, my friend."

Stephen chuckled. "Why, I do believe I'm being chastised. I admit, I'm guilty of leaving my office early as well. But the cause was a good one. I was just giving Elizabeth a history lesson, telling her the local lore about the pirates, thieves, and highwaymen hanged on the Common. And since she's not been out of the house since she arrived, I thought she might enjoy a carriage ride so I could show her around a bit."

"Not now, Stephen." His gaze slid to Elizabeth. "Elizabeth, would you mind waiting in my study? I'd like to speak to you."

"Certainly." Her carriage slim and straight, she flashed a smile at Stephen as she gathered her skirts in her hands. "Stephen, thank you for a most entertaining afternoon." With a swish of her skirts, she was gone.

"Well, well," Stephen remarked when the two men were left alone. "One might think you the lord of the manor and she the lady."

Morgan's jaw might have been etched in stone. "I have no idea what you mean," he said tersely. "Though I think perhaps a reminder is in order—she's already been spoken for, Stephen."

Stephen's brows winged skyward. "You surprise me, Morgan."

"Indeed. How so?"

"Frankly, I find it strange that you protect your brother's interests, very strange indeed."

Morgan gritted his teeth. Such was hardly the case. Yet if not that, then . . . what? He didn't know—and he didn't dare search for the answer.

"In fact," Stephen continued lightly, "I find myself wondering if you don't have eyes for the lady yourself."

Morgan's mouth was a grim slash in his face. He said not a word.

"I must say, it's perfectly understandable. She's a fetching sight indeed. Wouldn't you agree?"

"Very," said Morgan between his teeth.

Stephen sighed. "But you're right, I'm afraid. She belongs to neither of us." He paused thoughtfully. "Frankly, I just can't envision her with me, though I admit, I still have a difficult time picturing her with Nathaniel. Just think, your brother with an English lady, a genuine lady of the realm!" He laughed in obvious mirth. "And the idea of her with you . . . why, it's utterly preposterous! But altogether amusing, don't you think?"

Morgan glared.

"No? Ah, well." Stephen untangled his legs and got to his feet. "Oh, and by the way, I've seen you so seldom, I almost forgot to tell you . . . I'm having a ball tomorrow evening. I thought it might be good for Elizabeth to get out amongst people. Besides, it's time we introduced the lady to Boston society, don't you think? Oh, and you needn't worry. I won't let it be known she's been staying with you. I thought I might say she's a distant cousin of mine. And I'll arrange it so that she arrives before the other guests and leaves afterward."

Before Morgan could say a word, Stephen ambled forward. "I think it's time I took my leave. No need to call Simmons, I'll see myself out," he said with a wave of his hand.

Morgan was already at the entryway to his study by the time the front door closed. Yet he didn't enter straightaway. His gaze swept the room until it found Elizabeth. She was sitting in the low-backed chair before his desk, her back to him. She was as still as a statue, her head bowed low and her hands clasped in her lap. Her hair was swept high upon her crown. A few stray wisps escaped, curling almost lovingly against the sweep of her nape.

What held him there, Morgan didn't know. Instead he stood on the threshold, his eyes fixed on the delicate span of her neck, her nape bare and enticing. He knew instinctively that if he were to touch her there, her skin would be smooth and downy soft . . . Abruptly he became angry with himself. What nonsense was he about, to have such thoughts about his brother's intended? It was merely what Stephen had suggested, outrageous though it was. He wasn't attracted to her—no, not in the slightest.

At length he approached her. She glanced up when he took a seat behind his desk.

Her gaze eagerly searched his features. "You wished to speak to me about Nathaniel, didn't you?" Her tone was breathless. "You've had news of him then?"

He hesitated. "The detective I sent out learned nothing," he heard himself say. "He searched the entire East Coast, but there's been no sign of him. For all we know, he could be clear across the continent."

Her face fell. It was as if he could see her spirit plunging. In that moment he almost hated himself.

"Can't you keep look— No, no, of course you can't." He heard the ragged breath she drew. "I'm sorry. It's just that I was hoping so . . . and when you said he'd probably return eventually—"

"That could be a year from now. For all I know, ten years from now."

She averted her gaze, and he knew she was fighting for control. "I'm grateful for all you've done, Mr. O'Connor. Truly I am."

Morgan, he wanted to shout. *My name is Morgan*.

Instead he said, "Of course, you see now there is no point in staying. Go back to your father, Elizabeth. Go back and—"

"I can't." Her tone was almost wild. She was wringing her hands. "Don't you see? I *can't!*"

"No, frankly, I don't see—"

"He's dead. My father is dead. He was buried two weeks before I set sail for Boston."

It was his turn to look away. The raw pain in her voice made him feel like the world's biggest fool. "Forgive me. I don't mean to be insensitive."

"Of course. You couldn't have known. I never told you."

Morgan frowned. "You look a trifle pale. Would you like some brandy?"

"Yes. Please."

He moved to pour a generous splash into a crystal snifter. As he handed it to her, their fingers barely touched—hers were as cold as a winter wind.

She choked a bit on the first hearty swallow. Her eyes began to water and she coughed.

Morgan smiled faintly. "Sip it," he cautioned. "Otherwise it will burn."

He positioned himself on the corner of his desk, arms crossed over his waistcoat, long legs stretched out before him. He watched as she followed his advice, lifting the glass to her lips again and again. Gradually two spots of color began to bloom on her cheeks. He waited until she was more calm before he spoke. "I'm a bit confused, Elizabeth. You said before that you'd been disinherited. Why would your father do such a thing?"

"Oh, he didn't," she said quickly. "It was his wife."

"His wife . . . your mother?"

Her generous mouth turned down. "Heavens, no. My mother died when I was just a child. It was my stepmother who disinherited me. In Papa's will, he left matters almost entirely in her hands. But Hayden Park, our country estate in Kent, was to pass to me on the occasion of my marriage. But Papa—faith, but I can't imagine what he was thinking!—left the task of finding a husband to Clarissa."

Morgan frowned. "What about Nathaniel?"

Her eyes darkened. "Well, I hadn't yet told Papa about Nathaniel's proposal . . . He was so very ill . . . he died before I could. And Clarissa never did like me, you see—or Nathaniel either. So when Papa died, she proposed to marry me to Lord Harry Carlton." She shuddered. "Oh, what a horrid man! I hated the way he looked at me! Strange as it sounds, it was as if he wanted to—to eat me with his eyes!"

Morgan's gaze dropped to her mouth, wandered down the slender length of her throat, and back to her lips. He didn't find it strange at all. But he listened quietly, though he had a very good idea indeed what had happened.

"I didn't need Clarissa to find a husband for me," Elizabeth went on. "I'd already found one! But she simply wouldn't accept Nathaniel as my choice. And when I refused to marry Lord Harry instead, she disinherited me!"

The softness of her lower lip thrust out in a pout. Morgan struggled to withhold a laugh. She reminded him for all the world of a child who was angry and resentful that she hadn't got her way.

By now her glass was empty. She gazed down at it, a faint consternation puckering her brow. Then she raised her head and held out the glass. "Might I have a bit more, please?"

Morgan moved to oblige. But as he handed it back to her, she frowned anew. He raised his brow in silent query.

"Won't you have some, too?"

He gently refused. "I drink but rarely, I'm afraid."

"Papa used to say he didn't know a man who wasn't fond of his port, if you know what I mean."

Morgan allowed a faint smile to curl his lips. "I suspect that's all too true, I'm afraid. Indeed, my own father partook far too freely, which is why I resolved at an early age not to make the same mistake." He paused. "Didn't Nathaniel tell you?"

She shook her head. "He talked mostly about the places he'd been, what he'd done there. And his home here, as well as the shipbuilding . . ." She stopped short, as if she'd just realized what she'd said. "That is to say, *this* house, and *your* business. Why, if you recall, I didn't even know he had a brother."

Morgan said nothing, for what was there to say? It came as no surprise that Nathaniel had embellished his own worth quite outrageously. He hesitated, then almost in spite of himself, he spoke. "How on earth did the two of you ever meet?"

"We met at an afternoon garden fete given by

the daughter of an acquaintance of my father."
She sighed. "He was quite dashing, you know. I
confess, I'd heard about him before we met. He
was the talk of London—handsome and charming and ever so debonair. I daresay every young
lady in London was half in love with him."

Morgan stiffened. He had no wish to hear tales
of his brother's prowess with the female gender.

But Elizabeth didn't seem to notice. "At first I
couldn't believe he actually fancied me," she
went on. "Me, can you imagine? Why, I've always been more country mouse than London
miss."

Morgan was rather stunned. Didn't she know
she was beautiful? Oh, not in the ordinary way.
But she was a beauty nonetheless.

She stopped suddenly, her expression rather
forlorn as she contemplated her glass. "Oh,
dear," she murmured. "It seems I need more
brandy." She held it out once more.

Morgan didn't move. His regard sharpened.
Her voice sounded slightly different. Why, if he
wasn't mistaken, he'd say she was—

"Feeling lazy today, are you? Well, then, I'll
simply fetch it myself."

She rose, only to sway dizzily as she began to
straighten. She would have fallen if Morgan
hadn't moved like a streak of lightning, catching
her beneath her arms. He stared down at her. He
was right—she was drunk! God, if only he could
laugh! Yet all he could feel was her body against
his, warm and soft, the undeniable swell of her
breasts against his chest.

As soon as she was steady, he released her and
stepped back.

She smiled across at him. "Oh, dear. I feel rather strange. Won't you please fetch my brandy?"

"No more for you," he said firmly. "You've had quite enough, Elizabeth."

Her smile withered. She looked as if she'd been struck. To his shock, her mouth began to quiver. "You hate me, too, don't you?"

Bewildered, Morgan spread his hands wide. "Of course not—"

"You do. Just like Nathaniel."

"Oh, come now. Surely Nathaniel doesn't hate you—"

Quite suddenly, she began to cry. "Of course he does. And he—he really isn't coming, is he? Oh, the—the wretch! I believed him! I-I was truly convinced he wanted me to be his wife. And now everything is ruined!"

Morgan had no patience with women's tears. He sought to reassure her. "You were duped, Elizabeth. You aren't the first. Unfortunately, you'll probably not be the last either."

She paid him no heed, only buried her face in her hands and sobbed harder.

At his sides, Morgan's hands opened and closed. He swallowed, and swallowed again.

He'd thought himself distanced from such feelings. Yet a voice deep in his brain reminded him that once . . . once he'd been capable of such things. Of comfort. Of tenderness. But he'd lost all that, thanks to Amelia. He would never trust again, least of all another woman.

Yet the sound of Elizabeth's sobs was like a knife ripping into his gut. And it was that which swayed the battle.

His arms stole around her slowly, as if he were very uncertain. But Elizabeth's response was immediate. She ducked her head beneath his chin and clung to the lapels of his jacket. It seemed totally illogical that she should find comfort in his arms, yet she did. And indeed Morgan found it odd as well. He couldn't help but feel sorry for her.

Perhaps because they'd both been fooled by Nat.

He stroked the valley of her spine, a soothing, monotonous motion. "Stop this, Elizabeth. Stop this now. Things will look better in the morning, I promise you."

She turned her face in to his shoulder and wept; hot tears scalded the front of his jacket. This time Morgan didn't hesitate. He swept her into his arms and climbed the stairs to her room.

By then, her tears had distilled to a watery sigh. He lowered her slowly to the floor. "Here," he whispered. "It's time you were in bed."

She made no effort to move, nor to undress. Indeed, she appeared numb as he stepped behind her. His fingers went to the myriad hooks at the back of her dress. Any second now he expected her to whirl on him in indignant rage for daring to undress her. But she only turned listlessly as he urged her around with a touch on the shoulder.

Holding his breath, he tugged her gown down over her shoulders and let it drop to the floor. He relieved her of her petticoats next, then guided her down to remove her stockings and slippers. Next he removed the pins from her hair, feeling his way along her scalp. One last tug and it tumbled down around his hands, a heavy waterfall of spun gold.

His heart had begun to pound. He ignored it. Leaving her clad only in her underclothes, he tugged the counterpane aside and wordlessly motioned her inside. She slid obediently between the covers, though she had yet to say a word.

But her eyes were fixed on his face, wide and questioning and still brilliant with the sheen of tears.

He snuffed out the candle, then sat on the edge of the bed, close but not touching her. "What is it?" he asked quietly.

Her eyes roved his features. "You—you don't look like Nathaniel, you know. He smiles. You never smile." She startled him by reaching up and tracing the hardness of his mouth.

Morgan did not move. "Don't," he warned, in a voice that was but a breath.

Her fingers stilled. "Why not?"

Her hair caught the light of the moon. It glistened as if it were shot through with moonglow, silver and gold combined. Morgan took a deep breath. "Because you just might get more than you bargained for."

"What?"

"This," he whispered. His head was lowering, even as he spoke.

His mouth closed over hers. He heard her swiftly indrawn breath at the contact, but he didn't withdraw. Sweet heaven, he couldn't. A heady satisfaction filled his chest. God, she was sweet. And Lord, but she tempted him. Beneath the thin cotton that covered them, he'd glimpsed the outline of her limbs, long and impossibly slender. It made him want to feel them locked around his hips as he thrust deep and hard inside her.

God, now he knew why he hadn't sent her packing the very day she'd appeared on his doorstep. He could lie to himself no longer. Stephen was right. He was drawn to her. To her sweetness. To her youth.

And there was fire in her. He could feel it in the way her lips molded against his. But there had been fire in Amelia too. That was one of the things he'd found so captivating—her vivaciousness, her spirit.

His breath came heavy and fast. It struck him like a blow then . . . He wanted her. Lady Elizabeth Stanton. He wanted her more than he'd wanted any woman in a long, long time.

Not since Amelia.

Why? The question turned over and over through his mind. Because she was Nat's? Because in some strange way he didn't understand, he felt the need to get even? No. *No.* It was more. Desire pooled thick and heavy in his loins, swelling his manhood to marble-hardness. Yet he didn't want to feel this way. Not about any woman. Especially not *this* one. She was Nat's, he reminded himself. She belonged to Nat . . .

But the battle he fought was already lost. It was dangerous. It was mad. God might see him in hell for wanting his brother's fiancée . . .

He didn't care. By God, he didn't care. Nothing mattered but this driving need turning his blood to fire. He ached with the need to spend himself deep in her body.

He fed on her mouth greedily, as if he couldn't

get enough of her. She arched into him as if she were made for him. Unable to stop himself, he traced his fingers along the lacy neckline of her chemise, then dipped to the succulent flesh beneath. Her breast filled his palm, firm and ripe. He teased the tip to a quivering peak against his skin, reveling in the way she gasped into his mouth.

A low groan rumbled deep in his chest. Unable to stop himself, he broke the fervor of their kiss. But it was only to stretch out beside her and pull her full and tight against his length. She slid her arms around his neck and smiled faintly.

"Nathaniel," she sighed. "Oh, Nathaniel."

The name was like a flood of icy seawater full in his face. In a heartbeat, Morgan was up and on his feet beside the bed.

Elizabeth's eyes opened, sleepy and dazed.

"Go to sleep," he said harshly. "Go to sleep, Elizabeth."

Her eyes fluttered closed. Within seconds her breathing grew deep and even.

But Morgan knew sleep wouldn't come so easily for him. He stood by the bedside, both hands balled into fists at his sides.

He'd been right, he realized. The sooner she was out of his house—out of his life!—the better.

Chapter 6

Elizabeth awoke with a raging headache and a terrible thirst—and the undeniable sensation that there was something she *should* be remembering . . . yet did not. Though she tried and tried, all she could remember was the most outrageous dream—that Morgan O'Connor had *kissed* her. That he'd lain beside her and touched her. Her body. The naked flesh of her breast . . . No. *No*. It was but a dream—a *horrid* dream.

And then there was Nathaniel. A hollow emptiness filled her chest. Oh, but she had gambled foolishly—and lost! Regret lay heavy on her heart, yet she spared no tears. Odd as it was, the hurt she might have expected was simply not to be.

It was afternoon before she appeared downstairs. She gave a silent prayer of thanks that Morgan had departed for his offices as usual. But Simmons commented that she seemed a trifle pale. Somehow she managed a weak smile.

"Oh, by the way, ma'am. Dr. Marks sent word that he's sending over his carriage for you at six o'clock sharp."

Stephen's ball! Lord, but she'd completely forgotten it! Her first thought was to plead illness, for in all honesty she had no heart to attend such a festive affair. Yet Stephen had been such a dear, tending her in her illness, visiting her afterward. In truth, he'd been her only source of enjoyment. How could she disappoint him, when he'd gone to so much trouble for her? She could not, she realized.

The rest of the afternoon was spent in a frenzy of preparations. She had brought with her her favorite ball gown. Of white satin and lace, it had a daringly low-cut bodice, yet was both classic and elegant. Of course, it needed to be pressed. And her hair . . . Annie, the upstairs maid, came to her rescue, dressing it in a shining twist on the back of her head.

Stephen accompanied the carriage. As she descended the staircase, his gold eyes lit with unguarded appreciation. She knew then she'd made the right choice.

Morgan had yet to arrive home . . . For that, Elizabeth was eternally grateful.

From the start it promised to be a grand fete. Stephen's home was every bit as magnificent as Morgan's, if not more so. Indeed, it seemed ablaze with the light of a thousand candles. As Stephen introduced her to first one and then another of his guests, it struck her she was having a far better time than she ought. She laughed and smiled as she hadn't in a long, long time—so much so that she felt rather guilty. After all, shouldn't she be mourning Nathaniel's loss? Yet she was received with such warmth, she couldn't help but return it. When her last dance partner went to fetch a glass of wine, she found herself alone for the first time that evening.

There was a touch on her shoulder. She turned.

It was him—Morgan. Even in evening dress, he possessed an aura of raw masculinity unmatched in any other man she'd yet to encounter.

Her breath deserted her. A vibrating tension filled the air. All at once she feared this moment. She feared *him*, yet it was in a way she didn't fully understand.

"Would you do me the honor of waltzing with me, Elizabeth?"

She wanted to refuse. She *ought* to have refused. But words escaped her. Morgan took her silence for concurrence and reached for her hand. Elizabeth very nearly snatched it back, but his grip was firm.

"I do hope Stephen has kept you away from the brandy tonight," he murmured.

Her eyes flashed upward to his. To her shock, there was no mockery, no accusation.

"How are you feeling?" he asked.

"Much better than I did this morning," she blurted.

He didn't laugh, but he smiled, to her utter surprise. She blushed fiercely.

Something elusive tugged at her memory. All at once she couldn't help but recall the kiss, the pressure of his mouth upon hers . . . It was just a dream, she told herself. Just a dream.

But his nearness was overpowering. It seemed . . . familiar somehow, but immensely disturbing as well. He pulled her close, so close she could feel the breadth and hardness of his chest. The warmth of his hand on her waist burned clear through to her skin.

Her heartbeat quickened. She swallowed. "I must ask a very great favor of you," she said, her tone very low. "I-I realize that you are right—that I can no longer depend on Nathaniel. And so, untoward as it may be, I fear I must ask if I might impose on your hospitality awhile longer. But I-I won't return to London, you see. I won't marry Lord Harry."

A rakish brow rose askance. "Then what will you do?"

"I intend to stay here."

"Here? In Boston?"

"Yes," she said, praying she didn't sound as terrified as she really was. "I am extremely well schooled. And I thought I would try to find a position as a governess perhaps."

"You? The daughter of an English earl? A governess?" It was his tone more than anything that conveyed sheer skepticism.

Elizabeth's chin rose almost defiantly. "I don't see why not. And I will do anything—anything!—even scrub floors if need be. But I refuse to go back to London."

He spoke not a word, merely studied her with those piercing gray eyes, his expression giving away nothing. Elizabeth longed to scream in frustration—if only she could see into his mind!

"Of course you may stay on," he said at last. One side of his mouth curled upward. "Though we may well set tongues to wagging before you are settled." They whirled and dipped. "In fact," he murmured, "I do believe we've done so already."

At first Elizabeth didn't follow. But when he tipped his head to the side in silent indication, her gaze took in the other guests. Sure enough, a number of eyes were trained on the two of them.

A tiny jolt went through her. "Why are they all staring at me?"

There was a subtle tightening of his arm about her back. "Perhaps because you are with the most handsome man in all of Boston?"

"Ha! Perhaps because I am with the most *infamous* man in all Boston."

In that instant, something changed. *Everything* changed. The shoulder beneath her fingertips turned as rigid as stone. The fleeting camaraderie between them vanished, as if it had never been. Bewildered, Elizabeth stared up at him. His features were glacial.

"What? What is it?" There was no chance to say more. The music had stopped. Elizabeth found her arm snagged by an earlier dance partner, Gerald something-or-other.

"Lady Elizabeth, come here! My sister and her friends are anxious to hear about all the latest styles in London. It's so much closer to Paris, you know..."

Her protest died on her lips. Morgan had already turned his back and was striding away. Hurt mingled with anger, and then a simmering resentment overtook her. The cad! He was positively rude. It was little wonder that he was unmarried—he possessed the social graces of a toad!

She turned to her former partner with a gay smile. "Of course, I'm happy to, Gerald. But I warn you, I'm hardly a fashion hound."

From that point on, Elizabeth resolved not to give Morgan O'Connor another thought. Yet every so often, her gaze strayed over someone's shoulder as she searched for him among the throng.

After a while, the music and voices and laughter made her head begin to ache. More than anything, she wished the evening would end so she could go home and to bed. Hoping for a bit of quiet, she slipped out a set of French doors onto the terrace.

The night was a trifle cool, but Elizabeth welcomed the fresh-scented breeze. Several small lanterns lit the darkness. Beneath a towering oak tree, there was a small stone bench. It was there Elizabeth directed her steps. Sitting down, she took a deep breath to clear her head.

"It appears you are quite the belle of the ball."

The voice startled her. Elizabeth's hand flew to her throat. But it was only Morgan. She let out a huge sigh of relief.

He stepped from out of the shadows. "But then, I suppose such things are second nature to you, aren't they, Elizabeth? Oh, do forgive me. Perhaps I should say *Lady* Elizabeth."

His tone was stinging. Pride brought her chin up. Through the silvery darkness she confronted him calmly.

"When my father and I were in London, we entertained, yes. And of course, I attended parties, and the theater and opera. But it was our home in the country—Hayden Park, where I was happiest."

"Somehow you don't strike me as a simple country girl."

He took a step closer, his hands behind his back. Elizabeth swallowed a flicker of nervousness. She peered through the darkness, but his back was to the lamplight. He appeared dark and faceless.

Gathering her courage, she straightened her shoulders. "You know very little about me," she said quietly. "But I think you consider me spoiled. And I think you resent me for being born into a family of privilege." She tipped her head to the side and regarded him coolly. "Is that why you dislike me?"

"Contrary to what you obviously believe, I do not dislike you. So let us change the subject, shall we? Frankly, I'm surprised at you. I would think you'd realize it wasn't wise to come out alone."

Elizabeth's spine was ramrod straight. "I'm hardly alone," she pointed out. "*You* are here."

He continued as if he hadn't heard—no doubt he didn't, the wretch!

"To some men it might be construed as an invitation. What if someone chanced to see you slip out alone?"

"Someone did!" Her glare was as hot as fire. "Besides, what could possibly happen?" She started to rise, only to find her shoulders firmly gripped as he suddenly pulled her upright.

Her breath tumbled to a standstill. Stunned, she met his eyes.

"This could happen, you silly fool."

As his mouth came down on hers, she had a

fleeting glimpse of his eyes. They were no longer cold, but as searing and hot as the summer sun. For the space of a heartbeat she was too stunned to break his hold on her, and then the world swung away.

Morgan was kissing her . . . *Morgan*. It was almost too much to grasp. Her heartbeat quickened. Her breath caught halfway up her throat. God help her, it wasn't unpleasant—no, far from it! His lips were warm, drawing from her a response she was helpless to withhold. She shivered, swamped by sensation, pierced by a dark, sweet pleasure she'd never felt before . . . or had she? Something vaguely elusive tugged at her mind, just barely out of reach.

She broke away with a gasp. "Oh, God, it's true. I-I thought I'd dreamed it." She pressed her hands against her cheeks. Remembrance flooded her. "Dear God," she cried in horror, "you—you touched me . . . you undressed me . . . again! And you kissed me—as if I were a common trollop!"

An arrogant smile played about his lips. "What!" he mocked. "And Nathaniel hasn't done so?"

Before she knew what she was about, her hand shot out. She slapped him hard against the cheek; the resounding crack sounded like a shot. "Damn you!" she cried. "Why would you do such a thing?"

Rage fired in his eyes. For an instant she thought he might retaliate. But then his lips curved in a smile, a smile that was purely a travesty. "Well," he said softly. "I did promise you might slap me when you were able. I'm glad to see you're quite recovered." He inclined his head. "I do believe I'll take my leave now. Oh, and you needn't worry, Elizabeth. I've no thought of invading your bed—tonight or any other night. In fact, I believe I'll spend the night elsewhere."

He strode away, without a second glance.

Still flooded with the taste of him, Elizabeth touched her lips, numb and disbelieving.

They had no idea they were neither alone . . . nor unobserved.

Chapter 7

As luck would have it, Morgan arrived home in the middle of the night. He'd left Stephen's and gone straight to the apartments of Isabelle Ross. A reasonably successful stage actress, Isabelle had been both friend and lover to Morgan throughout the years. She was startled to see him, but welcomed him with open arms.

Clad in a pink silk negligee that revealed far more than it concealed, she slipped a hand into the crook of his elbow. Smiling up at him with full, painted lips, she pressed her breast against his side. "Morgan, what a wonderful surprise." Her tone was low and sultry; it could not be mistaken for anything other than the sensuous invitation it was. "What brings you here?"

In answer he threw his hat aside and pulled her into his arms. His mouth came down hard on hers. She responded immediately, thrusting out her tongue to duel wildly with his. He wasn't feeling particularly lusty, but he was at least looking forward to what he knew would be a most entertaining night. Isabelle was a woman who had perfected the art of pleasing her lover. Indeed, her talent matched her eagerness. With hands both daring and playful, she could bring a man to the brink of passion in mere seconds. And what she did with her mouth . . .

They proceeded directly to her bedroom. There, Morgan had a whiskey—well, actually, several. Oddly, he found himself in no particular hurry to proceed to the fleshly pleasures for which he'd come. Isabelle said nothing, but ordered the plate of food he requested. At last he set it aside.

As if on cue, Isabelle immediately stood, slowly letting her gown slip down her arms until she was naked. Boldly she touched herself, sliding her fingers around huge dark nipples until they stood quivering and erect. Then, a smile on her lips, her eyes half slits, she licked the tip of one finger and drew a wet path down her belly and into the thatch of reddish-brown curls, coming to rest at the pearly nubbin hidden deep within. And all the while she watched him watch her.

But Morgan was soon to find that however much he appreciated her voluptuous curves, his body exhibited little response. Ever patient, Isabelle kissed him lingeringly, allowing her hands to wander where they pleased . . .

All to no avail.

Isabelle was puzzled. Morgan was furious. What peace of mind he'd managed to regain since Amelia's death had been shattered. For even as he'd touched and fondled Isabelle determinedly in return, his mind refused to relinquish the image of huge green eyes and hair the color of spun gold.

And his body remained stubbornly disinterested.

Before he made a complete fool of himself, he cited too much whisky as an excuse and left.

After a near sleepless night, his vile temperament was not improved the next morning. He breakfasted in his study, tending to a number of household matters. It was after noon before he was ready to leave for the shipyards. But just then Simmons announced a visitor.

"Mr. Thomas Porter is here to see you, sir."

Morgan scowled. "Porter? I don't know anyone by that name," he said impatiently. "Tell him I can't see him now. If he's determined to see me, tell him to make an appointment with my assistant at the ship—"

"I think it would be to our mutual advantage if you did see me," interjected a strange male voice. "Please don't be so hasty, Mr. O'Connor."

Morgan glanced up to see a tall, thin man, clad in dark wool, standing in the doorway.

The man's eyes glinted. "Indeed, I think you'll regret it if you don't."

Morgan dismissed Simmons with a wave. The man closed the door after Simmons's departure, then walked boldly over to stand before his desk.

Morgan didn't ask him to sit. "Who the devil are you?" he demanded.

The man inclined his head. "Thomas Porter at your service, sir, reporter for the *Chronicle*."

Morgan's jaw hardened. God, but he despised reporters—and especially for the *Chronicle*. After Amelia's death, the wretched paper had gleefully crucified him with never a thought to his innocence.

Morgan leaned back in his chair, his expression unrelenting. "State your business," he said brusquely.

"Very well." The man called Porter pulled up a chair. "I'm an ambitious man who would eventually like to rise above covering the social events of the city. But on the other hand, I've discovered I have quite a knack for gathering gossip." He smiled. "And I confess, one never knows what juicy little tidbits one might uncover in the confines of Boston's little social circle." He tipped his head to the side. "You've been out of the circle for quite some time, haven't you, Mr. O'Connor?"

Morgan's mouth was a grim straight line. "I was never *in* the circle, and you damn well know it."

Porter gave a raspy chuckle. "Be that as it may, Mr. O'Connor. I, on the other hand, am always prepared to take full advantage of any situation that might present itself. And sometimes things turn up in the strangest places . . . Naturally, when I saw that Dr. Stephen Marks was having a little soiree last night, knowing of your friendship, I wondered if you might be in attendance."

Morgan fought the urge to stand up, seize the man by the throat, and throttle him. "What did you do?" he asked, his lip curling in disgust. "Hide in the bushes taking note of any and all who attended?"

"I admit, I'm not above hiding in the bushes." Porter gave a sly laugh. "It's amazing what one sees . . . Why, in fact, last night on the terrace I saw you share ... shall we say, a rather ardent embrace with a certain English ladybird?"

"One stolen kiss is scarcely a criminal offense." Morgan struggled to restrain his temper.

"No," Porter agreed. "But I admit to having been very curious indeed about this beauty, so I stayed a bit longer. Of course, I'd heard she was a distant English cousin of Dr. Marks, here for a visit. I was quite puzzled when she left at a rather late hour, so I followed her."

Across from him, Morgan clenched his fists.

"Fancy my surprise when she came here, to your home! I watched her go inside, and it wasn't long before I saw a light upstairs—imagine that!"

"Let me guess," Morgan said tightly. "You didn't leave because you were *curious*." He said the word as if it were an abomination.

Porter sat back in his chair, a smug, self-righteous expression on his face. Clearly he was enjoying himself. "Of course I did," he answered.

"Then you must have seen me arrive home at a much later hour. It should be obvious then that I was not with the lady."

"Only you can say, Mr. O'Connor, only you can say. Naturally I stayed a bit longer, and this morning I chanced to see a young boy helping the gardener. I was able to talk to him and I asked if he'd ever seen the young lady in question—oh, he was quite forthcoming! He told me the lady had been here for weeks, in fact. He told me she'd been ill, but still ... imagine. An unmarried young girl staying here, beneath your roof! Why, any number of things could have gone on, and no one suspected she was even here until now! Why, what would people think if they knew! As I'm sure you know, Boston's social circles can be very unforgiving."

Morgan had gone very still. "You bastard," he said through his teeth. "What do you want?"

Porter's eyes gleamed unpleasantly. "Unfortunately, I didn't inherit the family business—my elder brother did. I suspect your own brother would no doubt know what it's like to be a younger son. One never has enough money . . ." He named an outrageously high figure.

"Half that," Morgan snapped.

"Agreed! I'll stop by your bank late this afternoon." Feeling rather proud of himself, Porter stood and offered a hand.

Morgan ignored it. If he touched the man, he'd likely tear him in two. He strode to the door and called for Simmons. "Show this man out," he said tersely.

Back in his study, he tapped the tips of his fingers together, deep in thought. It would not end here, he concluded. The next time Porter found himself in need of a ready source of money, he would return, with more innuendo. More veiled threats. God knew he could survive the scandal. But what about Elizabeth?

The foolish girl was hell-bent on remaining in Boston. Even if she weren't, as the daughter of an English earl, her identity alone would pique interest. Shame and disgrace would follow her; rumors would multiply. No matter where she lived, her reputation would be blackened and her life ruined.

He shouldn't have cared. By God, he didn't.

He was hardly her savior. Why, he strongly suspected she disliked him intensely.

But she has no one else, argued a voice in his head, *no one to look after her.*

Certainly he had no desire to find himself tied to one woman again, especially one who fancied herself in love with his blackguard brother! He would be wise to avoid folly, he told himself harshly. God knew he'd learned his lesson—his only reason for staying with Amelia had been to avoid scandal, and that had turned into a fiasco.

Yet in the end, no matter how his mind circled and turned, he always came back to the same conclusion. He could think of only one way to save Elizabeth's name and avert disaster . . .

Heaven help them both.

Elizabeth managed to evade Morgan the entire day and well into the next—or did he avoid her? Either way, it didn't matter, as long as their paths didn't cross. Oh, she knew they would eventually, and she dreaded the moment, for what could she say? Should she apologize for slapping him? No! He had deserved it for treating her so—so abominably. On the other hand, it would be difficult to pretend nothing had happened, that he hadn't kissed her—Lord, not on one, but two occasions! Why, the very thought made her cringe inside—little wonder that for now she was content to keep things as they were.

But late afternoon had left her with little to do. She wandered into the library, idly noting that it was well stocked with a noble collection of books. But she felt too restless to sit, and found herself wishing Stephen would drop by.

She hadn't seen him for several days, since the night of his ball. Despite the disastrous ending to the evening, she realized she had enjoyed herself immensely. Humming a waltz, the veriest smile on her lips, she lifted her arms and whirled around.

There was a hearty burst of applause.

Elizabeth stopped cold. Her arms dropped to her sides like a puppet whose strings had been cut. Even before she spun around to confront her intruder, she knew it was he—Morgan.

The stinging heat of embarrassment flooded her cheeks, her entire body. But that was the only trace of it as she glared her displeasure.

"You might have knocked," she said coolly.

"Knock? In my own home? I see no need."

A dozen disparaging remarks sputtered in her mind. She pressed her lips firmly together to keep from spilling each and every one of them.

"Come now," he said mildly. "There's no need to be shy. You're still angry with me, aren't you? You look as if you'd dearly like to call me any number of unpleasant names, so why not simply say it and be done with it?"

Drat the man, for he seemed always to know what was in her very mind! "Because I'm too much of a lady to utter a word of any of them!"

"Yes," he said slowly. His mood seemed abruptly sober. "That you are, Elizabeth. That you are indeed." He paused. "Have you seen the morning paper?"

Elizabeth shook her head. It seemed a rather odd question to ask her, especially coming from him.

"Then come. I've something to show you."

He gestured her through the doorway. Taking her elbow, he strode toward his study. Elizabeth fought the urge to dig in her heels and halt. All at once she felt distinctly wary—and much like a lamb being led to the slaughterhouse.

He stopped before his desk, flicking a finger at the newspaper that lay open atop his desk. He released her arm, and she stepped back hurriedly.

He paid no heed. "I daresay you'll find the *Chronicle*'s social column of particular interest today, Elizabeth."

Her guard went up immediately. It struck her that he was acting very strangely. "I cannot think why," she said bluntly. "I'm afraid I don't remember half those I met at Stephen's ball."

"That's not what I mean. However, I'll save you the trouble of reading it for yourself. You see, today's paper contains an announcement concerning my future." He paused. "Congratulations are in order, Elizabeth. I'm soon to be wed."

Now, this, she was more equipped to deal with. "Oh, dear," she said cheekily. "Well, then, my condolences to your intended."

"Ah, but there's the thing, you see." A smile that could only be called devilish lurked on his lips. "You, sweet"—his tone was soft—"well, you are my intended."

Chapter 8

His smile should have served as a warning. Oh, but she should have known he was up to something . . . !

For the space of a heartbeat, all she could do was gape. Then she snatched up the paper for herself; quickly her eyes scanned the newsprint. It read:

> *Boston shipbuilder Morgan O'Connor is pleased to announce his upcoming nuptials to Lady Elizabeth Stanton, daughter of the late Earl of Chester. The pair plan to wed within the month.*

Elizabeth's head came up. She stared at him in utter horror. "Who did this? Who would dare to make such an announcement?"

"I placed the announcement," he said calmly.

"Why?" she cried. "As some—some monstrous joke?"

"It's hardly a joke, Elizabeth. I fully intend to make you my wife." His expression was almost grim. There was no doubt he meant what he said.

The floor beneath her feet seemed to dip and twirl. "You-you cannot mean it," she said faintly. "You cannot mean to—to marry me." She could scarcely dare to say it.

"Oh, but I do."

Elizabeth was aghast. She swayed, all at once feeling rather dizzy.

Hands on her shoulders, Morgan guided her to a chair and gently pushed her down. "Come now. Surely it's not that bad." There was the veriest hint of amusement in his tone.

Elizabeth pressed cool hands to her flushed cheeks. Closing her eyes, she fought to regain her composure. When she opened them, speech was still beyond her.

An imperious voice sounded above her head. "There, now. It's not so bad as all that. Take a slow, deep breath and calm yourself."

She did as he ordered. She lowered her hands to her lap, her mind churning. She noted distantly that they were trembling. She clasped them together to still them. At last when she was able, she said the first thing that popped into her mind. "You're mad!"

"I assure you, I am not."

"But . . . dear heaven, why? I-I cannot think why you should want to marry me!"

One side of his mouth turned up. "Need I point out that you came here to be married?"

"Not to you!" she said wildly.

His expression grew chill. Too late Elizabeth realized her insult.

"It's just that I don't understand." Her tone

was as shaky as her hands. "This is so sudden, so"—she groped for the right word—"so unexpected."

Her heart seemed to shiver. *Marry* him. It still seemed too much to take in. How could she marry this strange, brooding man who was so unlike his brother? She didn't like the way he made her feel. So odd. So unlike herself. Especially when he'd kissed her.

The memory flooded her mind—his mouth on hers, warm and demanding. Tenderly she touched her mouth.

He spoke suddenly. Coolly. "The other night, Elizabeth . . . the kiss we shared? I do hope you realize it was but a moment's idle fancy." His gaze met hers, cool and remote. "I've shared many things with many women," he said with a shrug. "Just so we understand each other, I'm hardly enamored of you."

Elizabeth went icy cold. Never had she resented him more! "Then frankly," she snapped, "I fail to see why you should be so magnanimous!"

"Magnanimous? Indeed, I'm being far more magnanimous than you realize. And I see no reason why you shouldn't know the truth. Unfortunately, you see, the two of us were seen on the terrace that night. Yes," he went on when her eyes widened, "caught in that very same kiss."

"By whom?"

"By an unscrupulous man named Thomas Porter."

Elizabeth strained to recall. "I remember no one by that name," she began.

"Oh, he was not a guest." Morgan's mouth

thinned. "He is a reporter for the *Chronicle* who specializes in digging up dirt. At any rate, he paid me a visit yesterday morning and gleefully divulged what he'd seen. Unfortunately, he didn't quite believe the story that you were Stephen's cousin visiting from England—especially when he followed you here later that night. The next morning, he spoke to a young lad helping the gardener and learned you'd been here in my house for quite some time." Those devilish brows rose high. "Need I say more, Elizabeth? He hinted at the scandal that would take place should others learn of the incident. All in all, he was most eager to line his pockets. Unfortunately I had no choice but to oblige him, and at a tidy sum, I might add."

"You paid him?" she cried out. "But you know I have no money. I cannot repay you—"

"I dislike being the brunt of such scandal." His tone was clipped. "But I would no doubt fare better than you, Elizabeth. If you still insist on remaining in Boston, your reputation will be in shreds, no matter that you are an earl's daughter—indeed, *because* you are an earl's daughter. People will not soon forget. Your morals will be suspect. If you are lucky enough to obtain a position as governess, the master of the house might well consider it his right to rut between your thighs whenever he wishes; whether it be in the nearest bed, or up against the nearest wall—"

"Say no more!" she cried. His bluntness shocked her. *Up against the wall* . . . Did people do such things? No. Not *decent* people. But Morgan was right—she would be no better than a whore.

Still, she was confused. "But the announcement
. . . When did you—"

"I saw to it yesterday afternoon."

Her gaze was wide and distressed. "But why?
Why announce that we . . . that you and I . . ."
She faltered.

"Because I've no intention of letting that bastard Porter bleed me for the rest of my life. And
that's exactly what will happen if we do nothing.
If we are already wed, he can do no harm."

Elizabeth fell silent. It seemed he'd thought of
everything. And so now they must both sacrifice.
Oh, she didn't fool herself. No doubt it was his
own reputation that concerned him far more
than hers.

She glanced down at her hands, now knotted
tightly in her lap. "I hardly know you," she said,
her voice very low. *And what little I know of you,
I do not like,* she amended silently.

His laugh was biting. "You know me far better
than you know Nathaniel."

Nathaniel. For an instant wild hope flared
within her. Perhaps if she simply waited, Nathaniel would yet appear . . . But Morgan was
right. A man was far better able to survive disgrace than a woman.

Once again, he read her mind as if it were his
own. "Good God," he said disgustedly. "Not a
soul knows where Nathaniel is, or when he'll return. I thought you understood that. Even if he
did return—tomorrow—and the two of you married, what then? You choose not to believe me
when I tell you he is not the man you think.
There exists a very good possibility that you
would wake up one morning and find yourself

alone. What then? And what if you were with child?"

Elizabeth blanched. A baby. Certainly that was something she hadn't considered. "I—I understand that. Truly I do. It's just that I"—suddenly it just spilled out—"I don't love you! And—"

"Love only complicates marriage."

Elizabeth stared at him, taken aback by his coldness. He sounded so callous. So cynical and so very certain. Oh, she knew it was seldom so, but she wanted a husband she could love, and a husband who loved her in turn, as wildly as she loved him.

"If that's how you feel, then clearly you have no more desire to marry me than I—"

"On the contrary, Elizabeth. I find myself liking the prospect more and more."

Her mouth opened, closed, then opened again. What kind of man was he? Just when she thought perhaps she'd begun to glean some inkling of his reasoning . . .

"Surely you do not mean that." She found the notion that he might truly wish to marry her oddly disconcerting.

"Oh, but I do." He had moved to stand near the window. As he paused, cold sunlight washed over the stark angles of his face; his features might have been cast in stone. His profile revealed nothing whatsoever of his thoughts or his emotions. Yet she was struck by the feeling there was much held deeply in check, and much he chose *not* to reveal . . .

He turned. "I am a wealthy man, Elizabeth— wealthy, successful, as worthy as any. I possess the looks of a gentleman and I've acquired the manners to accompany it. I live in a home many would envy. I've entertained grandly. Yet Boston society is not particularly appreciative of a man with my lowly past. Unlike most of them, I earned my money—I didn't inherit it. In short, though I've mingled with those in the most elite society circles, they've yet to accept my right to stand among them."

Elizabeth was puzzled. "And you think marriage to me would make a difference."

"Most definitely."

"But . . . how?"

The merest of smiles dallied on his lips. "To put it bluntly, I'm hardly well connected. As I'm sure it is in England, here in Boston, breeding is all-important, no matter how much money one has. But my background—my breeding, or lack of it—is something I cannot change. And so it occurs to me I must marry well. And marriage to you, an English *noblewoman* . . . why, no one would dare to look down on me."

Elizabeth's expression was faintly troubled. "Does it truly matter?" She posed the question very quietly. "It's just as you said. You are a wealthy man, as worthy as any. What does it matter what others think?"

There was a subtle hardening of his smile. "Then I would ask you the same," he challenged. "What if you went to the theater and you knew everyone there whispered behind your back? Would you continue to make your way about the city? Or would you hide behind closed doors and live *in* this world, but never a part of it? What if you walked out this very instant and someone called you whore?"

Her breath caught. Faith, but he could be cruel! Yet she knew she could not live her life like that—it would be completely untenable.

In her silence lay her answer.

"I thought so. You could not stand it either." Morgan's voice turned harsh. "Why, you ask me. Call it a matter of pride. No more, no less." He paused. "So tell me, Elizabeth. What is your answer? Will you marry me?"

Even as their eyes collided, a hundred thoughts rallied in her mind. What did she know of him . . . truly? Very little. He wasn't close to Nathaniel. Indeed, she suspected he didn't even *like* his brother. But he had taken her in when she was ill. He'd fed her and saw to it that she was well. He'd been more than generous, she admitted grudgingly.

But to marry him . . . !

His voice prodded her. "You came here to start your life anew, Elizabeth. I offer you that chance."

She lowered her head. Despite her best intentions, hot tears stung her eyes. Her heart cried out. This was scarcely the marriage of her dreams.

She bit her lip to keep from weeping. She struggled to speak, her head lowered in defeat. "Very well," she said, her voice low and choked. "I-I will marry you."

They set the date for two weeks hence.

The day after the announcement appeared in the *Chronicle*, Morgan informed her that Stephen had made arrangements for her to stay with his aunt Clara Fleming, who had just returned from Paris the afternoon before.

Elizabeth felt rather uncomfortable at being thrust upon a stranger, yet she acknowledged the necessity. Indeed, she found it rather ironic, for things might have turned out quite differently had Clara been here in Boston the last few months rather than Europe; she could have stayed with Clara, and Thomas Porter would never have spied her entering Morgan's home. Marriage to him might well have been averted . . .

As it was, the day approached with frightening speed.

Clara had obligingly offered her the use of her home and carriage. Though the old lady's hair was white as snow, she was surprisingly active. Indeed, she was gone so often that Elizabeth joked to Stephen that the only time she saw Clara was on her way in and out of the house.

Soon there was but one more day until the wedding.

The afternoon was spent with the seamstress on the final fitting of her gown. When Morgan had informed her he'd made arrangements with the finest seamstress in Boston to make her gown, Elizabeth had protested the need for a new gown at all.

"As you once pointed out," she reminded him, "my clothing is hardly that of a pauper."

His smile was annoyingly autocratic, and all too familiar. "Nonetheless," he had informed her, "you will have a wedding gown that befits a lady of your standing."

Her gaze flew to his; there was just the

slightest emphasis on *lady*. Did he mock her? She
had the oddest sensation he did. Yet as he returned her regard with faintly lifted brows, she
could find no trace of anything but a cool polite-
ness.

But the gown was lovely; she couldn't deny it.
As she stood before the full-length mirror in her
room, she scarcely recognized herself. Yards and
yards of pale cream satin cascaded to the floor;
she appeared fragile and doll-like. As the seamstress tugged a fold of the train, her assistant
clasped her hands together. "Oh, miss, I've never
seen anything quite so magnificent! Why, you
will surely melt Mr. O'Connor's heart!"

How? Elizabeth wondered vaguely. She was
sorely inclined to believe he *had* no heart.

When the seamstress finally departed, she cast
the gown aside while her spirits ebbed lower
with every second. When a maid came up to announce that Stephen was waiting to see her in
the parlor, she was very tempted to make her
excuses. But she knew that he would think
something was wrong, and she didn't want him
to worry.

Somehow she made it through tea without displaying her melancholy mood. She looked on as
he replaced his empty china cup in the saucer.

"So," he said lightly. "Tell me, Elizabeth. Is the
bride-to-be ready for her wedding day?"

It was the wrong thing to say. A burning ache
stung her throat. She couldn't prevent the
thought that came next. Why hadn't Nathaniel
waited as he had vowed? Why had he forsaken
her? What was wrong with her that he didn't

love her? For she was suddenly very certain that he did not.

She ducked her head, but not in time. Stephen was peering at her oddly. "Why, Elizabeth, you look ready to cry!"

Perhaps because she was, she nearly blurted.

Gently he laid a hand on her shoulder. "Tell me," he urged. "Elizabeth, what is wrong? If there's something I can do—"

She shook her head. "There's nothing," she murmured.

His eyes remained dark with concern.

She swallowed the lump in her throat. "It's just so—so different than what I thought it would be when I left London." She spoke the words with difficulty, her voice a mere whisper. "I came here to marry Nathaniel. I never expected to marry his brother. I never expected to marry a—a stranger!"

Stephen's hand tightened ever so slightly. "Elizabeth—"

There was a sound near the doorway. They both looked up and saw him at the same time— Morgan. Stephen was on his feet in an instant.

"Morgan," he said easily. "We were just discussing you."

Morgan's gaze had yet to leave Elizabeth's face. "So I see." At last he glanced at Stephen. "Would you excuse us, Stephen? Elizabeth and I have several matters to attend to."

Stephen was ever the gentleman. "Why, of course." He glanced at his pocket watch. "It's time I left anyway. I need to check on several patients before I return home."

Elizabeth smiled and walked with him to the

entry hall, all the while conscious of Morgan's unrelenting scrutiny.

Stephen departed. She had scarcely returned to the parlor than Morgan's imperious voice stabbed at her like the point of a knife. "I do hope you had the good sense not to go out with him."

Elizabeth bristled. "What if I did?"

His look was withering. "I do not think it wise to risk further scandal, Elizabeth. Need I remind you?"

She stiffened, as if a hand had dug into her spine. She'd done nothing to warrant such a rebuke. "Stephen is a friend," she informed him stiffly.

"And I am the man who will soon be your husband. I do not begrudge you a friend, Elizabeth. I know that you are alone in a land far distant from your own. But I'll have no one question your behavior, so let us see that that's all he remains."

"My behavior . . ." She glared her displeasure. "Need I remind *you* that it was *your* behavior which caused this—this sham of a wedding to begin with? Thomas Porter would never have followed me if you hadn't kissed me—"

"But I did. And now we must both pay the consequences."

Oh, but he was so cool, so always in control, and she was suddenly very irked with him. "Is that why you came here?" she demanded. "To accuse me of philandering with Stephen?"

"I've accused you of nothing. I trust Stephen, though I've yet to come to trust you."

Elizabeth was speechless with anger . . . but there was more.

"Our marriage will be an arrangement," he went on, "an arrangement that serves both our needs. You will open doors I thought forever closed to me. In return, I will provide you with a home and money. But I give you fair warning, I'll not be made a fool of."

"A fool?" she shot back. "Since you obviously consider me feebleminded at best, perhaps you should explain yourself."

"Certainly. I'll tolerate no other men in your life. To be blunt, I'll tolerate no *lovers*."

Elizabeth was too furious to speak. How dare he question her morals in such a manner. How dare he dictate to her as if—as if he were her master!

He reached inside his jacket and withdrew a narrow oblong box. "Now, on to other matters. Actually, I came to bring you this." With a fingertip he loosened the catch. "I thought you might wear it tomorrow."

Snuggled upon a bed of velvet lay a strand of gleaming translucent pearls. Under other circumstances she would have exclaimed with sheer delight, for they were lovely beyond compare. As it was, her temper still simmered. How dare he give her a dressing-down and then proceed to grace her with pearls!

But before she could say a word, he had turned her around and fastened the clasp around her neck. A hand at her elbow, he tugged her before an oval gilt-framed mirror on the adjacent wall.

Behind her, he tipped his head to the side.

"Well?" he queried. "What do you think?"

Their eyes met in the mirror, one pair snapping, the other coolly inquiring. "Lovely," she said through her teeth.

A devilish brow rose. "Come now, Elizabeth. That's all you have to say?" As he spoke, his gaze traveled down to rest on the circlet of pearls . . . and still further.

Elizabeth froze. The heart-shaped neckline of her gown was hardly immodestly low, yet all at once it was as if he saw right through her. And he was so close—almost frighteningly close! The scent of his cologne swirled all around her. She could feel the wool of his jacket flush against her back, the heat of his body permeating through to hers.

"Lovely," she said again, this time more brightly. She would have stepped away with all due haste, but he stopped her. His hands closed on her elbows. To her horror she was bodily turned to face him.

"Why, I do believe your manners have forsaken you, Elizabeth. Such an extravagant gift warrants some gratitude, don't you think?"

"Oh, but of course! I didn't mean to be rude." One small hand nervously touched the pearls. "Thank you. Thank you so very much."

Hard lips curved in a smile that was purely tormenting. "I had in mind," he murmured, "a more demonstrative token." He pretended to study her. "A kiss, I think. Yes, I do believe one small kiss will suffice." He turned his head just a hair and presented her with the angled plane of one lean cheek.

Elizabeth inhaled sharply. He toyed with

her—oh, and well he knew it! But she was anxious to be free of him and so she knew she would comply. Hauling in a deep, fortifying breath, she closed her eyes and levered herself up on tiptoe.

But her lips never met the raspy hardness of his cheek. Instead she found herself caught up against the unyielding breadth of his chest, strong arms taut against her back. What small sound of protest she would have made was swallowed by his lips.

Indeed, the kiss was never hers to give. His mouth captured hers, the pressure of his lips deep and demanding. A jolt tore through her, even as the fleeting thought traveled through her mind that it was just as before . . . Her stomach felt weightless. She felt ridiculously light-headed. Though she longed to fight it—to fight him—she possessed neither the will nor the strength. Trapped between their bodies, her hands opened, as if to push him away. But then her lips parted before the insidious persuasion of his. Her limbs melted against him as if she sought to make herself a part of him.

Abruptly he released her. The tension reached a screaming pitch as they stared into one another's eyes. Elizabeth had the oddest sensation he was as confused as she. But then his fingers closed over hers where they lay upon his vest. His grip tightened, and he stepped back . . . or did he thrust her away? Her senses still reeling, she watched as he strode to the door.

There he paused. "After tomorrow you'll be mine, Elizabeth. Remember, I'll not be cuckolded."

The chill of his tone washed over her like icy

brine. When he'd gone, she gave a half sob of mingled fury and frustration. What was wrong with her that she allowed herself to be touched— to be held and kissed!—by this cold, hard man who had accused her of dallying with another, then kissed her as if he owned her! She didn't understand him . . .

Nor did she understand herself very well at that moment.

Chapter 9

⌒∽᠀᠀∽⌒

Morning came too soon, and with it the arrival of her wedding day.

Rising from the bed, Elizabeth walked barefoot to the window, pushing away the disheveled curtain of her hair. Sleep had been elusive last night. She was as exhausted as she had been when she climbed into bed. Peering through the lacy curtains, she saw that the sky was gray and cloudy. A rumble of thunder greeted her.

A dismal day . . . for a dismal bride.

There was a knock on the door. It opened and a maid peeped in at her. "Ma'am? Are you ready for your bath?" It was Mary, the cheery little maid who had attended her the past two weeks.

"Yes. Thank you, Mary." The smile she sought simply would not come.

Though the bath refreshed her tired muscles, it did nothing to revive her spirit. If not for Mary's aimless chatter while the girl helped her dress and tended her hair, the room would have been silent as a tomb.

At last she was finished. At Mary's insistence, she stood before the mirror in her room. The girl stood beside her, her eyes round and shining. "Oh, ma'am," she breathed, "you look like an angel. Truly you do."

Elizabeth stared at her image. Her hair was piled atop her head, with soft ringlets framing the oval of her face. Her color was heightened— not from excitement, as Mary surely thought, but from nerves. Two frightened eyes gazed back at her, dark with distress.

"Here, ma'am, I almost forgot. Here are your pearls." Mary fastened the clasp at Elizabeth's nape. She sighed, a dreamy sound. "Oh, ma'am, he surely must love you to buy you such a beautiful necklace."

No, Elizabeth thought. There was no love. No duty. No obligation. She stifled a bitter laugh. What would Mary think if she knew that marriage was simply Morgan's answer to blackmail—and a way to elevate his status in the eyes of Boston society?

All at once she longed to fling away the pearls in spiteful defiance.

But she didn't quite dare.

All too soon she was being ushered downstairs. Stephen was there, for he had offered to escort her to the church. Morgan had also asked him to stand as witness to the wedding. When she reached the entry hall, he took both her hands. His gaze swept the length of her, his approval obvious. "You take my breath away," he said with a smile.

Elizabeth flushed. Her mind veered straight to Morgan. Would she take his breath away as well? Oh, silly question, that! Indeed, most of the time, he looked right through her. She was stunned at the pinprick of hurt the thought provoked. Why should she even care what he thought of her appearance? She chastised herself firmly. Their marriage was solely for the sake of convenience. An *arrangement*, as he had called it.

It had seemed the only answer.

Now she wasn't at all sure it was the *right* one.

Stephen offered her his arm. "Shall we?"

It took every ounce of willpower she possessed to force herself to take his arm—even more to walk out the door.

She was silent in the carriage, her mood as bleak as the weather. Stephen glanced over at her. "I have the feeling Morgan wasn't particularly pleased to find you with me yesterday afternoon. I felt it best to leave." Stephen paused. "I hope he didn't prove difficult."

Elizabeth's mind sped straight to his kiss. "He made no secret of the fact he trusts you," she said before she thought better of it. "But he actually had the audacity to suggest that I might be . . ." She stopped, suddenly realizing what she was about to divulge.

Stephen tipped his head to the side. "Unfaithful?" he supplied.

Elizabeth colored. "Frankly, yes."

He chuckled, but his amusement was rather short-lived. His smile withered. "Morgan can be a bit disagreeable at times," Stephen said slowly. "But he is not a man to shirk his responsibilities. He is not like—" He stopped short.

Now it was her turn to finish. "Like Nathaniel?" she guessed.

"Now I'm the one who is trying not to prove difficult," Stephen said gently. "I do not mean to hurt you, Elizabeth. But if I were a drowning man about to be rescued, and both Morgan and Nathaniel extended their hands to me, there's no question I would take Morgan's." His expression was earnest. "You'll find no better man, Elizabeth."

He seemed to hesitate then. She had the oddest sensation he wanted to say more, but just then the carriage stopped.

They had arrived at the church.

Her legs felt wooden as she alighted from the carriage. Indeed, were it not for Stephen behind her, no doubt she'd have bolted the opposite way as fast as she was able.

The ceremony began all too soon. At a signal from Stephen, she began to move forward.

The walk seemed endless. Distantly she noted that while the church was not crowded, there were quite a few people. And then she caught sight of *him* . . .

Morgan.

He awaited near the altar, tall and darkly handsome. Elizabeth couldn't take her eyes from him; his presence was such that it blotted out all else.

As usual, he was unsmiling, his face an iron mask. No hint of emotion—neither approval nor disapproval—crossed his features as she breached the last step between them.

Her knees began to shake. Panic surfaced in her mind. She couldn't do this. Just as her legs would have buckled, he reached for her. A hard arm slid tight about her waist and drew her close—so very close!—against his side. One lean, dark hand reached for hers. Hers was like ice, his like a blast of heat. All that kept her upright was the pressure of his fingers locked tight around hers.

When it was time for the vows that would unite them forever, he spoke his with unfaltering determination.

She whispered hers.

Then it was over. The clergyman pronounced them husband and wife. "You may kiss the bride," he announced.

Tears glazed her eyes, tears she couldn't withhold. This was her wedding day, the day she had dreamt of many a night, yet never had she been so—so miserable! She had married, not out of love, but out of necessity.

A painful wedge of emotion trapped in her throat, she raised her chin and sought to blink away her tears, praying Morgan wouldn't see. But she knew from his scowl that he did.

Nor was his kiss the chaste, perfunctory brush of their lips she expected. His kiss was deep and hard and so long, the clergyman finally cleared his throat.

Morgan raised his head. Elizabeth was stunned at the strange glitter reflected in his eyes . . . triumph? His hand atop hers, he turned and led her from the church. Elizabeth felt numb, as if this were happening to someone else and not to her.

A small group of people clustered at the foot of the stone steps. Elizabeth barely saw them. Morgan paused, raising their joined hands high.

One man broke apart from the others. "You'd best take care, lady," he shouted, "or you'll end up dead like the other one!"

Beside her, Morgan's entire body went rigid. He dropped her hand. What might have happened then, she would never know. Suddenly Stephen was there. He thrust out a hand toward Morgan, as if to block him. "Let me handle this," he said, already turning for the stairs.

Elizabeth blinked. "What on earth—"

Morgan had already recovered. "Don't worry," he said curtly. "It's nothing to be concerned about." As he spoke, he was already steering her toward his carriage.

They were soon back at his home, which was alive with activity. The next hours passed in a haze. Servants were everywhere. To her dismay, Morgan kept her close, introducing her to the guests. Soon the names and faces began to blur. There was his banker, Wilson Reed. His attorney, Justin Powell. A dozen more.

A table had been set with roast and ham, bread and vegetables. Elizabeth could barely eat, but she accepted the glass of wine Stephen pressed into her hand. Finding herself alone, she slipped out the French doors onto the terrace. Her head pounded dreadfully, and there was a heavy ache in her breast. Eyes downcast, she stared at the band of gold on her finger, twisting it around and around; it seemed as heavy as her heart.

All at once her spine prickled.

She knew he was there even before she slowly raised her head.

He stood not three feet away. He regarded her coolly, his arms crossed over his chest. "Regrets already?" he inquired.

The bite in his tone brought her chin up. She glared at him.

He smiled rather tightly. "Now, that's better, Elizabeth. For an instant I feared I'd married a crushed blossom."

A scathing retort sprang to her lips. "You may find I'm more than you bargained for."

His brows shot upward, even as his gaze slid down to the roundness of her breasts. His tone was lazily suggestive, his study long and thorough. "A prediction, Elizabeth? Or a promise?"

"Neither!"

"A pity then, for I find the possibility rather intriguing. Indeed, I—"

"Morgan?" The door was thrust open. It was Stephen. "There you are. Come inside, the both of you. Justin would like to offer you a toast."

Elizabeth was only too glad to comply. Picking up her skirts, she preceded the two men inside.

Champagne was immediately pressed into their hands. Morgan's attorney, Justin Powell, slapped his shoulder as they reentered the room. "Now, now, you shouldn't be so selfish with your bride!" he chided the younger man. "There's time enough for that later, eh?" He laughed uproariously.

Elizabeth's smile was rather sickly. It was obvious Justin was enjoying himself immensely—and imbibing rather liberally. His nose and cheeks were flushed and ruddy.

He raised his glass high. "And now for a toast," he went on. "To many years together"—he winked—"and many children."

Elizabeth's smile froze. Embarrassment flooded her like a crimson tide, for this was the one aspect of marriage to this man that she had tried hard to eradicate from her mind. To her horror, she felt the touch of Morgan's eyes on her profile.

She couldn't look at him—faith, but she could not! At a loss for words and deed, she lowered her gaze and tried to smile.

From that point on, Morgan didn't leave her side. Occasionally his hand grazed her arm, skimmed her shoulder, flitted to the curve of her waist. Fire seemed to sizzle wherever he touched.

Again and again her gaze strayed to his other hand, the hand that held the crystal goblet. He had yet to drink, while her own was empty. His fingers were long and brown and strong looking, yet his touch was almost delicate on the fragile stem. Her mouth went dry, her thoughts rampant.

She knew how the basic act of procreation was done, of course. But since she had no mother to guide her, she knew very little else. She'd heard rumors in the ladies' school she'd attended in London, things that couldn't possibly be true. And according to gossip, there was kissing involved. And touching, too . . .

She couldn't tear her eyes from Morgan's hands. What would those hands feel like against her skin? And his body . . . would it be like the man himself, hard and unyielding?

The thought evolved. Would she be naked? Dear God, would *he*?

"Elizabeth."

The sound of her name rattled her out of her daze. Her eyes caught his.

"Yes?" Her voice sounded high and tight, nothing at all like her own.

He removed the empty glass from her hand

and set it on the tray of a passing maid, along with his own, which was still untouched. He bent low, so that his lips grazed her ear. "Enough for you, love," he murmured. "I'd hate for you to spend the first night of our marriage rather tipsy."

Elizabeth blanched. Until now, it seemed the evening was never-ending. Now she found herself wishing it were not over so soon!

The merest hint of a smile dallied at his lips. "It's been a long day," he observed. "Since most of the guests are gone, I'll have Annie show you upstairs."

She could hardly speak for the cold lump of dread in her throat. "As you wish," she said, her voice barely audible.

"Elizabeth?"

She had already turned away. She glanced back over her shoulder. "Yes?"

"You may as well retire. There are several matters I need to discuss with Justin. I may be some time yet."

Elizabeth could have jumped for joy. *Take as long as you like*, she thought silently.

Annie awaited her near the bottom of the stairs, her face glowing. Elizabeth's heart twisted. No doubt the girl thought it hopelessly romantic that she and her master had married. Sure enough, Annie was a step ahead all the way up the stairs. On the landing, Elizabeth instinctively began to turn right. The room she'd previously occupied was just a few doors down.

Annie stopped her with a hand on her arm. "Oh, no, ma'am. Not that way."

Elizabeth frowned. "But my room is there—"

"Not anymore, ma'am." Though her cheeks grew red, Annie's smile was priceless . . . or would have been under any other circumstances. "You'll be in the room that adjoins Mr. O'Connor's. I've already unpacked all your things and put them away in the wardrobe." She beamed. "Come now, ma'am. It's this way."

Elizabeth lagged behind her, her spirits as sluggish as her steps.

The room was spacious and lovely. Cream-colored carpet covered the floor. Pale blue damask hung at the window and covered the bed. A matching ruffle draped the dressing table. At any other time, Elizabeth would have clapped her hands in wondrous appreciation.

Now all that captivated her attention was the door on the far wall, the door she knew intuitively led to Morgan's room.

There was no lock.

"I thought you'd like a bath to freshen up," Annie said brightly. "The water's still piping hot, ma'am."

With Annie's help she was soon divested of her wedding gown. The girl was right. The water was steaming hot, yet Elizabeth had never felt so cold! Heedless of her mistress's anxiety, Annie chattered on while she scrubbed her back, then held out a fluffy towel when she was done.

"I hope you don't mind that I laid out your nightgown. I picked it out myself," Annie declared.

Elizabeth swallowed when she saw the sheer silk nightgown already spread out on the bed. "It's a bit cool for such a thin gown, don't you think?"

Annie's expression plummeted.

"But it is lovely, isn't it?" she added hastily.

Annie's smile returned full bloom. "And you've someone to keep you warm the night through, remember?"

Soft silk was whisked over her head and twitched into place. Elizabeth winced as she glimpsed her reflection in the mirror—the outline of her body was clearly visible.

Her arms stole around herself. "Oh, dear, I'm afraid I'm still rather cold after that nice warm bath. I think I'd like the robe as well, Annie."

Annie gave a telling sigh but went to the wardrobe. The girl draped it around her shoulders—and added more wood to the fire blazing in the hearth.

Then she was left alone, the only sound that of a small gilt clock on the bed stand . . . that and the pounding of her heart.

She paced restlessly, her mind consumed by just one thought. A husband had the right to lie with his wife. It was expected—it was a duty. And if he wanted, she must endure it over and over . . . Her thoughts grew wild. Perhaps it would be a blessing after all to be with child. Perhaps then Morgan would leave her well enough alone . . .

She'd avoided thinking about the night to come. If she didn't think about it, it wasn't real. But now the reality was nearly upon her, and so was the hour.

She lay down, but didn't sleep. The clock ticked slowly, so loud and so long she wanted to scream. Her ears strained for any sign that Morgan had come upstairs.

There was no sign of him.

Finally she arose, tugging her robe over her nightgown. Before she knew it, she was across the floor, one hand poised on the door that led to Morgan's room. Holding her breath, she slowly twisted the handle, then gently pushed it open.

The hazy glow of lamplight filled the room. It was empty, thank heaven. Drawn by a curiosity she couldn't deny, she ventured farther into her new husband's domain.

The furnishings were starkly masculine. A massive four-poster bed dominated the opposite wall, and it was that which captured Elizabeth's attention for a timeless moment.

"I must say, Elizabeth, this is a most unexpected surprise."

Chapter 10

It was him.

For an endless moment she couldn't move. Her feet felt heavy as iron. Then her hand fluttered to her throat. All at once her chest felt suffocatingly hot.

She turned to face him slowly, aware that her cheeks flamed scarlet. He stood there, as wholly at ease as she was flustered. Even as she watched, he discarded his jacket and vest, dropping it carelessly on the chair near the door.

"I-I'm very sorry." She grappled for poise—and for an explanation. Yet what could she say when she'd been caught in a place she should never have been . . . sweet heaven, his *bedroom*! "I-I didn't mean to intrude."

"Oh, it's no intrusion." As he spoke, he rolled up his shirtsleeves, displaying strong forearms liberally coated with silky-looking dark hair. He looked impossibly masculine—oh, there was no denying it!—impossibly virile . . . and suddenly she felt impossibly weak.

He glanced up and caught her gaze. Elizabeth

was horrified to discover she'd been caught staring.

"After all, where else would a wife be on her wedding night?" He smiled—oh, surely it was a demon's smile! "In fact, if I'd known you waited for me here, I'd have come up aeons ago."

She caught her breath, for the very idea that she . . . ! "You are mistaken."

"Indeed. How so?"

Blast the man! Must he toy with her so? Uncertainty rent her breast. "I beg your pardon," she said, clasping her hands together before her. "I'm afraid I was merely being unforgivably inquisitive."

"Indeed. I presume your room is to your liking?"

She nodded.

"You may have it redecorated if you like."

"Oh, no! It's lovely just as it is."

A heavy brow arched sharply, as if he'd expected otherwise.

The tension mounted as the silence continued. Her gaze slipped to the connecting door that led to her room.

He stood between her and the door, blocking her escape. His gaze followed hers. One corner of his hard mouth turned up in a faint smile.

"Are you anxious to leave, Elizabeth?"

Her reply came haltingly. "I am. I-I'm very tired."

"Oh, come now. After all, here we are, husband and wife"—his smile turned mocking—"and finally alone."

Her courage returned. "You know very well I didn't enter your room to offer myself to you!"

He moved a step closer. "Nonetheless, we are wed. And I would tell you, Elizabeth, that as your husband, I don't need your permission to take what is mine by right of the vows we spoke only this morning."

Her stomach clenched, for his matter-of-fact statement was like a slap in the face. The beast! Why must he remind her?

Her chin came up a notch. "Is that what you intend?" she asked stiffly.

He parried quickly. "Is that what you want?"

"Hardly." Only when it was out did she realize how scathing was her tone. One look at his taut expression and she knew she'd made a grave mistake.

"And what if I should insist?"

"I pray that you will not." Her tone was fervent, her features imploring.

He paid no heed, merely stepped closer. His gaze drifted over her, lingering on the thrust of her breasts. Only then did she realize her robe had fallen open.

She clutched the edges to her breast. Her heart was beating so hard, she feared it would choke her. "You said our marriage was an arrangement." Her voice was breathless. "A business arrangement. I-I see no reason why it should be anything else."

"A marriage in name only then?"

"Y-yes."

"I see. Why then, do you like it when I kiss you?"

"I-I don't!" Denial sprang quickly to her lips.

All at once he was there before her. "You do." He caught her by the arms, pulling her full and tight against him. His mouth hovered dangerously near. "And I'm more than willing to prove it once again."

Heaven help her, he did.

At first she kept her lips tightly closed against him. But his mouth on hers was infinitely knowing, infinitely sweet . . . and infinitely patient. She felt her defenses crumple as if they had never been.

He was right. She *did* like it when he kissed her.

Her mind screamed, even as her senses seemed to widen and flower. He did not demand—he compelled with subtle persuasion, his lips sweetly warm upon hers. His kiss drew from her a dark pleasure she could not fight. There was a peculiar tightness in her middle. In some hidden part of her, she longed for the kiss to go on and on . . .

Yet why? Why was it so? Her pulse pounded a frantic rhythm in her veins. Something tantalizing but elusive stirred in her breast. Never had it been like this with Nathaniel, she realized. Never! In her heart she was appalled at her helpless response to this man.

The man who is now your husband, whispered a niggling little voice in her mind. Yet she couldn't help it. She couldn't help but feel guilty that she should feel such things with Nathaniel's *brother*.

Nimble fingers breached the barrier of her robe, parting it with unswerving intent. His touch as bold and brazen as the man himself, he molded the cushioned swell of her breast in his palm, flesh that had known no other man's touch.

Reality surfaced with a jolt, even as a flurry of panic assailed her. If she did not stop this, *he* would not stop. Inexperienced as she was, intuitively she knew it was so.

She tore her mouth away, pushing blindly at his chest. "No. No, I say!"

He was as immovable as a pillar of stone. Slowly he raised his head.

"I-I cannot do this. Do you hear me? I cannot do this!"

His eyes seemed to burn her. "Cannot do what?" he asked, his tone dangerously low.

Desperation filled her breast. "I cannot lie with you!"

"You cannot lie with me," he repeated.

"No!" she cried wildly. "I cannot lie with you. I *will* not lie with you! Not now. Not tonight. Not—" She broke off abruptly.

The silence that followed was awful.

"Not ever?" Flatly he spoke the very words implanted in her mind.

Only now did Elizabeth notice his expression had iced over. She nodded, unable to tear her gaze from his face. His jaw was knotted and bunched, his lips drawn in a relentless line.

He released her abruptly. "My dear girl, I don't recall asking you to."

His tone was as cutting as his look. Elizabeth gaped, staggering back a step. "But downstairs you said . . ."

"I said you should not spend your first night as a bride feeling rather tipsy."

"You mean you will not—" She stopped, unable to bring herself to say more.

"No, I will not. But I *will* have the truth, Elizabeth." Before she could break away, strong hands closed around the soft flesh of her upper arms, guiding her until they stood toe to toe. "So tell me, and tell me true. Would you withhold yourself if Nathaniel stood before you and not I?"

Her eyes flitted away. She was not cruel, yet why did she suddenly have the strangest sensation she had hurt him?

No. It was absurd. Impossible.

He was insistent. His knuckles beneath her jaw, he prodded her chin up. "Answer me, Elizabeth. Would you deny Nathaniel what you now deny me?"

"No!" she cried, though in truth her thoughts had never carried her to that point. Anger and frustration broke loose inside her. She tossed her head, her eyes flashing. "I did not want this marriage, or you!" she said fiercely. "If you thought I liked it when you kissed me, 'twas because I did. But only because I pretended you were Nathaniel. Do you hear? I pretended you were Nathaniel!"

"I see," he said tightly. "Then if I can't come to you for carnal pleasures, I assume you'll have no objection if I seek satisfaction elsewhere."

Her breast was heaving. "I would welcome it!"

He freed her so suddenly, she stumbled backward. "Then you need worry no longer," he informed her tautly. "I have a mistress, and you've made it plain you would rather I lie with her than with you. So rest easy, Elizabeth. You'll spend your wedding night alone, while I spend mine in far more satisfying company."

He turned away. His movements were fierce, almost violent as he snatched up his coat and was gone.

Left alone, Elizabeth stared at the door he'd just passed through, shaken to the core by the anger she sensed in him. A hard knot of dread tightened in her belly. A dozen questions tumbled in her mind. She'd been spared . . . but for how long? And why did she have the awful feeling this was not the end of it?

For now, all she could do was pray—pray that he didn't have a change of heart.

Morgan didn't return home that night.

Nor did he go to Isabelle.

Instead he walked and walked. At such a late hour, the streets were deserted. The sharp rapping of his footsteps was the only sound. Curling wisps of fog swirled all around. Before long, he found himself on the docks.

A briny wind had sprung up. Morgan stared seaward, oblivious to the damp and the chill. Everything inside him was hard and brittle.

A muscle in his jaw tensed. *I did not want this marriage, or you!*

For an instant, when he'd come upon her in his room, he'd thought . . . But no. He was a fool, he decided with no little amount of rancor. She had come to Boston expecting to find Nathaniel. She had *wanted* Nat.

If you thought I liked it when you kissed me, 'twas because I did. But only because I pretended you were Nathaniel . . .

Her deception made his blood boil all over again. Yet why, he didn't know. After all, he had lied to her. And he'd lied to himself.

He wanted her.

From the moment he'd first seen her in his room, her eyes huge and uncertain, he'd wanted her. He longed to brand her as his own. Deep inside, he was convinced that had he tried, he might have swayed her with kisses of flame, touches of fire. In time, she would have yielded. Perhaps not at first . . .

But the very thought of taking her when it was Nat she longed for . . . An acrid bitterness seared his veins. That had halted his intentions as nothing else could have. He'd never taken an unwilling woman in his life; he wasn't about to start with his wife.

But buried beneath his studied indifference, he was angry—angry at her for tempting him. At Nathaniel for doing this to her—to him! At himself for his weakness, when he knew it was for Nathaniel she yearned.

He wanted her willing—by God, she *would* be willing. Even now, the very thought of plunging deep in her feminine warmth stirred his loins nearly to readiness. He thought briefly of Isabelle, then discarded the notion immediately— not because of any particular morality. After all, many men had mistresses. But the very idea of going from Elizabeth to Isabelle was completely unpalatable.

No, he hadn't been entirely truthful, even to himself . . . *especially* to himself. It wasn't to save Elizabeth's reputation that he had agreed to this marriage; it was for himself. And yes, deep down, perhaps there was a part of him that longed to take from Nathaniel what Nathaniel had taken from him . . .

The wind blew harder. The sea began to roil. Morgan stared out into the darkness, his mouth a grim line.

So much for marriage, he thought blackly. So much for love.

Elizabeth was not sleeping well. Her nights were spent listening, her ears straining. Waiting for her husband to come home, for her bedroom door to swing wide . . .

Her nerves were so tightly strung, she jumped at the slightest rustle or footfalls in the hallway.

It was soon apparent she worried for nothing, however. Her new husband had yet to seek out her company—for any reason. He was regularly very late arriving home. Often it was past midnight. There were some nights she was almost certain he didn't come home at all.

Last night was one of them.

So where had he been? With his mistress?

The nagging thought persisted, though she told herself she didn't care who the wretch bedded—as long as it wasn't her.

But there was the rub. On one hand, she was vastly relieved that he hadn't forced her to his bed. Yet the very thought of his mistress triggered a reaction faintly akin to hurt—yet why she should care, she couldn't imagine!

Still, the idea that a man should find pleasure outside marriage was one Elizabeth found she disliked—and heartily so. She was fairly certain that her father had never done such a thing—either with her mother or Clarissa—for he had valued loyalty and fidelity too much to make such a mockery of it.

Then one morning, she found a note scrawled in a bold, masculine hand on her breakfast tray:

I have tickets to the opera tonight. Be ready at seven.

In a rare temper, Elizabeth crumpled it and threw it across the room. "We shall see, my good man," she muttered hotly. "You may have to attend the opera alone." She was furious—he couldn't even do her the service of informing her in person!

Nor had he asked.

By the time the clock struck six her mood had softened. Perhaps a pleasant evening together would dispel the distance between them.

She dressed carefully, wanting to look her best. Annie swept her hair high and off her face, displaying to advantage the slender length of her neck. The midnight blue satin gown she wore was not new, but it was one of her favorites. The neckline dipped low, revealing the gleaming slope of her shoulders. Around her neck she fastened the strand of pearls Morgan had given her.

At last she was ready. The downstairs maid had dashed up twice to inform her that Morgan awaited her in the foyer. Descending the stairs, she saw him pacing impatiently, dressed in dark evening clothes.

Just as she reached the last step, he turned and saw her. His gaze traveled the length of her, from the top of her head to the toes of her slippers, and up again. Elizabeth held her breath and waited.

Their eyes collided. She saw nothing in his—no pleasure. Neither approval nor disapproval. Just a cool indifference. She might have been no more than a stick of furniture.

Something inside her seemed to wither, yet she was determined not to let it show. A single step placed him before her; he offered her his arm. Feeling curiously hollow, she placed white-gloved fingertips on his sleeve.

By the time they arrived at the theater, not a single word had passed between them.

Nonetheless, Elizabeth was determined not to spend the evening engulfed in misery. She maintained a smile as they alighted from the carriage. They were soon swept inside with a crush of people. To her delight, she found their seats were excellent. Situated on the balcony, they overlooked the center of the stage.

The curtains rose. From that moment on, Elizabeth leaned forward, scarcely aware of her stoic husband. From the moment the curtains parted, she was enraptured by the story played out below. The heroine was played by a lilting soprano with a voice of pure gold.

The intermission came far too soon. Along with the other patrons, they arose and moved to the lobby where refreshments were being served. The scents of perfume and eau de cologne mingled in the air, along with a medley of sound. Morgan brought her a glass of wine, but, as she was learning to expect, none for himself.

He handed it to her; their fingertips did not

touch. "I had no idea you were such a devotee," he observed, one dark brow aslant.

Her nerves were suddenly all aflutter. *How could you?* she nearly blurted. Quickly she thought better of it. Instead she smiled up at him rather shyly. "My father was very fond of the opera. When we were in London, we attended as often as we could."

"You were very close to your father, weren't you?"

Her smile faded. "Very," she responded quietly.

Several men and their wives came up and introduced themselves. Jewels flashed brightly. Elizabeth couldn't help but notice the unguarded looks of appreciation cast her way. Not that her husband seemed to notice. As for the women, they were overly gracious and prattled on about current fashions, how she would enjoy the social calendar . . .

The last couple had no sooner departed than he bent close to her ear. "Boston blue bloods," he murmured.

"Ah," she said gravely. Her soft mouth twitched with an irrepressible humor. "A haughty lot indeed, don't you think?"

Their eyes caught and held. His were startled, then something replaced it, a curious something that made her heart stop and her breath catch.

It was then, over his shoulder, that she noticed a dark-haired woman staring unabashedly at him. Dressed in a daringly low-cut gown of crimson satin, she was exotic looking and lovely. But her shiny red mouth was pinched and tight.

Even from this distance, Elizabeth sensed her displeasure.

But Morgan had noticed her distraction. "That woman is staring at you as if she would like to consign you to the devil himself," she said lightly. "Do you know her?"

He had turned and followed her gaze. "Yes," he said curtly. "But she's no one who concerns you."

Whatever had passed between them might never have been. She battled a sick feeling in the pit of her stomach. Suddenly she knew . . .

This beauty was his mistress.

She knew it for certain when the woman shot her a venomous look, then pointedly presented her back.

What pleasure she had experienced vanished. Her mood turned despairing, as despairing as her future. She spent the rest of the evening in abject misery.

They were nearly home when she addressed him. "I dislike the room next to yours," she announced. "I would like my old room back."

One look at his face and she knew it was a mistake. His profile was stark and unyielding.

"Out of the question," came his brusque reply.

She challenged him with a bravado she was far from feeling. "Why not?"

He turned on her, his features so forbidding, she shrank back in fear. "Because it would cause talk within the household—and eventually without. And I'll be *damned* if I'll tolerate any more gossip about the two of us."

Elizabeth couldn't believe her ears. "Gossip!" she burst out. "And what of you? Do you think they don't know how late you've been coming home? That many a night your bed is not slept in?"

"I was under the impression you didn't care whose bed I slept in as long as it wasn't yours."

No retort came readily to her lips—oh, but he was cruel to use that against her!

Nor was he prepared to let it go.

"Could it be that you find your solitary bed lonely, Elizabeth? Ah, but how can that be, when it was you who wanted nothing to do with me?"

Her chin tipped mutinously. "This marriage is a farce. I see no reason to continue with it. And just so you know, I—I fully intend to have my things moved back to my old room!"

His hands clamped around her shoulders. He drew her close—so close she could feel his breath strike her face. His eyes were glittering pinpoints of light.

"You'll have your privacy and I will have mine, Elizabeth. But you *will* occupy the room next to mine."

She cried out, angry at his power over her, angry that her life was in shambles. She sought to free herself, but his grip was too strong. "Then I demand a lock be put on the door between!"

Even through the dim light, she saw his jaw set tight. His voice was almost dangerously calm. "Let me speak plainly, Elizabeth. I will not have a door locked against me in my own house. Besides, I thought we had settled this. If I wanted you, no lock would keep me from you."

Even as he spoke, the carriage rolled to a halt. The door opened; Morgan leaped out. Elizabeth bit back her anger, aware that the driver could overhear. She would have shunned her husband's assistance in helping her down, but he wouldn't allow it. He lifted her down, then took her by the elbow.

"Let me go," she ordered the instant they were inside.

Fingers tight around her soft flesh, he steered her toward the library. "This discussion is not finished."

She muttered under her breath. In all her days, she'd never encountered arrogance such as his!

Simmons appeared. "Sir," he began, "I must tell you that your—"

"Not now, Simmons."

He guided her into the library, pulling the door tight behind them. Elizabeth jerked free of his touch and whirled to face him.

From the corner of her eye there was a swirl of movement across the floor. Before she could say a word there was a burst of husky masculine laughter.

"I must say, Morgan, you keep a very fine bottle of brandy—a pity you don't enjoy it."

It all seemed to happen in slow motion. From the wing chair near the fireplace, a figure rose in leisurely grace. A staggering horror seized hold of her. Elizabeth could only stare in shocked, frozen disbelief.

Dear God, it was Nathaniel.

Chapter 11

$\mathcal{F}$or the life of her, she didn't know who was more stunned—she or Nathaniel.

His smile withered. An oppressive mantle of silence descended.

It was Morgan who broke it. "I see you've made yourself right at home, Nathaniel." His hand caught Elizabeth's. He raised it high. "I'd like to introduce my wife, the former Lady Elizabeth Stanton, only daughter of the Earl of Chester. But I forget . . . the two of you know each other, don't you?"

She could almost see the confusion running through Nathaniel's mind. He shook his head, as if to clear it. "Elizabeth," he said hoarsely. "Sweet Lord, how on earth . . ."

"She arrived nearly two months ago." Morgan's tone was icy cold. "But of course, you weren't aware of that."

Nathaniel had yet to take his eyes from Elizabeth. He set aside his brandy and stretched out a hand. "Elizabeth," he said imploringly. "Tell me it isn't so. Tell me you didn't marry him!"

Elizabeth gave a tiny shake of her head. "I . . .

It's true," she said haltingly. "We've been married nearly two weeks."

"How could you? Dammit, Elizabeth, how could you?"

The hurt in Nathaniel's voice cut her to the quick. She might have gone to him, but Morgan had transferred his hand to her waist. At the precise moment she would have moved, he pulled her tight against his side. His arm slid around her waist, like a shackle of iron. Her lips parted, but Morgan was already speaking.

"We're husband and wife, Nathaniel. And not a soul on earth can change it."

Nathaniel's face underwent a lightning transformation. His eyes flamed as he snarled, "Stay out of this, Morgan. In fact, *get* out. I want to speak to Elizabeth alone."

"No." Morgan spoke but one word. Quiet as it was, never had a sound been more ominous.

The atmosphere was suddenly sizzling. Nathaniel cursed roundly. "Dammit, Morgan, this is between me and her—"

"Not anymore."

Nathaniel clenched his fists. "You bastard!" he hissed. "I knew her before you. She's mine! She's here because of me, and I have every right—"

"You have no rights, Nathaniel, nor is she yours. You see, I know the truth. I know how you claimed to be a rich Boston shipbuilder with a house on Beacon Hill—odd, how much you and I have in common, isn't it? I know how you charmed Elizabeth, how you professed to love her; how you asked her to marry you, when all the while you had no intention of following through."

The seconds crept slowly by. Nathaniel didn't deny it. Instead he glared at his brother, even as a betraying flush crept up his neck.

"But it no longer matters," Morgan went on, "because Elizabeth is now married to me. And as my wife, there is no aspect of her life that doesn't concern me as well. So if you'll excuse us, it's been a long and tiring day. And as I'm sure you can understand"—a half smile lurked on his lips—"we eagerly await our nights together."

Elizabeth was mortified beyond words. Grasping her elbow, Morgan propelled her from the room and up the staircase. Once they were outside her bedroom, she wrenched away. "That was rude!" she told him heatedly.

"He knows the way out."

Elizabeth was outraged. Aware that her cheeks still flamed scarlet, somehow she found the courage to speak her mind. "You only said what you did about us to—to taunt him!"

Morgan made no reply. Opening the door, he nodded for her to precede him into her room.

Elizabeth marched inside. "You could at least be civil!"

The door closed. He leaned against it, arms crossed over his chest, his expression coolly remote. "I'm sorry my manners fail to live up to your standards, my *lady*," he stressed. "But I wonder if you know exactly why my brother came here tonight."

"And I wonder if *you* do!"

"I can assure you, it wasn't because of any desire to see me. Surely that was apparent even to you."

It was indeed. The air between the two brothers was charged with something she couldn't even begin to understand. Striding to the bureau, where she stood before the mirror, she raised her hands to unfasten her pearls. "Perhaps he came to ask for your advice on some matter—"

Morgan stepped behind her. He addressed himself to her reflection. "Trust me, Elizabeth, he didn't. He came for one reason only." There was no give in his tone whatsoever.

She continued to struggle with the catch on the pearls. "And what, I might ask, is that reason?"

Suddenly his fingers were there, brushing hers aside. Everything within her seemed to leap. For the space of a heartbeat, his touch was warm and smooth on the bare skin of her nape. "What else?" he said flatly. "Money." In the next instant, the pearls were deposited on the bureau.

Only then did Elizabeth realize she'd been holding her breath. His nearness had an unsettling effect on her nerves—and her pulse. Quickly she stepped away, anxious to put some distance between them.

Her reply was just as unshakable. "You have a deplorable opinion of your brother."

"Deplorable? Now, there's a word that does indeed leap to the fore when it comes to Nathaniel." Morgan's laugh was anything but mirthful. "In time you'll come to see what I mean."

"Why do you dislike him?" she demanded.

Morgan's lips thinned. "I don't dislike him. I merely see him for what he is. And so should you."

Elizabeth gritted her teeth. "I'm quite capable

of thinking for myself, thank you. And I begin to see why the two of you cannot stand each other—you're too much alike." Her skirts swished as she moved to the connecting door between their rooms. "Now, if you don't mind, it really *has* been a long and tiring day."

"Then I won't keep you any longer." The faintest note of sarcasm in his voice, he bid her good night.

But he didn't exit through the connecting door between their rooms. Instead he strode into the hallway . . . A moment later she heard a door slam. The sound of hoofbeats soon followed.

An odd little hurt knotted Elizabeth's heart. Morgan had no doubts about Nathaniel. And she had no doubts about where he'd gone . . .

Back to his mistress.

It was late before Elizabeth roused the next morning. She woke as fatigued as she'd been only hours earlier, for it was near dawn before she'd finally fallen asleep. It was for that reason she declined a breakfast tray and waited instead for the noonday meal.

It was while she was eating alone in the dining room that Simmons carried in a small silver tray. "This just arrived for you, ma'am."

Elizabeth blotted her lips with her napkin, then reached for the small linen envelope on the tray. "Thank you, Simmons," she said with a smile. Thinking it was probably an invitation to a party or some such affair, she very nearly set it aside. But then she noticed her name alone was scrawled on the envelope.

A strange feeling tightened her middle as she

gingerly opened it. Her smile faded as she read the note inside.

It was from Nathaniel.

He wanted to see her. He listed an address on Hansen Street and asked that she meet him there that afternoon.

Elizabeth caught her lower lip between her teeth, her lunch forgotten. Instinct warned her that Morgan would not be pleased if he knew. Yet how could she refuse? Morgan had allowed no time last night for either questions or discussion. No doubt Nathaniel merely sought answers . . .

And she had some questions of her own.

Rising from her seat, she called for Simmons and asked that he have Willis, the driver, ready the carriage. "I've decided to do a bit of shopping," she told him.

Within the hour she was at the address Nathaniel had given her. Holding on to her bonnet, for the wind threatened to carry it from her head, she told Willis that she would hire a cab for the return trip home. He seemed puzzled that she didn't want him to wait, but she was firm. She waited until the horses had rounded the corner before hurrying down the walkway toward a small red brick building.

She couldn't help but note that the neighborhood was scarcely elite. Tufts of grass poked through the earth here and there. A window high above was cracked, the curtains a dingy yellow, the brass knocker rusty and stiff as she thumped it twice.

Footsteps sounded within. Nathaniel threw open the door. "Elizabeth! I knew you would come!" His smile was warm and welcoming.

Elizabeth felt distinctly ill at ease as she stepped inside. Something had changed, she thought vaguely ... *everything* had changed.

Nathaniel led the way into a small parlor.

But despite the shabby furnishings, Nathaniel was as usual, impeccably and fastidiously dressed in the height of fashion. He spread his arms wide. "As you can see," he proclaimed grandly, "my brother keeps me in the height of style."

"It should hardly be up to your brother to keep you at all!" The stinging retort slipped out before she could stop it.

His smile faded. "He's gotten to you, hasn't he? He's turned you against me!" He swore hotly. "Dammit, Elizabeth. How could you do this? How could you betray me?"

Elizabeth was speechless, first with shock, then with anger. "Betray you ... I did no such thing! You know it as well as I! We agreed that when Papa was well, I would come to you. Well, Papa *died*, Nathaniel. But still I did as I said. I came to you as soon as I was able."

Nathaniel had the grace to look sheepish. "I-I'm sorry. I didn't know about your father."

"How could you?" She confronted him with flashing eyes. "It was you who promised you would be waiting, Nathaniel! But you were not, and I think I'm owed an explanation. Your brother even hired an investigator to try to find you!"

"I left Boston soon after I arrived from London," he said quickly. "I was in New York visiting a friend I hadn't seen in years."

"Then why didn't you send word to me? I expected you would be here in Boston!"

"I should have, Elizabeth. I know that now. But frankly, I-I didn't expect you so soon. For all I knew, your father's illness might have dragged on for months."

"But it didn't, did it?" A faint trace of bitterness crept into her voice.

For the longest time he said nothing. "That still does not explain why you married Morgan."

Elizabeth laced her hands together before her. "When I arrived, I went to his home, believing it was yours. But I was very ill and collapsed when I saw your brother and not you. He and his friend Dr. Marks took care of me."

Nathaniel snorted. "You married him out of gratitude?"

"Necessity," she supplied curtly. "I had no choice. I could not return to England, Nathaniel—I *will* not. You were gone and I had no one to turn to for help. I had very little money and—"

"Very little money! Elizabeth, your father was hardly poor. Surely he left you something—"

"Papa left nearly all to Clarissa—the estate in Kent was to pass to me on the occasion of my marriage. But the task of finding a husband was left to Clarissa." She paused. "The only choice Clarissa would approve was Lord Harry Carlton. When I refused to marry him, I was disinherited."

"You were left nothing?" Nathaniel was aghast.

His reaction made her cringe inside. Outwardly she was calm and poised as she surveyed him. "Precisely."

"You mean to say you came to Boston knowing you'd been disinherited?"

Elizabeth knew then . . . she knew it was not she herself who had captured Nathaniel's fancy . . .

It was the thickness of her father's pocketbook. And indeed, there was a bitter irony in that his brother had married her not because of wealth, but simply because she was *Lady* Elizabeth Stanton, daughter of the Earl of Chester.

"So it wasn't me you loved—it was the size of my inheritance."

"Elizabeth, of course not! How can you even think such a thing?"

His wounded facade did not fool her. "You are not the one who was wronged here, Nathaniel. I did not posture myself as wealthy. I did not claim my brother's achievements. I did not promise to await the one I proposed to marry."

"I know," he said quickly. He sat down, running his fingers through his fair hair. "It's just that I-I did not expect you so soon," he said again.

"Let us at least be honest with each other, Nathaniel. You did not expect me at all." Strange, but the hurt Elizabeth expected to feel did not materialize.

Nathaniel's expression turned hopeful. "Perhaps if you returned to England, Clarissa would forgive you. You could divorce Morgan—"

Divorce! Why, such a thing was scandalous! "No, Nathaniel. *No.* I cannot. I have done nothing wrong and I will not pretend that I have."

She struggled to contain her mounting indignation and didn't entirely succeed. "I most certainly will not grovel before Clarissa for the sake of money! Whatever the reason, your brother and I are married."

Nathaniel got to his feet. His gaze sought hers, a tentative question on his lips and in his eyes. "Elizabeth, has he . . . Did he?"

There was no need to say more. Elizabeth colored deeply. She couldn't say yes. But dear God, she couldn't say no.

Nathaniel reached his own conclusion. His expression turned faintly belligerent. "He forced you to marry him, didn't he? Of course he did. I know Morgan and he—"

"No. He didn't." She was compelled to defend her husband, though she felt very much the hypocrite for being unable to divulge the true state of affairs between them. "An unscrupulous man discovered my presence at Morgan's house. He threatened blackmail. Morgan knew there would be no further scandal if we were wed. He proposed marriage to save me from ruin, to protect my good name, with no thought for his own. So you see, the choice was mine, Nathaniel. I married your brother of my own free will."

But Nathaniel's expression had gone rockhard. "God, but that sounds like Morgan," he sneered. "Always the savior. Always the rescuer."

"Whatever the reason, it's done. I couldn't live with myself if I didn't stand by my own choice." She glanced toward the door. "Please excuse me. I must get back before it gets any later." She turned, crossing the floor, her heels rapping sharply on the wooden surface.

Nathaniel was right behind her. Always the gentleman, he hurried to open the door for her. But before she could leave he turned to her. "Elizabeth, I want you to know . . . I did intend to marry you. Truly I did. If I hadn't had to leave so abruptly—"

"Then why did you?"

He sighed, his manner once again apologetic. "Elizabeth, if I could tell you, I swear I would. But I can't."

"No, Nathaniel. You *won't*. There's a difference. Surely you see that."

But he said nothing. Only when she started past him did he speak. "Please, Elizabeth. Don't do this. I know you can't be happy with Morgan. My God, he is—"

"He is now my husband," she broke in gently. "And it's already done, Nathaniel." She gave a tiny shake of her head. "We've all made our choices, and now we must live with them. Don't make it more difficult—for any of us. You must accept this marriage as"—she swallowed bravely—"as I have."

There was nothing more she could say. She turned and walked outside, grateful when she heard the door click shut a scant second later.

Back in her room at home, she undraped her shawl and dropped it on the bed, rubbing her fingers against her aching temples. Perhaps, she thought wearily, a hot bath would revive her. As for dinner, she would simply take a tray in her room.

Soon she was soaking in the huge wooden

tub. Plumes of steam rose all around her. Wanting to be alone, she dismissed Annie, then rested her arms atop the sides and leaned back. But the peace she sought simply was nowhere to be found. Her restless mind gave her no ease.

Accept this marriage as I have.

She winced. What on earth had possessed her to say such a thing!

Accept this marriage as I have.

Oh, if only she had . . . if only she *could*.

Behind her, a hinge creaked. Elizabeth frowned. Thinking Annie had misunderstood, she called out, "There's no need for your assistance. I can manage quite well by myself."

There was no reply, only several footsteps followed by a rustle of clothing . . . "But I'm only too glad to lend it," said a mockery-laden voice that was all too familiar.

It came from directly behind her. Elizabeth shot forward like an arrow, huddling her legs to her chest and hugging her knees tight. Her heart began to pound. Her husband proceeded to kneel at the side of the tub and dribble water from a sponge onto her naked shoulder—as if he had done so every day of their lives—as if he had every right to do so!

He did, chided an unwelcome inner voice. After all, he was her husband.

"Wh-what are you doing?" she stammered.

"I'm scrubbing your back in the hope that someday you'll return the favor."

And God in heaven, he did—with a touch that stole her breath and her very tongue. Discarding his jacket, he rolled up his shirtsleeves.

The sponge was tossed; it landed with a *plop!* near her right hand. Liberally soaping both hands, he laved every inch of her back from her nape to the dimpled valley above her hips. His touch was firm and bold; it left a wake of fire wherever he stroked. Elizabeth was too stunned to move.

And then she was afraid to do so.

Nor could she rid her mind of what he'd said. *I'm scrubbing your back in the hope that someday you'll return the favor.* It was outrageous enough that he was present at her bath, yet alone to bathe her so. But the very idea of touching him in such a way, sliding her fingertips down the muscled expanse of his back ... why, she'd never even seen a man in his natural state!

On and on her mind roiled. Finally he drew back. From the corner of her eye, she saw him shift to his heels. "The water grows cold, Elizabeth. Don't you think you should get out?"

She blurted the first thing that popped into her head. "How can I? You would see me naked!"

"So I would. But I've already seen you naked, remember?"

She would have preferred that he not remind her. "Ours is not the usual marriage," she managed to say.

"That it's not," he agreed, and now there was a note in his voice that sent a tremor of warning all through her. "Two weeks wed and you've yet to lie with your husband."

Her stomach dove. Somehow she braved a glance over her bare shoulder. He had risen and stood watching her, his regard somber and un-smiling.

"Please," she said, struggling for dignity—what little there was in such a predicament! "You promised I would have my privacy."

He slanted her a faint smile. "So I did, Elizabeth. So I did." He reached for his jacket. "I'll send Annie back up. I'll tell Simmons to have dinner served in . . . shall we say fifteen minutes?"

Her nod was absentminded, for her mind was racing. He planned to be home, then—so much for her plans for a relaxing dinner alone in her room. As soon as he was gone, she rose and hurriedly dried herself. She didn't linger over a choice for a gown but left it to Annie. The girl chose a deep burgundy satin that brought out the bright gold of her hair.

Morgan was waiting for her in the dining room. Elizabeth glanced at the clock as she hurried in—she was late. She apologized for her tardiness as he seated her. In return he was faultlessly polite, as he was throughout the remainder of the meal.

It was over coffee—a taste for which she was certain she would never acquire—that he turned his head and gave her his undivided attention.

"Simmons tells me you went shopping this afternoon. What did you buy?"

Elizabeth floundered. "I-I'm afraid I found I wasn't in the mood for shopping after all," she said lamely. "It was silly of me to have gone alone."

"I see." Cool gray eyes appraised her. "In that

case you should have asked Nathaniel to accompany you."

Elizabeth's gaze flew to his. What she saw smoldering in his eyes made her heart plummet like a stone. "You know," she said weakly. "You know I saw Nathaniel."

"Yes, Elizabeth, I do know. And I must say, you're hardly the accomplished liar that Nathaniel is."

She couldn't tear her eyes from his face. Never had she seen him so grim! She began to tremble, linking her hands together in her lap to keep them from shaking.

"I trust the two of you had a cozy reunion." His tone was less than pleasant.

She shook her head. "It-it wasn't like that—"

"Then what was it like?"

"Surely you can understand that he deserved an explanation," she said with as much calm as she could muster.

"An explanation. Yes, I suppose I can understand. But I wonder, Elizabeth"—his tone was almost lashing—"what else did he get?"

The usually soft line of her lips tightened. "You insult your brother's honor by suggesting such a thing," she said levelly.

"My brother has no honor."

She drew a deep, fortifying breath. "Put yourself in his place for once. I was to marry him. Instead he returned home only to discover I was already married—and to his brother yet. He has every right to know why."

Morgan's lip curled in disgust. "You owe him nothing, Elizabeth. He failed you, and you would give him pity! But Nathaniel is good at fooling people. A shame you haven't discovered that yet. But you will. Eventually, you will."

It was then that Elizabeth realized. Morgan did not dislike Nathaniel. Nor was he impatient or frustrated . . .

"Dear God," she said baldly. "You hate him. You hate Nathaniel . . ."

Deep within her she thought he would deny it. Assure her she was mistaken, at the very least . . . ! But he did neither. Instead, his silence was brutally condemning.

She was both stunned and appalled. What manner of man had she married that he would forsake his own brother?

She stood, drawing herself up proudly and facing him. "Believe what you will about Nathaniel," she said clearly, "and about me. It matters little, because I know the truth. I went to see Nathaniel, yes. I shouldn't have lied about my whereabouts, but I knew you would not like it if you knew. But that is the end of it, for my only purpose was to explain our marriage. It was hardly a lover's tryst—I did nothing wrong. And I will admit to nothing, for I have *done* nothing. Now, if you'll excuse me, I intend to spend the rest of the evening in my room—at the moment, I find my own company far more preferable than yours."

She waited for neither permission nor assent, but swept away in a swirl of skirts, the incline of her chin tipped high as a queen's.

By the time she reached her bedroom, her anger had dissolved into frustration. She changed into nightgown and dressing gown, then stood before the bureau mirror, unmoving. But it wasn't her own reflection she saw; Morgan's features swam before her, his expression taut as a drum, his mouth tight with disapproval.

Her conscience pricked at her. She truly regretted that she had chosen to mislead Simmons. But she was undeserving of Morgan's displeasure—and his veiled accusations.

Her mind was awhirl with unanswered questions. Why was he so openly suspicious of her? It was just as she'd said—she'd done nothing to warrant such behavior. Was it simply in his nature that he was so distrustful? Or had something happened to make him this way?

So engrossed was she in her musings that she didn't hear the connecting door click open and shut. She glanced up with a gasp when the figure of her husband loomed in the mirror behind her.

He wore only a robe, loosely belted at the waist, revealing a wedge of dark, hair-matted chest.

Their eyes caught and held. Hers were wide and startled, his were dark and unreadable.

Her question came in a rush. "What are you doing here?"

He merely shook his head. "I'm afraid you were wrong, Elizabeth. The evening is not yet over"—there was a weighty pause—"for either of us."

Along with his entrance came a seething awareness. Her pulse seemed to stumble. Her mouth went dry as dust. "Wh-what do you mean? What are you going to do?"

A dangerous half smile lurked on his lips. "What I should have done on our wedding night," he said softly.

Chapter 12

Deep in the darkness of his soul, Morgan had known it would come to this. He'd known it almost from the start. He'd been fighting it since the moment he'd kissed her . . .

He was done fighting.

But he resented her for doing this to him, for twisting his insides into knots. For making him want her when she gave her heart to his brother . . . How many nights had she lain here, in that very bed, thinking of Nat? Dreaming of him? Wishing she were married to Nat and not him?

All this . . . all this and more tormented him, burning like blisters inside him.

By God, she was his. *His*. She was married to him, not Nathaniel.

He stepped forward. It was time his lofty little bride knew it, too.

And indeed, Elizabeth had gone stiff with apprehension. It seemed to require a tremendous effort to force her lips to move.

"Please leave."

"No, sweet." His smile had yet to waver. "Not this time."

Her heart had begun to quake. "What do you want?"

His gaze, dark and silver, pinned hers. "You," he said softly.

Her mind seemed to stumble. "Wh-why?" she stammered.

He merely shook his head. "A silly question, Elizabeth. You are my wife. Need I say more?"

"But you—you said that you are hardly enamored of me."

"Good Lord, girl. A man and woman hardly need to be in love to share a bed—and the pleasure of each other's bodies."

An icy dread chilled her veins. "You have no right—"

"On the contrary. I have every right. I am your husband. You are my wife. Or were you tempted to forget that when you saw Nathaniel today?"

Elizabeth closed her eyes and fought desperately to bring her panic under control. If only this were a dream! But when she opened her eyes, he was still there.

"That's why you're here, isn't it?" The words came out low and choked. "Because I saw Nathaniel today. I-I saw the way you looked at him yesterday. It's just as I said. You hate him. Only now you would take out your anger on me!"

"Ah, but that's where you're wrong, sweet. I'm not angry. But there's one thing I've discovered I cannot tolerate. I won't have Nathaniel in your bed" —his eyes held hers, a wordless challenge—"and not me."

He was so cool. So utterly in control of himself and his feelings.

And somehow that frightened her even more.

She pressed her lips together to keep them from trembling. She felt as if she'd come face-to-face with her Maker only to be sentenced to some vast unknown world of darkness and cold.

Only now he had reached out and caught hold of her. His palms were disturbingly warm and big. All at once she felt small and helpless in a way that had never happened before.

She raised a hand between them, a halfhearted gesture at best, as if to push him away. "Please, I don't want—"

"But I do, Elizabeth."

Her hand was captured and brought high to rest on his shoulder. He did the very same with the other, even as his hands settled on her waist. And then she was being drawn close—so very close she could hardly take in enough air to breathe without pressing the whole of her body against his.

"So tell me, Elizabeth. What did you find so irresistible in my brother? Did he woo you? Seduce you?" His tone was almost lazy. She opened her mouth to speak, only to discover his eyes had locked on her lips.

"No matter," he murmured. "It's me you're with now." His fingers beneath her chin, he lifted her face to his. Elizabeth's eyes flew wide as she gleaned his intent, but then it was too late.

His mouth was on hers, not the forceful stamp of possession she'd expected, but hot and sweet. The sound of protest she might have made was never to be. It was drowned in the heat of his kiss. And if his intention was to drive all thought of Nathaniel from her mind, he succeeded beyond measure.

Nathaniel had never kissed her like this, she thought dimly, over and over, until her senses were awhirl and she could scarcely think. She was only vaguely aware of deft fingertips untying the belt of her dressing gown and sliding within. Her body seemed to ache—Lord, but she was secretly mortified!—especially there where her nipples grew taut and tingly. And there was a strange questing deep in the pit of her belly.

Over and over he fed on her lips, as if he were starving and she were his feast. Pleasure swirled in a dark mist all around her. If he had demanded and taken as he said he might, she'd have fought him kicking and screaming. But instead he cajoled and persisted, with only the artful pressure of his lips against hers, and she was powerless against such devastating persuasion.

His tongue skirmished boldly with hers. A low moan escaped, a sound of yearning, for what, she knew not. By the time he raised his head, she could only cling to him feebly, weak-kneed and dizzy.

Only now she was naked.

Her gown and robe lay pooled in a heap about her feet. She stood mutely, aware that he had retreated a step, aware that eyes the color of pewter scoured every bare inch of her flesh—no part of her was overlooked. Hot shame scalded her veins. She quivered beneath his unrelenting gaze, certain her face—indeed, her entire body—was the color of flames. Her arms came up to shield her breasts, an age-old gesture of defense she couldn't suppress.

He didn't allow it. His hands encircled her wrists as if she were caught in a clasp of steel, keeping them at her sides. Soft, masculine laughter rushed past her ear. "No, Elizabeth. There'll be no maidenly protests tonight."

Deep in the recesses of her brain, she knew there would be no stopping him; it was pointless even to try.

And Morgan knew it too.

Raw heat twisted inside him, shooting down to his loins, swelling his manhood. She was even lovelier than he remembered, her skin as lustrous as the pearls he'd given her. Long and slender limbs lent her an air of fragility, yet no woman had ever fired his desire as she did now. Her breasts were small but high and delectably round, tipped by nipples the color of ripe summer berries. Her waist seemed incredibly narrow, but her hips flared round and feminine. Between the span of her belly, a triangle of golden hair guarded the gates to paradise. Filled with a raging need, he swept her high into his arms and laid her on the bed.

Every muscle of her body tightened as he stretched out beside her. Then she was pulled close and tight against his length. His mouth claimed hers once more, hot and ardent. Only now he was not content with sampling just her lips.

One lean, dark hand closed around the fullness of her breast. Elizabeth tore her mouth away from his, stunned to the core at his boldness. She was wholly unprepared for the sight that met her eyes—her swelling softness fit his palm as if she were made solely for him.

In shock she watched his thumb trace a slow circle around the crest of her breast, a wanton, tormenting caress. Her nipples grew pebbly hard and achingly engorged. A strangled breath escaped; she hardly knew it came from her lips.

But there was more.

His mouth stole slowly down the arch of her throat, tasting . . . and seeking. For a timeless moment he was poised above the turgid peak of her breast. Her breath grew shallow and quick. His tongue touched her first, a delicate foray that went through her like a bolt of lightning. His lips grazed the swollen tip, the merest touch. Then his mouth closed around one pink, straining nipple . . . He sucked first one, then the other.

Elizabeth bit back a cry. Her fingers dug into the sleek flesh of his shoulders, but she didn't stop him. Sweet heaven, she couldn't. All else was forgotten. Her anger with him. All the reasons she hadn't wanted this to happen. But nothing existed save the exquisite torture he wrought on her body. Shameful as it was—crazy as it was—she was filled with a quivering excitement unlike anything she'd ever felt before.

It was no different for Morgan.

Never had desire raged so keenly within him, so deeply that he was robbed of all sanity, of all but the need to bury his rod hard and deep within her. His blood on fire, his hand drifted lower, tangling in her golden fleece before delving still further.

His fingers probed with daring intimacy. A lone finger sought and found her secret channel. She started with surprise. Her nails bit into his shoulder. He gritted his teeth. Lord, but she was small . . . A voice within whispered she was an innocent. No. She couldn't be. Oh, she was gently bred, to be sure. But she'd fallen for Nat, and he couldn't imagine that Nat would have let her be.

His hand left her. Rising, he shrugged off his robe and tossed it aside.

Unencumbered, his manhood sprang free.

Elizabeth caught the hard smile that curved his lips as she turned her head. Her mouth grew dry at the sight of him. His chest was wide and matted with curly dark hair. His hips were incredibly narrow, his belly flat as a board.

Her gaze strayed lower.

She stifled a gasp, for his arousal was thick and rigid and distended, framed within a dark, curling jungle. She couldn't look away as he came down beside her once more.

Her limbs were trembling, not with excitement but with a very real fear. Her lips parted, and then his mouth was sealed on hers once more. His chest pinned hers, wide and heavy. She could feel the press of his manhood against her thigh, like an iron probe, scalding hot. As he shifted to lever himself atop her, panic burst anew in her brain.

Somehow she managed to tear her mouth free. "Please. Please do not!" It wasn't a denial, but a frantic, desperate appeal.

He paid no heed.

"Please! I must tell you—"

"Not now." His whisper, low and hot, rushed by her ear.

"But I've never—"

"Hush," he said thickly. His fingers laced through hers, borne to the mattress beside her head. The weight of his thighs kept hers parted wide, open and vulnerable.

One burning thrust and he was deep—deep!—within her.

It happened too fast, before she could stop it. Her eyes flew open. She cried out at the sudden, tearing pain. She pushed at him, but he was like a rock above her, immovable as stone. "Please," she said tremulously. "Please!"

Above her, Morgan went utterly still, his features twisted into a grimace that might have been pain.

She pounded at his shoulders. "What have you done?" she choked out. "What have you done?"

"Elizabeth! Don't move!"

But Elizabeth was beyond hearing. Her writhing only made her aware of how deeply embedded inside her he was. Finally, in sheer and utter defeat, she ceased her struggles.

His shaft left her, but the burning pain did not. Squeezing her eyes shut, she turned her face to the wall. She scarcely noticed as he awkwardly covered her nakedness with the sheet, then rose to put on his robe.

The mattress dipped as he sat on the edge of the bed. "Dammit, Elizabeth! You should have told me."

Elizabeth stiffened. After all this, he dared to berate her? She twisted around and looked at him then, clutching the sheet to her naked breasts. "I did try!" she cried. "But you refused to listen."

"If I had known—"

"You'd have what? Let me be?" A high-pitched note of hysteria entered her voice. "It would have made no difference and you know it!"

Morgan drew a deep, unsteady breath. He reached out a hand to touch her shoulder. "Elizabeth—"

She shrank away. "Don't," she said brokenly. "Please don't. Just-just leave me alone."

His expression froze. All trace of emotion vanished in the blink of an eye. The hand extended toward her closed into a fist at his side. "Certainly." One fluid movement brought him to his feet.

He left her huddled into a ball, quietly weeping.

By morning the brandy decanter in the library was empty.

Chapter 13

Elizabeth rose the next morning feeling tired, achy and sore. The memory of last night flooded her being. Was this why women were reluctant to discuss such delicate matters? She went hot all over, the events of last night a scorching—and all too vivid—remembrance.

Her throat tightened oddly. For a time, there had been a promise of provocative pleasure, tantalizing and elusive. Recalling the way Morgan had touched her—*where* he had touched her—brought a heated flush to her entire body.

But it had been ruined by the thrusting pressure of him deep inside her, a part of her, as no man had ever done before . . . She would never be able to look in the mirror again. She would never be able to face *him* without thinking of all that had happened.

Yet in the end she did. When she happened to see him, she was always nervous and ill at ease. He was reserved and formal.

And his bed had been unoccupied almost every night since—Elizabeth was almost certain of it.

Then one evening Simmons told her Morgan wished to meet with her in his study. After the old man had left, she grappled almost frantically for an excuse to avert this meeting. Unfortunately, she could find none.

She approached his study reluctantly, uncertain why he should want to see her, and even more apprehensive. Every part of her was aflutter with nerves.

Just as she knocked, a vision flashed before her—her supine body, stretched out on the carpet before his desk, Morgan's long frame atop her ... Where it came from, she didn't know, for it was positively scandalous and wholly outrageous. In fact, it was so ridiculous, a bit of her trepidation fled. A man would hardly be about such husbandly pursuits in his study—let alone on the carpet!

Her knock was surprisingly firm. At his summons, she opened the door.

Seated at his desk, he looked up as she entered. Their eyes met for what was surely the most agonizing moment in her life. His features were noncommittal; he was apparently not at all beset by the awkwardness that plagued her.

He beckoned her forward. "Elizabeth. Please sit down." He indicated the chair across from him.

Once she was seated, he began, "I've been remiss in not discussing this with you earlier, but I'm afraid it slipped my mind until Simmons reminded me of it. At any rate, I'd like the handling of funds for household matters to be in your hands. Therefore, I've established an account at my bank which should prove adequate."

His manner was politely formal. "And should you need it, I also keep a sizable amount of cash in this drawer." He indicated the drawer adjacent to his left leg. "It's in a small metal box at the very back. The key is under the rose porcelain vase on the mantel." He gestured toward the fireplace. "Should you need additional funds for any reason, please don't hesitate to inform me."

Elizabeth folded her hands in her lap and murmured her thanks.

"I've also set up another fund for your personal use. If it meets with your approval, I'll continue to deposit a weekly allowance in the account." He named a figure that seemed outrageously high.

Elizabeth shook her head. "Truly, it's not necessary!" she said quickly. "I can think of nothing I need. Indeed, I already have much more than I need."

A dark brow hiked upward. "It's not a question of need, Elizabeth. I'm well acquainted with a woman's penchant for fripperies, so there's no point in depriving yourself." His tone grew rather stiff. "Besides, I'm fully capable of keeping you in the manner to which you've been accustomed."

Elizabeth lowered her gaze, feeling as if she'd just been thoroughly chastised. And why did she have the feeling he viewed her as greedy and grasping? Yet if she protested further, she might well risk offending him.

"Then I thank you for your generosity," she told him softly.

He acknowledged with a slight inclination of his head, then arose. Elizabeth's gaze followed him upward. Her breath caught as he rounded the corner of his desk and came nearer. All at once he appeared bigger than ever, his shoulders broad as the horizon. To her utter mortification, she found herself recalling how he'd looked without benefit of clothing—his body tall and spare, sleek, long muscles coated with curly dark hair.

He perched on the edge of his desk. His legs stretched outward, arms folded across his chest, he fixed her with a look. But his nearness was disturbing. She had to stop herself from swiftly drawing back her slippers beneath her chair. When his gaze settled for a disturbingly long moment on her lips, everything within her leaped wildly.

But his tone was purely matter-of-fact when he spoke. "I'd like to give a dinner party the week after next," he went on. "My attorney and banker will be among the guests, along with a man named James Brubaker. Mr. Brubaker is a designer of clipper ships. It's my belief he'll be much sought after in the future, and I'm very much interested in a joint venture with him."

Elizabeth listened intently. This was the first time Morgan had shared any aspect of his work with her. She couldn't help but be pleased; perhaps he'd finally begun to trust her.

She nodded. "Brubaker would design ships and you would build them?"

"Exactly." He paused. "Will you see to the dinner preparations?"

"Of course," she said promptly.

"There is just one more thing. Brubaker is from Liverpool, and I thought he might enjoy the company of one of his own countrymen."

Elizabeth's smile froze. Her enthusiasm vanished. "I see. And that's to be my task?"

A half smile curled one corner of his mouth. "I ask no more than what an aristocratic English lady is surely taught—to be charming and amiable and gracious."

All of Elizabeth's pleasure withered. A lady. Why must he always make it sound like an insult?

"Besides," Morgan continued, "certainly it can't hurt if Brubaker ends the evening in an amenable spirit. Perhaps then he'll be more receptive to my proposal." He paused. "I'd appreciate it if you would oblige me in this."

Oh, but she should have known! After all, wasn't this why he'd married her? To open doors that might otherwise be closed to him?

An acrid bitterness crowded her chest. She was not a wife, to be cherished and loved. She was nothing but a prize. A trophy on display at his side. A pawn to be used at his whimsy.

Never had he pretended otherwise, she reminded herself. Never.

So why did it hurt so much?

She inclined her head in silent assent, for what choice did she have?

The next days were spent in a flurry of preparations. There were invitations to be addressed and delivered. She pored over the menu with the cook. The silver must be polished, floors and furniture waxed until they shone with a mirrorlike sheen.

When the day arrived at last, Elizabeth found herself as nervous as she'd been on her wedding day. She scarcely slept the night before but rose at dawn, for there was still much to be done. Late in the afternoon, she escaped to her room for a brief nap. She woke tired yet a bit more refreshed—but it was growing late.

Thank heaven for Annie. Within minutes the girl had a hot bath waiting and ready. When she emerged, Annie dressed her hair and helped her into her gown, a deep, rich burgundy whose color lent her courage. The neckline was low and sweeping, leaving her shoulders and the rounded tops of her breasts bare.

Morgan awaited her as she descended the stairs. She sensed his impatience even before she saw his face. Picking up her skirts, Elizabeth stepped before him.

"I'm sorry. I didn't realize it was so late." Her tone was breathless.

His gaze traveled the length of her, a thorough appraisal that took in every detail.

Yet his only comment was, "You look well."

She started to say, "And you as well," for he was indeed as handsome a figure as ever, but there was no time to reply, for it seemed her arrival was in the nick of time. She had no sooner opened her mouth than the bell rang.

Within the next quarter hour everyone arrived. Elizabeth mingled with the guests, conscious of the fact that this was her first event as hostess and anxious for it to be a success.

Or did she merely want Morgan's approval?

She dismissed the niggling little doubt as nonsense. Why on earth would she want Morgan to be proud of her? He cared nothing about her and she cared nothing about him.

Or so she told herself.

By the time dinner was served and everyone had moved to the parlor for coffee and brandy, she found herself growing more relaxed and at ease. As for Morgan's request, she was sweetly attentive to Mr. James Brubaker, seating him next to her at dinner and engaging in a lengthy conversation with him afterward. Indeed, she found it no hardship at all.

Somehow she had expected an older, imposingly austere figure of a man. But she judged James Brubaker to be only slightly older than Morgan. Fair-haired and ruddy-cheeked—a bit on the gangly side—Brubaker was quiet but infinitely likable.

He was widowed, having only recently lost his wife and young son in a carriage accident. It was altogether apparent he had loved her deeply.

"I miss her and Gregory more than I can say," Brubaker said with sad wistfulness, "and yet I count myself blessed for each and every hour that God granted me with them."

Elizabeth's heart went out to him. A hollow ache rent her breast, for that was what *she* had hoped to find in marriage. She couldn't help but think of her father's will. Would he have done what he had—placed her happiness in Clarissa's hands—if he had known what fate awaited her?

Much to her dismay, the thought unfolded. What *would* her father have thought of Morgan? Would he have considered Morgan a more worthy husband than Nathaniel? She winced inwardly. Her father had been a man of integrity;

a man who valued honesty and truth above all else.

In the end, nothing could change what had happened. Nathaniel had deceived her, while Morgan had been nothing but honest . . .

Sometimes painfully so.

And now—now his eye was ever upon her . . . In the dining room. In the drawing room. From where he stood near the fireplace, talking with his banker.

Was there nothing he missed?

Before long the hour was late. She and Morgan stood together near the door, bidding everyone good night. Elizabeth almost dreaded the moment when the door closed for the last time.

For now they were left alone, she and Morgan. Her anxiety returned full bloom, yet she was determined not to show it. Conjuring up a smile, she said lightly, "That went well, don't you think?"

Her husband's regard was like an icy blast of frigid air. "Brubaker did seem to find you quite enchanting." There was a heartbeat of silence. "I must say, you certainly seemed to warm to the task."

Elizabeth's chin came up, but she remained pleasantly placid. "I was given to believe that was what you wanted."

"I suppose it was a success, since I'm meeting him tomorrow morning. But as I recall, I asked that you be charming"—his tone was lashing—"not that you *charm him*."

Elizabeth's spine went ramrod-straight. She held onto her temper, but only by a thread. "I did as you asked—no more, no less."

When she would have stepped away, his fingers curled into the soft flesh of her upper arm. "I tell you now, Elizabeth, I'll not have a bastard in my home. Not my brother's, or anyone else's."

Elizabeth jerked away. "If your opinion of me is so little, then why did you marry me?" A rash boldness seized her. "Oh, do forgive me! Because I possess exemplary bloodlines. Yet still you believe my behavior is that of a—a common slut, when you know very well that cannot be!"

Something flitted across his face, something that might have been fleeting guilt. Elizabeth experienced a brief moment of triumph.

"I know what was *not* the case before our marriage," he allowed at last. "But I also know what I will not permit."

"Oh yes, you made yourself quite clear. You said you would tolerate no lovers. Nor," she informed him heatedly, "will I."

He gazed at her as if she'd gone mad. "Precisely what does that mean?"

"I am not such a fool as you think!" she snapped. "The night of the opera there was a woman staring at you. I asked who she was. You told me she was no one that concerns me. But I'm afraid she does concern me when I know full well she is your mistress—and that's where you've been spending all your nights!"

He neither denied it nor confirmed it. "Need I remind you of our wedding night? You made it quite clear I could not seek pleasure from you."

Sheer bravado prompted her retort. "Nonetheless, I-I demand that you give her up! Now, if you'll excuse me, I'd like to retire."

Morgan said nothing. But his features were a

mask of stone as he watched her march from the room, her nose tipped high as a queen's.

Slowly he made his way to the library, where he sat in a velvet chair, long legs sprawled before him, his jacket discarded, his shirt unbuttoned. Darkness surrounded him, as black as his mood. Though his body was still, his mind was not.

Throughout the evening, no matter where he was—who he was with—his mind was encumbered by *her*. His wife. The wife who denied him in any way she could—in every way.

The longer he sat, the more the tumult within him squalled.

He'd married a stiff-necked Puritan, he decided darkly. But she didn't look like one. Her naked shoulders had tempted him throughout the evening. He couldn't help but recall that moment when he'd taken her; it was branded in his mind like fire. He hadn't forgotten how it felt to be buried deep within her, her body hot and tight around his swollen flesh. Christ, but he'd longed to complete the act he'd only started! Leaving her then had been the hardest thing he'd ever done. He'd wanted to explode within her again and again and again.

And now his blood was burning again, scalding his veins, blazing through his body like lightning.

But she was as forbidden to him as ever.

His jaw clenched hard. It didn't have to be that way. By God, it would *not* be that way.

He took the stairs two at a time.

Elizabeth sat before the vanity, clad in a simple high-necked, long-sleeved muslin nightgown.

Her hair hung like a golden curtain about her, loose and free. She pulled a brush through the gleaming strands, hoping the monotonous motion would calm her runaway emotions.

She didn't know if she should regret or applaud her angry outburst.

On one level, she was glad it was out, that Morgan knew she disapproved of his mistress and would endure a faithless husband no longer. On quite another, she was petrified of his reaction. Indeed, whispered an intrusive little voice, wasn't that the very reason she had fled?

I didn't flee, she argued silently.

You did, the voice reiterated. *You're a coward.*

No!

Yes . . . yes!

She paused in her ministrations, then let out a long, uneven breath. He was, she admitted at last, a formidable figure, this man she had married.

Never more so than now.

The hallway door swung open. Even as a prickle of grating awareness touched her spine, Elizabeth froze. Her heart lurched, but her fear lasted only an instant. She welcomed the surge of anger that began to simmer. Considering the subject of their exchange in the foyer, she couldn't believe he had the audacity to come to her room!

Four steps put him directly behind her. Elizabeth tensed but did not turn. Their eyes met in the mirror. Hers were guarded and wary; to her dismay, his were wholly unreadable.

"What do you want?" she asked curtly.

"I should think that would be obvious. I would like to speak with you."

"Can't it wait until morning? Can't we discuss it elsewhere?"

A dangerous smile curled his lips. "No, it cannot. *We* cannot. In fact, there's nowhere I'd rather be, my dear wife"—a hard smile edged his lips—"and you've nowhere to run."

Chapter 14

〜〜⟨O⟩〜〜

Elizabeth's heart began to thud. With deep-ening dread, she watched as he began to walk slowly back and forth, strong hands linked behind his back. His spotless white shirt was open at the throat, baring a tangle of wiry dark hairs. Elizabeth watched him, a cold lump of dread tightening her middle.

"You left before we finished our discussion, Elizabeth."

Elizabeth said nothing. The hand with the hairbrush had lowered to her lap. Her grip was white knuckled.

"Our so-called arrangement is not working out as expected. Do you agree?"

Elizabeth hesitated, then finally nodded.

"Then I think it's time we acted our roles. You've chosen to dictate boundaries. So be it." There was a pulsebeat of silence before he said softly, "But I'm afraid I have some demands of my own."

Quietly as he spoke, she sensed a harshness in him that could no longer be denied—and ah, how she suddenly regretted the rashness of her tongue!

She had to force her lips to move. "Such as?"

He had paused directly behind her, so close the fabric of his shirt brushed her hair. "We've been married over a month now." He spoke with cool deliberation. "Frankly, Elizabeth, I expect more from a wife."

That stirred her temper. "Perhaps I expect more from a husband!" she flared.

"Excellent. Because I find I am willing—even eager—to carry out my duties as a husband." His eyes had dropped to where the mounds of her naked breasts thrust against the cloth.

An unholy glint had appeared as well. His meaning was unmistakable. Once again she could almost feel him . . . the hot spear of his manhood stabbing into her flesh, as if to rend her in two . . .

Panic threatened to choke her. She could not bear it again . . . she could not! She lurched upward with a cry. "That's not what I mean—"

"But it *is* what I mean." Strong hands caught at her shoulders, bringing her around to face him. His gaze ran over her, making her feel stripped to the very bone.

His hands fell away from her. "Indeed, I feel cheated. You wore a gown of red this evening—red is the color of passion. Yet what warmth waits for me each night?" His lip curled. "My proper Boston wife—my very proper *English* wife whose welcome is colder than the sea."

Elizabeth made no reply, for what could she say? She stared at him, her eyes wide and uncertain.

A long finger flicked disdainfully at the neckline of her nightgown. "Remove it," he ordered curtly.

Even if she'd wanted to, Elizabeth couldn't have moved a muscle. She swallowed a rush of fear, for his regard was utterly unyielding. The very air between them seemed to sizzle with sparks.

A dark brow arose. "Unless you would rather I do it."

Elizabeth paled. Grasping for courage, she fought back with indignant outrage. "What kind of husband are you to make such demands?"

Morgan's jaw locked tight. Elizabeth quaked inwardly, for never had she sensed such danger. "I take what is mine—to have and to hold, as I recall." His tone was grating. "And I am a far better husband than you are a wife!"

Wildly she cried out, "No! You take what I would give!"

"And who would you give it to? Nathaniel?" He sneered. "Perhaps you should ask him why he wasn't here when you arrived from England; why he came when he finally did. I suspect the widow in New York grew tired of him. Or maybe he grew tired of her."

Shock rendered her immobile. The blood drained from her face as she realized what he was saying. He'd known Nathaniel was in New York. He'd *known*.

"You found him," she said faintly. "You found him, didn't you? You lied when you told me the man you hired had found no trace of him." Furious anger kindled in her voice. "What a fool I was, to believe you were an honest man!" She tossed her head. "But you're right, you know. It's Nathaniel I want. I've never *stopped* wanting him. And I-I intend to get a divorce as soon as I can!"

Morgan said nothing. A mask of ice descended over his features. Only his eyes shone like burning embers.

Her tongue ran wild and reckless. She plunged on, only half-aware of what she was saying. "Did you hear me? It's Nathaniel I want, not you! So damn you. Damn you anyway!"

For Morgan, it was an echo from the past. *It's Nathaniel I want, not you!* First Amelia. And now Elizabeth. Both scorned him. Faithless wives ... an untrustworthy brother. And all treacherous and disloyal ...

Something snapped in him then. Without warning his arms shot out. Blinded by rage—and passion—he dragged her up against him.

"No," he said fiercely. "Damn *you*."

His mouth came down on hers. His fingers slid through her hair. Long, golden strands tumbled down around his hands as he held her still for his kiss. Winding a handful around his fist, he caught her closer still against him.

His mouth was fiercely devouring, angry and punishing. Her low, choked cry was trapped between their lips. Her head spinning from the relentless pressure of his mouth on hers, she could make no protest as she felt herself lifted and laid on the bed. The weight of his body came down beside her. Once again he loomed above her, his features drawn by anger—and something else.

Caught in the ruthless hold of his embrace, she felt a tempest of pain swirling in her breast. His touch was sheer male mastery. She could feel it in the boldness of his caress—his hands roamed wherever he pleased.

He would not stop this time. Elizabeth knew it, as surely as the sun rose in the east. What use was there in protest? He wouldn't listen. Nor could she fight him. Even if she tried, she would never win.

Her gown had become tangled about her thighs, leaving slender white limbs naked and exposed. She lay passively while deft fingers worked the buttons on the bodice of her nightgown. Her chest ached as she struggled against a stinging rush of tears.

"You pretend to scorn me, Elizabeth. You deny me with words. But why is it your body always tells me otherwise?"

In all honesty, Elizabeth expected sheer, raw possession. What she got was something else entirely. His fingers barely grazed the tips of her breasts again and again, his play tauntingly provocative. Knowing he watched her, she was awash with hot shame. Yet to her utter mortification, her nipples began to tingle. Each roseate peak hardened into a tight, hard knot.

He smiled.

In an instant her gown was whisked up and over her head.

A lean, dark hand came down on the smoothness of her belly. Her whole body jerked.

There was the glint of steel in his regard. "I've yet to ever hear you say my name, Elizabeth."

Her eyes clung to his. She couldn't, she thought helplessly. The ache in her throat made speech impossible.

His gaze hardened. "Say it," he demanded. "Say my name."

Her lips trembled. Her throat worked. The silence spun out tensely between them, until with a low, choked sound deep in her breast, at last she turned her head away.

Everything constricted into a cold, hard knot in Morgan's belly. His fingers on her chin, he wrenched her face to his and took her lips in a bruising kiss. Maybe it was better this way, he thought furiously, with no angry words flying between them.

But there *was* something else between them. Something warm and wet and salty . . .

His head jerked up. Her eyes were huge and green and stricken, glittering with tears.

His entire body stiffened until he was taut as a board. "Damn you," he said tightly. The blistering curse was fairly flung at her. "Damn you, Elizabeth!"

For Elizabeth, it was suddenly all too much. Everything collided inside her. She began to sob. Wildly. Uncontrollably. Turning away from him, she curled into a little ball.

Defiant rebellion was certainly what Morgan had expected. But not this, never this. The sound of her weeping tore into him like the blade of a knife.

And God help him, he didn't know what to do. He was caught wholly off guard. He had little experience with the softer side of a woman's emotion. Amelia had always been too sure of herself and her beauty to display any vulnerability. And only now did he realize he'd fitted

Elizabeth into the very same niche. Never had he thought of her as vulnerable.

A tentative hand hovered above her. "Elizabeth," he said, and then again: *"Elizabeth."*

She didn't hear him. In some odd way, Morgan knew instinctively she'd withdrawn to a place where he couldn't reach her.

Warm fingers settled on her naked shoulder. He reached out for her almost tentatively. Yet when he turned her bodily in his arms, she nestled against him with a ragged sob, as if he were the cure for all her tears . . . and not the cause of them.

He covered them both with the coverlet. She was still crying, as if her heart were broken. His arms tightened unknowingly. His body still burning, he held her close, her head tucked into the hollow of his arms, her tears drenching his skin . . .

Thawing the heart he'd been convinced lay frozen and cold.

In time, the tears stopped. Her tremulous breaths grew slow and even. Held fast within the sheltering protection of his arms, she slept cuddled against him as if she belonged there.

But sleep eluded him. His thoughts churned, circling around this woman who gave him no peace. His expression bleak, he lay awake long into the night.

Elizabeth woke later than usual the next morning. Her mind blurry, she yawned and stretched . . . only to realize she was stark naked!

With a gasp her gaze flew to the pillow beside

her. There was still the slightest indentation in the center.

The events of the preceding night flooded back with a vengeance. Morgan had been so angry—so iron-hard and determined!

She remembered opening her eyes—it must have been near dawn, for it had begun to grow light—and staring sleepily where her small hand curled amid the furry darkness of his chest. She stirred slightly; the next instant there was a husky murmur against her ear, the featherlight brush of lips against her temple.

"Go to sleep," he had whispered.

Or had she only imagined it?

What on earth had possessed her? She didn't wonder at the reason she'd broken down—that was obvious. But it was madness, to find refuge in the very arms that shackled her. Only a day earlier, she'd have sworn that Morgan O'Connor was a man who possessed little compassion. Comfort, she had been convinced, was utterly foreign to his nature.

She pulled the counterpane tighter beneath her chin. When he'd entered her room last night, the thunder of his emotions seemed to charge the very air around him. Just thinking of it made her shiver. He had been so determined to possess her body—to assert his will over her own.

So why had he stopped? The question haunted her. And why hadn't he left her to cry alone? Instead, he'd spent the night here, holding her close . . .

And he hadn't gone to his mistress.

This she found altogether pleasing.

Still, her mood remained a trifle melancholy

throughout the morning—and weighted with guilt.

What was it she'd told Nathaniel? *Accept this marriage, as I have.*

She hadn't, she realized.

Perhaps it was time she did.

The thought caught hold. Perhaps it was time to put aside the distrust that existed between her and Morgan, once and for all. These past weeks had been filled with tension and strain. She didn't want to go on like that, she realized.

There was only one thing to do.

Early in the afternoon she asked that the carriage be brought around. Willis, the driver, helped her inside. "Where to, ma'am?" he asked cheerfully once she was seated.

"Mr. O'Connor's shipyard, please."

He looked startled. "The shipyard, ma'am?"

She smiled at him. "Yes. And please hurry. I'm a bit anxious." And so she was, she thought with a shaky inner laugh. Not for what she was about to do, but simply to have it done!

A short time later, the carriage rolled to a halt near the waters of the bay. The day was clear and warm, the sky an endless canopy of blue.

Willis opened the door and helped her out. "Would you like me to stay, ma'am?"

Elizabeth quickly considered. "Could you return in an hour?" That should give her plenty of time to gather her courage.

The name O'CONNOR SHIPBUILDING hung on a huge sign above the gate. Squaring her shoulders, she ventured within.

Inside the yard were two half-finished hulls surrounded by scaffolding. Men walked to and fro on the catwalks. The sound of hammering and an occasional shout filled the air.

All at once a tall, bearded man with bushy gray brows appeared at her elbow. "Can I help you with something, ma'am?" Deep, craggy lines scored his brow. His eyes were friendly and welcoming.

Elizabeth turned to him gratefully. "Yes. I'd like to see Mr. O'Connor."

Something flickered in his eyes. "Are you Mrs. O'Connor?"

Elizabeth nodded. She hadn't yet grown used to being addressed as Mrs. O'Connor.

White teeth flashed in the beard. "I'm Roger Howell, ma'am, your husband's assistant."

He'd already reached for her hand and was pumping it furiously. She smiled. "It's very nice to meet you, Mr. Howell, and you're probably just the one I need to see. Is my husband in his office?"

Howell gestured toward a vessel anchored off a dock a short distance away. "He's on board the *Windcloud*, ma'am. We did some repairs and he took her for a trial run."

Elizabeth turned to look. She couldn't help but catch her breath in startled surprise. At such close range, the vessel seemed enormous, but its lines were sleek and spare. With the sails a huge mass of snowy white canvas, it appeared like a majestic white seabird poised and ready for flight.

But the beautiful clipper ship didn't hold her attention for long. Sure enough, a tall, familiar figure stood on deck.

And he was staring directly at her.

For his assistant's benefit more than anything else, she raised a gloved hand and waved at her husband.

He didn't return it.

But there was no time for uncertainty. "Here, come along now." Mr. Howell had already taken her elbow. "Why don't you wait in Mr. O'Connor's office?"

He led her into a building just across from the yard, through a small reception area and into a spacious office. Even if she hadn't seen Morgan's jacket draped across a chair, Elizabeth would have known instantly this was his abode—the familiar scent of his cologne lingered in the air. Mr. Howell directed her to a seat, then quietly withdrew.

The door reopened far too quickly. Her heightened awareness warned her of Morgan's presence, even as he crossed the room to stand behind his desk.

No hint of greeting warmed his gaze or his expression. He folded his arms across his chest and waited, an air of impatient expectancy about him.

Much as Elizabeth suddenly longed to bolt and flee, it was too late.

Her lips felt stiff as she tried to smile. "I hope you don't mind that I came."

Her tentative statement met with cool indifference. "Not at all."

Clearly he wasn't going to make this easy for her. "I-I thought we might talk."

"About what?"

She found his bluntness disconcerting. "About . . . last night."

The silence thickened before he spoke. "As I recall, Elizabeth, when I tried to talk to you last night, you were in no mood."

That brought her head up. Their eyes clashed fiercely. "And as I recall, talking was the last thing you had in mind!" she flared before she thought better of it.

His jaw locked tight. "Yes," he stated grimly. "You were quite eloquent in conveying your feelings."

Too late Elizabeth regretted her rashness. A burning ache closed her throat. There was a sinking flutter in her heart. Tears rose perilously close to the surface. Why? she cried silently. Why was there always such tension—such distance—between them? She hadn't wanted this—indeed, with her presence here today, it was the very thing she had sought to avoid!

Her eyes grazed his, then quickly flitted away. Her hands locked convulsively in her lap as she tried to still their trembling . . . as she strived to find a courage that was maddeningly elusive.

"I-I'm sorry," she said, her voice very low. "I came to apologize for my behavior last night. I was shocked—and angry—when you said you'd discovered Nathaniel was in New York and you failed to tell me. But I should never have said what I did."

She paused, trying to gather her tumultuous emotions. Oddly, he was the one who broke the deepening silence.

"You had every reason to be angry, Elizabeth," he said slowly. "I'm not trying to defend myself. I'm not even certain I can explain. Perhaps I shouldn't have withheld Nathaniel's whereabouts. If I were faced with the same choice today, I can't honestly say my decision would be any different. But I think you mistook my intentions. It certainly wasn't to hurt you—or him." He paused. "If anything, I was trying to spare you."

A frown knit the smoothness of her brow. "From what?"

"From the truth," he said quietly. "He was with another woman, Elizabeth. How could I tell you that?"

Something that might have been pain flickered over her features. "It doesn't matter now," she said, her voice stifled. "What's done is done. I-I didn't marry Nathaniel. I married you. And—I'm afraid you were right after all. I-I haven't been a . . . a very good wife. I'm afraid I've been a—a miserable failure."

This time it was he who countered with a question. "How so?"

Her head bowed low. She stared as if in fascination where her fingers strained against each other. She couldn't look at him—she simply couldn't!

"I made a promise to you—a promise before God—to be your wife. And so I will. Because I-I know now it was wrong of me to deny you"— she faltered slightly—"on our wedding night. And again . . . last night." Her voice plunged to a mere wisp of sound. "But I—I won't deny you again."

Morgan had gone utterly still. He could scarcely believe his ears. But then triumph surged—triumph and a passion that made him long to drag her into his arms, kiss her mindless and let desire be his master.

Before he knew it he stood before her. Hands beneath her elbows, he brought her upright. He could feel her trembling and longed to reassure her. But the feelings that swamped his chest were as tangled as his mind.

His knuckles beneath her chin, he brought her face to his. Scarcely daring to breathe, he lowered his head. Their lips brushed, a featherlight caress. Again . . . and then again.

She sighed, a wispy exhalation of air. Her lashes fluttered closed. Slowly he deepened the kiss.

Her lips flowered beneath his, giving back all he sought and more. A hard arm curled around the slightness of her waist. With a low groan he brought her tight within the cradle of his thighs. She stiffened slightly, but she didn't withdraw as he thought she might. His free hand stole to her breast, cupping that sweet mound and claiming it for his own. With his thumb he circled the very peak, again and again.

It was a test—a test he despised himself for— but he couldn't help it. Her swiftly indrawn breath echoed in his mouth. He knew he had startled her . . .

Her nipple tightened into a hard little knot. With a breathy little sigh she arched into his palm.

His chest heaving, reluctantly he broke off the kiss. Trying to calm the wild racing of his heart, he pressed her face into the hollow of his shoulder.

"I have a small cottage on the coast north of

here." His voice wasn't entirely steady. "I was thinking . . . we could spend the next week or so there, just you and I." He leaned back so he could see her. His gaze roved her face intently. "Would you mind?"

Her cheeks flushed a becoming pink. Wordlessly she shook her head.

Morgan needed no further invitation. Like a starving man presented a sumptuous feast, he kissed her again, long and lingeringly. Coaxing her tongue out of hiding, he smothered a groan as she shyly began to learn the taste and texture of his mouth even as he explored hers.

His hands grew bolder still.

A groan erupted deep in his throat. It was heaven. It was hell, knowing she wouldn't stop him. But he didn't dare carry this through to its natural conclusion. Not now. Not *here*.

Besides, he wanted her too much. He didn't want to scare her off when she came willingly.

And this time he wanted their union to be all it hadn't been the first time.

Nonetheless, it was a very long time later before he finally raised his head. He had just one thing to say:

"We'll leave in the morning."

Chapter 15

_⤛⤜◦⤛⤜_

The coastline was rocky and rugged, but there was a wild, unrestrained beauty to it that Elizabeth found irresistible. Like a child on her first visit away from home, she peered eagerly through the glass, watching the landscape roll by. The day had dawned rather cloudy, but she didn't let it dampen her spirits. Her husband sat across from her, his expression faintly indulgent, long legs angled out before him. Though the pair had been silent throughout most of the journey, it was not an uncomfortable silence.

As they came around a jutting point of land, he sat forward. "There," he said softly, extending a finger. "Do you see it?"

Elizabeth leaned forward, straining to see. Below, a sandy stretch of beach lined a small cove. There was even a tiny, grassy island.

She frowned. "No—" she began.

Just then the sun emerged from behind a cloud. Streamers of sunlight unfurled, spreading like liquid silver on the waters below. It was then she saw it—a square, weathered gray house nestled amid a tall stand of pines. A wooden porch wrapped around the three sides visible to her. There was even a love seat that looked out over the ocean.

She couldn't help but catch her breath in wonder and surprise. It was lovely—and so she said.

Morgan made no reply, but she sensed he was pleased.

Once they arrived, Morgan helped Willis unload their bags and supplies onto the porch. "If we need anything else," he explained, "the town is only half a mile or so further north."

When they'd finished, Willis climbed back onto the seat and tipped his hat. "Enjoy your stay," he called.

He wouldn't return for one full week.

Somehow, even as she waved a cheery goodbye, that single fact was all she could think of. She would be alone with Morgan for the whole of seven days . . .

And nights.

She exhaled, a long, shaky breath. Thank heaven, Morgan didn't seem to notice anything amiss. He was busy fishing a key from the pocket inside his jacket. "You may be disappointed," he warned as they mounted the steps. "It's very small, and not at all grand."

Elizabeth couldn't help but be wounded. Did he truly consider her so pretentious? Never had she looked down upon another—never! Why couldn't he see that? The cry of hurt trembled on her lips, but in the end, she kept silent. Above all, she didn't want to begin this trip on a tense note.

Once they were inside, the thought was forgotten. True, the entire cottage would have fit in the drawing room of his house on Beacon Hill. Two plump chairs and a divan stood across from a huge fireplace. She exclaimed in delight over a built-in seat near the front window. It was piled high with cushions and looked out over the ocean.

Next came the bedrooms. There were two, Morgan explained. The smaller of the two, he had converted to a study where he could work when he was here. The other was bright and filled with afternoon sunshine.

There was but one bed.

The realization jumped out at her before she could stop it, and then it was all she could do to tear her gaze from the huge four-poster piled high with soft, downy quilts.

With a casualness she was suddenly far from sharing, she watched as Morgan retrieved their bags from the porch and set them on the bed. He turned to her.

"Would you like to look around outside?"

Her nod was of almost frantic relief.

"Let me change," he said, "and then we'll be off."

He rejoined her on the porch a few moments later, wearing a light cotton shirt and trousers any of his yard workmen might have worn. It seemed momentarily odd to see him dressed so informally, yet it struck her that even while his clothing lent him an undeniably rugged masculinity, his presence was far less intimidating than usual. Or perhaps it was simply that for whatever reason, the tension that always charged the air between them had dwindled. As she fell into step beside him, she acknowledged that the change was indeed a very welcome one.

A series of small stone steps led down to the beach, where gentle waves slapped the shore. Elizabeth's eyes widened when she spied a small boat resting on the sand.

"Oh, a boat!" she exclaimed.

"A dinghy," he corrected.

She wrinkled her nose at him, then glanced longingly toward the island. "Do you think we might row over there and explore?"

He hesitated. "Do you swim?"

A hand pressed against her throat, she feigned amazement. "What! You mean you won't rescue me?"

Morgan's middle tightened as if a fist had plowed into it. He suspected his lovely young bride had no idea of the enchanting picture she posed—her eyes green and sparkling, roses on her cheeks from the wind, wisps of bright golden tendrils escaping from her temples and nape. The vibrant promise of having her so near fired a hungry ache in his loins, an ache he prayed would manifest itself no further!

God, he thought. *And who will rescue me from you?* As if to torment him still further, a sudden burst of breeze swirled hard, outlining the lithe promise of supple young breasts beneath the fabric of her bodice.

He gritted his teeth against the fiery demands of his body. "Well?" he prompted, dark brow raised askance. "Do you swim?"

She made a face. "If you must know," she said with an exaggerated sigh, "like a fish."

His mouth turned up in a lazy smile. "In that case, how can I refuse?"

Minutes later they were rowing smoothly across the cove. They spent half an hour walking about, and Elizabeth was thrilled when she found a patch of ripening strawberries. Not far away she found a spot beneath a gnarled old oak tree that she pronounced a lovely place for a noonday picnic.

The sun was a fiery ball of bronze in the western sky when they finally pushed off towards shore. Just as he had when they'd left, without a word Morgan swept her high in his arms and deposited her in the dingy. He'd discarded his shoes and rolled his trouser legs up above his knees, as well as his shirtsleeves. The lines beside his mouth had softened. He appeared younger, far less stern. The muscles in his forearms flexed again and again as he commanded the oars with ease, slicing through the waves in perfect symphony and pushing them forward.

Elizabeth tipped her head to the side. "I must say," she remarked, "that doesn't look at all difficult."

Heavy jet brows shot up. "Would you like to try?"

A dimple appeared beside her mouth. "Actually," she confessed, "I would."

They exchanged places. Elizabeth swayed a little as she rose. Immediately strong hands closed warmly about her waist, holding her steady and guiding her to the seat now vacant. By the time she sat, she was breathless—doubtless from excitement, she assured herself.

Morgan showed her how to grip the oars. "The key is to think of them as extensions of your arms. Stroke in deep, wide circles," he instructed. "Dip and pull, up and return, all in one fluid movement."

Elizabeth nodded eagerly. Biting her lip, she tipped one oar daintily in the water.

His mouth had relaxed into a smile. "It won't break, Elizabeth."

In all honesty, the dratted oars were heavier than she'd expected, and rather awkward to handle. She wrestled with the pair, her brow furrowed in concentration as she tried to do as he'd instructed—dip and pull. Dip and pull.

Looking on, Morgan sat back and shook his head at her bewildered frustration.

The flat of one oar struck the water. A jet of water shot high, spraying her full in the face. "Oh!" she gasped.

"What's wrong, my highborn London lady?" he teased. "Afraid you'll melt?"

Elizabeth glared her indignation. So he thought she was amusing, did he?

Ten minutes later, she lost her grip on the right oar; it slid through the lock. Unthinkingly she pitched forward after it, trying to grab it. "No!" she cried. "Oh, no!" It was only Morgan's quick reaction that saved them both—herself and the oar. One hand caught the handle of the oar; the other arm wrapped hard about her waist and pulled her down beside him.

Unable to help himself, he laughed outright, the sound rich and full.

It was then the strangest thing happened. Elizabeth went very still. Her hands came out to touch his lips. "You laughed," she said slowly. Wonderingly. "I've never heard you laugh. And I've never seen you smile, the way you are just now." She touched the raspy hardness of his face, the tips of her fingers tracing the grooves etched beside his mouth, an unconscious caress.

His smile faded. For the span of a heartbeat—then another and another—their eyes caught and held. His grip on her waist tightened ever so slightly. And all at once she felt as if she certainly *would* melt, not from the water but from the searing heat of his gaze, so intense she felt scorched by it.

What might have happened, she would never know. The dinghy surged upward on the crest of a sudden swell, breaking the curious spell that had cropped up between them.

Morgan glanced out over the waves. "It's getting a little rough," he frowned, reaching for the oars. "We'd better get back."

They returned to shore. While Morgan beached the dinghy, Elizabeth went back to the cottage. The day had been warm, and she was still flushed from exertion. In the bedroom, she poured water from a pitcher into a flowered basin. Unbuttoning the bodice of her dress, she tugged it from her shoulders and let it drop to her waist. Wringing out a cloth, she wiped her face and neck, the valley between her breasts where they swelled above the top of her camisole.

There was a slight sound behind her. Elizabeth half turned to find Morgan filling the doorway. His eyes wandered from her face and down her throat.

It didn't stop there.

She could feel the rapid rise and fall of her

breasts. Her pulse began to thrum. Only days earlier, she might have counted his presence an invasion of her privacy. Now, she didn't retreat as he looked his fill; protest was the last thing on her mind. Indeed, all she could think was that she hoped her body pleased him. She wanted him to like what he saw . . .

Oddly, he was the one who turned away first.

Their meal that evening was simple: fresh bread baked that morning, a thick wedge of cheese, chicken that the cook had sent along.

Afterward they sat outside on the porch, while twilight's violet haze crept over the earth. One by one the stars came out. True to the day, a sense of serene contentment wrapped itself around her.

"It's so peaceful here," she said with a sigh. "I think I could live here forever."

"Summers are wonderful," Morgan said with a faint smile. "But it's rather wild in the winter. Storms blow in, and the wind howls like a banshee." There was a brief pause. "I like watching the storms. It's a little like being at sea all over again."

"You were at sea?"

He nodded. "I started out as a deckhand when I was fifteen."

Elizabeth regarded him, her head tipped to the side. "I didn't know you were a sailor."

His lips quirked. "I could hardly be a shipbuilder without being a sailor," he said dryly.

Elizabeth laughed. "Yes, I suppose so." She fell silent, lifting her face to the kiss of the evening breeze.

Morgan frowned. "Are you cold?"

"Perhaps just a little."

The next thing she knew, strong arms encircled her. She felt herself drawn back against the solid breadth of his chest. A tiny smile curled her lips, for he didn't withdraw. Instead his arms wrapped snugly around her. She was nestled fast within his embrace, his hands clasped atop her own.

"Do you miss it?" she asked after a moment.

"Sailing?"

"Yes." Her voice was slightly breathless.

"Not as much as I used to," he admitted. "At first I did it for the money. I signed on with a salty old captain named Jack McTavish." He chuckled. "Believe me, I earned every penny I made. But I managed to save most of what I earned so Nathaniel could go to a decent school. But it wasn't long before I realized I was free like never before."

His voice grew husky in remembrance.

"Most of the crew looked forward to docking and getting back to shore. But what I loved most was leaving port, the power of the ship gathering speed, watching the bow cleave the waves, hearing the sails clap like thunder. There was nothing like it—feeling the breeze in my hair, my skin scraped by the wind, the scent of brine heavy in the air."

A vivid picture bloomed in her mind, yet all she could feel was the rush of his breath in her hair, the warmth of his skin against her own, the familiar scent of bay rum swirling all around.

Silence reigned briefly. "I suppose you look down on that," he said after a moment.

There was an odd note in his tone, a note she'd never heard before. Elizabeth frowned, twisting slightly so that she could see his face. "What?" she asked.

"The fact that while there is nothing common about you, Lady Elizabeth, you are married to a man who was once a common sailor."

Her gaze searched his profile. The muscles of his forearms had grown stiff as a board. Though he revealed nothing of his feelings, she sensed that her answer—this very moment—was somehow important.

To both of them.

"Not at all," she stated with unshakable resolve. "You were only a boy when you went to sea, yet you faced the future alone and unafraid. I admire your courage."

He stared at her, so long and so hard, she grew uncertain beneath such penetrating intensity. He made no move to kiss her, as she thought he might—as she wanted him to!

Her emotions careened in every direction. Indeed, why should he? she thought wildly. He hadn't wanted to marry her. He'd been thrown into it, every bit as much as she. She was coming to know her husband, and he was not a man to shirk duty. He owed her nothing, yet he had done the right thing—the honorable thing—and married her. And in so doing, he had sacrificed his own happiness.

She inhaled deeply, tried to smile and failed abominably. "I'm sorry," she said shakily. "I've bungled things rather badly, haven't I? I've not only made a mess of my own life, but yours and Nathaniel's."

Heavy jet brows drew together. "Elizabeth—"

"No, please. I-I need to say this. I'm sorry. I don't know what else to say, except . . . I'm sorry. If it weren't for me, most likely you'd be with her"—a sharp pain ripped through her heart—"why, this very instant, no doubt."

Morgan's brow was furrowed. "Who?"

She averted her face. "The woman at the opera." She faltered. "Of course, I can see why. She—she's very beautiful, you know."

Gentle fingers curled beneath her chin. Slowly he guided her face to his. "She's not my mistress, Elizabeth."

She shook her head. "Please," she said, her voice very low. "I'd rather not know—"

"I *want* you to know," he countered. "I've let you believe something that was not true, and for that, I must apologize. But I want you to know the truth."

The truth. Why was she so afraid of it? Her heart was thudding so hard, her chest hurt. She didn't want the truth, didn't he see that? It would hurt too much. Yet there was something in his eyes, something so compelling she lost the will to stop him. Nor could she tear her gaze away.

He hadn't released her chin. Now the pad of his thumb swept back and forth along the delicate line of her jaw, a tentative caress.

His gaze was chained to hers. "I won't lie to you, Elizabeth. We had a relationship, she and I. But what we shared was purely physical, a mutual enjoyment of each other's bodies. But I haven't touched her, not in the way that you think, since the day you walked into my house."

The world seemed to reel and pitch. "But all those nights you've been gone . . . I thought you were with her—"

He was adamant. "I wasn't. When I first started my business, I often worked well into the night, so I put a cot in the room next to my office. I hadn't used it in years, until just lately."

Dazed, she gave a slight shake of her head. "So that's where you were? All those nights you've been gone, you were there?"

He nodded, his gaze chained to hers. "At first it was because I was angry, angry because you denied me. Then later, the temptation of having you so near was overpowering. You wanted a lock installed. I began to think you were right, because I didn't trust myself. So I did the only thing I could think of. I stayed away."

Elizabeth was speechless.

"God, if you knew the hours I lay awake in that room, thinking about you." His voice had gone very low. "Wanting you so much sometimes, I thought I'd go crazy."

He wanted her. *He wanted her.* It seemed impossible. Unbelievable. Yet even while her mind still sought to grasp all he told her, her body displayed a will of its own. Suddenly her hand was on the raspy plane of his cheek. Her fingertips moved, the merest caress.

"Truly?" she whispered.

He stood with her in his arms, then placed her on the floor before him. Her feet were planted squarely between his. His hands kept possession of her waist.

He nodded, his expression very grave as it searched hers. "I could show you"—his gaze delved deep into hers—"if you'll let me."

Chapter 16

All at once she was shaking from head to toe. She stared at the hollow of his throat where a tangle of hair grew dark and thick. "How?" The question came out before she could stop it.

He leveled on her a gaze of quiet intensity. "I think you already know, Elizabeth."

She did, and though she fought against it, her eyes shied away in mute confusion. She wanted to be close to him, to have him hold her tight and strong, not just in comfort, but in the heat of passion. And yet, a part of her was consumed with doubt.

One strong hand slid up to her nape. His touch was warm and strangely reassuring. A finger beneath her chin, he tipped her face to his. The kiss bestowed upon her lips was slow and undemanding, immeasurably patient. His touch was like a drug, a drug she had to have or die. She twined her arms around his neck and clung to him shamelessly. Over and over he kissed her until her limbs felt as if they were melting.

She had no recollection of being carried to the bedroom. The next thing she knew, she felt the softness of the mattress beneath her. Morgan stretched out beside her, the pressure of his mouth now sweetly fierce. Her lips parted, an unconscious invitation. He made a faint sound and caught the flutter of her breath deep in his throat.

"I want you," he said against her lips. "I want to feel you naked against me, your skin against mine."

Need vibrated in his voice. An undeniable thrill shot through her. Though her heart bounded clear to her throat, she made no protest as his hand deftly worked the buttons at the back of her gown. Cool air rushed over her as he tugged the bodice down to her waist, over her hips, until she was clad in only her camisole and petticoats. A flicker of fear fringed the edges of her mind, a fear she managed to push aside.

But when his hand went to the ribbon tied between her breasts, she stiffened.

Slowly he raised his head. "What?" he queried softly. "What's wrong?"

Her hand half lifted, a tenuous gesture that matched her feelings. "I-I want this," she quavered. "Truly I do. But I'm . . ."

She couldn't finish. Time swung away endlessly.

Her chest rose and fell rapidly. Morgan had yet to withdraw. His knuckles touched the silken valley between her breasts. Her mouth dry as dust, Elizabeth was quiveringly aware of the tension in his fingers. For a mind-splitting instant she thought he would ruthlessly cast aside her reticence.

His eyes snared hers. "Afraid?" he finished quietly.

Images of him plunging inside her flashed inside her head. "I-I don't want to be. I-I like it when you kiss me. I feel . . . carried away. And I like—being held by you. It's just that I can't help but remember—"

"I know." He cut her off. His expression was faintly grim.

"Perhaps it's me. Perhaps there's something wrong with me that such a thing happened." Elizabeth shook her head, her voice half-strangled. "But there was blood—"

"Only the first time, Elizabeth, only the first time. And there's nothing wrong with you, I swear." He moved then. Strong fingers captured her fluttering hand and brought it to his lips. Holding her gaze, he rubbed his cheek against her knuckles.

"I would very much like to hold you, too, Elizabeth. And I don't mean to frighten you, but I would very much like to hold you naked in my arms. With nothing between us, Elizabeth. Not your clothes, or mine. No shame or regret. But especially, no fear."

"But—that's not all you want!" Her cry emerged unbidden.

"No. But it would be different this time, Elizabeth. I promise, it wouldn't be the same at all." His voice grew low and intense. "There would be no pain, only pleasure."

Caught squarely between desire and desperation, Elizabeth could neither agree nor disagree. The silence seemed to go on and on forever.

It was Morgan who broke it. "Would it make

it easier if I were the one who undressed first?"

Elizabeth drew a deep, fractured breath. "Yes. No." It all tumbled out in a rush. "Oh, please forgive me, but I—I just don't know!"

Morgan stayed poised above her. The tension escalated to a screaming pitch. Just when she thought she could stand it no longer, he rose, moving to stand near the fireplace. His features remained somber, yet nonetheless determined.

No words passed between them. Indeed, none were needed.

As if he had all the time in the world, he began to undress, the outline of his form bathed in the hazy glow of the lamplight shining in the corner. He didn't face her directly; instead he gazed out the window. Little by little, he bared himself to her, to watch as she wished.

And God help her, she couldn't look away. Her eyes locked helplessly on his body. His shoulders seemed wide as the doorway, the muscles of his back cleanly sculpted, his skin like smooth walnut. He stepped from his trousers, his buttocks tight and round. Slowly—deliberately—he turned to face her.

His body awakened . . . before her very eyes.

Elizabeth inhaled sharply. Between the crease of his hips, his manhood stood rigidly erect, stiff and swollen. What he wanted to do simply was not possible. She could almost feel him prodding against her once more, inside her, tearing through delicate flesh.

She jerked her head away. Yet still she could see the shape of him even with her eyes averted, starkly raw and masculine.

"No, Elizabeth. Don't look away."

Words failed her—and courage too. There was a rustle, and then the mattress dipped as he resumed his place beside her. He touched her nowhere, yet she felt as if he did.

She looked at the wall, the ceiling, everywhere but at him.

His voice stole through the quiet. "Am I truly so ugly that you cannot stand the sight of me?"

"You are not ugly. Indeed, you are quite handsome." Her reply came unthinkingly.

"Then why won't you look at me?"

She did then, albeit reluctantly. He was propped on his elbow, facing her. Morgan couldn't help but notice her gaze strayed no lower than his nose.

"That's better," he said softly. "Now then, I have a proposition to put to you. If you are uncomfortable with anything I do, you have only to ask and I will stop."

Her tongue came out to moisten her lips. "You will?"

"I did before, didn't I?" He knew from her expression that if he hadn't been so utterly serious, she would have doubted him. God, if she only knew how he ached for her! In every pore of his skin. Through every bone in his body. Secretly he prayed this was the right thing to do; more important, the right *time* to do it. Because if it wasn't, he was very much afraid that this time he would *not* be able to stop.

"I think it's reasonably safe to say that your experience with men—*naked* men—has been rather limited. So I have a suggestion, Elizabeth. Why not indulge your curiosity?"

Her eyes flew wide. "I am hardly curious!" she

blurted. "Indeed, I've seen far more than I imagined I should ever see."

He chuckled. But then the laughter faded from his eyes. "Then indulge *me*," he said quietly. Slowly, giving her time to withdraw if she wanted, he brought her hand to rest on his side, near his waist. "Tell me, Elizabeth. Is this so frightful?"

"No," she said promptly.

"And this?" Holding his breath, he coasted her hand to the center of his chest. Even when he lifted his own, she didn't retreat. Instead her fingers uncurled, tangling through the dense, dark pale, barely grazing his skin.

Progress, he decided with satisfaction.

Lightly enclosing her wrist, he guided her hand to his mouth. She needed no urging to keep her fingertips pressed against the center of his lower lip.

His eyes captured hers. "And this? Does this frighten you?"

"No. But then, you already know I like it when you kiss me."

A surge of hot possessiveness surged through him. He had to stop himself from clenching his jaw. Lord, if she only knew how she inflamed him! "And I would like it if you would kiss *me*," he said gravely.

"Now?"

The word was a mere squeak of sound; her round-eyed expression was precious. He bit back a smile.

"Now," he invited, easing to his back.

Surprisingly, he didn't have long to wait. Leaning over him, she pressed her lips to his.

Morgan held himself very still, allowing her to taste as she would. It was she who touched her tongue to his. Raw heat splintered through him. His manhood jumped, but thank heaven, she didn't notice. His own tongue joined the play, lightly sparring.

For Elizabeth it was like nothing she'd ever experienced. They kissed endlessly, slow and deep and rousing; lost in the moment, lost in each other, lost in the feeling. And this time no protest broke from her lips when he flicked aside the edges of her camisole.

Because suddenly it was all she wanted as well—to lie against him, her breasts against the furry roughness of his chest, her hips bound tightly against his. Soon she was as naked as he.

With his thumbs he flicked the stiffened tightness of her nipples. She arched her breasts into the warm roughness of his palms. She thought she would die of sheer want as he brushed his lips over the naked mound of one breast. Heat rose, a spiraling tide within her. At last he gave her what she wanted. His tongue delicately touched the dark, straining center. Lashing. Circling. Teasing. She caught his head in her hands, threading her fingers through the silken darkness of his hair as he finally took her into his mouth and sucked strongly.

She was nearly delirious with bliss when he finally lifted his head. "Touch me," he said raggedly.

His intent was unmistakable. He caught at her hand and dragged it down across the flattened plane of his belly . . .

"Yes. *Yes.* Touch me, Elizabeth. *Touch me.*"

Elizabeth's pulse knocked wildly, yet his dark whisper compelled her to obey. Lean fingers atop hers, he guided her with heart-stopping deliberation. The plundering journey came to a halt only when her palm closed about the jutting ridge of his member. With the subtle pressure of his hand, he held hers trapped beneath his for a mind-splitting instant.

He was enormous, swollen and thick. Deep inside, she was appalled that she didn't snatch back her hand and leap from the bed. Yet the curiosity she'd denied now commanded her. She extended her fingertips, barely skimming his flesh, her touch as light as a feather. She was stunned at his heat and hardness, yet the arching crown seemed encased in silk.

"You see?" His voice sounded odd and strained. "There's nothing to be afraid of. No weapon. Just more need for you than my body can contain."

She gazed at him. His eyes were squeezed shut. The tendons of his neck stood taut. With the tips of her fingers, shyly she traced the length of his shaft and back again, gauging his reaction. She couldn't have withheld the question had her life depended on it. "You . . . like this?" she whispered.

His groan was all the answer she needed. Again his hand clamped hers, but it was only to show her how she might deliver the utmost pleasure.

A heady feeling of power consumed her. He was no less affected by her fledgling touch than she, and the knowledge gave her a boldness that would later make her cheeks flush scarlet.

But pleasure was not only hers to give, but to receive. "Stop," he said with an odd little laugh. "It's your turn now."

His mouth sought hers. His knuckles grazed a shattering path across the hollow of her belly. Boldly he weaved through the golden thatch at the juncture of her thighs. Elizabeth jerked when a daring finger breached tender folds of flesh, clear inside her.

But there was more. With his thumb he stroked a tiny little pearl of flesh where a pinnacle of sensation dwelled. His touch, maddening and elusive, made her moan and writhe. To her everlasting shock, damp warmth gathered there, in the furrowed cleft he claimed so boldly.

Her nails dug into the knotted hardness of his arms. Horribly embarrassed by that dampness, she drew a deep, shuddering breath. "Stop!" she pleaded. "Oh, please, I don't think—"

He understood. He gave a tiny shake of his head. "It's all right, sweet. It means you want me. You do, don't you?"

Something had surfaced in his voice, an uncharacteristic uncertainty that made her melt inside. She touched his cheek. "Yes," she whispered in a voice that wasn't entirely steady. "I do want you. I do." She wrapped her arms around his neck and clung.

It was all the invitation he needed. He crushed her to him, his embrace fiercely strong. She reveled in it, in the hotly demanding pressure of his mouth on hers as he rolled her to her back.

She felt the searing probe of his manhood against her thighs, but there was no time to be afraid. His breath filled her mouth, even as his shaft filled her body. She drew a shallow breath, somehow expecting the same arrowing pain as before shooting through her belly.

At last he was buried to the hilt inside her. He didn't move, but allowed her to grow used to the feel of his swollen manhood deep within her. She was stunned at the straining pressure of his invasion, yet her body engulfed him, all of him. Yet it was just as he'd said; even as she felt herself stretched to the limit, there was no pain, only the indescribable sensation of his thick rod imprisoned hot and tight in her silken sheath.

Slowly he raised his head. Silver eyes aflame, he stared down at her. "Are you all right?" His voice was gritty, his jaw tense.

Wordlessly she gave him her answer, pulling his head down to hers.

Slowly he began to move, sinking deep within her. Again. And yet again. She caught her breath at the wondrous friction of his manhood sliding against her—inside her—even as she sensed his restraint.

Her eyes glazed over. An emotion that was painfully sweet caught at her chest. Morgan O'Connor was not a man she'd have called tender. Yet it was there in every kiss; in the achingly slow caress of his fingers over her skin, in the care he'd taken to see that she was spared further hurt at his hands . . . hands that gave a pleasure she'd never dreamed could exist.

With each plunge of his hardness within her, heat flashed along her veins. A heavy ache unfurled low in her belly. She buried her fingers in the midnight darkness of his hair, touched his nape, ran her fingers over the corded smoothness of his back.

Hunger wound through her. Her body caught fire. Her hips met his, eagerly seeking, instinctively searching for what only he could give.

"Morgan," she cried against his throat. "*Morgan.*"

This was the first time she'd called him by name—they both knew it.

Above her, he went utterly still. But then it was like something burst inside him. He kissed her, his mouth like a hot brand. His fingers laced through hers.

Their hips came together again and again; faster and faster, with a desperation borne of desire and passion and need too long denied. He thrust harder, almost wildly, but Elizabeth gloried in it. Harsh, rasping breaths filled the air, his . . . and hers.

His fingers slid down her back. He filled his hands with her buttocks. "You're mine," he muttered hotly. "You know that, don't you?"

His possessiveness was thrilling. It sent her hurtling over the edge. Waves of ecstasy broke over her. Whimpers of rapture broke from her lips. His climax scalding his loins, he erupted inside her, bathing her womb with fire.

Afterward his fingers combed idly through the silken tangle of her hair across the pillow. Lazily he propped himself above her on his elbows. Lowering his head, he kissed her, the contact long and lingering. "Mine," he said into her mouth, a sound that reeked of satisfaction. But she didn't mind. No, not at all. Because he was smiling as he said it . . .

Morgan was the first to fall asleep, a hard arm locked around her waist, his head upon her breast.

He was still smiling.

Elizabeth wept with joy.

Chapter 17

◦◦◦◦◦◦

Their days were steeped in contentment and serenity, their nights ablaze with passion. Eagerly she surrendered her body, while Morgan gave of himself without restraint. For both of them, it was a time of teaching, a time of discovery, a haven from all the turmoil that had gone before.

Morgan didn't mind her shy exploration. He encouraged it with gentle words and tender whispers. Elizabeth blushed fiercely when she chanced to think of all he had done to her—and she to him! They fell asleep wrapped in each other's arms, their limbs an intimate—and wholly erotic—entanglement. They woke the same way . . .

And it was usually quite some time before they arose.

For Elizabeth, it was like sunshine spreading a fiery glow deep inside her. Morgan's entire demeanor was more relaxed. He seemed more at ease with himself and with her. The harshness she'd always sensed in him fled as if it had never been. This was a man she hadn't known existed . . .

A man she could love.

Hope flowered within her. She prayed that these days marked a sign of things to come. If so, marriage to Morgan would not be the struggle she had envisioned. Indeed, it could be so much more . . . She sent fervent pleas heavenward that it would be so.

While Morgan was out fishing one afternoon, she decided to walk to town. She spent the next few hours wandering among the booths at the local marketplace, pausing over a pretty shawl now and then, exclaiming with delight at a length of tiny seashells fashioned into a necklace.

She was just about to depart for home when she noticed a small booth at the end of the row where there were some dozen or so framed paintings of various sizes. Before them sat a young man wearing a faded shirt and baggy trousers, sketch pad and charcoal in hand.

His brow was furrowed in concentration. She couldn't help but notice that in the little time since she'd observed him, he had darted her several quick, intent glances before turning back to his sketch pad.

Rather intrigued, she started toward him. Intent on his work, he didn't notice her until she stepped up beside him. "I do hope you don't mind," she said brightly, leaning over to see what he was sketching.

It was her.

Elizabeth blinked. She'd left her hair loose and tumbling down her back, swept back from her forehead with a plain white ribbon. The expression she wore was faintly wistful.

The young man smiled weakly. "And I hope *you* don't mind."

She nodded at the paintings behind him. "You're quite talented."

"Thank you."

One by one she studied the paintings. But it was the last one on which her gaze lingered, that of a graceful clipper ship upon the sea. Standing on the bow was the likeness of a man, strong hands gripping the rail, booted legs braced wide apart, his profile lifted to the wind.

What was it Morgan had said? *What I loved most was leaving port, the power of the ship gathering speed, watching the bow cleave the waves, hearing the sails clap like thunder. There was nothing like it—feeling the breeze in my hair, my skin scraped by the wind, the scent of brine heavy in the air.*

She couldn't help but catch her breath. The artist had captured all the sleek majesty of the vessel, the wild turmoil of the seas, the dynamic pride of the captain.

In a trice she found herself standing before it. "This is lovely," she breathed. "So lifelike. You must have sailed many, many times."

The man chuckled. "A few," he admitted. "But I prefer solid ground beneath my feet. My father's the sailor in the family. He's one of the local fishermen."

Elizabeth clasped her hands together impulsively. "How much is it?" Her thoughts were already speeding forward. She had a few coins with her, but she hadn't spent a single penny of the allowance Morgan had deposited for her.

Once they were back in Boston, perhaps she could send back with the money.

"You'd like to buy it?"

"Oh, yes! Very much." She sighed. "But I'm afraid I have very little money with me. I'm from Boston, here on holiday with my husband. But if you could hold it for several days, I could send my husband's driver back with the remainder of the purchase price."

The young man stroked his jaw. "Well, it was rather forward of me to sketch you without your knowing it." He paused. "Tell you what. How about a trade of sorts? The painting is yours if you'll sit for a while and let me finish my sketch."

"Done!" Elizabeth very nearly squealed in delight. "Though I must say, I think I got the better bargain."

The artist grinned broadly, pleased with his deal. He introduced himself as Andrew. They shook hands and then he pointed her to a stool, with the coastline at her back.

Half an hour later, Elizabeth strode away, the painting wrapped in brown paper, hugged like a prize to her breast.

Morgan was sauntering up the beach when she arrived back at the cottage. Her heart tripped at the very sight of him. His hair tousled by the wind, he was barefoot and shirtless, the legs of his trousers rolled up to just below his knees.

"You look nothing like you did the day we met," she teased. Her gaze swept up and down the length of him. He had stopped on the step below her, and still she had to tilt her head far back in order to meet his eyes. "Why, I could easily imagine you a pirate, especially now that I know you were a sailor."

"A pirate?" His half smile made her toes curl. "Elizabeth, you wound me. How could you even consider me so nefarious?"

"Come to think of it, I do believe it fits! Why, my knees were shaking every time you spoke to me!"

He smiled—or did he? "Of course, there's no mistaking you for anything but what you are."

Elizabeth glanced at him sharply. As offhand as he sounded, she thought she detected ... what? Regret? Sadness?

"And what is that?" she asked brightly.

"A lady." Lean hands settled on her waist. He gazed down at her. "*My* lady."

His husky tone thrilled her, clear to the very bottom of her feet. He had only to look at her and she felt giddy and weak.

His eyes had dropped to the package she still held tucked against her breast. "What did you buy?"

"I can't tell you," she said promptly.

"Oh, come now. I'd like to see if I approve of your taste."

"I certainly hope you do!" Her eyes sparkled. "I saw it and thought immediately of you. I knew then I just *had* to have it."

One rakish brow arose. "This sounds rather fascinating." His expression warmed. "Why don't you go put it on and we'll see, hmmm?"

Her lips twitched in secret amusement. "Oh, it's not for me. It's for you."

"For me!" He was clearly astonished. "Why?"

She smiled at his dumbfounded amazement. "Must there be a reason?"

Something flitted across his features, something she couldn't quite place. It was gone in a heartbeat. "Well, then," he said, "why can't you tell me what it is?"

"Because you're simply going to have to see for yourself." She settled herself on the top step of the porch and patted the space beside her. He sat, and she pressed her gift into his hands.

He hesitated . . . forever, it seemed! Indeed, she wondered if he had any intention of opening it. At last he began to unwrap the paper slowly—almost awkwardly, she would always remember thinking.

At last he held the painting in his hands. But his reaction was hardly what she had hoped for. No smile of pleasure creased the hard line of his lips. He simply stared, motionless for what seemed like an eternity.

She swallowed a pang. He didn't like it, she realized, and she had been so certain he would! She blinked back stupid, foolish tears, feeling crushed inside, but determined not to show it.

"Oh dear, I-I'm very sorry, Morgan. It was presumptuous of me to assume you would like it." Her smile would surely make her face crack. "I'll take it back. Better yet, why don't *you* do it? That way you'll be certain to have something you like."

She lurched upward, her only thought to escape before she embarrassed herself further. But her husband's long arm snagged her by the waist and pulled her down beside him once more.

"Elizabeth, no! Don't! I-I love it, I swear!"

She battled a stinging rush of hurt. "You don't," she said with certainty. "But it's all right—"

"No, it's not! I love it, I swear on the grave of my mother. It's just that . . ." He ducked his head and gave an odd little laugh. "God, I'm making such a mess of this!"

She peered at him. He sounded so strange, so unlike himself. "No, you're not. Please, Morgan," she urged. "Just tell me."

She watched the muscles in his throat work as he swallowed. And there was a strange glaze over his eyes . . . She balked. No. No, it simply couldn't be . . .

"I-I don't know what to say, Elizabeth." He still didn't look at her as he spoke; the words were hoarse. "It's just that . . . I've never had anyone think to give me a gift before now . . ."

It dawned in an instant. Elizabeth's heart wrenched as she realized what he was saying. Her own childhood had been so full of love and wonderful memories, but Morgan's had been filled with emptiness. As she gazed at him, she saw the poor little boy who'd spent his childhood in a wretched dockside tavern. But she also saw the man he had become—the man who had risen above all that, a man who had made his way in life and acquired a considerable fortune.

Laying her palm alongside his jaw, she turned his cheek to hers.

"Well, now you have," she said softly. "And I'm very glad I was the one who thought of it."

Their eyes met. Something passed between them. Something they couldn't hold in their hands, yet was more precious than gold.

Setting aside the painting, Morgan drew her into his arms. He rested his forehead against hers. "So am I," he said huskily. His smile widened a fraction. "I only hope you didn't send me to the poorhouse."

Elizabeth turned her nose up. "For your information, it didn't cost me a penny. The artist said if I sat for him for a few minutes while he sketched me, I could have the painting as my fee." She laughed, a tinkling sound carried away by the breeze. "Though I can't imagine why he wanted to sketch *me*."

Morgan could. Granted, he found her lovely beyond words. But hers was a beauty that was more than a mere pretty face. It was a sweetness and warmth of spirit that came from deep inside her and, in so doing, spread its glow to others.

In all honesty, he'd had precious little experience with such sentiment. So many people he'd known were heedless of all others; they thought of themselves above all else. But his mother had been much like Elizabeth, unselfish and giving. And what about him? Shame bit deep, for in the last few years, whatever warmth he'd once possessed had vanished, as if it had never been . . .

He'd forgotten how to laugh.

But Elizabeth had taught him how.

He'd forgotten how to *live*.

She alone had returned the vitality of life.

His throat tightened oddly. This past week had been the most carefree—above all, the happiest—time of his life.

All because of Elizabeth.

But what if he should lose her? An awful fear

wrapped itself around his chest. No. *No!* That couldn't happen. It *wouldn't* happen.

They departed for Boston several mornings later, both of them wholly reluctant to leave.

They had no idea what awaited them.

Once they were home, the foyer echoed with gay laughter as Elizabeth and Morgan swept inside. Lifting her clear from her feet, he whirled her around and around until her senses were spinning and she was breathless and dizzy. One by one the servants came to gather around, gaping at their master and his bride in sheer disbelief.

"Enough!" Elizabeth gasped. "Morgan, please, I'll never be able to walk!"

Morgan's eyes lit up as he whirled to a halt. "Then I'll just have to carry you, won't I?" he teased. He startled her by bending and swinging her high in his arms.

Elizabeth's protests were but fleeting. Her tiny little smile was glowing. She dropped her head against his shoulder and sighed her satisfaction.

One by one the servants dispersed. As they turned away, every one wore a smug little grin.

But they were not alone.

"Quite an exhibition," boomed a low male voice. "Quite an exhibition indeed."

One booted foot on the bottom step, Morgan halted. He turned around, his precious burden still tight in his arms.

Nathaniel stood in the doorway of the library. He saluted them with a glass of amber liquid in hand. "I never did have the chance to toast the newlyweds."

All at once Morgan's arms were like steel. Elizabeth felt herself lowered slowly to the floor.

Nathaniel's smile was goading. He lifted his glass high. "Morgan, may you have better luck with this marriage." His gaze slid to Elizabeth. "Elizabeth. Dear Elizabeth, what can I say? May my brother make you happier than he made Amelia."

Elizabeth's mind reeled. She felt weak as the blood drained from her face. Huge eyes fixed on her husband's tight-lipped features.

"Amelia?" she echoed faintly. "Who on earth is Amelia?"

Chapter 18

❦

The room was steeped in silence.

"It's not who *is*, but who *was*." Nathaniel shifted his arrogant smile to his brother. "Morgan, I do believe this should come from you. Although frankly, I'm amazed you haven't told her by now."

Oh, but he was clever. Morgan regarded his brother through a blistering mist of fury. Nathaniel, the stinking cur, *knew* he would say nothing. He knew!

Bitter frustration clawed inside him. More than anything, he longed to tell Elizabeth the truth. But he could hear his mother's voice, calling out to him in some deep valley of his subconscious.

Your brother is so young . . . He will need someone, Morgan, someone like you. Guide him. Protect him.

A furious resentment seized hold of him. Most everything he'd ever done had been for Nat. *For Nat*, he had told himself many a time when he'd been tempted to give up. *Always for Nat.*

Blackness seeped into his soul. Maybe he was being selfish. Hell, he probably was. Oh, his mother had cared. But she'd left him alone, alone to take care of his brother, with a father who cared about neither of them. And since that day, no one had ever thought about *him*. His feelings. His well-being. His future.

No one . . . but Elizabeth.

Only now he could almost see her slipping like sand through his fingers. It wasn't fair, he raged inwardly. It just wasn't fair.

His hands closed into fists at his sides. He leveled a burning gaze on his brother. "You bastard." His voice rang with contempt. "Get out."

Elizabeth was stunned that two words could sound so deadly.

Nathaniel smirked. "Oh, come now, Morgan. There's no need for such testiness—"

Morgan took a single step forward. "Get out," he said from between clenched teeth, "or by God, I'll throw you out myself."

Unknowingly Elizabeth put herself between the two men. "Morgan! For God's sake—"

"I'll give you an answer to your question, Elizabeth, when we don't have an audience." He directed a drilling stare at Nathaniel, who assumed a role of affronted outrage.

"If that's how you feel, fine," he said, straightening the cuffs at his wrists. "I'll return when I can be more certain of my welcome."

Morgan gritted his teeth. "Don't return until you're *invited*," he stressed coldly.

If Nathaniel was distressed, there was no sign of it. He was whistling a merry tune as he walked out the door.

A pall descended once they were alone. Two pairs of eyes collided, one deeply green with hurt and confusion, the other as gray as storm clouds.

Wordlessly he gestured to the library. Elizabeth stiffened when he cupped her elbow and led the way forward. But once they were alone inside the library, she quickly stepped away.

Morgan's mouth thinned to a grim line, but he said nothing as she furthered the distance between them.

Elizabeth's calm was deceptive. The tempo of emotions jumping inside her was wildly erratic. She was furious with Nathaniel for provoking Morgan—he hadn't fooled either of them. But she was far more angry with Morgan.

Her mind was all ajumble. What was it Nathaniel had said to Morgan? *May you have better luck with this marriage.*

Realization dawned, a realization that nearly made her cry out. But she wanted to hear it from his lips.

She hid her hands in her skirts so he wouldn't see them shaking. "Who was she, Morgan?" The question came out clearly. "Who was Amelia?"

Something flickered across his features, something that might have been regret. Yet he made no response.

Something snapped inside Elizabeth. "Tell me, damn you! Who was she? Your wife?"

He inclined his head. "Yes."

Elizabeth battled a pain that nearly brought her to her knees. No doubt he hadn't married her because he'd been *forced* to. No doubt he'd married her because he loved her . . .

The pain was blessedly short. She welcomed

the anger that returned in its stead. "And where is she now?"

"She's dead." His tone was flat, as if he were completely indifferent. Suddenly her emotions were shooting in every direction. God! she thought jaggedly. What kind of man was he to say it with such lack of feeling?

"You were a widower?"

Again that aloofness. "Yes."

Elizabeth remained very still. Everything within her wound into a tight, hard knot. She felt betrayed. Rejected, though deep in her heart she knew it was silly to feel this way when the poor woman was dead yet!

Morgan's mouth twisted. "Don't tell me. You'd much rather have Nathaniel, wouldn't you? You wish you'd married him!"

"Right now I wish I'd never laid eyes on either of you!" she cried.

His jaw tensed. "Don't you see what he's done? This is what he wanted. He wanted to put us at each other's throats!"

Elizabeth's eyes blazed. "Don't lay this on Nathaniel. This isn't his fault. I just want to know one thing, Morgan. Were you ever going to tell me? Were you?"

Guilt flashed in his eyes. "I don't know," he said tiredly. "I really hadn't thought about it." He paused, then reached for her. "Elizabeth, please, you have to understand—"

She batted his hand away, ignoring his quiet entreaty. "Don't! Don't tell me that it was for my sake. Don't tell me that you thought I was better off not knowing the truth. I remember when I first came, you said there were some who would call Nathaniel a liar, a cheat. But you're no better!"

She didn't wait for his response. She whirled and started for the double doors. She flung them wide, then turned.

"Did you love her?"

She should have expected his silence.

"Tell me," she practically screamed.

"Yes."

"And did she love you?"

His smile was a travesty. "I thought she did. But Amelia loved no one but herself."

The pain Elizabeth felt was like fire in her lungs. Tears misted her vision. Seeing them, Morgan gave a muffled exclamation and started toward her.

Elizabeth shook her head wildly. "No. Don't touch me. Please"—her voice broke—"just leave me alone." With a half sob she picked up her skirts and ran headlong from the library.

The house was quiet as a tomb that night.

The peace and closeness they had shared at the cottage had been shattered.

Somewhere along the way, the pain and anger lessened. Yet still Elizabeth's heart remained torn. She wasn't proud of her outburst, yet Morgan should have told her long, long ago that he'd been married.

It hurt to think of Morgan with another woman. *Loving* another woman, though she reminded herself over and over that he had certainly never professed to love *her*. But in the end, she realized it was selfish and small of her to feel this way. Morgan had spent his youth in misery and drudgery. What did it matter that he had been married—or that he had loved his wife? The woman was dead. She could hardly begrudge him whatever happiness he had found with her.

Yet still a hundred questions buzzed in her mind. How had she died? Had she been ill? An accident perhaps?

She posed that very question to him the next morning at breakfast. He immediately dropped his napkin and rose from the table. "I don't have time to discuss this," he said curtly. "I have a meeting this morning." With that he walked out on her, leaving her bewildered and frustrated.

Later she checked the calendar in his study. He had no such meeting listed.

The morning passed slowly. By afternoon she'd had enough of being closeted inside. Hoping to rid herself of her restlessness, she went out walking. Soon she found herself before Stephen's house. Before she knew it, she'd climbed the steps and rung the bell.

A short, stout housekeeper with iron-gray hair opened the door. "Hello. Can I help you?"

Elizabeth smiled. "I hope so. Is Dr. Marks here?"

"He's in his office at the back of the house. Do you have an appointment?"

"I'm afraid not."

"Well, no matter," the woman said briskly. She beckoned Elizabeth inside. "I don't believe he has any other patients at the moment. I'm sure he'll see you."

As the woman led her toward Stephen's office, she couldn't help but feel she was going behind Morgan's back. Still, he'd left her no choice. She *had* to know about Amelia.

Stephen broke into a broad smile when he saw her. "Well, well," he said, moving to shut the door behind her. "I can think of only one reason you'd come here, Elizabeth. Feeling a little queasy in the morning, are we?"

"Not in the least," she answered. A puzzled frown furrowed her brow. "Why should I be?"

"Well," he said rather sheepishly, "I thought perhaps there might soon be an addition to the family."

Still she looked at him blankly.

His smile deepened. "A woman who's going to give birth is usually in need of a physician." His gaze lowered to the flatness of her belly.

His intimation finally dawned on her. She gasped. "You mean . . . a baby?"

"That's usually the end result of birth, my dear girl." He chuckled. "Being a married woman, I sincerely hope you're already acquainted with what precedes a child's birth."

"Of course I am!" she blurted, then went scarlet as she realized what she'd just admitted to. But even though she now knew precisely what resulted in babies, she had never considered it might happen to her.

Stephen threw back his head and laughed outright. "Good. Because I'd hate to be the one to have to explain it to you."

Planting her hands on her hips, she feigned outrage. "If it were anyone but you, Stephen

Marks, I'd have slapped your face for even daring to speak of such things."

He patted her shoulder. "A pity I'm not right," he said cheerfully. "But don't worry. No doubt it'll happen sooner or later—probably sooner than later."

Elizabeth blushed fiercely once more. "Stephen, you are—impossible!"

"So I'm told, Elizabeth. So I'm told." Crossing his arms over his chest, Stephen moved to prop a hip on the edge of his desk. "So tell me what brings you here, if not my skill as a physician."

Try though she might, she was unable to mask her distress. Her smile withered. She looked down, plucking at the folds in her skirts.

Stephen sighed. "Don't tell me. It has to be Morgan. What's he done now to put you in such a state?"

"I'm hardly in a 'state.' " Her attempt to smile was an abominable failure. "And it's not what he's done, so much as . . . what he hasn't."

Stephen probed very gently. "And what's that?"

A huge lump had lodged in her throat. It was a moment before she could speak. "I've only just learned about Amelia."

There was no need to say more. Stephen's expression had gone utterly sober. "Did Morgan tell you?"

She nodded. "But only because Nathaniel mentioned her name. Naturally, I wondered who she was . . . But all he would tell me was that she had been his wife, only now she is dead."

Stephen's tone was very quiet. "I see."

"Anyway, I thought, since you're Morgan's closest friend . . . and being a physician, I thought perhaps . . . was she ill?"

Stephen made no effort to hide his reluctance. "Elizabeth," he said with a shake of his head, "I'm not certain this should come from me. If I tell you, Morgan might well be angry with both of us."

"I know, Stephen. Truly, I hate putting you in such a position. But the truth is, it doesn't matter if Morgan is angry with me. He—he doesn't care a whit about me anyway," she finished, her voice very low.

"I don't for a minute believe that's true, Elizabeth."

"Believe it, Stephen." The ache in her heart had spread to her voice. "For a time, I thought perhaps he did care . . . We spent at week at his cottage north of here. He—he was so different! But now . . ." Her gaze dropped. She shook her head, the gesture speaking for her.

Stephen's gaze sharpened. "He took you to the cottage?"

"Yes." Her voice was scarcely audible.

"Then I think you underestimate him—and yourself—quite sorely, Elizabeth. That cottage is his hideaway from the world. To my knowledge, he's never taken anyone there before now. I know for a fact Amelia was never there. I remember once she pouted for days because he refused to take her. *I* have never even been there."

"So you did know Amelia?"

"Yes."

"Then tell me about her, Stephen." With her eyes she pleaded with him. "Tell me. Please."

He sighed. "Amelia was an alluring woman," he began, seating himself behind his desk. "Bright and vivid. Very alive and animated, a veritable social butterfly who thrived on attention. I used to think there was no one alive she couldn't charm."

"Was it a happy marriage?" It hurt to say it aloud, yet she had to know.

"At first. But later"—he hesitated—"Morgan never said a word, but somehow I don't think so."

"How long ago did she die?"

"About five years ago."

"What happened? Was she ill? You didn't say," she reminded him.

He was clearly torn. "Elizabeth—"

"Stephen," she implored, "please, I must know!"

He released a long, pent-up breath. "All right," he said at last. "She was . . . killed."

"Killed? How? An accident?"

There was a dragging silence. "She was murdered," he said at last. "Amelia was murdered."

Her eyes widened. For a mind-splitting instant she thought her ears had deceived her. "Murdered," she echoed. "But—how?"

"She was choked to death. Her body was found in her bedroom."

Elizabeth's jaw dropped. "My Lord," she said numbly. "Who would do such a thing—"

"There's one other thing, Elizabeth."

There was something in his tone . . . She held

her breath, all at once filled with trepidation. "Yes?"

His voice was very quiet. "Morgan was arrested and charged with the murder."

Chapter 19

~~~∽⃝G∽~~~

Morgan was arrested and charged with the murder.

The words dropped into the air with the weight of an anchor. Elizabeth's legs would have buckled had she been standing. A vague memory sifted through her mind. She suddenly recalled their wedding day, when a small crowd had gathered outside the church. A man separated himself, raised a fist high, and shouted, *"You'd best take care, lady, or you'll end up dead like the other one!"*

The other one . . .

It had made no sense then, but now comprehension descended like a thick black cloud.

The other one . . .

. . . had been Amelia.

She was shaking from head to toe. Her expression reflected her horror. Unknowingly she flung out her hands. "Dear God, I asked Morgan if he loved her, if she loved him. He said . . . he said Amelia loved no one but herself." A dry, choked sound escaped. "He seemed angry."

Stephen gripped her hands and pulled her to

her feet. "Listen to me, Elizabeth. He didn't do it. *Morgan did not kill Amelia.* He simply is not capable."

"But how can you be so certain?" she cried. "How can you know?"

"Believe me, Elizabeth, I do. I found him not long after he found the body. Amelia was already dead, but he was trying frantically to help her. And I was with him when he was taken into custody. I saw the fear in his eyes—the fear that he might be found guilty—but he scarcely said a word to defend himself! It was shock, I know. He planned to leave Amelia. We'd talked that very evening about how to tell her ... Then to go home and find her dead, only to stand accused of the crime ... ! But as God is my witness, I know he didn't kill Amelia."

Elizabeth gazed into his eyes. Stephen was so utterly convinced, and he knew Morgan better than anyone. The tension gradually seeped from her body. Gauging her reaction, Stephen squeezed her hands reassuringly, then let go.

"What happened then?" she whispered.

Stephen grimaced. "A trial was scheduled. God, what an ugly mess! But prior to that date, the prosecutor dropped the charges. He finally admitted there was no real evidence to point to Morgan." There was a small pause. "In short, Elizabeth, his only crime was in finding Amelia's body."

Elizabeth shuddered. To be subjected to such humiliation—it must have been awful for him!

"So many turned their backs on him, men that he'd dealt with for years. Thank heaven the yard workmen remained loyal. It's a miracle he didn't lose everything, but Morgan weathered the storm. There would be a lot of hungry mouths in Boston if it weren't for his shipyard. Eventually the city's businessmen realized they couldn't afford *not* to do business with him."

Elizabeth's features were somber. She recalled how, on the day Morgan had proposed to marry her, he'd said he disliked being the brunt of scandal.

Dear God, no wonder.

Once she was home, Simmons met her at the door. "Thank heaven you're back, ma'am!" He nodded toward the library. "The master's in there, fretting about your whereabouts. He's been asking after you for hours now!"

Elizabeth handed him her parasol. "Thank you, Simmons." Straightening her spine, she approached the library.

It didn't appear Morgan was fretting. *Steaming* was more like it. He jumped to his feet from behind his desk and came toward her, gray eyes glowing like liquid silver.

"Where the hell have you been?" he demanded.

"There's no need to be angry," she stated calmly. "I merely went out for a walk."

"You've been gone nearly three hours!" A muscle jumped in his cheek as he faced her.

She nearly faltered beneath his blistering glare. "I also went to see Stephen."

His eyes narrowed. Jet brows drew together over his nose as he returned to his seat behind the desk. "Why? Are you ill?"

Now came the difficult part. "No," she admitted. Shoring up all her defenses, she took a deep breath. "He told me how Amelia died."

His jaw clamped tight. Elizabeth winced inwardly, for she could almost see him struggling to hold fast to his temper. His expression tightened, storm clouds brewing over his thin-lipped countenance. He swore. "I should have known he would—"

"If you're going to be angry, be angry with me, not Stephen." Elizabeth moved to defend her friend—and his.

Morgan's fist crashed down on the desk. Lightning flashed in his eyes. "Dammit, the two of you had no right to sneak behind my back!"

Elizabeth paled, but she didn't retreat. Before he could say a word, she confronted him boldly. "We weren't sneaking around behind your back. Frankly, I don't see why *you* couldn't have told me how she died. But you refused to discuss it. And it wasn't that you *couldn't* tell me," she challenged. "You simply wouldn't!"

"It makes no difference. You shouldn't have gone to Stephen."

"I shouldn't have *had* to," she flared.

"Exactly what did he tell you?" he asked suddenly.

She took a deep, ragged breath. "Everything," she said, meeting his regard with a valiance she was far from feeling. "He told me about the charges, the dismissal. And he told me over and over that you didn't kill Amelia."

His tone turned scathing. "What! Don't tell me you weren't ready to believe the very worst of me!"

"Of course I wasn't!" Her retort was indignant.

"And what about now? Do you still believe I didn't kill her?" All at once he was there before her, his eyes glittering, the planes of his face thrown into stark relief by the afternoon sunlight. With only the ruthless hold of his eyes, he pinned her, as if her feet were rooted to the floor.

His hands, strong and lean, came down to frame the delicate span of her shoulders. He drew her close—so very close to him!—a sheer masculine presence so potent and powerful that her mouth grew dry as dust. For one heart-stopping moment, it spun through her mind that he had only to close his fingers about her throat and squeeze . . .

"Well, Elizabeth." His whisper, dark and hot, caressed the shell of her ear. "Do you still believe me innocent?"

With the pads of his thumbs, he traced the fragile line of her collarbone, a touch so achingly gentle, she went weak inside. She couldn't help but recall the night at the cottage when he had made her truly a woman . . .

Truly his wife.

These hands, so strong yet tempered with such tenderness, were simply not capable of such violence, no matter the provocation. She knew it with a certainty that surpassed all else.

No, she thought with a painful catch deep in her breast. The threat he posed was not to her person . . .

But to her heart.

She loved him. God help her, but she loved him.

Her hands threaded through the midnight darkness of the hair that grew low on his nape.

She brought his head down to hers, lifting her own so that their lips met and clung. "Yes," she breathed against his mouth, and then inside it: "Yes."

His arms nearly crushed her. His mouth opened on hers, hot and fiercely devouring. She could taste the desperation in his kiss, but her need for reassurance was no less intense than his. Passion flared, wild and recklessly consuming, spinning them both into a pool of molten desire.

She could feel the iron prod of his manhood, there against her secret bud of pleasure. Wanton joy surged through her. She circled her hips against his thickened spear, an erotic dance that drove them both half-mad. He tore at her clothing; she fumbled with his, clumsy in her haste to rid him of his clothes.

Soon she was naked. Morgan shrugged off his shirt. His trousers were the last to go, her nails scraping the ridge of his hips until his shaft, stiff and swollen, sprang eagerly free.

She had no recollection of sinking to the carpet, an intimate tangle of arms and legs. He kissed a fiery trail down the fullness of her breasts, straying down across the hollow of her belly, clear to the golden thatch clustered between her thighs. With the wedge of his shoulders, he spread her legs wide.

Elizabeth's heart beat high in her throat. It was unthinkable. Sweet Lord. Surely he would not . . .

There was a rush of hot breath, the damp heat of his tongue. Dipping and swirling. Sliding and tasting. Lapping and curling, there at the very pearl of sensation hidden deep within her secret cleft. Her fingers grasped at the rug. Burning raged through her like fire. Mindless pleasure streaked through her veins, building to a blinding crescendo.

The pleasure was so intense, she arched her back and cried out, a wanton cry of ecstasy. Morgan shifted suddenly, rolling to his back and pulling her astride him. Hands on her waist, he wordlessly guided her, holding her upright. She shivered once more at the feel of his fingers caressing the backs of her thighs. Her senses whirled. One smooth, fluid twist and he was buried to the hilt inside her, stretching her, filling her until they were both gasping.

The sensation was indescribable. The softness of her belly grazed the hardness of his. Never in her life had Elizabeth imagined a woman might ride a man so—never had she imagined she might want to! But she was an avid pupil as he dragged her hands to his chest. Her fingers weaved through the dark, curly pelt that grew there. With his thumbs he teased her nipples to quivering points of erectness. Elizabeth moaned, instinctively plunging down at the very instant his shaft filled her to bursting.

Their hips met in a driving, pagan rhythm. Elizabeth couldn't look away from the sight of his manhood lunging into her furrowed warmth, hot, torrid strokes, again and again. She began to pant and writhe, her pelvis churning wildly. Her limbs turned to water, even as a tight coil of heat gathered there, in the place he possessed so fully. Pleasure burst within her, shimmering along her veins. She cried out her ecstasy. With a hoarse groan he pumped his scalding seed deep within her, erupting at the very gates of heaven.

When the coolness of the evening air brushed her heated cheeks, Elizabeth realized what they'd just done—in the library yet! She hid her face against his neck. A giggle caught in her throat as she recalled how she'd once conjured up that very image in her mind.

Never had she thought the deed would indeed be done—or in the *way* it had been done.

She yawned, rubbing her cheek against the sleekness of his shoulder. The night had aged considerably when Morgan finally put her from him. Wrapping a shawl around her body, he carried her up to her room. Elizabeth stirred sleepily as she felt the mattress beneath her back. Her eyes fluttered open. Morgan stood naked beside the bed, tall and magnificent. A little thrill shot through her.

She held out her hand.

He sank down beside her, and soon they were flying among the clouds once more.

It was a long time later that her voice stole into the silence of the night.

"Morgan?"

"Hmmm." He lay on his back, a lean arm cradling her close against his side.

"Who *did* kill Amelia?"

Between one breath and the next, everything changed. One moment he lay relaxed and lazy against her; the next he was stiff as a wooden beam. She nearly cried out when he flung the covers away. His legs swung to the floor, every line of his body taut and unyielding as he arose.

Elizabeth clutched the sheet to her breasts and sat up. "Morgan. Morgan, please! What did I say that was so wrong? I just thought perhaps Amelia's murderer had been discovered—"

"He wasn't."

"But surely you tried to—"

"The subject is closed, Elizabeth, once and for all."

Her jaw sagged. "What! You mean you'll never discuss it again?"

"Precisely." He yanked on his trousers. "It's over and done with. Amelia is dead and there's nothing that can bring her back."

She stared at him, stung and confused by his cold withdrawal. "You sound as if you don't want to know."

"I don't." His voice was clipped and abrupt.

"My God, she was your wife!"

His lip curled. "My wife. You want reasons, Elizabeth? Fine. Let me tell you about my dearly beloved. In all but the first year of our marriage, there was an endless parade of lovers in and out of her bed. When she died, I just wanted to forget the hell she put me through. And that reminds me, I'll thank you not to question Stephen about Amelia again—or anyone else for that matter."

Angry tears burned her throat. "But I only went to him out of concern—"

"Concern for whom, I wonder. Were you worried I might murder you in your sleep?"

"I-I didn't even know she'd been murdered until after I spoke to him!"

He paid no heed. "Tell me, Elizabeth. Would you have married me if you'd known I'd once been charged with murder—the murder of my wife no less?" His mouth twisted. "The proper English lady married to a common criminal."

"You're not a criminal."

"But I might as well be." His tone fairly dripped with contempt. "Rest assured, the good people of Boston have never forgotten. Why should my highborn English wife?"

"Highborn? I would remind you I was nearly penniless when I arrived here!"

"It didn't have to be that way, Elizabeth. All you had to do was stay in England and marry. Then you'd have had your share of your father's money. I won't stand in your way, if that's what you want. Go back to England. I don't care one way or the other."

Elizabeth clenched her fists. "You have made that quite clear," she managed to say. Her rage suddenly fired as hot as his. "You tell me nothing. You *feel* nothing. Well, let me tell you something, Morgan O'Connor. I feel like a fool. I feel used."

Her voice vibrated with the tenor of her outrage. "At the cottage, I thought we had something we could share. But it seems I'm no better than—than your mistress! What was it you said? 'We shared nothing but a mutual enjoyment of each other's bodies.' "

She swept a disdainful hand wide across the rumpled bedclothes. "Is that what *this* was? Is that what you intend our marriage to be?"

His silence was oppressive. He said nothing . . . and in so doing he said everything.

Elizabeth gave a low, choked cry. "Well, that's not a marriage," she said feelingly. "That's nothing but a prison, for both of us."

She thought it could get no worse.
She was preparing the next week's dinner

menus in the drawing room the next day when
Simmons announced Nathaniel was waiting in
the foyer.

Elizabeth couldn't help it. Morgan's warning
the day they had returned from the cottage re-
verberated in her mind like a cannon.

Don't return until you're invited.

She bit her lip, then made a split-second decision. She set aside her paperwork. "Please
show him in, Simmons."

Nathaniel entered a moment later. He was
dressed as impeccably as always, but there were
dark circles under his eyes. He looked positively
unwell.

"Hello, Nathaniel." Her smile was tentative.
"Please sit down."

Nathaniel glanced around, his expression distinctly wary. "Morgan's at the office?"

She nodded, watching as he took the chair opposite her. He appeared visibly relieved. "He
had business out of town this morning," she said
quietly. "He won't be back until evening." What
she didn't say was that Morgan hadn't told her
himself; he'd left it to Simmons to tell her.

"Would you like coffee or tea?"

"No. I just came to—to apologize to you." He
had the grace to look sheepish.

"About what happened the day before yesterday?"

"Yes."

Elizabeth clasped her hands in her lap. "You
don't owe me an apology, Nathaniel." There was
a significant pause. "But I think you owe one to
Morgan."

"Morgan!" His snort was rather eloquent. "Why should I apologize to him?"

His regard had turned belligerent. Elizabeth met it with chin high, refusing to back down.

"Your behavior was rude and insensitive, to say nothing of inexcusable," she said evenly. "You wanted to stir up trouble. You wanted to belittle him in front of his wife."

"And what if I did? He took you from me—he stole you away!"

"No, Nathaniel. I did what I had to—what was right for me. I married Morgan of my own free will. You have to understand that." She was firm. "It was my choice to marry him."

"You don't love him, Elizabeth!"

Her heart wrenched. Her gaze flitted away. *Not then,* she thought achingly. *But God help me, I do now.*

But she couldn't tell that to Nathaniel. Just as she acknowledged that she'd never really loved Nathaniel, not in the way she loved Morgan. She'd been swept away. By the glitter of London. The gaiety of life. By his charm and laughter.

No. She could hardly tell him so. She couldn't wound him like that. It simply wasn't in her nature to deliberately hurt another.

She didn't realize that something of her melancholy mood must have shown. Nathaniel seized on it.

"You see? I was right. He'll make you miserable. He has already, I can see it! Elizabeth, he'll do the same thing to you that he did to Amelia. He'll rob you of any chance at happiness—"

"Don't!" The word was rapier-sharp. Her eyes were snapping. "Don't say another word against him, Nathaniel. If you do, I'll have to insist you leave."

His lips pressed together sullenly, but he said no more. Instead he surged upward and thrust his hands in his pockets. Back and forth he paced. Back and forth. It was on his third pass that Elizabeth's delicate nose caught the distinct aroma of spirits.

She was up and on her feet in an instant. "Nathaniel!" she cried in dismay. "You've been drinking again!"

He stopped abruptly. For the first time Elizabeth noticed his eyes were red rimmed and bloodshot.

His mouth turned up in a hard smile. "Just so you know, Elizabeth, it's a rare occasion these days when I'm *not* drinking."

"Nathaniel! I hardly think it's anything to boast about!"

He scowled. "Why shouldn't I? I've got nothing better to do. And it helps to pass the time."

She was horrified. "That's why you do it? To pass the time?"

He shrugged.

"But there are dozens of other things you could do!"

"Such as?" His tone was sullen.

Elizabeth's lips pressed together. "Something useful," she said baldly. "Something constructive."

"Constructive? You mean Morgan hasn't told you?" he sneered. "I'm a good-for-nothing, Elizabeth, as he's so fond of saying."

Frustration bit deep. Why were the two constantly at odds? Why? screamed a tiny voice in her breast. She was more certain than ever that there was something she didn't know, something vitally important.

"Then prove him wrong, Nathaniel! Not to spite him, but for yourself, your own pride! There must be some kind of work you could do. Find something to occupy your time—your mind!"

"I'm surprised Morgan hasn't told you. That fancy education he paid for was a waste. I've been let go from every position I've ever had."

Elizabeth shook her head. "Nonetheless, you need to work, Nathaniel." She linked her hands together before her, her mind turning furiously. "Wait!" she exclaimed. "I have the perfect solution. What if I spoke to Morgan about a position at the shipyard?"

"Elizabeth—"

She waved aside his protests. "There must be something you could do," she mused aloud. "Are you good with figures?"

"I used to be," he admitted.

"Good! Perhaps you could take on some of the bookkeeping. I know Morgan finds it tedious . . ." She was adamant—and convinced this was quite the thing to do.

She laughed softly to herself as the evening wore on. If Morgan were to see that Nathaniel was capable of proving his worth, surely his opinion of his brother would improve. Perhaps this might well be the first step toward healing the breach between the two.

It was quite late when Morgan arrived home, but Elizabeth was ready and waiting. Downstairs she heard his footsteps. The door of his study opened. Good. He'd missed dinner, so she'd asked the cook to prepare a plate for him; there was a generous slice of ham, savory beans, and bread. Picking up the tray, she went downstairs.

Her slippers made no sound as she entered the study. The yellow glow of a lamp lit the corner. Morgan stood near the window, staring out at the moon-drenched sky. For the space of a heartbeat, she drank in the sight of his cleanly etched profile. His features were utterly somber. There were deep channels carved beside his mouth. Even his posture was subdued. He appeared so incredibly weary that she couldn't help it. Her heart went out to him.

The rustle of her night-robe alerted him to her presence. He turned.

Holding her breath, she held out the tray. "You missed dinner," she said breathlessly. "I thought you might be hungry."

For a moment he didn't move. Elizabeth had the oddest sensation she'd startled him. Finally he came forward, taking the tray from her. Their fingertips just barely brushed, yet heat streaked through her like a fork of lightning.

"Actually I'm famished," he admitted.

She smiled. The relief that flooded her was immense. After her outburst last night, she'd been afraid his reception would be distant and unyielding. While he took his seat behind the desk, she settled herself in the chair directly across from him. As he ate, she chattered idly about how warm the weather had been of late, Simmons's rheumatism, the dinner party at the Porters' next week.

When he'd finished, he pushed away the plate

and arose. Rounding the desk, he came to stand in front of her. Before Elizabeth knew what he was about, he'd pulled her upright.

Small, slippered feet were aligned squarely between his. He had yet to release her hands.

"Thank you," he murmured. "This was very thoughtful."

She smiled up at him, all at once feeling absurdly happy. "You're very welcome," she told him. "I-I just wanted to do something special for you. I hope you don't mind."

"Not at all." His gaze roved the upturned beauty of her features. Her eyes were green and sparkling, her cheeks were pink and becomingly flushed. Her hair fell down her back, a rippling, golden waterfall. Her nightgown was just barely visible beneath the edge of her night-robe. Delicate white lace covered the ripe mounds of her breasts; it stirred with every breath she drew, more an enticement than if she had stood naked before him.

Desire struck like a fist planted low in his belly. More than anything, he longed to lay her down, strip away their clothes, and drive hard and deep within her silken flesh.

His grip on her hands tightened. But before he could say a word, he heard her.

"I'm so glad you're not angry about last night."

Last night. God, he could barely think, let alone remember last night. His pulse was clamoring. His blood had begun to heat.

"I hope you don't mind, but I've a favor to ask of you."

Lord, she was sweet. She could have asked for

the moon and the sun and the stars, and he'd have done anything in his power to see that she got what she wanted.

"Morgan, about Nathaniel . . . He needs something with which to occupy himself. I'm convinced he could make something of himself, if only he tried. And I was thinking . . . perhaps you might allow him to come work for you . . ."

Her request was slow to register. When it did, it was like an icy wave of seawater.

"Nathaniel? He was here, wasn't he?" All at once the atmosphere was stifling.

"Yes. I know you told him not to come back until he was invited," she clarified quickly. "But he came to apologize." She wasn't about to let on that Nathaniel came to apologize to her, not him.

Morgan went utterly still. "You want me to hire him? To give him a position?"

"Yes. You see—"

The pressure of his hands around hers tightened so that she nearly cried out. Then she was practically flung from him.

"No."

Elizabeth blinked. "Morgan," she began, hoping to make him see reason. "Of course, he doesn't expect to work hand in hand with you—"

"He won't be working *with* me, Elizabeth. He won't be working *for* me. Do I make myself clear?"

"But—"

His tone was brittle; he was completely unyielding. "There will be no discussion, Elizabeth.

I won't have him working for me. It's out of the question.''

Her eyes were riveted to his face. His expression was dark and dangerous. The air around them seemed to thunder and pulse. He swept an arm toward his desk, the tray and empty plate. "All this was on behalf of poor Nathaniel, wasn't it? You were hoping to convince me, to soften me so I wouldn't refuse."

Elizabeth was aghast that he could think so little of her. "No. No, of course not!"

His lip curled. His gaze raked over her from head to toe. Elizabeth was left feeling stripped to the bone, naked and exposed.

"You surprise me, Elizabeth. I thought you were more of a *lady*." He said it as if it were a curse. "Tell me, did you intend to seduce me? Just how far would you go for your beloved Nathaniel? Would you whore for him too?"

Elizabeth's temper boiled over. Her hand shot out before she thought better of it. There was a loud crack as she delivered a stunning open-handed slap to the hardness of his cheek.

His reaction was instantaneous. He snatched her against him, so close she could feel the iron brand of his legs taut against hers. His hold was ruthless, his hands like shackles circling her delicate wrists. His eyes impaled her with their fierceness.

"If I were you," he said between clenched teeth, "I would think twice before daring to do that again. Because I promise, my dear wife, the next time won't go unpunished."

Elizabeth managed to wrench herself free. There was a suffocating tightness in her breast.

"Damn you," she burst out. "Nathaniel is your brother! You owe him no less than a chance!"

Morgan's expression was rigid. "By God," he said tightly, "I owe him no more!"

Elizabeth's voice shook with the depth of her rage. "Then you are a man with half a heart, a man with half a soul! If I had a brother or sister, there is nothing that could break the bond between us. I would do all I could to help him, while you—I do believe you would do anything to be rid of him! How can you hate your own brother—your own flesh and blood? How, I ask you?"

The question hung between them, the tension never-ending. When she realized no reply was forthcoming, she gave a choked little cry and darted from the study.

Morgan remained where he was, his entire body taut. Though his expression was carefully blank, an unseen hand seemed to close about his heart and squeeze.

I don't hate Nat, came his answer at last. *He's my brother. My brother . . .*

Pain ripped through him, like a sword drawn from his throat to his belly. For locked fast in those two words lay a wealth of pain, a world of heartache.

His shoulders slumped. He dragged a hand down his face, a gesture of weary resignation.

No, he thought again. He didn't hate Nat. He loved him. After all the ugliness that stained their past, he still loved him . . .

That was the hell of it.

Chapter 20

There was another man in Boston who was less than pleased with Nathaniel O'Connor.

Only this man's intentions were far more devious, far more ominous.

Perhaps even deadly.

His name was Jonah Moreland. He'd arrived in Boston several weeks earlier from New York; prior to that he'd come from London. In the little time he'd been here, he'd formed the opinion that these Yankees were brash and bold, surely the most uncivilized lot on the face of this earth.

And the one particular man he'd tracked here was not especially bright.

Ah, but quick and easy was not his way. Jonah enjoyed his profession far too much. He preferred the fervor of the chase, the battle of wit and will, the culmination of the hunt. That was what gave him such zest for his work. Still, he prided himself on his fairness—and his shrewdness.

Ah, yes, Nathaniel O'Connor would be given a chance to repay a debt long overdue. If Jonah was feeling particularly generous, perhaps two chances.

But never more.

His employer on this particular case was Viscount Phillip Hadley. He and Hadley had done business on several other occasions. Admittedly, few men were daring enough—or foolish enough—to try to cheat Viscount Hadley.

That was Nathaniel O'Connor's first mistake.

His second was failing to make restitution.

His third was failing to expect retribution.

It was no accident that Jonah had chosen this particular establishment. Indeed, his quarry was a frequent patron at the Crow's Nest. Even now, Nathaniel O'Connor sat in the corner, swilling his liquor like water, an arm about the harlot with whom he'd spent the evening.

Jonah's pale eyes narrowed to thin slits. He absently rubbed the scar on his cheek. No doubt Nathaniel O'Connor had thought himself so very clever when he'd fled London all those months ago. But in Jonah's estimation, the wretch was incredibly stupid.

He was also amazingly predictable.

Jonah glanced at his pocket watch. Unless he was mistaken, O'Connor would soon rise and depart. He would make his way home, where he would sleep off the effects of his indulgence. Late the next afternoon, he would repeat the routine of the previous day. He would spend the evening gambling and imbibing, with some well-dressed whore at his side. In short, it appeared Nathaniel O'Connor had but three interests—gambling, spirits, and women.

Just then O'Connor staggered upright, said his

good-byes to his companion, and ambled toward the door.

Jonah Moreland swallowed the last of his wine, carefully blotted his mouth with his napkin, and flipped his pocket watch shut. He lagged four paces behind O'Connor as he passed through the doorway and out into the night.

O'Connor never even noticed.

He didn't make his presence known until O'Connor was nearly home. With the quickness that was his trademark, he collared the younger man and dragged him into an alleyway between buildings.

At O'Connor's throat he held his instrument of choice, shiny and glinting.

Jonah smiled. "I must say, O'Connor, you've led me quite a merry chase from London."

"Wh-who are you?" Nathaniel gasped.

"Think of me as a messenger from Viscount Hadley. Were you aware he has no tolerance for thieves? No, I don't expect so, considering where we are. I must warn you then. He was generous enough to loan you a considerable sum—why, half a fortune! But as you can imagine, he was quite distressed when you left London without repaying him so much as a farthing!"

The pressure on his throat eased. Jonah allowed him to slowly turn around but kept the dagger pointed straight at his heart. O'Connor swallowed as he beheld his assailant. He couldn't take his eyes from the thin white scar that bisected Jonah's cheek from his ear to the corner of his mouth.

His smile was pure menace. "Of course, you realize that's the reason for my presence here.

Viscount Hadley doesn't like loose ends."

O'Connor's voice was a hoarse croak. "Wh-what do you want?"

"Only what is due the viscount, my good man. Only what is due."

"How soon? I'll need some time to—"

"Three days," Jonah said coldly. "You have three days. I'll collect the money at the establishment you just came from. Is that understood?"

The younger man nodded. By now speech was clearly beyond him.

"Good." As he spoke, he ran his fingers up and down along the blade of the dagger. "Now, be off before I change my mind."

Nathaniel spun around and ran headlong toward home.

Jonah smiled, dusted off his jacket, and sauntered away.

Elizabeth was miserable.

The foundation of her marriage had always been shaky. But now it was as if it crumbled further with every day that passed. She and Morgan behaved like strangers. Though she longed to put aside the bitterness of their quarrel, it seemed neither could forget. She tried on several occasions to engage him in simple conversation, but he was distant and formal; it was clear he was hardly so inclined, which only riled her temper all over again. No, it was impossible to behave as if nothing were wrong, when she felt the world was collapsing all around her.

Her heart knew no peace, particularly when she realized her monthly cycle was late—never before had such a thing happened. Good heavens, she couldn't have a baby, not now! Yet Stephen's prediction echoed in her mind. *No doubt it'll happen sooner or later—probably sooner than later.*

She wavered between wonder and despair. A child of hers . . . a child of Morgan's. What would he or she look like? A girl, she thought longingly. She would so love a tiny baby girl.

But what about Morgan? Should she tell him? No. She wasn't even certain of her condition yet. Besides, now was not the time. But what, she asked herself half-hysterically, if the right time *never* came?

The night of the dinner party at the Porters arrived. Elizabeth dreaded the occasion—and for good reason, as it turned out. It proved every bit the ordeal she feared.

In the carriage, a thick silence was all that passed between them. She'd worn her pearls, with a fragile blossom of hope he might admire how they looked—how *she* looked.

She hoped in vain.

Not long after they were greeted by the Porters, they were separated. Morgan was seated at the far end of the dining room table, while she sat near their hostess. He spared neither a smile nor a look toward the woman he'd married.

After dinner there was music in the drawing room. Elizabeth smiled and chatted until her face felt frozen, speech an endless blur in her mind. Her eyes swept the room. She hadn't seen Morgan in quite some time . . .

It was the woman she saw first, dressed once again in crimson, her profile lovely and flawless. Elizabeth's eyes cut back to her.

It was her, the woman from the opera. His mistress. Morgan's *mistress*.

Just then someone stepped aside. Elizabeth was afforded a glimpse of the woman's companion.

It was Morgan.

Pain, stark and raw, clamped around her heart. The world swam dizzily, dark and gray. How she remained upright, she never knew.

When she looked again, the pair was still there. The woman's head was lifted to Morgan's. Her lips hovered just beneath his. Her hand lay possessively on his arm.

Anguish welled inside her so that she nearly cried out. Had she driven him back to the arms of his mistress? *Stop it!* a voice inside her reasoned. He'd been at home every night of late. In the very next room . . .

But what about tonight?

"You're looking a bit peaked, Elizabeth. Are you feeling all right?"

Elizabeth nearly jumped out of her skin. But it was only Stephen.

"No," she said, hating the catch in her voice. She couldn't stay. She couldn't stand to look at them. If she did, she would burst into tears, tears that might never stop . . .

"Actually, I have a terrible headache. I'm hardly very good company, so I may as well leave." She tried to smile and failed. "Would you mind asking someone to have the carriage brought around?"

"Of course not," he said. He raised his head, his gaze scanning the crowd. "I'll tell Morgan you're ready to leave—"

"No," she protested quickly. "There's no need to ruin his evening, too. After Willis takes me home, he can return and wait for Morgan."

Stephen frowned heavily. "Are you sure you're all right?"

"Yes . . . yes, of course."

"Then why don't I come with you, just to make—"

"No, Stephen. Truly it's not necessary. I just need to lie down and I'll be fine. Really. I just need to have the carriage brought around. And please tell Morgan I'm indisposed . . ."

Half an hour later she was upstairs in her bedroom. After Annie unhooked the back of her gown, Elizabeth dismissed her, wanting nothing more than to be alone. She changed into her nightgown and robe, her movements slow, as if it hurt to move.

She sat down at the dressing table and freed her hair from its tight coil at her crown. Would Morgan even come home tonight? The ache in her breast was nearly unbearable. His mistress— heavens, she didn't even know her name!—was so beautiful, like a bright, fragrant flower in full bloom. No doubt Morgan found her fascinating and exciting, alluring and beguiling . . .

. . . while he found his wife nothing but a tedious nag.

She stared at her reflection. Her hair tumbled thick and heavy over her shoulders. Green eyes stared back at her, dark as jade. Her skin was rather ashen. All at once she felt like a pale, wilted blossom. Frowning, she picked up her brush and began to stroke it through her hair. It was then she noticed she'd forgotten to take off her pearls. Her fingers were clumsy, but she managed to undo the clasp. The pearls were dropped in a small heap on the dressing table. She would return them to their case tomorrow. For now, she was simply too tired.

Just then there was a small sound at the hallway door—a knock? Her head cocked to the side, Elizabeth turned and listened. It wasn't Morgan. He wouldn't have knocked. But there it was again, a small, hushed knock.

The door was thrust wide just as she opened her mouth. Nathaniel stepped inside.

Elizabeth rose with a gasp, clutching her robe over her breasts. "Nathaniel!" she cried. "What are you doing here? You can't be in here!"

"I had to see you, Elizabeth." His tone was urgent. "When I saw that Morgan didn't come home with you, I knew it had to be now, so I sneaked in through the kitchen."

She shook her head. "Nathaniel, if it's about the position, I'm sorry. I spoke to Morgan and he refused—"

He waved his hands. "It's not that, Elizabeth."

A flicker of unease went through her. Nathaniel's hat was slightly askew, his manner harried. He seemed out of breath, as if he'd been running. "What then? What's happened?"

He crushed his hat in his hands and began to pace. "Elizabeth, I need money. A lot of it. I can't ask Morgan. I know he'll refuse. So I came to you."

Elizabeth was stunned. "Money," she echoed. "Nathaniel, whatever for?"

"I don't have time to explain now. I'll tell you tomorrow, I swear. Elizabeth, please, you have to help me! I need whatever I can get my hands on.''

Her unease sharpened to apprehension. ''You're in trouble, aren't you?''

His laugh was short and harsh. ''Yes. Yes, you might say that.''

''What sort of trouble?''

He thrust his fingers through his hair. ''Elizabeth, I don't have time now. I swear, I'll tell you the next time I see you. For now, I need whatever money you can lay your hands on.''

He sounded so frantic; she couldn't help but sense his desperation. She shook her head helplessly. ''I-I'm not sure I can help you. I've an allowance at Morgan's bank—I don't know how much since I've never used it—but it won't be open until Monday.''

He groaned. ''Christ!'' he swore. ''If I don't come up with enough to—''

''Wait!'' she cried. ''The household funds are in Morgan's study. I don't know how much there is—''

''Anything at all will help, Elizabeth. Anything.''

She nodded. ''Wait here. I'll get it for you.''

Her feet fairly flew down the stairs. In Morgan's study, she grabbed the key from beneath the porcelain vase. Hurriedly she pulled open the drawer and unlocked the small metal box stashed at the very end. She grabbed the pile of bills inside, slammed the lid down and locked it. Her hands were shaking as she jammed the key back beneath the vase.

Back in her room, Nathaniel was standing near the window. He glanced around as she entered.

Wordlessly she held up the wad of bills.

He broke into a laugh. "Bless you," he beamed. "You are truly a godsend." He took it from her and stuffed it into the inside pocket of his jacket. Turning back to her, he paused. Something flashed across his face, something that might have been regret.

Elizabeth glanced toward the door. "Nathaniel," she pleaded, "you'd better hurry. Morgan may be home any second now."

His eyes glimmered. "A kiss," he proclaimed with the same teasing grandness that had so charmed her in London. "Grant me one last kiss, Elizabeth, and I'll be gone."

"Nathaniel, no! It's not proper!"

His laugh was deep and hearty. "When have I ever done what was proper? Come now, Elizabeth. All I ask is a kiss. I won't leave until you agree."

Elizabeth's mouth opened, but there was no time to protest. Hands on her shoulders, he drew her to him. His mouth came down on hers.

It was odd, how she felt nothing, no excitement, no warmth, no shivery tremors the way she did with Morgan. The magic was gone, she realized. She allowed the kiss to linger a heartbeat more than she should have, but there was a part of her that needed to know for certain that all she had once felt for Nathaniel was no more . . .

Now she knew.

She broke it off and stepped back. "Nathaniel," she urged, "you must hurry."

With a nod and a wave, he departed. In her doorway, Elizabeth watched as he blended into the shadows. When she was certain he'd escaped unnoticed, she breathed a tremendous sigh of relief. If Morgan knew Nathaniel had been here, he would be livid . . .

Morgan did know.

And he was indeed livid, for behind the sheer lace curtains was the unmistakable silhouette of man and woman locked in a long, ardent embrace.

His eyes remained fastened on the window of his wife's room. From around the corner came the rustle of bushes, then thudding footsteps.

That would be Nathaniel.

Morgan's hands clenched into fists at his sides. He didn't go after him. He didn't dare. If he touched him, he would tear him limb from limb.

Inside the house he strode straight to the library—and the brandy decanter. His fingers closed around the neck of the decanter; he filled a crystal glass nearly to the brim. But he didn't drink. His jaw clenched. He stared at the ruby liquid as if it had been brewed by the devil himself.

Once before his lofty wife had pushed him to this point, a point at which he despised himself for his weakness, for sinking to such depths. He reminded himself savagely that if he gave in yet again, he was no better than his drunken father—no better than Nathaniel.

But the temptation to forget, to cast himself into oblivion, was too strong. Too powerful to fight.

The glass tipped. Brandy burned a path of fire as it slid down his throat.

By the time it was empty, his thoughts and actions had blurred, but his anger was fired as hotly as ever.

He climbed the stairs to his bedroom. He stood for a moment, staring blackly at the connecting door that led to Elizabeth's room.

Bitterness crystallized within him. He remembered how she'd looked the other morning, her naked form shaped against his side. The sweep of her nape lay bare and delicate, the smoothness of her shoulders fragile and white, feminine and vulnerable. Much like the woman herself . . . But no—no, that wasn't right. Elizabeth wasn't vulnerable. She was strong and possessed a will of her own. Just like Amelia.

Just like Amelia.

He flung his jacket to the bed, cursing himself for the blind stupid fool he was. He'd been duped twice. *Twice*. First Amelia. Now Elizabeth.

A crimson mist of rage clouded his vision. In his mind's eye he pictured Elizabeth and Nathaniel once more, lips clinging, arms wrapped around each other.

Directly across from him was the framed painting of the clipper ship she'd given him. Snatching it from the wall, he hurled it to the floor. It hit with such force the frame splintered into pieces.

So did his heart.

Elizabeth paused, one knee poised on the bed. The other slim leg was extended downward, bare toes still curled into the plushness of the carpet. She cocked her head toward Morgan's room.

She could have sworn she heard something strike the floor.

All was quiet.

A yellow sliver of light glowed beneath the connecting door. Moving very quietly, almost stealthily, she crept across to the door, still straining to hear.

Still there was nothing.

Holding her breath, she let her fingers curl around the doorknob. She twisted it slowly, possessed by a force she couldn't deny. Pushing it ajar, she peered inside. There upon the floor, the frame splintered and scattered in pieces, lay the painting that had been her gift to her husband.

No accident had rendered it so.

Sheer pain throbbed in her breast. This was what she'd heard, and the knowledge was like a fist crashing down on her heart.

Suddenly the door was wrenched from her hold and thrust wide. A tall, masculine form replaced it. Her eyes wide and stricken, Elizabeth looked up at her husband.

He regarded her with frightening intensity. His eyes were bloodshot but glittering. They stood so close, not even the span of a hand separated them; it was then she caught the pungent fumes of liquor.

He was drunk. The man she had never seen partake of spirits in all these weeks ... was drunk.

She was suddenly terrified.

With a cry she whirled and tried to bolt. Quick as she was, he was quicker. Strong arms imprisoned her, dragging her back against the unyielding breadth of his chest. She strained against his hold, but it was useless. Three steps brought them back within his room.

Half-afraid to move, even to breathe, she turned to face him.

For once his gaze was unshuttered. But the look in his eyes was terrible. She could almost believe he *had* killed Amelia . . .

"Morgan," she cried. "What is wrong? Why are you acting like this?"

He released her, only to walk in a slow circle around her. Elizabeth's heart was in a frenzy. She flinched when a blunt fingertip came out to trace the delicate sweep of her collarbone, yet his touch was as gentle as fleece . . . a touch wholly at odds with the venom in his eyes.

Several paces separated them, yet the gulf between them seemed far more immense. Her lips barely moved. "Please let me go, Morgan. You're drunk."

"So I am, Elizabeth. So I am." His smile was brittle. "But I wonder—is there something you'd like to tell me, sweet?"

She blanched. He knew. Heaven help her, he knew . . . "Oh, no," she whispered numbly. "Don't tell me you saw—"

His smile had vanished. "Oh yes, Elizabeth." His tone was lashing. "I saw my oh-so-virtuous wife in the throes of an embrace with my *brother*."

Elizabeth's mouth had gone dry. She stared at him, wanting to tear her eyes away but unable to do so. His gaze seemed to burn clear through to her very soul.

"Tell me, though. If I hadn't seen him here for myself, would you have told me?"

Her insides twisted in dread. She swallowed. Speech eluded her.

"I told him not to return until he was invited, Elizabeth. So tell me—did you invite him into your bedroom?"

At last she found her voice. "No!" She shook her head frantically. "Morgan, it's not what you think!"

"Then what was it, Elizabeth? How does one mistake two lovers caught in an embrace?" His voice was drilling. With his eyes he pinned her, a ruthless echo of his condemnation.

She stared at him beseechingly. "Morgan, I swear, it wasn't what you think! Nathaniel was here, yes. But I didn't know he was coming, nor did I invite him. He's in trouble, Morgan. He needed money, so I—I gave him the cash set aside for the household—"

"And what else did you give him, Elizabeth? What else?"

The words were like a slap in the face. Elizabeth went pale, but she held her ground. He couldn't argue with the truth, could he?

"I won't lie, Morgan. He—he kissed me. He wouldn't leave until he had. But if you must blame anyone, blame me. I should have stopped him sooner, I know. But it showed me once and for all that what I once felt for Nathaniel is no more. Don't you see? I felt nothing! All I could think about was you!"

His jaw was clenched hard. Yet something flickered in his eyes. "Then show me, Elizabeth. Come to me and show me."

The gauntlet had been thrown. Elizabeth realized she had no choice. She must take up his challenge or he might never believe her.

Slowly she crossed to him, her knees quaking so that she feared her legs would fail her. She moistened lips that were suddenly parched. "I-I don't know what you want me to do," she whispered.

His eyes were on hers, glittering points of silver, his expression stormy. "Kiss me, Elizabeth. We're brothers, Nathaniel and I. Brothers should share, don't you think? Even wives."

Elizabeth cringed inside. Must he forever mock her? But it was too late to change her mind. If she did, he might never forgive her.

Forgive her. Oh, but that was rich! Morgan O'Connor was surely the most unforgiving man alive! He had yet to forgive Nathaniel, for whatever misdeed Nathaniel had done! She didn't know how or why, but she'd never been more certain of anything in her life.

"I'm waiting, Elizabeth."

Her insides quivering, she placed her fingertips on his shoulders. Levering herself upward, she pressed tremulous lips to his.

He was cool and unresponsive, his lips pressed into a grim line. His stance was wooden. She could feel his tension; his body was rock-hard and unyielding. Intensifying her efforts, she deepened the kiss, turning her head first one way, then the other. She molded her mouth against the hardness of his, wordlessly urging him to yield. Her hands stole to his nape, an unconscious caress. Bringing her tongue out of hiding, she traced the beautifully sculpted outline of his mouth. His lips parted ever so slightly; their breath mingled and meshed.

Her head was spinning when at last she drew back. Their eyes cleaved together. His were still blistering—not with anger . . . but with something else, a fiery blaze of hunger that nearly sapped her courage.

"Undress me." His voice had thickened.

Her pulse leaped. She was sorely tempted to spring around and run, yet she couldn't deny the very thought of being the aggressor—the initiator—was oddly exciting.

Her fingers fell to the buttons of his shirt. Inwardly she was quaking, but she managed to free them without clumsiness. He said nothing as she drew the shirt from his shoulders and arms and let it drop to the floor.

His trousers were next. Elizabeth sank to her knees before him. The buttons there were more difficult, rendered so by the straining pressure of rigid flesh beneath. But at last they were free; a tug and the trousers fell to his ankles. The spear of his manhood sprang free and unencumbered. His trousers were kicked aside.

He would have bent to lift her to her feet, but with a slight shake of her head she stayed the movement. Glancing upward, she shyly beseeched him. Her fingertips framed the bony ridge of slim, narrow hips.

His hands on her shoulders grew still. For the space of a heartbeat it was as if the entire world held its breath.

With her mouth she touched him, delicately tasting his essence. With her tongue she discovered the shape of him, darting and swirling. He seemed to swell to even greater dimensions.

His fingers slid into her hair. "God," he said hoarsely, and then again: *"God!"*

Knowing she pleased him heightened her own excitement. Her fingers dug into his hips. He cast back his head and groaned his pleasure aloud.

When he could stand no more he caught her and pulled her upright. Tumbling her to the bed, he plunged the spear of his manhood deep— deep!—inside her satin cave. She clung tight to his shoulders, crying out her yearning. It was a union that was fiery and tempestuous, with heated, wanton whispers and breathless cries of rapture . . .

The first of several that night.

Chapter 21

It might have been just a dream.

But Morgan awoke to find his wife huddled close against his side, gloriously sleek and naked. Though his head pounded and his mouth was as dry as sawdust, the night just spent had been the most incredible night of his life.

And also the most painful.

Remembrance swept in like the rushing tide.

I won't lie, Morgan. He—he kissed me. He wouldn't leave until he had. But if you must blame anyone, blame me. I should have stopped him sooner, I know. But it showed me once and for all that what I once felt for Nathaniel is no more. Don't you see? I felt nothing! All I could think about was you!

He clenched his teeth hard. He couldn't forget what he'd seen so easily. Yet despite all, he wanted to trust Elizabeth. He wanted to believe in her.

He didn't dare.

It was too much like before. Amelia and Nathaniel. *Elizabeth* and Nathaniel. True, Elizabeth had fallen for Nathaniel long before he'd ever laid eyes on her; yet neither Elizabeth nor Amelia had been immune from his roguish brother's charms.

And that was what he couldn't forget. What if it happened again? What if Elizabeth succumbed once more?

One long arm tucked beneath his head, he stared at the hazy spears of sunlight spreading on the ceiling. His thoughts were brutally tormenting. He gritted his teeth, recalling how her hips had churned madly beneath his. A bittersweet shadow crept over him. Sweet as they were, her lips might easily lie, though her body did not. She *had* found pleasure in his arms.

But had she also found pleasure in Nathaniel's arms?

And then there was Nathaniel. What the devil had he gotten himself into now? Elizabeth had been adamant that he was in trouble. His lips thinned. That sounded like Nathaniel. He'd always had a knack for finding trouble. Or was it another of his lies—a pretense—a way to elicit Elizabeth's sympathy?

Elizabeth was awake by the time he'd finished bathing and dressing. Clad in pale gray trousers, jacket, and vest, he was so tall and handsome, he stole her very breath. He looked up just as he finished snapping shut a small leather bag.

Intercepting Elizabeth's questioning glance, he came to sit on the edge of the bed, very near but not touching her. "I'm leaving for New York this morning to check on some investments," he said by way of explanation. "I won't be back for several days."

Elizabeth sat up slowly, running her fingers

through sleep-tousled long curls, careful to keep the sheet tucked over her bare breasts. Morgan's manner wasn't cold, but he appeared very somber and reserved.

Impulsively she spoke. "Are you still angry about last night?" She held her breath and waited, forever, it seemed.

His gaze darkened. "I don't know. Wary, perhaps." His eyes held hers in a thorough study. "And frankly, Elizabeth, I often wonder where your true loyalty lies—with me or with Nathaniel."

Elizabeth caught her breath. There was no bite in his tone; she had the feeling he wasn't lashing out, but was merely being unfailingly honest.

Her hand came out to cover his lightly where it rested atop the counterpane. "I can understand why you should feel skeptical. But it's just as I told Nathaniel. You are the one I married, Morgan. *You*," she stressed softly. "My loyalty will always lie with you." *And so will my heart*, she thought achingly.

Eyes the color of storm clouds roamed her upturned features, as if he would search out the very depths of her soul. Elizabeth didn't flinch from his scrutiny, but met his gaze evenly, her own eyes wide and unwavering.

He made no answer. Instead his gaze was drawn to their fingers. Elizabeth couldn't look away as he lifted her hand, weaving their fingers together. The contrast was startling. Bronzed skin against fair. His so long and lean, hers so dainty and small.

At last he sighed. The merest of smiles grazed the stark beauty of his mouth. "I must be off," he murmured. He brushed his lips across her knuckles and rose.

She sensed his reluctance. Her pulse bounded forward. Her heart leaped with wild elation.

Halfway to the door, she called his name. "Morgan."

He turned, his bag in hand.

Elizabeth slid from the bed, wrapping the sheet around her nakedness. She ran to him, her cheeks flushed a rosy pink as she stopped before him. One small hand crept to his chest. "Come home soon," she whispered. Closing her eyes, she wordlessly offered her lips.

Morgan's free arm caught her close. His mouth came down on hers. From that moment, the kiss raged out of control, a storm of desire unleashed. Her body arched against his. There was no hiding the answering upsurge of desire in his.

His chest heaving, he raised his head. His gaze rested on the moist temptation of her lips. "I'd better go," he muttered hoarsely.

"Yes," she murmured, "you should." But she was smiling. Her lids fluttered open. The gleam in her eyes was half-teasing, half-sultry. She wound her arms around his neck.

The sheet puddled around her ankles.

Morgan's bag dropped to the floor.

A groan erupted from his chest. He swept her high in his arms and carried her to the bed. It was a long time later before he once again said his good-byes . . .

Elizabeth was humming when she finally made her way back into her own room. Hands on her hips, Annie stood in the center of the floor. Her ruddy features were utterly perplexed as she gazed at her mistress's bed, which clearly hadn't been slept in.

Behind her, Elizabeth cleared her throat. Annie whirled around. Her eyes grew wide as the moon; they shifted from her mistress to the connecting door, which still stood ajar, and back to Elizabeth. Her shocked expression was precious. Elizabeth couldn't help it; a bubbly laugh escaped.

"Good morning to you, too, Annie."

The little maid recovered quickly. "Yes," she beamed, "it is a fine morning, isn't it, ma'am?"

The rest of the morning was lazy. Elizabeth enjoyed a leisurely soak in the bath, savoring the memories of the past few hours.

Her husband was a man who was sparing in his praise. But he had whispered of his passion, his fiery hunger for her, how exciting he found the abandon of her hips driving wild and wanton against his, how he loved the feel of her mouth and hands wandering over his aroused flesh.

Nor was he a man to declare his emotions for all and sundry to hear.

She paused, standing near her bureau. Her hand crept unknowingly to her heart, for it was there that a frail tendril of hope took root.

For the first time, she allowed herself to wonder if it was more than just mere desire that Morgan felt for her. More than just the yearning for a woman—any woman—to ease his masculine needs. As she had lain in his embrace in the sweet aftermath of love—not an hour since—there was no more need for words. His arms were possessive. Protective. But far more important, she had felt herself surrounded by a feeling of closeness—of oneness—that surpassed all else. Did she dare to think he might love her after all?

She was afraid to believe . . . just as afraid not to.

She sighed, shaking herself from her reverie. Glancing idly down, she noticed that the lid on her jewelry case was ajar. Inside, a black velvet case was open and empty. She remembered then that she'd neglected to put away her pearls last night.

They weren't on her dressing table. Her brow furrowed in concentration, she stared down at the spot where she'd thought she had dropped them. She was almost certain she'd left them there on the dressing table, but it must have been elsewhere.

Only they were nowhere to be found.

Alarm clamored in her breast. She called for Annie, and together they searched every drawer and crevice in her room, under and behind furniture, all to no avail.

When Annie left her to go about her duties, Elizabeth tried to piece together the events of last evening. After leaving the Porters', she'd come home and immediately prepared for bed. It was while she was brushing her hair that she'd noticed the strand still encircled her neck. Yes! That was when she'd removed them, just before Nathaniel . . .

Nathaniel.

"No," she said faintly. "Oh, no . . ."

An awful assumption crowded her brain. Nathaniel had come for money. She didn't want to believe it, yet what choice did she have? Nathaniel had remained in her room while she was in Morgan's study. *Nathaniel*, she thought. *Oh, Nathaniel, how could you do this?*

Ten minutes later, she was sitting stiffly inside the carriage, her lips pressed firmly together. She hoped she was wrong, that Nathaniel hadn't stolen her pearls; not so much for her sake—or even because they'd been a gift from Morgan—but for his.

She alighted from the carriage almost as soon as it rolled to a stop before the shabby redbrick building. Willis hadn't even stepped down from the driver's box. Intent on her purpose, she gave only a cursory glance at a tall, thin man wearing a brown derby who had just emerged from the alleyway behind the building.

She waved Willis back to the seat. "Please wait here," she instructed crisply. "I shan't be long."

Her posture square and upright, she marched down the walkway. Her indignant anger kindled with every step that carried her closer to Nathaniel's door. She rapped the brass knocker sharply against the wood.

Nathaniel didn't come to the door.

Under normal circumstances, Elizabeth would have left, assuming that he wasn't at home. Instead she knocked harder with her closed fist. If he was sleeping off the effects of last evening's indulgence, perhaps he hadn't heard. If so, she was determined to wake him. This was no casual affair to be swept aside.

Still no answer. Elizabeth persisted. From the carriage, Willis gazed at her, then tipped his hat back. "Would you like me to help, ma'am?"

"No, thank you, Willis."

She turned back to the door. In sheer frustration, she wrapped white-gloved fingers around the door handle, intending to jiggle it soundly.

It turned easily.

So. He was home after all, the wretch! Elizabeth pushed the door wide and stepped inside. "Nathaniel!" she called. "Nathaniel, I know you're here, so you may as well come out."

Empty silence greeted her.

But no—there was a faint sound from the rear of the house. Too angry to be afraid, Elizabeth charged forward to the drawing room.

She stood in the doorway, the tilt of her head conveying her disapproval. The curtains were still tightly drawn. The room was dim. It took a moment for her eyes to adjust to the gloom, but Nathaniel wasn't here. The lazy scoundrel must still be in bed, she thought stingingly. She was just about to search out his bedroom when she heard something—the faintest of sounds, almost like a low moan.

It was then she saw what she had overlooked—a long form sprawled on the floor before the fireplace. He lay facedown, his head turned away from her.

She stepped toward him. "Nathaniel!" she scolded. "Nathaniel, for heaven's sake, it's afternoon! Don't you have sense enough to—"

Abruptly she stopped. Her eyes flew wide. All at once her heart began to pound. There was a huge stain on the floor next to him.

She emitted a horrified gasp. Dear God, it was blood!

She was beside him on her knees in an instant. "Nathaniel!" she cried, struggling to turn him over.

She succeeded in rolling him to his side. As she did, he moaned. "Oh, thank God, you're alive!" She gave a dry half sob. But his face was white as flour. The front of his shirt was bright crimson, nearly soaked through with blood.

Lurching upward, she picked up her skirts and ran for the door. She burst outside as if she were half-daft. The startled driver blinked at the sight of his mistress tearing down the walk. "Willis!" she nearly screamed. "Come quickly!"

Chapter 22

⟋⟍⟋⟍⟋

"Knife wounds," Stephen said grimly. "Two of them. Not a very pretty sight, I'm afraid."

Dread coiled heavy and tight in the middle of Elizabeth's belly. Stephen was right. It wasn't a pretty sight. There was a long, jagged wound in Nathaniel's left shoulder, yet another tearing slash just below his rib cage on the other side.

They stood in an examining room at Stephen's office. Nathaniel lay stretched out on a high, narrow table. Willis had driven at breakneck speed to get there. Panic-stricken and desperate, Elizabeth had raced into his house. She was certain his housekeeper was convinced she was a madwoman.

Stephen finished cutting away the rest of Nathaniel's shirt and dropped it into a basin at the bedside. Beneath was a tightly wadded swath of Elizabeth's petticoat. She'd used it to try to stanch the bleeding in his shoulder, the worst of the two. Using a pair of tongs, Stephen plucked it away. That, too, was tossed into the basin.

Fresh blood welled bright and crimson. She winced at the sight. Swearing under his breath, Stephen swabbed it away. "They're both deep," he muttered, "especially this one. I'll have to close them both or he'll never stop bleeding."

Elizabeth's gaze was riveted on Nathaniel. He looked ghastly. His skin was almost colorless, nearly as white as the sheet beneath him. He lay pale and motionless, his breathing weak and shallow.

"He's still unconscious. Is that normal?" She battled to keep the hysteria from her voice.

Stephen was bent over his patient. "I wouldn't worry yet. Besides, it'll be easier to close these wounds if he's not awake." He straightened. "Are you up to giving me a hand? Otherwise I'll call Mrs. Hale." Mrs. Hale was the housekeeper and also served as part-time nurse.

Elizabeth swallowed bravely. "I'll stay."

After scrubbing her hands, she stepped up to the table, steeling herself for what would come next. With steady hands and unfaltering gaze, she held a small tray of instruments and bandages, watching as Stephen worked. The point of the needle punctured Nathaniel's skin again and again, dipping and pulling.

At last the wounds were closed, jagged edges pulled together. By the time the last stitch had been secured, Elizabeth was feeling quite proud of herself. Stephen proceeded to bandage both gashes with snowy white gauze. Oddly enough, it wasn't until Nathaniel's torn, mangled flesh was hidden from sight that reality finally hit. Her stomach began to churn.

"There. It's done. Fine job, Elizabeth." Stephen

turned to find his makeshift assistant looking decidedly peaked. "Are you all right?"

Her smile was as shaky as her legs suddenly felt. "I'm afraid I'm feeling a bit strange." She swayed. Stephen chuckled and quickly set aside the tray in her hands, then pushed a chair behind her knees.

"Sit," he ordered. "Now breathe deeply. Deep and easy. Yes, that's the way."

After several minutes, the dizziness passed. Elizabeth raised her head. "Feeling better?" he asked.

She nodded.

"Good." Stephen reached for her wrist. "Your color's coming back." His fingers were on her pulse.

"Stephen, really, I'm fine," she protested.

He frowned at her good-naturedly. "I'm the doctor here, Elizabeth."

"But I feel silly, having you look after me while poor Nathaniel..." Her voice trailed away. Her gaze cut back to Nathaniel. Her eyes darkened. "Will he be all right?"

Stephen dropped her wrist, but gave her shoulder a reassuring squeeze. "I think he'll be fine. The only question now is whether we should move him to a hospital."

Elizabeth bit her lip. "Is it really necessary? I just hate the thought of leaving him all alone in a hospital."

"He won't be able to do much for himself these first few days. Rest and quiet is what he needs."

Elizabeth's mind was off and running. "Can he be moved?"

"Yes. Very carefully, of course."

"Then what if he comes home with me? There's an entire household to help look after him."

"I have no problem with that. I can look in on him there just as well as the hospital." An odd expression flitted across his face. She sensed he wanted to say more.

"What, Stephen? What is it?"

He hesitated. "I was just wondering what Morgan will have to say about all this."

"Morgan is in New York for several days. We can hardly wait until he returns to make a decision about Nathaniel's care. Besides, he can hardly object to his own brother recuperating at his home. There's certainly plenty of room. As I see it, there's just one thing to be done. Nathaniel must come home with me."

She was adamant. But in truth, it was bravado, pure and simple. She didn't dare speculate on what Morgan's reaction might be. But one thing was for certain . . .

She would soon find out.

Come home soon.

Since the moment he'd departed Boston, Morgan was chafing to do exactly that.

There was no denying it. Elizabeth had startled him—and pleased him beyond measure—with the sweetness of their parting. Time and time again he had imagined having her, warm and trembling and eager, in his arms. He had ached with the urge to fire her desire as hotly as his own; that it had finally happened was beyond his wildest imaginings.

Throughout the next few days, she was never far from his mind. He fell asleep tasting the heady nectar of her kiss; he woke yearning for the very same in the morning. After such a farewell, Morgan couldn't help it. He dared to dream that she was finally—truly—within his reach.

She was all a man could want—all *he* wanted.

And the searing passion that ran hotly through his veins was more than just desire . . . much more.

But that was not the only thing on his mind.

He couldn't entirely dismiss the twinge of doubt that gnawed at him. It bothered him that Nat had kissed her—that by her own admission, she had let him.

Nat's a rogue, a bounder, reasoned a voice in his mind.

But she didn't have to let him kiss her, argued another.

And she didn't have to admit it either. She could have blamed Nat completely, and she didn't.

Certainly Amelia had never protested her innocence.

But Elizabeth was not Amelia, he conceded at last. And perhaps it was time he stopped hiding from the truth. Elizabeth possessed a warmth of spirit, an openness and giving, that Amelia had never had.

Elizabeth was right for him . . . in a way that had never happened with Amelia—a way that never *could* have happened. And with that admission came a quiet satisfaction he'd never before experienced. For the first time in all his years, Morgan realized he had a chance to be happy—happy as he'd never been.

He'd be a fool to throw it away.

So it was that there was a spring in his step, a buoyant lightness in his heart, as he arrived home. He felt like a sailor on his first visit back after months at sea.

He set down his bag on the polished floor. "Elizabeth? Simmons?" he called out. "I'm back."

His only greeting was the hollow echo of his voice in the entrance hall.

He scowled. This was hardly the welcome he'd envisioned.

Just then Simmons stepped out of the library. He hurried forward when he spotted Morgan.

"Sir! I didn't realize you were here!" Simmons reached for his bag. "Would you like me to unpack for you, sir?"

Morgan gave a preoccupied nod. "Is my wife at home, Simmons?"

"Yes, indeed, sir. She's tending Master Nathaniel."

One foot already poised on the stairs, Morgan stopped abruptly. His gaze swiveled back to the old man. "I beg your pardon?"

Simmons gestured toward the ceiling, unaware of his master's glower. "Upstairs in the north guest room, sir. We've had quite a bit of excitement while you were gone, with your brother being injured and all. But thank heaven he's doing much better now."

Nathaniel had been injured? The plane of his jaw clamped shut. If this was another one of his tricks, by God, he'd have his hide!

He took the stairs two at a time.

Sure enough, Elizabeth was in the guest room.

In one sweeping glance he took in the scene. Elizabeth sat on the edge of the bed, partially eclipsing his view of a bare-chested Nathaniel. But Morgan could see quite clearly the tender press of slender fingers resting on his brother's brow.

"What the *hell* is going on here?"

Elizabeth was up and on her feet in a flash, striding toward him. Her small mouth pursed tight in disapproval, she tried to push him into the hall.

Morgan stood rooted to the spot. "Well?" he demanded.

"Keep your voice down! He's finally sleeping, and I don't want you to wake him!" She spoke in a whisper, yet her admonishment was utterly fierce.

Morgan's gaze slipped back to Nathaniel. For the first time he noticed the bandages crossing his shoulder. "What happened?" he asked tersely.

"He was knifed. In the shoulder and side. We don't know who attacked him, or why. The police have been notified, but they say unless Nathaniel saw the attacker, he'll likely never be found."

"When was this?"

"The day you left for New York."

Morgan's eyes narrowed. "Where did it happen?"

She shook her head. "I don't know for certain. But he was at home when I found him."

"*You* found him?"

Her gaze flitted away. Too late she'd realized her mistake, he noted furiously. "Yes," she admitted.

Morgan's voice was almost deadly quiet. "What were you doing there, Elizabeth?"

She linked her fingers together before her, bowed her head low, and said nothing.

The lid ripped off of his temper. "A spate of conscience, Elizabeth? I can certainly see why you'd be ashamed."

That brought her head up. Defiance blazed in her eyes. "I'm not ashamed!" she shot back. "I've done nothing wrong. Not that you seem to care, but I probably saved your brother's life!"

His lip curled. "How commendable. In the course of being unfaithful to your husband, you save your lover's life."

"Oh, for heaven's sake! Nathaniel isn't my lover! And I wasn't being unfaithful!"

"Then what *were* you doing there?"

A little of the fire went out of her. "I can't tell you. Not yet anyway. If you'll just be patient—"

"It seems to me I've been more than patient. And you don't fool me, Elizabeth. It's not that you can't tell me. It's that you *won't*."

"That's right," she stated coldly. "I *won't*. Because your accusations are utterly ridiculous. So if you'll excuse me, I need to get back to Nathaniel." Pointedly she turned her back on him.

Morgan's tone was blistering. "Tell me, Elizabeth," he called out. "If it were me instead of Nathaniel lying there, where would you be? Out digging my grave?"

In his study Morgan grabbed a bottle of brandy. He knew he shouldn't; yet once again he couldn't stop himself from downing the first glass. Or the next.

His emotions were a seething tangle. He was furious that she'd had Nathaniel brought here, under his very roof. But of course, she would want him near . . .

Deep in his heart, he was appalled at his anger. A part of him recognized that she'd had no choice. Yet he couldn't seem to conquer the blind, irrational fury that churned inside him like a raging, boiling sea.

He'd known from the start that she cared nothing for him. She'd married him because she had no other choice. Yet still his outrage boiled inside him. Why must he forever put his own feelings aside? Why must Nat forever come before him?

A stark, wrenching pain seemed to clamp around his heart and squeeze. Always his mother had thought of Nat first. Always . . .

And now it was Elizabeth's turn.

A brooding mask descended over his features. Christ, he was in love with her—and he'd actually begun to think that she loved him!

His mouth twisted. *Love*, he thought scathingly. The thrust of a blade. The turn of a knife. That was woman's love . . .

He'd not be imprisoned so again.

How long he sat there, he didn't know. His hand dangled over the arm of the chair. In it was an empty crystal glass. He was only half-aware of the front door opening and closing. There was the distant murmur of voices, followed by firm footsteps.

He didn't turn when the door behind him creaked some time later.

His voice rang out harshly. "I don't want to

be disturbed, Simmons. I thought that was understood."

"Simmons may have understood," said a dry
male voice. "But I certainly don't."

It was Stephen. Morgan swung around to face
his friend, who bore a look of stern disapproval.
Nor did the other man waste any time venting
his thoughts.

"I must say, you've outdone yourself this time,
Morgan."

Morgan's lips thinned. "Stay out of this, Stephen."

"Not this time. I stopped by to see Nathaniel.
Elizabeth was crying when I came in. It takes no
great power of deduction to figure out why."

Morgan regarded him in stony silence.

Stephen was calmly determined. "If you don't
want to talk about Elizabeth, fine. Let's talk
about you. You arrived back from New York this
afternoon?"

"Yes."

"What was your reaction when you learned
what happened?"

Morgan glared. "You're the great intellect
here. *You* figure it out."

Stephen studied him a moment. "You were angry. That much is clear. My God, man, he's your
brother. You should be glad she found him when
she did."

Morgan practically hurtled himself from his
chair. He prowled restlessly around the room,
like a caged animal.

"My point exactly," he said tightly. "She
found him, Stephen. My wife found him. The instant I was gone, my wife hurried over to see my

brother. Did you even bother to ask yourself why?"

"And did it ever occur to you the reason might be totally innocuous?"

Morgan stopped short. He whirled to face his friend. "How could it be innocuous?" he demanded. "You forget, she came here intending to marry him!"

"But she didn't, did she? Morgan, she merely has a soft heart—"

"And eyes for my brother! My God, Stephen, don't you see how I feel? It's happening all over again!"

"I don't think so, Morgan. I think she sees him as the man he really is. She doesn't condemn him, or judge him."

Morgan didn't argue, though his stormy features were a good sign he wanted to. His mind turned to his brother. "He'll be all right, won't he?"

His gruffness didn't mask his underlying concern. Stephen hesitated. "It's odd," he ventured slowly. "But I have the feeling whoever stabbed Nathaniel didn't intend to kill him. This may sound crazy, but maybe it was meant as some kind of warning."

"It doesn't sound crazy at all, knowing Nathaniel." It could have been anything, Morgan reasoned. Gambling. Cheating at cards. Dallying with another man's woman.

His eyes darkened. Broodingly he said aloud, "She's a fool if she thinks he'll ever change."

Stephen smiled faintly. He clapped his hand on Morgan's shoulder. There was a fool in this house, all right. But it definitely wasn't Elizabeth . . .

Chapter 23

Nathaniel's recovery was coming along quite nicely. No one was more relieved than Elizabeth. But she was greatly saddened by the state of affairs between the two brothers. She'd secretly hoped this incident might lead to a reconciliation of sorts. But Morgan remained as stubborn and unyielding as ever. As far as she knew, not once did he set foot in Nathaniel's room to see how he fared.

It was Stephen who told her that Morgan inquired daily as to his brother's condition, a fact that Elizabeth pondered long and hard.

While she had once been so very certain Morgan hated Nathaniel, she was no longer convinced. If Morgan didn't give a fig about his brother, why would he ask after him?

He still cared about Nathaniel. The bond between brothers had perhaps been blunted, but not broken. More and more she came to believe that. Yet why couldn't Morgan show it? What had happened that so cleanly divided the two? What could possibly be so terrible that they were forever at each other's throats?

Nathaniel was weak, not wicked. He wasn't as strong as Morgan. So why couldn't Morgan be more accepting of him, more tolerant?

Several days passed before Nathaniel was up to talking at length. Elizabeth had a number of questions for her brother-in-law.

She was determined to get answers.

He'd just finished his lunch one afternoon when she entered his room. A mound of pillows behind him, Nathaniel was sitting up in bed. A chestnut brow cocked high when Elizabeth pulled a chair up to his bedside.

"My, my," he said, a faint teasing light in his eyes, "this looks serious."

Elizabeth didn't return his smile. "Yes, I would say two knife wounds are quite serious. In fact, I'd say the subject demands further scrutiny."

He sighed. "I already told the police, Elizabeth, when they stopped by yesterday to talk to me." He shrugged his shoulders. "I didn't see whoever it was that stabbed me," he went on. "I was jumped from behind."

"Yes, so I heard. But I'm far more interested in what you *didn't* tell them."

Nathaniel was clearly taken aback by her conviction. "What makes you say that?"

"Nathaniel, I am not a featherbrain. You came here one night asking for money. You admitted you were in trouble. The next day you were stabbed. It's no coincidence, so please don't try to convince me that it was."

There was every indication he intended to do exactly that. A look of confusion and hurt flashed across his face—oh, but he was quite the actor, she would grant him that! Then all at once his shoulders slumped. "I suppose I owe you an explanation," he murmured.

Her eyes were snapping. "You owe me the truth."

He shoved his fingers through his hair, a gesture of frustration. "Hell," he muttered. "I don't even know where to start."

The pinched tightness of Elizabeth's mouth foretold a warning. He'd not get off so easily!

He sighed. "Remember when I left London so abruptly?"

"How could I forget? You said it was business. Obviously it wasn't."

"No," he admitted. "I'd been incredibly lucky at the gaming tables the first weeks I was in London. Elizabeth, I—I couldn't lose! It was like everything I touched turned to gold, and I—I wanted more."

Her gaze was steady on his face. "Go on."

He took a deep breath. "I learned about a man who would loan money—Viscount Phillip Hadley. So I borrowed twenty thousand pounds, certain that I could turn it into a fortune."

"You got greedy," she said softly.

Nathaniel didn't deny it. Instead he shook his head. "But my luck changed. I lost it, Elizabeth. I lost every last pound."

Elizabeth was aghast. "All of it?"

"One roll of the dice and it was gone—gone!" He made a disgusted sound low in his throat. "So I borrowed more."

"From Viscount Hadley?"

"Yes. I'd heard rumors that he could be . . . nasty, shall we say. But it was the only way I could think of to try to repay him."

"But you lost again, didn't you?"

He nodded. "Hadley demanded I repay him. But I didn't have it, Elizabeth. One night he sent several thugs after me. They roughed me up and said if I didn't repay the loan within a week, I'd be sorry." His tone had turned grim. "I was desperate, Elizabeth. There was no way I could repay him."

Elizabeth had a very good idea what happened next. "That's when you left, isn't it?"

"I-I didn't know what else to do. I didn't deliberately try to cheat him, I just wanted to save my own skin! I didn't think he'd follow me all the way across the Atlantic, but I needed to make sure. I figured they'd expect me to return to Boston."

"But instead you went to New York."

"Yes. I waited until I figured it was safe, then came home to Boston. But the other night someone followed me."

A sick feeling knotted in Elizabeth's stomach. "One of Hadley's men?"

Nathaniel had gone a trifle pale. "He held a knife to my throat and said he'd give me three days to deliver the money at a place called the Crow's Nest."

Elizabeth inhaled sharply. "That's when you came here, isn't it? You said you needed whatever money you could get your hands on."

"Yes. I told him I'd have the rest soon. But I guess it wasn't enough to satisfy him. Later that night when I arrived home he was waiting for me. He said he wanted to give me a taste of what would happen if I didn't pay up in full the next time."

"Dear God," she said numbly. "So that's when he stabbed you." She paused, then snapped her fingers. "Wait! The day I found you, a man walked out from the alleyway. He was tall and thin and wore a brown derby—"

"That's him. That's the one."

Elizabeth's mind was awhirl with all he'd told her. "Nathaniel," she said quietly. "Is that why you took my pearls?"

He nodded. His gaze slipped away. "I was hoping you wouldn't miss them for a while," he admitted.

"Why? So I would think I'd lost them? Or misplaced them?"

His silence was admission enough.

"I'm sorry," he said after a moment. "But Hadley's man has them now." He fell silent. "Does Morgan know I took them?" he asked suddenly.

"No. But you have to tell him about Hadley, Nathaniel."

"No! Promise me you won't tell him, Elizabeth. I can handle this on my own!"

"Nathaniel, don't be foolish! You need his help. If you won't tell him, then I will."

"No! And I don't want the police involved either."

"Nathaniel, don't be absurd. This is your life we're talking about—"

"Exactly," he broke in sharply. "It's *my* life. I'm responsible for this mess, Elizabeth. It's up to me to fix it. I don't need Morgan looking over my shoulder."

Elizabeth gazed across at him, her indecision

reflected in the troubled depths of clear green eyes.

Nathaniel's gaze softened. "You don't understand, do you?"

"No, I-I do. Or at least I think I do." She gave a tiny shake of her head. "But I'm afraid for you, Nathaniel."

"Don't be. I've made my own choices for a while now"—his smile was wholly self-derisive—"usually the wrong ones. But Morgan's always been back in the shadows, looking over my shoulder. Perhaps it's my own fault."

He seemed to be speaking more to himself than to her. "You were right when you said I shouldn't have to look to him to keep me. But I always have. I've looked to him for money when I needed it. To bail me out of trouble. It was . . . easiest, I suppose. God knows I've never been the hardworking sort. I left that to Morgan. Ah, yes, he's the industrious one. I'm the carefree one. Carefree and—careless." He gave a rueful glance at his bandaged shoulder.

Once again his eyes sought hers. "Elizabeth, please don't tell him. I need to handle this on my own." He shrugged. "Oh, no doubt I'll botch this, too. Lord knows I've failed at enough other things."

"Don't talk like that," she scolded gently. "You're not a failure."

He shook his head. "Oh, but I am." His smile was purely devilish—purely Nathaniel. "I'm a rogue. A scoundrel. The worst kind of reprobate."

"You're not."

"I am."

"Then—then you can change. I'll help you, Nathaniel."

"Such a tender soul," he mocked. "No self-respecting woman would have me, Elizabeth. Why, half the mothers in Boston hide their daughters from me." He gave an exaggerated sigh. "Ah, well, it's probably a good thing we didn't marry. You'd never have been able to reform me, and I'd have ended up disappointing you. In fact, I'd probably have broken your heart."

Though she smiled at his teasing, there was a painful stab in the region of her heart. Morgan's grim-faced visage flashed in her mind's eye. When she'd first arrived in Boston, she'd been hurt by Nathaniel's deception; she couldn't deny it. But that hurt was but a pinprick compared to the hurt Morgan could deal her. He possessed the power to wound her far more than Nathaniel. With but a word—a look—he could leave her feeling utterly devastated.

A shadow seemed to slip over her. It was strange, she reflected, all at once feeling lonely and pensive. Somehow she had always imagined that when she fell in love, it would be a joyous, blissful state, a world of happy contentment. And yes, she'd discovered love to be the most powerful stirring imaginable of heart and body and spirit . . .

But never—*never*—had she dreamed that love could be such deep, rending agony.

Fool, goaded a voice inside. The hurt is not in loving . . .

It was loving . . . and not being loved in return.

"Now," Nathaniel said, jarring her back to reality. "Will you promise you'll do as I ask and not say a word to Morgan?" Light as his tone was, his gaze was pleading.

Slowly, reluctantly, she nodded. "I promise," she allowed. And even as she spoke the words, she prayed it would be a promise she could keep.

"Good. And now that I've poured out my very soul, I have a question for you," he said.

"Yes?" Elizabeth tipped her head to the side and waited.

There was a heartbeat of quiet. He gazed at her, his regard deep and penetrating. "Are you happy?" he asked softly.

A tiny jolt went through her. The question was something she hadn't expected.

Something she wasn't prepared to answer.

Her smile wavered. It was all she could do to speak. "Nathaniel, ask me anything, but please don't ask me that."

His features were suddenly stormy. "Damn his hide!" he swore. "It's Morgan, isn't it? That bastard. He's made you completely miserable—"

"No. No! It's not what you think, Nathaniel. It's not that at all! It's just that . . ." She stopped, unable to go on. She bowed her head low so he wouldn't see the tears that sprang hot and stinging to her eyes.

Yet somehow he knew. "Dear God," she heard him say, "don't tell me you love him."

A single, scalding tear slid down her cheek.

"My God, you do!"

She took a deep, ragged breath. "Nathaniel, I-I'm sorry. I don't mean to hurt you."

He reached over and gripped both her hands. "Don't be sorry," he said intently. "Elizabeth, you were the best thing that ever came into my life. I was simply too foolish to realize it. So if there are regrets, let them be mine."

She raised her head and gave him a watery smile. "Nathaniel—"

"Forgive me for intruding on such a cozy scene," injected a voice from the doorway, "but I'd like to speak to my brother alone."

Elizabeth did the very thing she probably shouldn't have—she snatched back her hands guiltily and stood upright. Her heart plummeted. Oh, damn—damn! Why must this always happen?

She was stunned when he chose to overlook it.

"Do you mind, Elizabeth? I'd like to speak to my brother."

He was icily polite. "Of course." Flustered, Elizabeth grabbed her skirts and brushed by him. She didn't dare look at his face for fear of what she might see.

Nathaniel leaned back against the pillows, wincing a little as he crossed his arms over his bare chest. A brittle smile rimmed his mouth. "Come to inquire as to my health, Morgan?"

Morgan folded his hands behind his back. "Actually I came to deliver some good news. Stephen won't be by until tomorrow morning, but he's quite pleased with your recovery. He said you should be up and about by tomorrow. After that he sees no reason why you can't resume your normal activities."

Nathaniel gave a shout of laughter. "You didn't come as the merry messenger. You came to make certain I don't stay a minute longer."

"Not at all, Nathaniel. Of course, you may stay until you're well."

"Oh, come now, Morgan." Nathaniel openly jeered. "I know I'm not welcome here. If it weren't for Elizabeth, I wouldn't even be here."

Morgan neither agreed nor disagreed. "There's one other matter, Nathaniel." Morgan's gaze was as frigid as his tone. "You have a tendency to forget Elizabeth is my wife. I want your assurance it won't happen again."

Nathaniel's chin thrust out. "I haven't forgotten."

A dark brow arched. "No? And what about the night you kissed her?"

Nathaniel's eyes flickered. There was a long, drawn-out pause. "She's forgiven me for that," he said finally. "Besides, I was drunk."

"That excuse becomes rather old after a while."

Nathaniel's mouth twisted. "You can't tell me how to live my life any longer, Morgan."

"No. But if you'd ever listened to me, you wouldn't have made such a mess of it."

Nathaniel was suddenly as angry as Morgan was calm. "You know, you haven't changed a bit. You're still as rigid and inflexible as ever. If I don't do things your way, then my way is always the *wrong* way. Tell me, Morgan. Are you like this with Elizabeth, too?" He gave no time to answer, but charged on. "Do you even *care* that you make her life miserable?"

Morgan went utterly still. "Is that what she said?"

"She doesn't have to!" Nathaniel's voice was

fired as hotly as his glare. "All I have to do is look at her to know it!"

Morgan's entire body was taut with the effort it took to control his fury. His burning gaze settled on his brother.

The breath he drew was deep and slow, his tone deadly quiet. "A word of warning, brother. I won't let you ruin this marriage."

"No, I suppose you won't," Nathaniel flung at him scathingly. "You can do that quite well yourself, can't you?"

Chapter 24

∽◯◯∼

At midmorning the next day, Elizabeth hurried from her room, for it was late. Faith! but she didn't know what had come over her these last few days. No matter how long or how late she slept, she woke as exhausted as when she'd retired. Yesterday she'd taken a brief nap, yet still it made no difference.

Errant shafts of sunlight streamed through the stained glass windows that arched high above the landing of the stairs. Preoccupied though she was, Elizabeth caught her breath in wondrous amazement at the dazzling display. The entire entrance hall was filled with soft, translucent colors of pink and rose, gold and yellow; it was like being cast in the midst of a rainbow.

Halfway down, she spied Morgan talking to Simmons. The old man nodded and turned, but not before he'd spotted the lady of the house. A smile of greeting softened the many fine lines of his face. He exchanged a few more words with Morgan and then was gone.

Morgan had glanced up as well. He was waiting as she came down.

Her smile was tentative. "Good morning," she greeted.

There was no answering smile in return. He merely gave a slight nod. Though she'd been kept busy seeing to Nathaniel these past days, he was doing much better—in fact, he would be going home tomorrow morning.

In all honesty, she hoped Nathaniel's departure would put to rest the tension in the household that had arisen since his arrival. It was Stephen who gently pointed out that perhaps Morgan felt neglected because of all the time she spent with Nathaniel. Somehow Elizabeth had never considered such a thing, yet now that she did, it made perfect sense.

If anything, the strain had made her long to recapture the tender closeness she and Morgan had shared at the cottage. They might never agree about Nathaniel—indeed they probably would *not*. In the hope that it would make the days a little easier for both of them, Elizabeth had resolved to put their differences about Nathaniel aside and start each day anew, with no anger, no strain, between them.

As she reminded herself of this, she summoned a bright smile and slipped her hand into the crook of his elbow. "Would you have breakfast with me?"

"I can't. I was due at the shipyards an hour ago."

Elizabeth struggled not to pull her hand back. He'd glanced at it as if her touch offended him. "Oh," she murmured. "Perhaps dinner then?"

"Actually I've asked Wilson Reed, Justin Powell, and James Brubaker over for dinner. We have just a few loose ends to discuss regarding our agreement. You may find yourself bored, but perhaps it's just as well if you attend."

Elizabeth bit her lip—his banker and attorney, and James Brubaker. She winced, recalling the last time these three had come for dinner. Morgan had been so jealous—and she had been shrewish. He'd questioned her morals, and she had been provoked into confronting him about the woman who had been his mistress.

Still, this was business. And she reminded herself that she and Morgan hadn't dined together since Nathaniel's stabbing; with the wound in his shoulder Nathaniel had a bit of difficulty with meals, so she had tried to be present at mealtime. But now Stephen's observation echoed in her mind. *Perhaps Morgan feels neglected.* If she refused, would Morgan believe she favored Nathaniel over him?

That was the last thing she wanted.

She met his eyes. "You don't mind?"

He shrugged. "It makes no difference to me."

It was hardly a gracious invitation. She tried hard not to feel stung. "I'll be ready then," she murmured.

As the day wore on, she faced the evening with burgeoning hope. Perhaps dinner together would break some of the ice between them. When the guests were gone, they might linger downstairs for a while. And once they were alone, a measure of harmony might be restored. She could ask him to escort her to her room. If the evening proceeded as she hoped, she might wordlessly tug him inside her room and let the night lead where it would.

She wanted that, she realized wistfully. She wanted that quite badly. Oh, it wasn't just the pleasure to be had in his lovemaking. She missed the silent intimacy that followed. She missed being held tight against his body. She missed waking up in the haven of his arms.

He hadn't touched her—even the most casual brush of the hands!—since their terrible row over Nathaniel. Had he truly locked her out of his heart and mind? No. *No!* She couldn't give in to despair. That would change, she vowed determinedly. That would change *tonight*.

She dressed very carefully that evening. The deep rose chiffon gown she wore brought out the creamy ivory of her arms and shoulders. Annie knotted her hair atop her crown, leaving bare the fragile sweep of her nape.

She had just finished dabbing perfume at the base of her neck when a knock sounded on the connecting door. "Come in," she called, hoping she didn't sound overly eager.

Morgan strode in, as devastatingly handsome as ever. The scent of soap and bay rum filled the air; his hair shone damp and gleaming.

Elizabeth rose from her seat at the dressing table. Her heart bounded when his gaze traveled the length of her and back to her face.

"You look breathtaking, as usual."

Elizabeth flushed with pleasure.

"But something's missing." He frowned. "You should be wearing your pearls with that gown."

Her smile froze.

"I'll wait if you like."

Elizabeth's hand rested self-consciously on her bare throat. She was at a complete loss for words, for indeed, what could she say? *I'm sorry, Morgan, but Nathaniel stole the pearls you gave me to wear on our wedding day.*

She cringed inside. Morgan would never understand. He would never *forgive* such a transgression.

Her face grew uncomfortably warm. Little did she realize her expressive features were a mirror to her soul.

He nodded at the tall lacquered jewelry case atop her bureau. "I'll put them on if you'll get them." Mild as his tone was, all at once it was less than pleasant.

She stared at him, her eyes huge and stricken.

"Elizabeth!"

Her name was like thunder in the night. She nearly jumped out of her skin.

She swallowed. "I c-can't," she stammered.

His scrutiny sharpened. "Why not? Aren't they in your jewelry case?"

"No," she whispered. She couldn't tear her gaze from his face. His expression was terrible to behold. He knew, she thought sickly. Somehow he knew . . .

His mouth was ominously thin. "You wore them just last week. Where are they now?"

"I don't know!" That, at least, was the truth.

"Are you telling me that you lost them?"

"Yes. Yes!" She seized on the lie desperately. Now all she had to do was convince him . . .

"You're lying," he stated baldly. "I know a lie when I hear one. God knows I've had plenty of experience."

Elizabeth was nearly in tears. "All right," she cried. "Remember the night Nathaniel came to me for money? I-I didn't know what else to do, so I—I gave him my pearls."

Two white, angry lines had appeared beside his mouth. "You said you gave him the cash in the household account."

"I-I did."

His voice was dangerously low. "You gave him money *and* your pearls?"

Her gaze clung to his. She nodded.

"You should have come to me, Elizabeth. If he needed money, *you should have come to me.*"

"When the two of you are constantly at each other's throats? I was trying to avert a calamity, not start one!"

Never had she seen him so angry. "So you always say," he said tautly. "So you always say. But at least now I know exactly where I stand with you." He glanced at the clock atop her dresser. "We'd better hurry," he said coldly. "We have guests waiting."

She knew then it was an evening destined for disaster.

How she made it through dinner, she never knew. Her smile was forced; she felt as if her face might crack into a thousand pieces at any time. Justin's wife had been ill with a summer cold; Elizabeth inquired politely as to her health. She chatted with Wilson Reed between courses.

And all the while, Morgan looked right through her, as if she weren't there.

Elizabeth felt like weeping. He sat at the end of the table, nodding and listening as James Brubaker talked, his attention confined solely to

James—and business matters. Her gaze was unwillingly drawn to him again and again. There was a painful tightness in her chest. It had been like this since the night Nathaniel had been stabbed. There was never a smile for her. Never a look or a touch.

"We're going to have brandy in the library, Elizabeth." With a start she heard her name. "I'm sure you'd much rather retire for the night."

At last he looked at her. He awaited her response, dark brows lifted in cool expectation. He might have been addressing a wooden stick, for all the interest he showed. Elizabeth bit back foolish tears. This was the first he had even acknowledged her presence at the table, and he wanted her to leave!

She dropped her napkin on her plate. "Yes, of course. I-I'll leave you gentlemen to your brandy then." Her voice sounded nothing at all like her own. She was only half-aware of Morgan glancing at her sharply.

Hot tears burned just beneath the surface. Her heart began to bleed. It was all she could do not to burst out sobbing. She rose hurriedly, her only thought being that she had to escape before she embarrassed them both. Quickly she turned and headed toward the door.

But something was wrong. Her heart was pounding heavily. A gray haze swirled all around. She stopped short, for the ground seemed to be sliding away from beneath her feet. The world around her was reeling, a twisting kaleidoscope of sound and color. Dimly she heard someone shout her name. It was Morgan, she decided fuzzily, and he was angry again. Was there nothing she did that pleased him . . . ?

The next thing she knew there were a number of faces peering down at her. She blinked, struggling to focus. She tried to move, but her limbs were trapped against her body . . . No. No, it was only Morgan, cradling her against his chest. His arms were so strong, so comforting. She reached toward his face, wanting to trace the sculpted beauty of his profile.

But he was staring down at her with stern features, and it was suddenly too much. Her hand fell limply to her breast. She gave a dry, heartbreaking sob and turned her face aside. Dimly she felt herself being borne upward in a surge of power.

"Send someone for Stephen!" a voice shouted.

She must have lost consciousness again. When she next awoke, she was in her bedroom, the softness of the mattress at her back. A lamp glowed dimly in the corner. Morgan sat beside her on the bed. One of her hands lay snugly swallowed between both of his.

His eyes scoured her face. "How do you feel?"

She put a hand to her brow and considered. "Fine," she murmured. She started to rise.

"No." A firm hand on her shoulder restrained her. "You're not going anywhere until Stephen's had a look at you. He's on his way now."

"Morgan, truly," she protested, "I just felt rather odd for a moment. There's no need for all this fuss."

"We'll let Stephen be the judge of that."

"But shouldn't you be with your guests—"

"Simmons is seeing them off."

She leaned back against the pillows, feeling

pleasurably warm inside. She liked knowing he'd chosen to remain with her instead. Indeed, she was highly disappointed that Stephen chose to appear as soon as he did.

He strode inside, a small black bag in hand. He halted and arched a brow. "My, my," he said crisply. "This is becoming a habit, isn't it?"

"A habit!" Morgan's gaze lingered pointedly on his wife.

"She had a dizzy spell last week," Stephen explained. "But I think you're right. This warrants a closer look."

With Morgan's assistance, Elizabeth sat up slowly. Stephen came around and sat beside her. He listened to her heart and gently probed her scalp for any hidden bumps. Morgan looked on from the foot of the bed, his gaze piercingly intent.

Stephen cleared his throat and glanced at his friend. "I'd like to examine her a little further, Morgan. But I think it might prove easier for Elizabeth if we had a bit more privacy."

Morgan grimaced. "I'll wait in the hall," he said.

Once they were alone, Stephen proceeded with the examination, occasionally asking questions. Elizabeth's face was scarlet by the time he'd finished. She clamped her skirts to the bed as soon as he leaned back. He gave her a hand and she quickly swung her legs to the floor.

"It's just as you said, isn't it? Just a dizzy spell?"

"Yes. But there's a reason for those spells, Elizabeth."

Her eyes went wide with horror.

He chuckled. "You needn't worry. You haven't been stricken with a dreary, deadly disease."

She let out an audible breath. "What then?"

He paused. "You're going to have a baby," he said softly. "I'd say in—oh, a little more than seven months or so."

A baby. So it was true. *A baby*, she thought again, with an awestruck mixture of wonder and fear.

Stephen smiled and snapped his bag shut. "I'll leave it to you to break the news to Morgan."

Morgan. Elizabeth's pulse raced frantically. Her mind leaped forward. Her nails dug into her palms, but she didn't feel the discomfort. What would his reaction be? Would he be surprised? Of course he would! Ah, but would he be pleased? Having a child was something they'd never discussed. She was almost afraid to wonder, to hope! Of course he would be pleased. Every man wanted a child, didn't he? A son to carry on his name. A daughter to bring him joy.

Morgan strode in, clearly vexed. He resumed his seat on the edge of the bed and reached for her hand. "Are you all right? Stephen wouldn't tell me a damn thing!" he said irritably. "All he would tell me was that it would be better if it came from you."

She curled her fingers through the lean hardness of his. Moistening her lips, she lifted her face. Hope shone brightly in her heart and the vivid green of her eyes. "Morgan," she said breathlessly, "I . . . *we* . . . we're going to have a baby, Morgan."

Everything changed between one heartbeat

and the next. There was a suffocating silence. One moment he was the tender, considerate man she knew he could be, the next he was a harsh, cold stranger.

His gaze slid down to the flatness of her belly. It lingered there as if in horror—as if in accusation. He dropped her hand—as if she were a leper!

In that moment, something shriveled up and died inside her.

Without a word he spun around and walked through the connecting door into his room. A bag was hauled out from his closet and pitched onto the bed.

Elizabeth followed behind him, numb with hurt. She stood on the threshold, wavering and vulnerable. Her eyes skipped between the bag and his face. She was afraid to speak. "Where are you going?"

His features were a rigid mask. "To the cottage."

His flat statement was like a blow. She recalled vividly what Stephen had told her not so long ago. *That cottage is his hideaway from the world.* Raw pain throbbed in her breast, for now it would be his haven from *her*.

Her eyes stung painfully. She tried to arm herself against his coldness and failed miserably. "What's wrong? We're going to have a baby, Morgan! I-I hoped you would be happy, as happy as I am!"

His silence was like a slap in the face.

Her lips trembled. "May I go with you?" she whispered.

"No!" His denial was like the lash of a whip.

Every breath burned like fire with the effort it took not to cry. "Morgan," she pleaded. "You sound as if you blame me . . . What have I done that's so wrong? I-I don't know what's happening—what you're thinking!"

He tossed a shirt into the bag. "You don't want to know."

"Yes, I do! Morgan, please tell me!"

He whirled on her, and now there was no escaping the determined glitter of his eyes. Three steps brought him before her. His fingers bit into the soft flesh of her arms, dragging her close.

"No, Elizabeth, you tell me! Which of us is the father? Nathaniel? Or me?"

"How can you even ask such a thing!" she gasped. "Why, the very idea is preposterous—"

"Is it?" Morgan's voice cut sharply across hers. "Remember the day after Nathaniel returned? You went to his house, Elizabeth, and then you lied to me about it. You said you'd gone shopping, when in fact you were *alone* with my brother! So tell me, Elizabeth." He grabbed her shoulders and shook her. "Who is the father? Nathaniel or me? Or do you even know?"

The crippling anguish that splintered through her was immense. That he could even think she'd been unfaithful was completely beyond her comprehension—beyond words.

A scalding rush of tears filled her eyes. Her throat closed. She could only shake her head over and over. Morgan made a sound of impatience. He swung away and grabbed his bag.

Then he was gone.

She collapsed to the floor, her soul in tatters. A strangled sob tore from deep in her chest, and it was just as she feared. Once she began, she cried as if her heart were broken.

And so it was.

It was Nathaniel who found her, huddled against the wall, utterly defeated, her face ravaged by tears and despair.

He dropped down on one knee before her, a hand on her shoulder. "Elizabeth! Good God! I heard you clear in my room. Has someone died?"

She raised her head, her tears nearly blinding her. Her throat was raw. "No," she croaked.

"What then? Why are you crying like this? And where the hell is Morgan?"

"He's g-gone. T-to the cottage."

"Why?"

"B-because I'm going to have a b-baby."

Nathaniel sat back, stunned.

"And d-do you know w-what? He asked me if it was y-yours!" The breath she drew was jagged and tear choked. "I married h-him, not you. I could never be unfaithful—never! But he doesn't trust me, and I-I don't understand! What have I done that could make him believe I would do such a thing?"

Nathaniel sucked in a harsh breath. Carefully he lowered himself to the floor beside her, bracing his good shoulder against the wall next to Elizabeth's.

"It's not you," he said quietly. "It's me. *I'm* the one he doesn't trust."

"But you're his brother. Of all people, surely he would trust his brother with his wife."

Nathaniel had gone very still. "No," he said quietly. "He wouldn't. And for a very good reason." He sighed, all at once feeling the burden of guilt on his shoulders.

It was a weight he could no longer carry.

"Elizabeth," he said softly. "I think it's time you knew the truth."

She frowned, her gaze searching his face. There were deep grooves etched in his cheeks; he was incredibly solemn. Nathaniel was usually so gay and lighthearted, she knew whatever admission he was about to reveal was somber indeed.

"The truth?" she echoed.

"Amelia was carrying a child when she died, Elizabeth." There was a heartbeat of silence. "*My* child."

Chapter 25

Nathaniel had been Amelia's lover.

Elizabeth berated herself furiously for not guessing it herself. Too late she recognized the signs. The night she'd learned Morgan had been married . . . What was it he'd said?

Let me tell you about my dearly beloved. In all but the first year of our marriage, there was an endless parade of lovers in and out of her bed.

That wasn't the only clue. The night he'd seen Nathaniel kiss her, he'd been so angry. Half of what he'd said then had made no sense to her.

It made perfect sense now.

Kiss me, Elizabeth. We're brothers, Nathaniel and I. Brothers should share, don't you think? Even wives.

"I knew I wasn't the first," Nathaniel was saying. "I knew she'd been unfaithful to Morgan almost from the start. Everyone knew about her relationships. There were so many, I think Morgan had stopped caring long before.

"Amelia was always an outrageous flirt. If there was a man in the room, it was as if she had to have his attention—his admiration. Oh, I'd always thought she was beautiful. I don't think there was a man alive who didn't. And yes, there had always been a bit of innuendo between us, but that was just her way."

His eyes darkened. "But one summer things suddenly changed. I didn't initiate it, I swear. You see, once Amelia set her sights on a man, she could be . . . I don't know what else to call it . . . irresistible. I'm not trying to excuse what I did, Elizabeth. We both knew what we were doing, Amelia and I.

"Morgan didn't know, not at first. There was a part of me that couldn't believe I'd sunk so low. My God, I was his wife's *lover*. But I wouldn't let myself think about that. All I thought about was her. All I wanted was her. She was like—like a drug I had to have or die!"

Elizabeth listened, stunned at all he disclosed. He talked. And he talked. In some way she didn't fully understand, she sensed it was like a catharsis, a purging of the guilt he'd carried all this time.

"To this day, I don't know why I let it happen," he said. "I shouldn't have, I know. Morgan is my *brother*. For as long as I can remember, he's always been there, looking out for me. Except there's always been a part of me that's been . . ." He hesitated.

"Jealous?" Elizabeth finished softly. It wasn't hard to guess. The guilt in his expression was only too easy to interpret.

He nodded, staring where his hands were linked between his knees. "He was more a father to me than our own," he acknowledged, his voice very low. "I remember when I was young,

I wanted to be like Morgan. He was bigger. Stronger. My father had a vicious temper. If he didn't want us near, we'd get cuffed alongside the head. But Morgan wasn't afraid to stand up to him, even when he knew what was coming."

A shadow crept over Nathaniel's face. "I think I knew even then I could never be like Morgan. I used to steal things from my father. A coin here and there. Food. And he always found out; he always confronted us. Morgan knew it was me, but he took the blame. *Always*. Even though my father took a cane to his back every time. He never cried. He never made a sound, though it had to hurt like the very devil. Not even once. He didn't even cry when Mama died, though I know he loved her more than anything."

A cane to his back. Elizabeth nearly cried out. It was monstrous that anyone could be so cruel to a child. Yet she could almost see Morgan as a child, standing proud and tall and defiant.

"When he went to sea, he sent back every dime he earned. It was his money, not my father's, that paid for the clothes on my back, the food in my belly. He sent me to the best schools, did you know that? God," he said hoarsely, "I don't think I ever considered all he gave me until now!

"But by then I'd discovered I could never be like him. I could never be as *good* as he was—at anything. I wasn't smart like he was. I wasn't responsible. I'd never build a fortune the way he did. He was always the hero, always the rescuer. I remember the day he married Amelia. I envied him because he was lucky enough to marry someone so beautiful. And I knew that *I* would never be so lucky."

"You resented him," Elizabeth murmured. There was no bite in her tone, just a curious kind of sadness.

"Yes," Nathaniel admitted. "Odd, isn't it? The only thing he took on that failed was his marriage to Amelia." He shook his head. "And I was glad, Elizabeth. I was glad he'd finally failed at something. And when I fell in love with Amelia, it was as if Morgan didn't exist—as if he weren't my brother. I didn't care what he thought. I didn't care if he was angry. If he was hurt. If he hated me. If he felt like a fool. I didn't care if he even knew about the two of us. I didn't care *who* knew."

But there was more.

"Then Amelia discovered she was pregnant. I was ecstatic. I thought she'd leave Morgan, he'd divorce her, and we could get married. I *begged* her to."

Elizabeth was puzzled. "Wait. Amelia and Morgan still lived together?"

He nodded.

"Then how could you be certain the baby was yours and not Morgan's? How could she have been certain?"

"It was mine," Nathaniel stated with absolute finality. "Morgan hadn't touched her in months. He'd told me so ages before he realized we were having an affair. And Amelia used to rail on about how remote he was, how indifferent he was to her. Amelia was a woman who—who wanted to be worshiped and adored. Morgan had ceased to see her like that, and I think sometimes she hated him for it."

Elizabeth bit her lip. Perhaps Amelia's procession of lovers had been her way of punishing Morgan. This she kept to herself, however. Aloud she asked, "What happened then, Nathaniel?"

"Morgan had only recently learned about us. I remember Amelia saying how she'd enjoyed telling him—how she'd flaunted it. And when she told him she was pregnant with my child, she said she—she laughed. Can you imagine? She *laughed*. It was then I discovered how cruel she could be."

Nathaniel's hands were clamped on his upraised knees. His knuckles were white. "Amelia married Morgan for his money—the things it could buy. God knows why he ever stayed with her, but that's why she remained with him."

Elizabeth's heart twisted. How Morgan must have suffered!

Nathaniel swallowed; she heard his deep, ragged inhalation of air. "That's when I asked her to divorce Morgan and marry me. But she said ... she said she'd really only gotten involved with me to spite Morgan. But now she was bored with me, and there was someone else . . ."

Elizabeth's stomach knotted. "And what about the baby? Did she plan on claiming Morgan as the father?"

A spasm of pain flitted across his features. "No," he said in an odd voice. "A baby didn't fit into her plans, you see. She told me she was going to get rid of the baby . . . that there were ways . . . She knew a woman who'd helped her once before . . .''

Elizabeth's face had gone pale, but she laid an encouraging hand on Nathaniel's arm. "What happened then?"

She wished she hadn't asked. Dear God, but she did . . .

Nathaniel's arm was like a pillar of steel, his voice choked. "She just kept saying she didn't want me. How she'd already found someone else, another lover . . . a *better* lover. She was laughing . . . I remember thinking this time she wasn't laughing at Morgan. She was laughing at *me*. Over and over and over . . .''

Nathaniel was staring toward the shadows, his gaze wide and unblinking. An eerie chill prickled her skin as his hands came up. He clutched at thin air.

"I grabbed her. I remember shaking her. Putting my hands around her throat, just to make her stop *laughing*. I just wanted her to be quiet. And then suddenly she . . . she wasn't laughing anymore."

Elizabeth stuffed her fist against her mouth to keep from crying out.

Nathaniel had killed Amelia.

His voice was thick and unrecognizable. "I killed her, Elizabeth. I killed her, the woman I loved! I didn't mean to. God, I swear I didn't mean to!" His breath came jerkily. "I remember holding her, crying . . . Suddenly Morgan was there . . .''

Elizabeth closed her eyes. It was suddenly so very clear—why Morgan had seemed so callous when she'd asked if he'd discovered the identity of Amelia's murderer. And Stephen had said Morgan's only crime was finding Amelia's body.

But he'd found his brother as well.

Elizabeth had to struggle to speak. "No one else knows, do they? No one but you and Morgan."

He nodded. She saw that his eyes had grown suspiciously moist. "Elizabeth, that's not all. The police arrested Morgan for—for her murder."

"I know," she said quickly. "Stephen told me he was charged and held, but eventually the charge was dropped."

"You don't understand. Elizabeth, I was such a coward. I let him take the blame for me." There was raw shame etched into every word. "I killed her, and Morgan took the blame. I let him sit in jail. I would have let Morgan go to prison—for *me*. If it had come down to it, I would have let him"—Nathaniel's voice cracked—"I would have let him *die* for me."

He buried his head in his hands and wept.

Elizabeth's throat was achingly tight. She slid an arm around Nathaniel's shoulder and held him, like a mother giving sheltering comfort to a child who'd been hurt.

She wasn't afraid. She didn't judge Nathaniel. She didn't condemn him, for Nathaniel had just confirmed what she had always known to be true.

Morgan was the leader. The strong one, the rock to lean upon, the one to shoulder the burden.

But no one could be strong forever.

And no one should *have* to be.

*   *   *

North of Boston, darkness had settled over the coastline. The sky was moonless and cloudy, the monotonous swell of the ocean a dull murmur. The inside of the cottage was thick with shadows, as black as the night without.

Morgan slumped in his chair. He wasn't drunk, for he'd already discovered there was no solace in drink. He was merely incredibly weary beyond measure, though he hadn't moved a muscle in hours.

He'd arrived at the cottage late last night, and already another day had slipped by. Yet still the tumult in his mind—in his heart!—gave him no respite.

He'd guarded his feelings closely, since the day he'd lost his mother and found himself completely alone; afraid that to reveal them might very well open the door to heartache and pain.

And indeed it had. He'd risked his heart once—*once*, with Amelia. But from the day he'd learned of her first illicit love affair, he'd vowed he would open his heart no more.

But that was before Elizabeth.

He should have been ecstatic. He'd given up his dreams of having children long ago. Amelia hadn't wanted to ruin her figure. And with Elizabeth, well, she'd married him to avoid scandal. He hadn't dared to hope she might someday want to give him children.

And of course, there was Nathaniel . . . always Nathaniel.

A storm swirled within him, a blustering squall of suspicion and deceit. He couldn't banish the jealousy eating away at his insides. God, but it was like a knife turning inside him! It was all so much like before . . . Nathaniel and Amelia. Nathaniel and *Elizabeth*. Even the news of the baby had been much the same.

We're going to have a baby, Morgan.

Amelia's image danced before him. Morgan cringed inside, remembering what came next.

Oh, and surely you've guessed. Nathaniel is the father.

God, he remembered how Amelia had goaded him. How she'd laughed in loathsome glee as he'd walked out the door.

We're going to have a baby, Morgan.

He steeled himself once more. This time it was Elizabeth's voice ringing through his mind, the velvet green of her eyes abrim with vibrant promise.

Unlike Amelia, whose eyes had gleamed with undisguised malice.

I-I hoped you would be happy, as happy as I am.

Unlike Amelia, Elizabeth hadn't been laughing. She'd been crying, her expression stricken and bruised . . .

He could still hear her heartbroken sobs in every corner of his soul.

Unlike Amelia.

The taste of self-disgust was a bitter brew indeed. God, but he was a fool, a fool even to think of the two in the same breath.

But no more, he vowed. No more . . .

He got to his feet, his muscles protesting the movement. Crossing the floor to the window, he saw that the clouds had parted. A single, twinkling star winked down at him.

A faint smile rimmed his lips. He would leave

tomorrow, he decided. It was time to go home. Home to Boston.

Home to Elizabeth.

As was his way, Jonah was well aware of all that had gone on since he'd last seen Nathaniel. He watched from nearby when Nathaniel was delivered home once more. He watched as Nathaniel once again gradually began to go about his business. Jonah relished the wariness in his manner. Jonah could see it in the way Nathaniel surveyed his surroundings whenever he left home . . .

. . . which only made it all the more amusing when Nathaniel returned one day to find Jonah sitting in his drawing room, a goblet of Nathaniel's finest wine in hand.

Nathaniel did not find it so amusing. He was most disconcerted but determined not to show it.

"What do you want?" he demanded of the Englishman.

Jonah smiled. "I do believe that's already been established." His gaze shifted to Nathaniel's shoulder, where the thickness of a bandage stretched his jacket tight. "I'm glad to see you've recovered so quickly."

Nathaniel clenched his fists. "You bastard. You tried to kill me!"

"I beg to differ. If I'd wanted to kill you, you'd be dead. No, my fine young sir, that was merely a warning—a warning which wouldn't have been necessary if you hadn't decided to run off again." An imperious brow arose. "That was what you intended with that meager bit of cash upon your person, wasn't it?"

Nathaniel clenched his jaw and said nothing. What did it matter if he knew?

"If I were you," the Englishman went on, "I'd bear in mind there will be no more warnings. Though I do believe I've been going about this all wrong."

"If I'm dead, you'll never get your money," Nathaniel stated flatly.

"Ah, but what about your brother? He's done quite well for himself, your brother Morgan. What if he were to ... suddenly meet with a deadly accident?"

Nathaniel had a very good idea where Moreland was taking this discussion. Coolly he met the other man's arrogant scrutiny. "His wife would inherit, not me."

Moreland made a show of swirling the wine in his goblet and studying it. "A pity," he said lightly. "Perhaps, then, it might be just as well if they both have an accident. Poor couple. 'Twould be a tragedy, really, being newly married and all." He raised his head, his eyes glinting. "But then there would be no impediments to *your* inheriting. And you certainly would have no shortage of funds with which to repay Viscount Hadley, now would you?"

Nathaniel's regard was stony. "You'll get Hadley's money. But I'll have to borrow it from Morgan. Give me until afternoon tomorrow."

"Excellent!" Moreland set aside the wine and got to his feet.

Nathaniel watched him amble toward the door. "Should we meet here?"

Moreland smiled and tipped his derby. "Oh, I think not. But don't worry. I shall notify you before then of the place and time." He sauntered through the door.

Nathaniel's face was grim. There was a cold, hard knot in the pit of his belly. God, but that man was a snake! He'd never considered that the devil would drag Elizabeth and Morgan into this.

But he had threatened her life—and Morgan's life. The wounds in his shoulder and side were proof enough that Moreland meant business. Moreland wouldn't let up until he'd gotten what he came for. But he couldn't ask Morgan to repay his debt—not this time.

It seemed he had some pride left after all.

And maybe, just once in his life, it was time to do the noble thing . . . the right thing.

Chapter 26

For Elizabeth, the last few days had passed in a haze, as she'd wavered between feeble hope and wrenching despair. In the face of all Morgan and Nathaniel had suffered, her own heartache seemed almost small and insignificant.

But no less difficult to bear.

Her days were alive with helpless frustration, her nights with endless yearning. When would Morgan return? If only she knew! And how could she convince him the child in her belly was his? Would he leave her as he'd wanted to leave Amelia?

All this and more weighed heavily on her mind—to say nothing of her heart.

On this particular afternoon, Annie had convinced her to try to nap briefly before dinner. She was just about to stretch out on the daybed when she heard the sound of footsteps below in the entrance hall. She raised her chin and paused, her head tipped to the side, her ears straining. Then she heard it, the low buzz of male voices. Morgan! she thought joyously. Her pulse raced as she fairly flew down the stairs.

It was Nathaniel.

Simmons had just taken his hat. He glanced up at her, his handsome features guarded. "Hello, Elizabeth."

"Nathaniel." She smiled and beckoned toward the drawing room. "Please, come in." She was surprised but pleased to see him. He, too, had been on her mind. She'd wanted him to stay until the matter of his debt to Viscount Hadley had been settled; at least until the threat of danger from the man with the brown derby was over. But he had refused, adamantly.

Sitting on the edge of the divan, she smoothed the folds of her skirts. "Would you like tea?"

"No, thank you." Nathaniel took the wing chair across from her. "I won't be staying long."

Elizabeth's eyes held him in a quick but thorough appraisal. His color was good, and though the set of his shoulders was a bit stiff, he seemed fit. "You're looking much better," she observed.

"I'm doing quite well, actually." It was his turn to study her. "Is Morgan home yet?"

All the light went out of her eyes. Nathaniel cursed his brother for the world's greatest fool.

"He'll come to his senses, Elizabeth."

There was a stark pain in her eyes. "Will he?"

"The situation is entirely different than with Amelia." He sought to reassure her. "He cares about you, Elizabeth, in a way he never cared for her."

"I wish I could believe that," she said wistfully. "It seems I have little choice but to wait and see." Her gaze followed his form as he arose. "You're leaving already?"

He nodded. "I have something for you, Elizabeth." He fumbled in his jacket pocket and withdrew his fist. "Here. Hold out your hand."

Curious, Elizabeth obeyed. Something cool and smooth dropped into her palm.

Her pearls.

Stunned, she gasped. "You said you'd given them to that horrible man—"

"I lied," he said with such aplomb that she couldn't withhold a bubbly laugh. "Would you like me to put them on?"

"Please." She obligingly presented her nape. When he finished, she turned and touched the strand with her fingertips. "Thank you," she said softly. "I-I can't tell you how glad I am to have them back." Softer still, she added, "They were a wedding present from Morgan."

"Then I'm glad you have them back."

A dimple appeared in her cheek. "You know, you aren't such a scoundrel as you think, Nathaniel O'Connor."

He gave a rusty laugh. "Oh, I am, Elizabeth. But it seems I've suddenly developed a conscience." His smile withered. "I probably shouldn't be here. But I would like to know that you don't hate me."

"Of course I don't hate you! You will always be dear to my heart, Nathaniel. Always."

Guilt flitted briefly across his face. "And so you forgive me?"

"Yes. Yes, of course!" She reached up and impulsively gave him a hug.

She walked with him to the entrance hall. There he turned to face her. Some of the tightness around his mouth eased, yet he seemed so somber.

"When you see Morgan, will you give him a message for me?"

"Of course."

"Tell him if he hurts you, I'll come back to haunt him." He bent and kissed her cheek. "Good-bye, Elizabeth."

With that he was gone. Elizabeth stood at the door and watched as he sauntered down the walk and out of sight. A troubled frown wrinkled the smoothness of her brow as she climbed the stairs to her room. Over the course of the next few minutes, the elusive nagging within her only grew stronger.

She couldn't banish the uneasy feeling that something wasn't right. Nathaniel had not been himself. Granted, between his injury and his startling confession, she could hardly expect his usual jovial spirits. But he had been so somber, almost sad.

She retraced her steps to the drawing room. There she began to pace back and forth. It was on her fourth pass by the wing chair where Nathaniel had sat that something caught her eye. Bending over, she retrieved a tiny, wadded scrap of paper. Nathaniel had stood in this very spot when he'd pulled her pearls from his pocket. This must have fallen out with the movement.

She tugged it apart. A huge knot of dread had lodged in her chest, though for the life of her she didn't know why. The paper was so crumpled, she had to squint to read the writing scrawled across the surface:

6 o'clock. 200 Ferry Lane.

Once again she scanned it. It was an address.
Was Nathaniel meeting someone . . . ?

The man in the brown derby.

Her hand began to shake. Her skin turned
clammy. The thought came from nowhere, an
awful premonition that sent a shiver all through
her. Nathaniel was going to meet the man in the
brown derby, the man who had stabbed him.

There was a sudden commotion in the entrance hall. She glanced up just as her husband
strode boldly through the door.

She was running before she even knew it.
"Morgan! Oh, thank God you're back!" Unthinkingly she flung herself straight into his arms. She
would have sobbed her joy were it not for the
fear mounting ever higher in her breast. "Morgan, we have to hurry! Nathaniel's gone to meet
the man who stabbed him . . ." She was babbling,
half-hysterical.

Strong arms caught her. For just an instant she
was held close against his heart; then he drew
back so he could see her. "Elizabeth, calm down!
Where is Nathaniel?" Such behavior was unlike
her. He knew from her desperate air that something terrible must have happened.

It came out in disjointed phrases, yet somehow
she made him understand. "Nathaniel's being
blackmailed . . . that's why he was stabbed . . .
He came by and gave me back my pearls. I knew
something wasn't right . . . I found this slip of paper on the floor . . . There's an address on it . . .
Oh, I know it sounds crazy, but I think he's going to meet him—the man who stabbed him!"

Morgan's heart lurched. He snatched the scrap
of paper she waved and scanned it quickly.

"This is near the shipyards." He glanced at the clock on the mantel and swore. "Damn, it's six now! Say a prayer, Elizabeth. I'll be back as soon as I can, I promise." He tore out the door, yelling for Willis.

Elizabeth was fast on his heels. She wouldn't stay here, not when he might be in danger, too! When Morgan realized her intention, he spun around with a sharp rebuke.

She faced him with blazing eyes. "You're not leaving me behind, Morgan O'Connor, not this time!"

Without a word he extended his hand and pulled her into the carriage.

They traveled to the waterfront at breakneck speed, on a wild, swerving ride that nearly sent the pair tumbling to the floor more than once. Yet through it all, Elizabeth managed to tell Morgan the details of the entire story: the loan from Viscount Hadley that Nathaniel had lost gambling; how the man with the brown derby had tracked Nathaniel from England to reclaim the debt, which was why she'd given him money the night Morgan had seen Nathaniel kiss her. She left out nothing . . .

Except that Nathaniel had stolen her pearls. Perhaps it was unwise, but she decided it best to let Morgan believe she'd only been trying to help Nathaniel with his troubles.

They jolted to a halt. Morgan thrust open the door. Elizabeth tumbled out directly behind him. He whirled around and dropped his hands on her shoulders.

"No, Elizabeth! Stay here where you're safe!"

She wasn't listening. She was busy searching

over his shoulder. "There!" She pointed and cried out sharply. "There they are. The man with the derby, that's him with Nathaniel! They just went down that alleyway!"

Morgan turned and bolted. Heedless of his warning, Elizabeth picked up her skirts and ran as fast as she was able. But all too soon her lungs felt as if they would burst. Just as she reached the alley she stumbled and fell forward, bruising her knees and scraping her hands. She tried to rise, but a stitch in her side pained her so that she was unable to stand up and follow Morgan. Biting back a sob of despair, she raised her head.

There between two buildings a grisly scene was being played out between Nathaniel and the man in the brown derby. She saw it as if in slow motion. Nathaniel raised a clenched fist high and thrust it at the Englishman's face. Angry shouts were exchanged. Morgan was less than ten steps away from the man with the derby.

The Englishman ripped something out from his breast pocket.

A fading ray of sunlight glinted on shiny metal. He held the dagger poised in his hand for a never-ending moment. Then everything blurred together.

"No!" Morgan launched himself through the air.

Lightning-quick, the dagger sliced forward.

Elizabeth gave a piercing scream.

Nathaniel slumped to the ground.

But it was far from over.

The Englishman toppled over beneath Morgan's diving weight. Together they rolled and skidded forward. The dagger clattered across the cobblestones, coming to rest an arm's length away from the pair. Sheer terror clogged Elizabeth's veins. Two arms lunged outward, grappling for possession. But only one came up with that coveted weapon . . .

The man with the derby.

Morgan lay on his back, his gaze trained upward. The man with the derby rose to his knees, a feral smile on his lips. Once again the dagger gleamed bright and deadly.

There was a shattering explosion. Smoke filled the air, acrid and thick. Through the murky haze, Elizabeth saw the man with the derby pitch forward and land on the cobblestones, sprawled facedown.

Nathaniel lay on his side. A small pistol dangled from his fingers. A muffled exclamation broke from Elizabeth's lips. He was alive. Nathaniel was alive! She staggered upright and ran to him.

Morgan was there as well, kneeling beside him. But the frantic look on his face struck a shaft of fear into her heart once more.

"Dear God," he breathed jerkily. "We need a doctor. We need a doctor!"

Throughout the house the air was heavy and thick with an oppressive silence. Thank heaven Willis had already had the foresight to go after Stephen. Nathaniel hadn't been down for more than a few minutes when Stephen came running up. Mercifully he was unconscious when they bore him to the carriage, but Elizabeth had seen the dark red stain that soaked the front of his shirt and jacket.

A feeling of dread clutched at her insides.

They'd taken him home straightaway, to the bedroom he'd so recently occupied. Stephen had been closeted inside with Nathaniel ever since, while Morgan and Elizabeth stood vigil in the hall outside. The wait was agonizing. The minutes dragged by like hours.

They both looked up with a start when the door finally opened. Stephen stepped into the hall.

It was Morgan who spoke first. "How is he?"

Stephen shook his head. His expression was bleak. "I've done all I can," he said quietly. He dropped a hand on Morgan's shoulder. "He's asking for you." His eyes slid to Elizabeth. "You, too, Elizabeth."

Morgan was already through the door. Elizabeth trailed behind him. She nearly cried out at her first sight of Nathaniel. He lay back upon the pillows, his skin nearly as white as the sheets. His eyes were closed, and for a mind-splitting instant she was convinced he was dead.

But then he opened his eyes and gazed on her form as she came through the door. Though rimmed with pain, his eyes shone with a glimmer of light that beckoned her forward.

Elizabeth stepped close to the bedside. Summoning a strength she hadn't known she possessed, she blinked back a burning rush of tears. "Hello, Nathaniel."

"Elizabeth," he said weakly. "You see, I was right. I told you I was a scoundrel."

The smile she forced to her lips was the hardest thing she'd ever done. "Never," she vowed.

"Always," he countered.

His gaze slid to Morgan. In silent understanding, she bent and kissed his cheek, then quietly retreated.

Morgan stepped close. "Maybe you should try to rest," he said quietly.

Nathaniel's head twisted slightly on the pillow. "You never quit, do you?" he murmured teasingly. "Still trying to tell me what to do after all these years." He shivered, as if with cold.

Morgan drew the quilt up over his chest. His hand came out to close around Nathaniel's where it rested on the sheet. His chest was so tight, he could hardly speak. "And you're still as feisty as ever."

"I did put you through hell, didn't I?"

"You sure did." Morgan's voice was husky. "And you enjoyed every minute, didn't you?"

"I always wanted to be like you, you know." Nathaniel's throat worked. "God, but I'm sorry! I owed you so damn much—"

"No," Morgan said firmly. "You saved my life. That took courage, Nathaniel. I owe you, more than I can ever repay."

It was a moment before Nathaniel could draw in enough air to breathe. "I did, didn't I?" he murmured.

"Yes. You did." Morgan's grip on Nathaniel's hand tightened. For a moment the two were linked together, brother to brother, spirit to spirit.

A ghost of a smile drifted across Nathaniel's lips. "Who would have ever thought, Morgan? This time I got to rescue you. This time I was the hero." His voice thinned to a wisp of sound. "Remember that, will you, Morgan? Remember that when you think of me . . ."

His eyes drifted shut. The crushing pain in his chest lifted. Peace settled over his features.

Little by little the strength seeped from his fingers.

Morgan bent close. "Nat," he cried hoarsely. *"Nat!"*

Chapter 27

⌒◦◦⌒

He was buried the next day. The cemetery was within walking distance, small and peaceful, atop a grassy hill that looked out across the Charles River. The gravesite was beneath the shady canopy of a stately oak tree, dotted here and there with wildflowers.

Morgan stood apart from the others during the service, a stoic figure garbed in black. When it was over, he spoke to no one, not the minister, not Stephen, not even Elizabeth. He went home and locked himself in his study. It was left to Elizabeth to field condolences from those who stopped by or sent notes of sympathy.

For the next four days, only Simmons was allowed entrance to his study. Elizabeth was a trifle hurt at being shut out so completely, yet she could understand Morgan's need to be alone to deal with the tragedy of Nathaniel's death.

Stephen thought it best simply to leave him be. "Just give him a few days more," he suggested. "I know Morgan. He'll come out of it."

At first Elizabeth was convinced he was right. Whatever Morgan was going through right now would pass. But she watched with ever-increasing concern—and yes, disapproval—as bottle after bottle of brandy was delivered to the study. As she confided to Stephen, "He hasn't eaten a thing since he's been in there. Simmons has tried, but he refuses. Nor does it appear he's slept in all that time. I swear he's determined to drink himself into the grave after his brother."

"You may be right. It isn't like him at all," Stephen admitted. "Would you like me to try to talk with him?"

Stephen did try on several occasions.

He failed on all.

By the fifth day Elizabeth determined to take matters into her own hands. Morgan might forever hate her, but he could not go on like this.

Outside the study she intercepted Simmons, who was about to deliver the evening bottle. She took the tray from his hands, saying, "You and the staff may have the rest of the night off, Simmons."

Simmons looked uncertain. "Ma'am, he's been in a devil of a temper—"

"Please do as I ask, Simmons. Oh, and please knock on the door and tell Mr. O'Connor you're here with his brandy."

Simmons inclined his head. "Of course, ma'am." He knocked three times and did what was requested of him. Elizabeth motioned him away. When the door swung open she neatly stepped inside and shut it with her heel.

The study was steeped in shadows, the air thick with the scent of stale brandy. The drapes had been drawn tight against the outside world.

Elizabeth peered across the room, trying to find him.

"What the *hell* do you think you're doing?" His voice sliced at her from a point just to her left, startling her so that she jumped.

Mercifully, she recovered quickly. She raised her chin high and said with quiet dignity, "I came to ask you that very question."

Her eyes had adjusted to the dimness; they ran over him as she spoke. Dear Lord, he looked terrible! His face was haggard and drawn, his jaw dark and unshaven, half-obscured by five days worth of growth. His clothing was rumpled and untidy. His eyes were red rimmed and bloodshot.

"Leave me alone, Elizabeth." The anger had gone out of his voice. He merely sounded incredibly tired.

Her heart constricted as she watched him walk across to his desk. He moved like a man thrice his age.

Swallowing, she steeled herself against all emotion. "Why? Because you feel sorry for yourself?"

Morgan spoke from between his teeth. "No! So I can forget!"

She finally moved, setting the tray with its bottle of brandy on the corner of the desk. "You're not trying to forget, Morgan. You're trying to torture yourself."

"So get the hell out and let me do it alone!" An ugly snarl twisted his face. He reached for the bottle.

But Elizabeth was quicker. Stung by a sudden fury, she knocked it aside. It fell with a crash to the floor. She paid no heed to the amber liquid that streamed onto the carpet.

"Don't you care?" she asked fiercely. "Don't you care about me? Don't you care what this is doing to me?"

Morgan was on his feet. "If you have any sense, you'll leave before I ruin your life, too."

"That's nonsense, Morgan, and you know it!"

His features were a frozen mask. "No, Elizabeth. You don't know what happened. You don't know—"

"I do know! I know everything. I know Nathaniel was Amelia's lover. I know he killed her."

His face had gone pale. "How? How do you know?"

"Nathaniel. He told me everything, Morgan. *Everything*."

His reaction was exactly what she feared. He turned his back on her, as distant from her as ever.

Something snapped inside her. Three steps put her directly behind him. She punched at his shoulders with her fists.

"Damn you, you're going to listen to me, Morgan O'Connor."

His powerful shoulders went taut, but he didn't move.

"You know what else he told me? He said when you were a boy your father used to whip you with a cane when you took the blame for things he'd done. But you would never cry— never. Well, go ahead and cry, Morgan. Scream because it hurts that he's gone. Rage because God took him away too soon. But then be done with it. Don't hide what's inside. Let it go, Morgan. Let *him* go."

Tears streamed down her face, tears she wasn't aware of. But Morgan gave no sign that he'd even heard.

Something broke inside her then. Her spine wilted. With a jagged sob she sagged to the floor and hugged her knees to her breast, rocking back and forth.

"I need you," she wept. "I need you, too, Morgan. Please come back to me. *Please . . .*"

He squeezed his eyes shut. The sound of her sobs was like a knife in his heart. He turned and dropped to the floor. His arms stole around her shaking form. His fingers brushed aside her hair.

"Oh, damn. Damn. Elizabeth, don't do this to me!" he groaned. "I-I can't deal with any more pain."

She wrapped her arms around him and clung. "You took care of Nathaniel alone, Morgan. You suffered through Amelia's betrayal alone. But you don't have to be alone anymore. Just—just let me hold you," she pleaded. "Let me help you, Morgan. Let me . . . let me love you!"

He closed his eyes again. The ache of remembrance battered him. "When my mother died, she asked me to—to take care of Nathaniel. I remember she said . . . Guide him. Protect him. But I-I did everything wrong. Did I give him too much? Or too little. Christ, I-I just don't know!"

His breath came raggedly. "It's my fault this happened. It's my fault Nathaniel's dead. If I had done things differently . . . I would have helped him, Elizabeth, if only he'd been able to come to me. But I kept him away." His voice turned raw.

"That whole sordid mess with Amelia . . . I pushed him away. I-I couldn't forgive him and he knew it. Don't you see? He knew it!"

Her hand touched the crispness of the hair that grew low on his nape. "You didn't fail him, Morgan. You were loyal—to the very end, so don't burden yourself like this. Nathaniel's life was his own. You did what you could. Why, he told me himself that he made his own decisions—often the wrong ones, he knew! He was ashamed, Morgan, ashamed of the hell he put you through. But he didn't blame you. You have to stop blaming yourself!"

Morgan buried his face in the fragrant cloud of her hair. "You should hate me," he muttered hoarsely. "I've said so many awful things . . . accused you of things I knew weren't true . . . I-I don't know what came over me. God, I haven't even asked you how you feel!" Drawing back, he lightly grazed his fingers over the swell of her belly.

Elizabeth smiled mistily. The relief that poured through her was immense. "I'm fine," she said softly. Her smile widened ever so slightly. "*We're* fine."

His throat worked. "Do you . . . really love me?"

Her eyes brimmed and overflowed. She nodded.

Even as the sight tore him in two, the swell of emotion that rose in his chest was too much to contain.

"Would you say it?" he whispered.

She ducked her head low, all at once afraid. What if she had bared her soul for nothing?

What if he didn't love her in return? "No," she said tremulously, the word more breath than sound.

But then his fingers captured her chin, guiding her eyes upward. "Yes," he whispered, and then again against her lips . . . into her mouth. "*Yes.*"

She trembled with the force of her emotions. "I-I love you, Morgan. *I love you . . .*" The confession was torn from her, but his lips were there to smother it.

And then she heard the words she'd never thought to hear . . . She saw in his eyes the very thing that she'd never thought to see, a tenderness and love so pure and shining, she could only stare in wonder.

"I love you, Elizabeth." His arms engulfed her. "I love you. My lady. My heart."

Elizabeth wept all over again.

Night found them wrapped in each other's arms, limbs entwined, the beat of their hearts as one.

Daybreak found Elizabeth stirring lazily in the depths of her husband's bed. Her mind slowly registered the absence of warmth, and she lifted her head.

She was alone.

More puzzled than fearful, for the hours past had put to rest all of her doubts, she rose with a sleepy yawn. But Morgan was not in his study, as she'd thought. Nor was he in the library, or, indeed, anywhere in the house.

She paused, her mind taking flight. In the next instant she whirled and flew up the stairs. Suddenly she had a very good idea where her husband had gone.

A short time later, she pulled a cloak over her dress and quietly left the house. Her slippers made no sound as she hurried up the hill.

Very soon her feet took her down a narrow pathway, across damp earth and glistening blades of grass. And it was there, bathed in the amber glow of dawn's first light, that she saw her husband.

He stood before Nathaniel's grave, the posture of his body stiff but proud. His head was bowed low, the somber cast of his features etched in stone.

She halted, her heart aching, for she knew why he was here.

He'd come to say his good-byes to Nathaniel.

She stood there, still as a statue and holding her breath in an all-encompassing silence. She was unerringly certain she made not a whisper of sound.

Yet somehow he knew she was there.

He half turned. Their eyes met and meshed. He opened his arms . . . and his heart.

Her feet carried her forward. She slid her arms about his waist and held on to him desperately, as if he were her last anchor to the world. He rested his forehead against hers, then kissed her tenderly. The salty warmth of tears mingled with hers, trapped between their lips. And it was there that he showered upon her a gift beyond price.

He cried without a sound . . . but without shame.

Only the strongest of men could cry without shame.

No words passed between them. None were needed.

The sun was just rising over the treetops as they left, hand in hand, their heads bent together.

It was the dawning of a new day. A new beginning. A new life.

Epilogue

It was early August, and the weather was divine. The heat of summer hung in the air, but the coolness of the ocean breeze kept the temperature at a comfortable level.

As they did whenever they were able, Morgan and Elizabeth chose to spend the weekend at the cottage.

And if his squeals of delight were any indication, their son—nearly sixteen months old now—loved it here as much as his parents.

Robert Nathaniel O'Connor—Robbie, as he was called—possessed the deep green of his mother's eyes, the midnight darkness of his father's hair, and at times the reckless daring of his uncle, which often caused his mother's heart to lodge high in her throat . . .

As well as a sweetness of nature that was all his own.

His chubby legs pumped furiously as he ran along the beach. His father was right behind him, bare-legged and shirtless. The boy gave a high-pitched shrill of laughter as he was caught and swung high against his father's chest.

Morgan dipped his head down. A tremor of emotion rushed through him, and for a moment he was overcome. Never had he dreamed that life could be like this. Never had he dreamed that love could be like this. He had so much. A son. Another on the way, or perhaps a daughter. Yes, he would like that. A daughter . . .

He liked to think that some good had come of Nat's death.

He had turned his face to the future; to the happiest of times and precious new memories; to a love that filled every corner of his soul to bursting.

And it was his greatest love who sat there on the porch, wearing that sweet, serene smile he would carry in his heart forever.

Elizabeth.

It was later that night, when passion's fire had been quenched, that she snuggled close against his side.

She twined a fingertip in the curling hair on his chest. "Do you know," she mused aloud, "that it was here I first realized I was in love with you?"

"What!" he chuckled. "Not until then?"

She tweaked the hair and made him yelp in pain. "You were horrid to me, Morgan O'Connor! I thought you detested me. You certainly acted as if you did!"

"I didn't want you to find out how I really felt," he teased. "And I was convinced you detested *me*."

Her eyes grew soft. "Now it's your turn to confess. When did you first know?"

A secret smile curved his lips. "Before we were even married," he said lightly.

"Oh, you!" She frowned at him playfully. "The truth, now. When did you know?"

His arms tightened possessively. "Remember the night of Stephen's ball?"

The golden cloud of her hair tickled his chin as she nodded. "You kissed me, and that wretched reporter saw it!"

He weaved his fingers through her hair and tipped her head back so he could see her. He looked at her, uncaring that his heart was in his eyes.

"Well, that's all it took, love." He brushed her lips with his and smiled. "Just one kiss . . ."

Avon Romantic Treasures

*Unforgettable, enthralling love stories,
sparkling with passion and adventure
from Romance's bestselling authors*

LADY OF SUMMER *by Emma Merritt*
77984-6/$5.50 US/$7.50 Can

TIMESWEPT BRIDE *by Eugenia Riley*
77157-8/$5.50 US/$7.50 Can

A KISS IN THE NIGHT *by Jennifer Horsman*
77597-2/$5.50 US/$7.50 Can

SHAWNEE MOON *by Judith E. French*
77705-3/$5.50 US/$7.50 Can

PROMISE ME *by Kathleen Harrington*
77833-5/ $5.50 US/ $7.50 Can

COMANCHE RAIN *by Genell Dellin*
77525-5/ $4.99 US/ $5.99 Can

MY LORD CONQUEROR *by Samantha James*
77548-4/ $4.99 US/ $5.99 Can

ONCE UPON A KISS *by Tanya Anne Crosby*
77680-4/$4.99 US/$5.99 Can

Avon Romances—
the best in exceptional authors and unforgettable novels!